AMONG THE TITLES IN

The Universal Library:

-- and over 100 other equally distinguished titles

SHORTER NOVELS
OF
HERMAN
MELVILLE

WITH AN INTRODUCTION BY
RAYMOND WEAVER

Grosset's UNIVERSAL *Library*
GROSSET & DUNLAP
NEW YORK

CONTENTS

SHORTER NOVELS OF
HERMAN MELVILLE

INTRODUCTION

I

On Monday, September 28, 1891, at 104 East 26th Street, New York City, an obscure and elderly private citizen quietly died in bed. His funeral, at Woodlawn Cemetery, was attended by his wife and his two daughters—all of his immediate family that survived—and a meagre scattering of family acquaintances. The *New York Times* missed the news of this demise, but published a few days later an editorial which began:

"There has died and been buried in this city, during the current week, at an advanced age, a man who is so little known, even by name, to the generation now in the vigour of life, that only one newspaper contained an obituary account of him, and this was of but three or four lines."

In 1885, Robert Buchanan, in speaking of a pilgrimage he had made to these shores, wrote of Melville in the London *Academy:* "I sought everywhere for this Triton, who is still living somewhere in New York. No one seemed to know anything of the one great writer fit to stand shoulder with Whitman on that continent."

The man who had created Moby-Dick had, in early manhood, prayed that if his soul missed its haven that it might, at least, end in utter wreck. "All Fame is patronage," he had once in the long past written to Hawthorne; "let me be infamous." But as if in contempt even for this preference, he had, during the last half of his life, cruised off and away upon boundless and uncharted water; and in the end he sank down into death, without a ripple of renown.

Though for the twenty years between 1866 and 1886, Melville had been employed as Inspector of Customs, and the world at large had seemed utterly to have forgotten him as a man-of-letters, his wife, though temperamentally unfitted to understand him in any profound essential, had borne with him gallantly through poverty, sickness, and apparent failure, and on his certificate of death she declared her faith by giving his "Occupation" as that of "Writer." And the funeral once over, Mrs. Melville returned to his bedroom study, with its black, narrow bed, its black bookcases lined with volumes of poets and philosophers, with its prints and etchings that Melville had collected, and at the massive and ornate desk (brought over from France by Melville's father before Melville's birth) she went through Melville's papers. What was destroyed will never be known. What has survived she sorted, tied with pink tape into orderly bundles frequently labelled in pencil in her hand, and deposited the slight bulk of it all into a miniature trunk hardly larger than an average sized suit-case, where they reposed untampered with for twenty-eight years.

Mrs. Melville died; and then the older of her two daughters. The other daughter had married, and to *her* daughter, Mrs. Eleanor Melville Metcalf, descended this trunk.

As a small girl, Mrs. Metcalf had been perhaps as intimate a companion to Melville's solitude as any human soul alive. In recollection of Melville, Mrs. Metcalf has written:

"I was not yet ten years old when my grandfather died. To put aside all later impressions gathered from those who knew him long and coloured by their personal reactions, all impressions made by subsequent reading of his books, results in a series of childish recollections, vividly homely scenes wherein he formed a palpable background for my own interested activities.

"Setting forth on a bright spring afternoon for a trip to Central Park, the Mecca of most of our pilgrimages, he made a brave and striking figure as he walked erect, head thrown back, cane in hand, inconspicuously dressed in a dark blue suit and a soft black felt hat. . . .

"We never came in from a trip of this kind, nor indeed from any walk, but we stopped in the front hall under a coloured engraving of the Bay of Naples, its still blue dotted with tiny white sails. He would point at them with his cane and say, 'See the little boats sailing hither and thither.' . . .

"Once in a long while his interest in his grandchildren led him to cross the river and take the suburban train to East Orange, where we lived. He must have been an impressive figure, sitting silently on the piazza of our little house, while my sister and I pranced with a neighbour's boy and his express wagon, filled with a satisfied sense of the strength and accomplishment of our years. When he had had enough of such exhibitions, he would suddenly rise and take the next train back to Hoboken.

"Chiefly do I think of him connected with different parts of the 26th Street house.

"His own room was a place of mystery and awe to me; there I never ventured unless invited by him. It looked bleakly north. The great mahogany desk, heavily bearing up four shelves of dull gilt and leather books; the high dim bookcase, topped by strange plaster heads that peered along the ceiling level, or bent down, searching blindly with sightless balls; the small black iron bed, covered with dark cretonne; the narrow iron grate; the wide table in the alcove, piled with papers I would not dream of touching—these made a room even more to be fled than the back parlour, by whose door I always ran to escape the following eyes of his portrait, which hung there in a half light. Yet lo, the paper-piled table also held a little bag of figs, and one of the pieces of sweet stickiness was for me. 'Tittery-Eye' he called me, and awe melted into glee, as I skipped away to my grandmother's room, which adjoined.

"That was a very different place—sunny, comfortable and familiar, with a sewing machine and a *white* bed like other peoples'. In the corner stood a great arm chair, where he always sat when he left the recesses of his own dark privacy. I used to climb on his knee, while he told me wild stories of cannibals and tropical isles. Little did I then know that he was reliving his own past. We came nearest intimacy at these times, and part of the fun was to put my hands in his thick beard and squeeze it hard. It was no soft silken beard, but tight curled like the horse-hair breaking out of old upholstered chairs, firm and wiry to the grasp, and squarely chopped.

"Sad it is that he felt that his grandchildren would turn against him as he grew older. He used to forebode as much. . . ."

In the case of Mrs. Metcalf, at least, his persecution pattern was misplaced. She it was who elected herself to the trust of preserving all possible records of her grandfather. And with Mrs. Metcalf it was my privilege to examine the trunk of Melville papers just arrived in her possession, and to untie and examine the neatly docketed parcels that Mrs. Metcalf had preserved.

Not the least exciting bundle in the trunk was a batch of some 340 sheets of yellow paper, about six by eight inches, covered with an incredibly crabbed manuscript in pencil in Melville's hand. A posthumous novel it turned out to be: *Billy Budd*. "Friday, November 16, 1888, Begun," it started off; "End of Book, April 19, 1891," it concluded. Here then seemed a completed work finished within a few months of Melville's death: a last testament to a world he had come to rate as being too inconsiderable to address, written in the room that had filled Mrs. Metcalf with such mystery and awe, and by the man whose beard she had crumpled in her hands,—the man whose published works had marked him as the most completely disillusioned of American writers.

This, as everything else, I was permitted to copy. In 1924, in a limited edition, *Billy Budd* was published for the first time by Constable and Company, in England,—and never since. And between that edition and this present one there are certain minor variations which need a word of comment.

Such is the state of the *Billy Budd* manuscript that there can never appear a reprint that will be adequate to every ideal. In the first place (though this is not the worst difficulty) the script is in certain parts a miracle of crabbedness: misspellings in the grand manner; scraps of paragraphs cut out and pasted over disembowelled sentences; words ambiguously begun and dwindling into waves and dashes; variant readings, with no choice indicated among them. More disheartening than this even, is one floating chapter (Section IV in both this and the Constable Edition) with no numbering beyond the vague direction "To be inserted." The manuscript is evidently in a more or less tentative state as to details, and without some editing it would be in parts unintelligible. In such editing for intelligibility with the least possible departure from accuracy, I have only occasionally varied from the Constable text. In several cases I have been persuaded to change a single word; less frequently, the order of words; and once, in Section XXV, I have shifted a paragraph.

The three other narratives herein contained—*The Encantadas, or Enchanted Isles; Bartleby the Scrivener; Benito Cereno*—appeared originally in *Putnam's Monthly Maga-*

zine in 1853-4-5, and were included by Melville among the six pieces of *The Piazza Tales* (1856). *The Piazza Tales* have been but once reprinted—in the limited Constable Edition of Melville's Works; *Benito Cereno* separately has been once reprinted again—in a limited edition of the Nonesuch Press. Until this volume, these things have been practically unavailable. They are of prime importance, not only for their inherent qualities as works of art, but because of the very peculiar position they hold in Melville's development both as an artist and as a man.

II

The early effulgence of Melville's genius, and its long obscuration—the brilliant early achievement, the long and black eclipse: here is the most striking single aspect of his career. Yet, in its popular statement, this apparent discontinuity in his development has been surrounded by a lot of unnecessary mystery, with whispers from elegiac synods that he went insane. Romantically and irresponsibly viewed, Melville's career is like a star that drops a line of streaming fire down the sky—and then the dark and blasted shape that sinks into the earth. The figure is profoundly misleading. It is a fact that Melville was thirty-two when he produced *Moby-Dick*, his undoubted masterpiece and his sixth narrative. It is further true that the forty years which lay ahead of him after this were largely spent in sedulous isolation, and deepening silence. But it is at once both true and perniciously deceptive to say that he gave up the attempt to support himself and his family by writing books "because of some odd psychological experience that has never been definitely explained."

In the midst of the composition of *Moby-Dick* Melville

wrote to Hawthorne: "My development has been all within a few years past. I am like one of those seeds taken out of the Egyptian pyramids, which, after being three thousand years a seed and nothing but a seed, being planted in English soil, it developed itself, grew to greenness, and then fell to mould. So I. Until I was twenty-five, I had no development at all. From my twenty-fifth year I date my life. Three weeks have scarcely passed, at any time between then and now, that I have not unfolded within myself. But I feel that I am now come to the inmost leaf of the bulb, and that shortly the flower must fall to the mould." From a superficial view of Melville's life this seems strict history and sound prophecy. It is neither.

Not the least remarkable part of this pronouncement of Melville's is its discounting of the crowded years of his early manhood,—years of whaling, and captivity among practising cannibals, and mutiny, and South Sea drifting, and service in the Navy. His youth and early manhood he had spent in barbarous outposts of human experience. When, in October, 1844, Melville was in Boston discharged from the Navy, he made the dizzy transition from vagabondage in Polynesia to the stern yoke of self-supporting citizenship—and he made it at the age of twenty-five. "From my twenty-fifth year I date my life." And the first two steps in that initiation were singularly momentous: Melville sat down to the feverish making of books; he married the only daughter of Chief Justice Shaw of Massachusetts. The manuscript for *Typee* was bought in London by John Murray, by an agreement dated December, 1845. Melville was married to Elizabeth Shaw on August 4, 1847.

Although the evidence is almost wholly circumstantial, it would appear that at the time of his marriage there was every promise of a happy and brilliant career ahead. Behind, it is true, lay morbidity, bitterness, and rebellion: traits that are manifested, after all, in the green immaturity of many of our most upright and seasoned pillars of society.

His childhood had been spent in Albany and in New York. Both of his parents were of powerful family connections. His father had been merchant importer of French notions: a man who, by the extensive records of him which survive, was a snob, a prig, an epic bore;—and by Melville's own intimation, a hypocrite besides. Though he died rich in ostentatious respectability, he died with no corresponding abundance of corruptible riches. And nothing in his life more ill became him than his failure in business and his bequest of poverty to his wife and eight children.

Herman, the second son and third child, was not thirteen years old at the time of his father's decease: young enough to cherish up into early manhood the most extravagant idealization of his male parent. His first venture to sea as a youth, for example, though provoked in part by poverty and discontent, had as one of its most clearly defined goals a pious pilgrimage to retrace the steps of his father in Liverpool as they were mapped out in an old dog-eared guide-book which Melville cherished.

But as Melville grew in years, he did not grow in charity towards either of his parents. In his novel *Pierre*, he draws a vindictive delight in pronouncing, under a thin disguise, an unsubstantiated libel upon his father's memory. This dark wild book of incest and disaster is of the greatest importance as a document in autobiography. Most of the characters in *Pierre* are unmistakably idealizations of actual people. The hero, Pierre Glendinning, is a glorification of Melville's self; the widowed mother, Marie Glendinning, owes more to Melville's mother, Marie Gansevoort, than the initials of her name. And in this book Melville exorcises the ghost of his

father, and traces the ambiguous steps by which Pierre, at
the age of nineteen, arrived at the staggering conviction that
his sainted parent had in his youth been a lecherous rake.

As a child, Melville's imagination had been unusually
active. "I always thought my father," he says "a marvellous
being, infinitely purer and greater than I was, who could not
by any possibility do wrong or say an untruth." With this
"dangerous predominance of the imagination" it was inevitable that he should early begin to experience a poignant in-
compatibility between reality and heart's desire—between the
worlds of fancy and of fact. From his infancy, it would
seem, he began to view perfect happiness as a possession
lurking always just beyond the horizon. But to him, paradise were less than paradise if he could not return to the
humdrum world to make an ostentation of his enviable superiority. He confesses that as a boy he used to think "how
fine it would be, to be able to talk about barbarous countries;
with what reverence and wonder people would regard me,
if I had just returned from the coast of Africa or New Zea-
land: how dark and romantic my sunburnt cheeks would
look; how I would bring home with me foreign clothes of
rich fabric and princely make, and wear them up and down
the streets, and how grocers' boys would turn their heads to
look at me as I went by." The Narcissism here playfully
flaunted—a trait fundamental and persistent in Melville's
character—is more strikingly indicated where Melville asks
in *Moby-Dick:* "Why did the old Persians hold the sea
holy? Why did the Greeks give it a separate deity, and own
brother to Jove? Surely all this is not without meaning.
And still deeper the story of Narcissus, who because he could
not grasp the tormenting, mild image he saw in the fountain,
plunged into it and was drowned. But that same image, we
ourselves see in all rivers and oceans. It is the image of the

ungraspable phantom of life; and this is the key to all."
When he thus compares himself to Narcissus tormented by
the irony of being two, he was perhaps hotter on the trail of
the truth about himself than he was at the time aware.

"I am tormented," he said, "with an everlasting itch for
things remote." This disorganizing appeal of other times
and other places emerged early in his childhood. "We had
several pieces of furniture in the house," he says, speaking of
his early years, "that had been imported from Europe. These
I examined again and again, wondering where the wood
grew; whether the workmen who made them still survived,
and what they could be doing with themselves."

It is one of the few certainties of life that a boy who sits
abstracted in this mood, with his eye fixed upon a table leg,
is not likely to die an efficiency expert. At the age of fifteen,
introspective and morbidly sensitive, a poor relative in a
family of well-to-do uncles and aunts, Melville found himself faced with the premature necessity of coming to some
sort of terms with life on his own account. Helped by an
influential uncle, he tried working in a bank. The experiment was not a tempting success. His next venture was
clerking in his brother's fur-and-cap store. Banking and
clerking drove him to the farm of another uncle, who had
lived twenty-one years in France, where he alternated agri-
culture with rustic school teaching. The end result was des-
peration and the luxury of self-pity. "Talk not of the bitterness of middle-age and after-life," he wrote in retrospect;
"a boy can feel all that, and much more, when upon his
young soul the mildew has fallen. . . . Before the death of
my father I never thought of working for my living, and
never knew there were hard hearts in the world. . . . I had
learned to think much, and bitterly, before my time." Had
he been endowed with less impetuosity, with less abundance

of physical vitality, he might have moped tamely by the family hearth and "yearned." As it was, he resolved to slough off the irksome respectabilities of well-to-do uncles and cousins and aunts. Goaded by hardship, and lured by the mirage of distance, he decided to view the watery world. "With a philosophic flourish Cato throws himself upon his sword; I quietly take to the ship. This is my substitute for pistol and ball."

Redburn: His First Voyage. Being the Sailor-boy Confessions and Reminiscences of the Son-of-a-Gentleman (1849) is the only surviving record of Melville's initial attempt "to sail beyond the sunset." In the words of Mr. H. S. Salt: "It is a record of bitter experience and temporary disillusionment—the confessions of a poor, proud youth, who goes to sea 'with a devil in his heart' and is painfully initiated into the unforeseen hardships of a sea-faring life."

Before the time of Melville's hegira, many a young man of good family and education bade farewell to a home of comfort and refinement and made his berth in a smoky, fetid forecastle to learn the sailor's calling. Ships were multiplying fast, and no really lively and alert seaman need long stay in the forecastle. The sea was then a favourite career, not only for American boys with their way to make in the world, but for the sons of wealthy men as well. And Melville's relatives would doubtless have been agreeably surprised had he attempted to justify his sea-going by reminding them that at this time it was nothing remarkable for seamen to become full-fledged captains and part owners at the age of twenty-one, or even earlier. Melville's brother Tom chose such a career. But Melville was unmoved by any such vulgar and mundane considerations. "At that early age," he says, "I was as unambitious as a man of sixty."

In any event, this early recourse to the ocean was a

heroic measure, calculated either to take the nonsense out of Melville, or else to drive him straight to suicide, madness, or rum-soaked barbarism. It did none of these things. But he did return to his family still harbouring in his heart a fatal longing to repudiate the restrictions of the world of reality into which he was plunged, hankering still for a return to the happy omnipotence of infancy, for an escape into some land of heart's desire.

Of the details of his existence upon his return we have but the most sketchy records. In the brief record of his life preserved in the Commonplace Book of his wife, this period between Liverpool and the South Seas is dismissed in a single sentence: "Taught school at intervals in Pittsfield and in Greenbush (near East Albany), N. Y." In the interims between pedagogy, Melville "desired to write." In *Pierre* he devotes a whole book—half-satirical, half of the utmost seriousness—discussing his *juvenalia*. Two of the effusions of this period survive: and these ghastly attempts to be "literary" are, indeed, as Melville says in *Pierre*, "equally removed from vulgarity and vigour"—"characterized throughout by Perfect Taste." Melville proceeds ironically to praise these earliest writings for possessing those very defects which his maturer work was damned for not exhibiting. But Melville surely deceived himself if he in any degree believed that had he gone on in the dull and shallow tameness of his first manner he would thereby increase his royalties.

In the beginning, evidently, they brought him neither recognition nor release from poverty. His teaching, while keeping him fit by demanding pugilism as an instrument for discipline, was without further advantage. He did not comfortably fit into any recognized socket of New England respectability, and he had not disciplined himself against the teasing lure of some stupendous discovery awaiting him at the rainbow's end. One night, during the years immediately ensuing, out on the Pacific, and in the glare and the wild Hindoo odour of the try-works of a whaler in full operation, he fell asleep at the helm. "Starting from a brief standing sleep," he says, "I was horribly conscious of something fatally wrong. I thought my eyes were open; I was half conscious of putting my fingers to the lids and mechanically stretching them still further apart. But, despite all this, I could see no compass before me to steer by. Nothing seemed before me but a jet of gloom, now and then made ghastly by flashes of redness. Uppermost was the impression, that whatever swift, rushing thing I stood on was not so much bound for any haven ahead as rushing from all havens astern."

In headlong retreat from all havens astern, on January 3, 1841, Melville sailed from Fairhaven in the whaler *Acushnet,* bound for the Pacific Ocean and the sperm fisheries.

Just what were the immediate and specific circumstances which precipitated Melville into this drastic step will probably never be known: what burst of demonic impulse, either of anger, envy, or spite; what passionate disappointment; what crucifixion of affection; what sinister discovery. But this is certain: that when a youth of Melville's temperament and history concludes the Christmas holidays by a mid-winter plunge into the filthy and shabby business of whaling, this shifting of whereabouts is hardly a sign of mere jolly animal exuberance.

Melville was away three and a half years. His experiences during this time, while beyond the pale of civilization, are widely known, and the basis of what popularity as a writer he enjoyed during his life. During his far driftings, however, Melville had sentimentally clung to thoughts of home, —his imagination treacherously caressing those very scenes whose intimate contact had filled him with revulsion. "Do men ever hate the thing they love?" he asks in *White-Jacket*, perplexed at the paradox of his perpetual recoil. And until the final peace of his extreme old age, the present was always poisoned, for him, by bitter margins of pining and regret.

Of his impressions immediately upon his return he has left no account. Such was the calibre of his imagination, that he must have found the familiar scenes and people unbelievably like he knew they must be, yet incredibly different from what he was prepared to find.

Tanned with sea-faring and exuberant in health, he was effulgent with amazing tales. Deep in his heart, too, was the proud warm memory of a companionship which was to prove itself to be perhaps the happiest in his life. On board the man-of-war in which he had returned from the South Seas, Melville had been immediately under command of Jack Chase, first captain of the top. In *White-Jacket*, Melville glows with the same superlative admiration for Jack Chase that Ouida or the Duchess exhibit in celebrating the conquests of their most irresistible cavaliers. Of no other human being is Melville known to have spoken with such admiration and love, finding in him something heroic yet all human: an educated man, wise as Ulysses, shining as Nelson, azure-eyed, bright-hearted—"wherever you may be rolling over the blue waters, dear Jack, take my best love along with you." It would almost seem that Jack did, and that for this reason Melville lived unhappily many years afterward. This was the one glamorous and exultant attachment of Melville's that time never marred. And it was particularly appropriate that in the ultimate serenity of his old age he should have dedicated *Billy Budd* to Jack Chase.

Though bodily he was in a suburb of Albany, his companion image was the distant adventurer he saw mirrored in the admiring eyes of his friends. With what melancholy —if any—he viewed this reflected image of himself, and to what degree he was, Narcissus-wise, conscious of its irony, we do not know. But if the gay exuberance of *Typee* and *Omoo* be any index of his mood, he returned home happier and wholesomer than he was to be at any other period of his life. Before many years, unsolved problems of his youth were to reassert themselves, heightened in difficulty and in pertinacity. *Typee* was an almost instantaneous success; and its success was none the less brilliant because it was in part a *succès de scandale*. The appearance of *Omoo* on January 30, 1847, augmented Melville's notoriety and his income as well. Abetted by reviews, and encouraged by royalties, Melville began more hopefully to look at the world. He seemed at last to have stepped decoratively and profitably into his assigned niche in the cosmic order. It was delightful to rehearse outlived pleasures and hardships, and to discover that one's reveries and dreams sold for cash on the open market. Under this exhilaration, he married.

To Elizabeth Shaw, according to Melville's diagnosis of himself, he transferred his boyhood idealization of his mother. In *Pierre* he spends a chapter of dithyrambic in celebration of that sentiment, which, "inspired by one's mother, one transfers to all other women honourably loved." And during his courtship of Elizabeth Shaw, it seems that in Melville were these "audacious immortalities of divinest love."

Soon after the marriage, Melville and his wife moved to New York, where, at 103 Fourth Avenue, in a household made up of his brothers Allan and Tom, his sisters Augusta, Fanny and Helen, his mother, his wife, with incursions of Shaws on visit from Boston, Melville started his third book,

Mardi. On April 14, 1849, two years after Melville's marriage, *Mardi* appeared simultaneously here and in England. Of the adverse reviews it provoked, Melville wrote to his father-in-law: "These attacks are a matter of course, and are essential to the building up of any permanent reputation—if such should ever prove to be mine—but Time, which is the solver of all riddles, will solve *Mardi.*"

The riddle of *Mardi* goes near to the heart of the riddle of Melville's life. "Not long ago," Melville says in the preface to this book, "having published two narratives of voyages in the Pacific, which, in many quarters, were received with incredulity, the thought occurred to me, of indeed writing a romance of Polynesian adventure, and publishing it as such; to see whether the fiction might not, possibly, be received for a verity: in some degree the reverse of my previous experience. This thought was the germ of others, which have resulted in *Mardi.*"

Mardi, as *Moby-Dick,* starts off firmly rooted in reality. But after less than quarter way through, it swings abruptly into allegory—and there it was that Melville first tried his hand at the orphic style.

This allegorical part of *Mardi* defies simple characterization, though its purpose is simple enough. It is a quest after Yillah, a maiden from Oroolia, the Island of Delight. A voyage is made through symbolic realms, and around the civilized world, in quest of her. But Yillah is lost beyond recovery. In its intention to show the vanity of human wishes it is a kind of *Rasselas*—though a *Rasselas* which, for its "dangerous predominance of imagination," Dr. Johnson would have despised. The happiness sought in the person of Yillah is the total and undivined possession of that holy and mysterious joy that touched Melville during the period of his courtship. When he wrote *Mardi* he was married, and his wife was with child. And *Mardi* is a pilgrimage for a lost glamour.

In these wanderings in search of Yillah, the symbol of this faded ecstasy, the hero is pursued by three shadowy messengers from the temptress Hautia; she who was descended from the queen who first incited the kingdom of Mardi to wage war against beings with wings. Despairing of ever achieving Yillah, the hero in the end turns towards the island of Hautia, called Flozella-a-Nina, or "The-Last-Verse-of-the Song." "Yillah was all beauty and innocence; my crown of felicity; my heaven below:—and Hautia, my whole heart abhorred. Yillah I sought; Hautia sought me. Yet now I was wildly dreaming of finding them both together. In some mysterious way seemed Hautia and Yillah connected."

The hero lands on the shore of Hautia's bower of bliss. "All the sea, like a harvest plain, was stacked with glittering sheaves of spray. And far down, fathoms on fathoms, flitted rainbow hues:—as skeins-full of mermaids; half-screening the bower of the drowned." Hautia lavished him with flowers, and with wine that like a blood-freshet ran through his veins,—she the vortex that draws all in. "But as my hand touched Hautia's, down dropped a dead bird from the clouds." And at the climax of the surrender into which Hautia had betrayed him, it was, between them, "snake and victim: life ebbing from out me, to her."

Later, in *Pierre*, Melville came to reflect upon "the inevitable evanescence of all earthly loveliness." The nuptial embrace, he says, "breaks love's airy zone." The idealities of courtship, he wrote, "like the bouquet of the costliest of German wines, too often evaporate upon pouring love out to drink in the disenchanting glasses of matrimonial days and nights." And Pierre exclaims: "By heaven, but marriage is an impious thing!"

This darkly figured hieroglyph of Melville's discontent was neither acclaimed by the public nor deciphered by Melville's wife. Withal, Melville was now not only a husband, but a father besides; and for his income he depended solely upon the earnings from his books. The reviewers had, in effect, given him clear warning that he could not support his family in luxury by the sale of cryptic libels upon it. *Mardi* had been followed rapidly by *Redburn*. Though his household at 103 Fourth Avenue was populous with relatives and visitors, he had shut himself away from the distraction of this varied company. In a letter to Hawthorne he later confessed: "The calm, the coolness, the silent grass-growing mood in which a man *ought* always to compose,—that, I fear, can seldom be mine." Endless bustle within the house; outside, as Mrs. Melville writes to her mother, screams of street venders "continually under our windows in every variety of cracked voices"—screams in which the guests from Boston "find much amusement." Mrs. Melville further writes that "Herman thinks I had better go back to Boston with Sam to see if the change of air will not benefit me," but she could not bring herself selfishly to follow Melville's solicitude: "I don't know as I can make up my mind to go and leave him here—and, besides, I'm afraid to trust him to finish up the book without me!" It was a life to enamour even a misanthrope to the family hearth. To quiet them all momentarily, Melville would put them copying manuscript. Yet, despite everything, Melville had stuck to his desk. In three years he had published five volumes: *Typee, Omoo, Mardi* (in two volumes), and *Redburn*. Though he had attracted wide attention as a writer, he was, nevertheless, in debt to his publishers. Another book—*White-Jacket*—he had finished in manuscript. Some very drastic step was necessary. So, five years after his return from the South Seas, and two years after his marriage, Melville for the third time decided to resort to a ship.

He was away eleven weeks. Most of the time he was in England, making personal intercessions with publishers, hoping thereby to improve his income from the other side of the Atlantic. After signing a contract with Bentley, he took a running jaunt through Paris, Brussels, Cologne, and Coblenz, returning in time to sail from Southampton on Christmas Day, 1849. Mrs. Melville, in her Commonplace Book, says of this trip: "Took little satisfaction in it from mere homesickness, and hurried home, leaving attractive invitations to visit distinguished people." As surprising as this "homesickness" may sound, it is repeatedly confessed in the journal of this trip which survives. This is but another instance of Melville's sentimental preoccupation with distance. As it had been with his mother, so was it with his wife: together, he craved to put oceans between them; estranged, he was restless to return. And it was thoroughly characteristic that, once back again to his household of wife, mother, and maiden sisters, he should have written companion sketches of moments in his life home and abroad entitled *Paradise of Bachelors and Tartarus of Maids.* Of the Paradise of Bachelors he wrote: "We were a band of brothers. You could see that these easy-hearted men had no wives and children to give them anxious thought. Almost all of them were travellers, too; for bachelors alone can travel freely, and without any twinge of their conscience touching desertion of the fireside."

The summer following his return, in search of less disorganization than New York offered, he and his wife and infant son Malcolm boarded at Broadhall, near Pittsfield,—

the old home of his uncle, where he had visited as a boy, and since converted into a hotel. In the autumn of the same year, with money advanced by his father-in-law, he took possession of a neighbouring farm which he named "Arrowhead." This was his home from October, 1850, to October, 1863. And it was, at once, the scene of the apex of his achievement, and of the blackest night of his defeat. Here *Moby-Dick* was to be written and dedicated to his neighbour, Nathaniel Hawthorne. In the headlong and desperate out-pouring of himself in this friendship, and in this agony of creation, he was to spend himself to the verge of utter exhaustion. And with his recognition of Hawthorne as a case of mistaken identity, and the popular fiasco of *Moby-Dick*, Melville for the first time would have been a perfect artist if he had put a bullet through his head. Instead, as if in a rage of vindictive and self-righteous defeat, he wrote *Pierre*.

Mrs. Melville records of the first years at Arrowhead: "Wrote *White-Whale* or *Moby-Dick* under unfavourable circumstances—would sit at his desk all day not eating anything until four or five o'clock—then ride to the village after dark—would be up early and out walking before breakfast—sometimes splitting wood for exercise. Published *White-Whale* in 1851—wrote *Pierre*, published 1852. We all felt anxious about his health in the spring of 1853." In a letter written to Hawthorne in the midst of *Moby-Dick*, Melville says: "The reason I have not been up to Lenox is this,—in the evening I feel completely done up, as the phrase is, and incapable of the long jolting to get to your house and back. In a week or so I go to New York, to bury myself in a third-story room, and work and slave on my *Whale* while it is driving through the press. *That* is the only way I can finish it now,—I am so pulled hither and thither by circumstances. Dollars damn me; and the malicious Devil is for ever grinning in upon me, holding the door ajar. My dear Sir, a presentiment is upon me,—I shall at last be worn out and perish, like an old nutmeg-grater, grated to pieces by the constant attrition of the wood, that is, the nutmeg. What I feel most moved to write, that is banned,—it will not pay. Yet, altogether, write the *other* way I cannot. So the product is a final hash, and all my books are botches." Letters of Melville to Duyckinck written at this time tell the same story—with the added detail that he seems going blind. "I keep one eye shut and wink at the paper with the other," he says; or again, "My evenings I spend in a sort of mesmeric state in my room—being unable to read"; or yet again, "Like an owl I steal about by twilight, owing to the twilight of my eyes." These were the eyes which Mrs. Hawthorne objected to in a dissertation to her mother because they were neither large nor deep. "They are not keen eyes, either, but quite undistinguished in any way." One full section of *Pierre* recounts under thin disguise the torture of those days in New York, mentioned above to Hawthorne, during which Melville wrestled with *Moby-Dick*, not only half blinded, but dropping in the streets from sudden vertigo.

It was in this state of exhaustion and hyper-excitability that Melville found himself a neighbour of Hawthorne's. When Hawthorne moved to Lenox, he was forty-six years old—Melville's senior by fifteen years. "He had recovered his health," his son says, "he had done his work, he was famous, and the region in which he dwelt was beautiful and inspiring. . . . Had *The Scarlet Letter* not achieved so fair a success, he might have been long in recovering his normal frame of mind. But the broad murmur of popular applause, coming to his unaccustomed ears from all parts of his native country, and rolling in across the sea from academic England, gave him the spiritual refreshment born of the assurance that our fellow-creatures think well of the work we have striven to make good. Such assurance is essential, sooner or later, to soundness and serenity of mind." And such assurance Melville had never known, nor was he ever to know it. At the time of his meeting with Hawthorne, he was ravished in solitude by his alienation from his fellows, and eager, to the point of hysteria, for a Utopian friendship that might solace him for all his earlier defeats. His letters to Hawthorne are amazing documents: exultant in worship, absolute in surrender. He craved of Hawthorne an understanding and a sympathy which neither Hawthorne, nor any other human being, perhaps, could ever have given. His impetuous soul rushed out to embrace Hawthorne's as that of a brother in despair. At this time, so his son says, "Hawthorne became a sort of Mecca of pilgrims with Christian's burden on their backs. Secret criminals of all kinds came to him for counsel and relief." Hawthorne was weary, perhaps, of souls harrowed and in voluble crucifixion; and when Melville came to him, not for counsel, but in headlong and absolute devotion, and in the intimate fraternity of the disenchanted, Melville had totally misread the temper of Hawthorne's disenchantment.

Emile Montégut, it is true, has described Hawthorne as a *romancier pessimiste*. Pessimist Hawthorne doubtless was—if pessimism be an absence of illusions. And in this sense, every worldly-wise man is a pessimist. Hawthorne was, of course, as W. C. Brownell has taken pains to show, "distinctly the most hard-headed of our men of genius." His son said of him: "He was the slave of no theory and no emotion; he always knew, so to speak, where he was and what he was about." His nature clearly was cool and self-sustaining, and like a star he dwelt apart; though no flower that ever bloomed could ever fill *him* with thoughts too deep for tears. For one of his nature, his family life was ideal. He was worshipped, idolized, canonized, and on his side it seems to have required small effort worthily to fill the rôle a more ardent nature would have either merited less or found more irksome. With his vital interests bounded by his domestic periphery, he had the good sense, the lack of enthusiasm, the disillusioned pessimism of the man of the world.

Though both Hawthorne and Melville were, in a sense, pessimists, they were pessimists in diametrically opposed usages of the word. Both were repelled by reality; both were quite out of sympathy with their time and its tendencies. But they had arrived at this point of meeting from opposite points of the compass.

Whereas Hawthorne's pessimism was an expression of lack of ardour and illusion, it was the very ardour of Melville's illusions, and the passion to discover that reality was cast in their mould, that was at the basis of Melville's hurt and embittered defeat. Both men, from their youth, had felt the flagrant and stubborn discord between the actual and the ideal, between fact and aspiration. But Hawthorne, unlike Melville, found no great difficulty in accepting the obdurate universe of people and things with a serene and robust fatalism. He accepted the universe as unalterable, and, as fame came to him, towards his own destiny he felt satisfaction without elation. It was his good sense to behave as if he felt that, in so far God had seemed to botch His job as a creative artist, that God's masterpiece, such as it was, was amenable to but trivial modification. The world of fact, and the world of illusion, he viewed as essentially exclusive realms; and, as Thoreau has counselled, he contented himself to live in "one world at a time." He was without hope in the sense that he never expected the order of nature to swerve of itself one hair's-breadth in the direction of his heart's desire. And this very hopelessness steadied him to the faith which no reasonable man can be without: faith, that is, in illusions as such, without the naïve and romantic exuberance which expects by the mere magic of wishing and the fever of locomotion, to find paradise in any local habitation. The realm of illusion,—which is the realm of the imagination, the realm of reverie and of art: his craving for omnipotence he restricted to that realm. And herein lay Hawthorne's superior adjustment to the world.

Hawthorne's was an adjustment that seems to have been an easy fulfilment of an essentially cool and self-possessed nature. Melville's was a more primal temperament, for the domestication of which, centuries, and not a mortal span of years, were best adequate. He was born with an imagination of very extraordinary vigour, and with a constitution of corresponding vitality. In sheer capacity to feel, most denizens of Christendom look pale beside him. Fired by a lust for life, a dogged unwillingness to learn from experience, a contempt for rationality, he launched forth in search of the seacoast of Bohemia. Few men have compassed such a volume of the raw material of experience as he crowded within the thirty-two years of his quest. Such was his naïve fulness of hope, his innocence of faith, that it was inevitable that, as one by one he put his illusions to the test, the bolts of his imagination, discharged against reality, but blazed out charred avenues to despair. And when on a bleak and snowy November day in 1851, the Hawthorne family, with its trunks, got into a large farm wagon and drove away from their little red house, Melville had dreamed the last of his avenging dreams. At Arrowhead there remained a very sick man in his thirty-second year, and a desperately poor one, with no source of income but from the writing of books which didn't sell, his soul solitary in its desolation.

Other than suicide, and short of miracle, the number of choices which were open to Melville in this extremity were limited in the extreme. He and the world had come to bitter and intolerable odds; and the world, not he, had, to all appearances, the upper hand. Something was drastically wrong somewhere, either with himself, or the world, or both. If with him, he might attempt to examine his conscience and reform; if with the world, he might defame and despise what he could not mend, protest thereby his own deep righteousness, and draw sweet solace besides, from feeling sorry for himself. More difficult than either, by rising superior to his emotions, as a disinterested spectator he might try to understand both himself and the world. Already he had discovered that when he put his earnest convictions on paper, the value of the paper deteriorated thereby. Though sick in body and soul, he was, none the less, married and twice a father: and but for the charity of relatives, debtors could be held at bay only by the point of his pen. Under these circumstances he behaved with incredible subtlety, passion and perverseness. Acting under no single one of the choices enumerated above, but alternating among them all, he sat down to write an apologia of his life, which he defiantly flung into the public's face.

Melville wrote *Pierre; or, The Ambiguities* (dedicated, this time, not to Hawthorne, but to the mountain Greylock), with no intent to reform the ways of the world. But he did write *Pierre* to show the impracticality of virtue; to give specific evidence, plagiarized from his own experience, that "the heavenly wisdom of God is an earthly folly to men," to put on record the reminder that the world's way is a hypocritical way in so far as it pretends to be other than the

Devil's way also. When he sat down to write, what seemed to him the holiest part of himself—his ardent aspirations—had wrecked itself against reality. So he undertook to present, in the character of Pierre, his own character purged of dross. For the other characters he drew upon relatives and intimate enemies, including Hawthorne (under the name of Plotinus Plinlimmon). Then he started his hero forth upon a career of lofty and unselfish impulse, intent to show that the more transcendent a man's ideals, the more certain and devastating his worldly defeat; that the most innocent in heart are those most in peril of being eventually involved in "strange, *unique* follies and sins, unimagined before."

And yet even the purest of impulses, Melville is intent to show, are less immaculate than superficially they seem. "In reserves men build imposing characters," he remarks; "not in revelations." And here in the character of Pierre, Melville seemed resolute to exhibit before a scandalized public a human soul, naked and unashamed. The subtlety of the analysis is extraordinary; and in its probings into the winding ambiguities of our self-deceptions, it is prophetic of some of the most recent and savoury findings in psychiatry. Beside it, *Jude the Obscure, The Idiot,* and *Women in Love* seem rather obvious and wholesome tales.

Pierre is a double-edged apologia of Melville's own defeat, in the sense that in *Pierre* Melville attempted to show that in so far as his own defeat—essentially paralleling Pierre's—was unblackened by incest, murder, and suicide, he had escaped these rewards of seraphic virtue through accident and inherent defect, rather than because of superior merit.

After *Pierre,* any further writing from Melville was both an impertinence and a moral defection. Melville was convinced of the futility of writing and effort; he wanted only

tranquillity for thought.   But his health was seriously breaking, and his family had to be fed. Writing had proven itself
an arduous way to starvation.   On April 29, 1851,—six
months before the American publication of *Moby-Dick*,—
Melville drew up an inventory of his earnings as author, in
an effort to demonstrate to himself and to Harpers that he
was a valuable business venture. To that time, the five
books that he had produced in five years of prodigious con-
centration, had brought him in $8,069.34: prodigal wealth,
when compared with what was to be his later driblets of
income.   To that time,—as thereafter,—Harpers was liberal to him beyond the strict letter of the bond.   Though
he was then nearly $700 in debt to Harpers, he asked for a
further advance on royalties,—counting against hope, apparently, that the supreme effort of *Moby-Dick* would bring
corresponding rewards.   Harpers denied this advance.
Moby-Dick appeared, and left Melville still in debt to Harpers. In publishing *Pierre*, Harpers made certain drastic
modifications of contract with Melville. Whereas before
Pierre, Melville and Harpers had shared, half-and-half,
cost of manufacture of books and profit from sales, with
Pierre Harpers agreed to pay Melville twenty-five cents on
the sale of any volumes after the first 1,190 copies. Melville's first royalties on *Pierre* were $58.25: an amount
greater than the sum of royalties that *Pierre* accumulated
during all the years that were to follow. During 1853—
the year after the publication of *Pierre*,—54 copies of
Typee were sold; 56 of *Omoo*; 42 of *Redburn*; 49 of
Mardi; 29 of *White-Jacket*; 48 of *Moby-Dick*; and 27 of
Pierre.   After his initial burst of popularity, it was a
miraculous year, indeed, that brought him in $100 royalties.
By working his farm, he succeeded in producing some of the
barest necessities of life. He had tried farming in the

prime of his youth, and had sailed for the South Seas soon after instituting the venture. In his present state of health it was a more difficult and no more luring occupation. And he had taken hostages of fortune to make impossible another escape to the watery world. So he looked about him for some other and unliterary source of income. Attempts were made by Hawthorne, Richard H. Dana, Jr., and by his brother Allan, to get him a consular appointment,—preferably in the South Seas, but that failing, anywhere. All attempts unavailing, Melville did the one thing he could: he sat down to try to turn out stuff that would sell.

Between 1853 and 1856 Melville published, in *Putnam's Magazine* and in *Harper's Monthly*, a serial novel and fifteen sketches and stories. The novel, *Israel Potter*, appeared in book form in 1855. *The Piazza Tales*, which appeared the following year, was a book of short stories, five of which had appeared in either *Putnam's* or *Harper's*.

Having followed Melville's career to this point, one would expect, with every apparent guarantee of mortal certainty, that this novel and these stories, done under economic compulsion, and by a man in Melville's state, would be worse than negligible; and most of the sketches and stories undoubtedly are. The unqualified failures are those in which Melville tries to imitate Hawthorne. Of himself Hawthorne once wrote, with engaging candour: "Whether from lack of power, or an unconquerable reserve, the Author's touches have often an effect of tameness." Of Hawthorne at his best this statement is false in every part. But of Hawthorne as Melville unconsciously parodies him, it is a flattering description. In these pieces Melville evidently recognized his failure; for he never republished them nor violated the anonymity under which they appeared.

Surprisingly enough, *Israel Potter* is a decidedly competent and entertaining picaresque story, half of it strictly historical. And, as Mr. John Freeman observes: "As if the attacks and sneers at his natural exuberance had indeed entered his soul, he resolved no more to cast his style to the swine but to restrict himself to the dry husks of language, putting an external constraint upon his genius." This book is to be dismissed as insignificant only by those who value Melville but for his eccentricities. It was praised by Hawthorne for its delineations of Franklin and John Paul Jones, and doubtless deserves a wider recognition than has ever been given it.

With *The Piazza Tales* we come upon one of the most totally amazing of all the surprises of Melville's career. For, though the book dropped from the press into almost perfect silence and neglect, the two chief stories of the volume—*Benito Cereno* and *The Encantadas*—are slowly coming to be chosen as marking the supreme technical achievement of Melville as an artist. When *The Encantadas* first appeared, it was read by Lowell; and according to a letter from the editor of *Putnam's Monthly* to Melville, Lowell was so moved that "the figure of the cross on the ass' neck brought tears into his eyes, and he thought it the finest touch of genius he had seen in prose." But Lowell was an isolated admirer; and in so far as is known, no other word of praise of these stories ever reached Melville. It was not until 1922, when all the happiness and hysteria of the Melville boom was upon us, that this book was singled out for special mention: and then, very quietly, in a kind of minority report. I quote at some length from Mr. Michael Sadlier's *Excursions in Victorian Bibliography:*

"The respective merits of the outstanding books of Melville are already (and will remain for long enough) the sport of literary publicists, to whose views and counter-views

I refer the curious. One feature, nevertheless, of contemporary opinion challenges to protest my amateur temerity. Apart from *Moby-Dick*, the neo-Melvillian has little beyond patronizing approval for the books of his hero; *Typee* (1846) and *Omoo* (1847) are interesting records of travel, remarkable mainly for the early date of their appearance and as forerunners of the South Sea School in letters and in painting. *Mardi* (1849), *Redburn* (1849), and *White-Jacket* (1850) claim respect as autobiography and for passages that reveal their author's genius struggling towards a more complete expression. These are the rising steps to the unique summit of Melville's work. There, unique and peerless, stands *Moby-Dick;* beyond it the terraces fall away again, and even more steeply than they rose.

"Is this opinion a just one? I am a little uncertain. With no desire to denigrate *Moby-Dick* or to deny it the first place in *importance* among Melville's books, I would venture that his genius is more perfectly and skilfully revealed in a volume of stories belonging to the so-called decadence. *The Piazza Tales* are liable to be dismissed by the critic to-day with kindly condescension as 'the best of the later work,' a judgment as misleading as it is easily explained. In some degree the worship of *Moby-Dick* and the comparative neglect of the other work are inevitable corollaries of the Melville boom at its present stage. During the first period of any new æsthetic wonder, the peculiar transcends the normal in the imagination of the disciples. Let the case of Melville be paralleled with that of Tintoretto's pupil, Greco. When first set in the revival of interest in this painter's work, he was most admired when most bizarre. He won favour for the contrast he presented to his immediate forerunners and his contemporaries. The name of Greco stood for certain mannerisms in colour and composition, and, the more a Greco picture revealed those mannerisms, the better a Greco it was judged to be. Already, from the hand of time, this formula of appreciation is suffering adjustment, but Melville is to-day precisely at the point where yesterday Greco stood. Like the master of Toledo, he has peculiar and noticeable tricks of matter and of style. Because *Moby-Dick* is of those tricks more redolent than the author's other books, it tickles the palate of contemporary enthusiasm more thoroughly than do they.

"*Moby-Dick* for all that it is unmistakably Melville is far from flawless. What if Melville recognized its weaknesses? What if he deplored those very characteristics that are to-day lauded as his priceless individuality and chief claim to fame? With all its vastness and its wonder, the epic story of Ahab and the great white whale displays the faults of its author as strikingly as it reveals his talents. In years to come, when the glamour of oddity has paled a little, it will be admitted that the book labours under a sad weight of intolerable prolixity. Nor is this prolixity implicit in the greatness of Melville's writing. This is proved by the two chief stories in *The Piazza Tales*. *Benito Cereno* and *The Encantadas* hold in the small compass of their beauty the essence of their author's supreme artistry. They are profound and lovely and tenderly robust, but they are never tedious and never wilful. Surely it were generous to admit that Melville sought to improve on *Moby-Dick* and that, in the matter of technical control, he succeeded. These two stories cannot as literary achievements compare with their vast and teeming predecessor. That is natural. But they may not be ignored as the last glimmer of a dying lamp. They mark the highest technical achievement of their author's work, and, had not within a year or two of their appearance the darkness of distrust descended upon him, might well have proved a revelation of something yet to come from the brain of Herman Melville, something destined—but for the treacherous inhibition of human frailty—to excel in power everything to which that brain had previously given birth."

With the appearance of Mr. John Freeman's *Herman Melville* in 1926, another deliberate and competent critic spoke out against the neglect of *The Piazza Tales*. Mr. Freeman characterizes *Benito Cereno* as "a flaming instance of the author's pure genius. . . . An astonishing story that must have brought tears of pride to Melville when he looked back upon it; and only a little less wonderful is an episode in another of the series, *The Encantadas, or Enchanted Isles*."

All this has been mounting to the pronouncement of Mr. Edward J. O'Brien. In the *Forum* for June, 1928, Mr. O'Brien has published his choice of "The Fifteen Finest Short Stories." *Benito Cereno* heads the list. Mr. O'Brien says:

"I regard this as the noblest short story in American literature. The balance of forces is complete, the atmosphere one of epic significance, the light cast upon the hero intense to the highest degree, the realization of the human soul profound, and the telling of the story orchestrated like a great symphony. Although it is the greatest short story in American literature, it has been practically inaccessible and is known to very few people. All Conrad's strivings reach fulfilment in this story, and its music lingers in the memory long after Conrad's music is forgotten."

To an incorrigible romantic, these tributes to works of Melville's "decline" must appear impious to *Moby-Dick*. For to the romantic, the prime excellence of any work of art is the volume of its passion; and to such a temperament, a work may be inchoate and ill-digested, a volcanic eruption that tosses itself blindly into the sky, and for that very reason be a glorious and successful achievement. The power to stimulate is surely the beginning of greatness. But a red-hot irrationality that can utter the wildest cries, surrender itself with the most absolute passion, heap up the most indiscriminate wealth of images, is not the perfection of genius. Melville himself, in the midst of the composition of *Moby-Dick*, confessed to Hawthorne a feeling that headlong turmoil botched creation.

It was Melville's great misfortune to drift into manhood without education: with no discipline of the will, no training in the uses of the practical or theoretical intellect, no initiation into the lessons of the past. After all, there is profound and disastrous significance in Melville's boast: "for a whale-ship was my Yale College and my Harvard." When Melville states that his development began in his twenty-fifth year he congratulates himself unduly. Marriage and authorship "developed" him in the sense that they made more explicit his capacity for chaos. During the vagrancy of his first twenty-five years he had gone about among the latitudes expressing his "spontaneous Me," like Rousseau, "burning with desire without any definite object." As a writer, he had put the highest premium upon "sincerity" and earnestness; and these, as he had yet to learn, are very questionable virtues in an artist. His case was similar to that of the amateur musician who, with gorgeous native endowment, tries to make up in "feeling" for what he lacks in mastery of technique. A man who is mastered by an emotion is in no state to calculate how that emotion were best communicated. As Richard Strauss exclaimed of Wagner's *Tristan:* "Such fire of sustained passion! It could have been written only by a man of ice!" Melville's career as a writer, up to and including his outburst in *Pierre* in praise of folly, is marred by a deepening of "sincerity." And in such a state he could not portray emotion, which demands detachment; at best he could betray it. The overwhelming bulk of Melville's writing is self-expression and satire; the hero is always himself, either in his own undisguised person or else thinly masked in all sorts of romantic and allegorical finery. And, since he was so much in earnest in his fiction, since he threw himself so unreservedly into his creations, since his imagination was so exclusively a vent for his personal preoccupations, Melville's most enthusiastic readers have been those primarily interested in him as a tortured and cryptic personality—not readers who have valued him for being a first-rate creative artist.

It was in *Benito Cereno* that for once, at least, he saved his soul as an artist, by losing it in something outside of himself. In this story he rose to the vantage ground of universal reason, above the passionate experiences which he overlooked and upon which he reflected. And for once he composed in the spirit of true beauty: a work devoutly finished, simple, and truly just.*

A brief moment of equilibrium—a momentary brightening of the embers into pure flame! Then, totally unencouraged by sympathetic friendship, by enlightened criticism, or by a glimmer of appreciation from the public, Melville for ever abandoned letters as a career.

The long remaining years were a struggle against poverty and ill health. In 1856, such was his growing moodiness— bursts of rage, followed by periods of silence and depression—that with the generosity of his father-in-law it was made possible for him to try to get away from his immediate worries and disappointments. He was away seven months;

---

* In *The Publication of the Modern Language Association of America*, Vol. XVIII, No. 2, June, 1928, Mr. Harold H. Scudder reprints the Eighteenth Chapter of Delano's *Voyages and Travels* (Boston, 1817): Melville's source for *Benito Cereno*.

but the difficulty was, he travelled with himself. At Liverpool, "a little paler, perhaps, and a little sadder, with his characteristic gravity and reserve of manner," he saw Hawthorne for the last time. Hawthorne goes on to say: "He informed me that he had 'pretty much made up his mind to be annihilated'; but still he does not seem to rest in that anticipation, and I think will never rest until he gets hold of some definite belief. It is strange how he persists—and has persisted ever since I knew him, and probably long before— in wandering to and fro over these deserts, as dismal and monotonous as the sandhills amidst which we were sitting. He can neither believe, nor be comfortable in his unbelief; and he is too honest and courageous not to try to do one or the other." From Liverpool he moved on to Constantinople and the Holy Land. In Melville's journal of this trip, his agonized scepticism is repeatedly recorded; and if not precisely homesick, his conscience tortured him for truancy from his obligations at home.

Back to Pittsfield, he earned what money he could from the produce of his farm, and from lecturing. For his own private behoof, he expanded the journal of his trip to the Near East into an amazing poem of 571 pages, which in 1876 was printed at the expense of a maternal uncle. *Clarel: A Poem and Pilgrimage in the Holy Land* is of prime importance as a document if not as a poem.

In 1863, after a residence of thirteen years, Melville and his family left Pittsfield, and by financial arrangements with his father-in-law bought the house at 104 East 26th Street, New York.

It was not until he was forty-seven that he succeeded in finding some non-literary employment that would assure him against starvation. On December 5, 1866, he was appointed Inspector of Customs. And for twenty years, morning and evening, between 26th Street and the foot of Gansevoort Street, East River, an inconspicuous and elderly private citizen—a man whose history had been partly told and partly foreshadowed in *Bartleby the Scrivener*—walked with his own private thoughts.

All the while, except for the associations at home and in the Custom House, Melville sedulously avoided human contacts. His leisure he spent in reading, and in worrying over the problem of the freedom of the will. But his impulse to write he seemed to have been unable ever to completely strangle. Most of his indulgence was in verse. Of these he printed two small volumes—*John Marr* (1888) and *Timoleon* (1891)—at his own expense and in editions of twenty-five each. Tied up in the trunk of Melville's papers was the manuscript of another volume of verse: *Weeds and Wilding Chiefly: With a Rose or Two*. There is a longish dedication to his wife which concludes: "But take them. And for aught suggestive of the 'melting mood' that any may possibly betray, call to mind the dissolving snowflakes on the ruddy oblation of old, and remember your 'Tears of the Happy.'" On the title page he had inscribed as legend: "Alms for Oblivion," and "Yes, decay is often a gardener."

Another manuscript volume, apparently unfinished, is a mixture of prose and verse. It is chiefly interesting because of Melville's preoccupation therein with a character called the Marquis de Grandvin, and his friend and disciple, John Gentian. Both the Marquis and his friend are old gentlemen but are men endowed from birth with personal beauty, moral charm, keen wit, and an amplitude of worldly belongings. In their lives, Melville suggests, they have so fully realized themselves they have never been urged to the vicarious fulfilment which is the function of the arts. And since, because of the very superiority of their gifts, these

men will make no exertion to rescue their names from oblivion, Melville proposes to exert his lesser gifts to perpetu-
ate their superior endowments. The scheme of the book is
best indicated in the most protracted of the five title-pages
Melville designed: AT THE HOSTELRY. *Literally rendered from the rhythmic inspiration of the Marquis de
Grandvin; being a piece introductory to* AN AFTERNOON IN
NAPLES IN THE TIME OF BOMBA *(herein included); the
latter digested into metre from the desultory narration of
John Gentian, Esq., of the Burgundian Old Fellows' Club,
a man the cherished lover of the aforesaid Marquis. The
Whole supplied with expository headings to the parts by the
Editor.* Except for the glimmer of an attempt to present
a life of overflowing sociability as being superior to a life
cramped to authorship, the book is as pretentious and dull
as its five title-pages.

It was not until Melville's sixty-ninth year that he was
for the first time to know the taste of leisure and economic
security. His wife had come into an inheritance from
her family. Melville resigned from the Custom House on
January 1, 1888, and before many months he was at his desk
—writing the last and not the least remarkable of his novels.
He had come to the end of his long ordeal. The passionate
urgencies within him had been tempered by years, and his
worldly defeat had gone into the recollections of things
past. He had money. Of his four children, both sons were
dead; one daughter was well married. His household consisted only of his wife, nobly loyal to him through forty-one
years, and an unmarried daughter approaching middle-age.
Then it was, and so protected and surrounded, that time and
circumstance were to bring Melville into that innocence and
serenity from which, by his own striving, he had been more
alienated the more he had striven to take them by violence.

A robust conscience had never been part of Melville's vigorous endowment. When he married and took hostages of fortune, he suffered profoundly from his inability to earn a decent income, dependent constantly upon his father-in-law's liberality. The quick succession of his books at the beginning of his career, an outpouring of his vital powers sustained at enormous length, was not the behaviour of a man primarily disposed to expect unearned increments from the world. He challenged the world with his genius, and the world defeated him by ignoring the challenge and starving him. He stopped writing because he had failed and because he had no choice but to accept the world's terms: there is no mystery here. This was not insanity, but common sense.

But in his personality and in his defeat in all human contacts there is mystery. In his books is revealed the secret fury of his essential nature. By every known record he was, to all external appearance, a man of extraordinary reserve; and the face that he presented to the world in his day, and to us still, is a mask.

Julian Hawthorne has written: "There was vivid genius in this man, and he was the strangest being that ever came into our circle. Through all his wild and reckless adventures, of which a small part only got into his fascinating books, he had been unable to rid himself of a Puritan conscience; he afterwards tried to loosen its grip by studying German metaphysics, but in vain. He was restless and disposed to dark hours, and there is reason to suspect that there was in him a vein of insanity. His later writings were incomprehensible. When I was in New York in 1884, I met him, looking pale, sombre, nervous, but little touched by age. He died a few years later. He conceived the highest admiration for my father's genius, and a deep affection for him personally; but he told me, during our talk, that he was convinced that there was some secret in my father's life which had never been revealed, and which accounted for the gloomy passages in his books. It was characteristic for him to imagine so; there were many secrets untold in his own career."

To call a man crazy when you cannot understand what he says, is an easy way to rest the intellect. But in detecting a consciousness of suppression in Melville, and in noting that he imputed it to others, Mr. Hawthorne is an acute and valuable witness. It is, of course, inadequate to say that Melville was merely hiding his disappointment at the failure of fame, and renouncing his gifts because they were no longer recognized. Year after year to go on perpetually writing books that would not sell was a luxury he could not afford. But his personal isolation, the infelicity of his marriage, his friendlessness, his growing sense that contact with men was an embarrassment rather than a refreshment—these suggest some fatal and hidden maladjustment within himself. The whole known record of his life seems insistently to indicate that veiled and deep-seated impulses from his nether-consciousness resolutely blocked the way to singleness of purpose and whole-heartedness of surrender; suppressions the more eloquently betrayed by his efforts both in his writings and in his life, to conceal them from himself. His was a soul so divided against itself that in the failure of self-mastery was mastered by life.

According to the myth which Plato puts into the mouth of Aristophanes, there was, in the beginning, a race of beings terrible for their strength and might: round in shape, with four feet and four hands, back and sides forming a circle, one head with two faces looking opposite ways, and the remainder to correspond. When this race in their might and insolence made an attack upon the gods, Zeus, after doubt, hit upon a scheme to mend their manners and humble their ways: he cut them all in half. Since then, each human creature, being but a mutilation, is in endless quest of his other half. And this is the nature of love: to reunite our dissevered selves, making one of two, healing the state of man. "And if we are not obedient to the gods," Aristophanes warns in conclusion, "there is danger that we shall be split up again." With Christianity, his prophecy was fulfilled, and this second severance became a fact. Man was divided against himself into body and soul, into flesh and spirit, crucified between the war of the members. "For the good that I would do I do not; but the evil which I would not, that I do. I delight in the law of God after the inner man: but I see another law in my members, warring against the law of my mind, and bringing me unto captivity to the law of sin which is in my members."

With very remarkable intensity of ardour, Melville's most relentless craving was to discover and dissolve himself into his other Platonic half. But his own nature was so disintegrated by the New England contamination from Saint Paul, that he viewed any such dissolution as a surrender to iniquity. Sexual strife and bodily surrender were not to him (as they were to Blake, whom in other ways he strikingly resembles), an ultimate fulfilment rehearsing the reconciliation of the vaster conflict between man and God, between Time and Eternity; it was a grossness and a shame, only to be annulled. Sex, to him, was not the consummation and dedication of ideality, but its filthy reverse.

His demoralization—as seems to be true of every other Galahad—had begun at home. His father,—who from Paris had characteristically written of the lascivious temptation of France and the rectitude of his own New England uxoriousness,—had infected his offspring with corrupt ideals of "innocence." Melville's extravagantly affectionate nature had, moreover, from the cradle haloed his mother with the wonder and mystery of sanctified womanhood: without blemish—unclouded, snow-white, terrible, yet serene. Between this ideality and the gymnastics of passions wherein he had been conceived, was a revolting antinomy that he was able to resolve neither at home nor in any latitude of Polynesia. "By heaven, but marriage is an impious thing!" he exclaims after his own marriage, in the person of Pierre; "Hard fate, that Love's best verdure should feed on tears."

No one can read Melville's work extensively without being struck by the almost complete absence of women and his almost complete avoidance of any mention of sex except either in glib parroting of traditional "literary" attitudes or else in dark and ominous evasion. As Mr. Freeman has said: "A cold nature his assuredly was not, and passages in *Pierre* have a power so unholy that one reads shrinkingly. But except in *Pierre* and one or two of the lesser books, and also *Clarel* among the poems, there is scarce a hint that Melville was aware of what it is that teases, exalts, ennobles, and destroys men. The sharpest sexual passion in his work, and it is an all but solitary instance, is incestuous." In *Timoleon*, the book of poems that appeared the year of his death, there is one piece amazingly apart from all the rest of this otherwise serene volume. *After the Pleasure Party* is the title, and the subject is the sting of sex. And here, with a directness unparalleled elsewhere in his work, he speaks out plain of "the sexual feud that clogs the aspiring life." "Drear shame," he exclaims, asking bitterly, "And kept I long heaven's watch for this?"

Viewing women as he did in the double capacity of Yillah and Hautia—"Yillah was all beauty and innocence; my crown of felicity; my heaven below;—and Hautia my heart abhorred"—it was in manly friendship, as offering ideality without sex—that he hoped for the fulfilment that marriage denied. That the volcanic and unenlisted energies of his sex might be roused in the fullest integrity of any such passion: that, by the evidence of his books and his behaviour, was of such nauseating repugnance to him that his whole nature seems to have fended against the very thought of such a possibility. And yet, in his writing, as in his life, is an abundance of masculine passion, an extremity of devotion, which suggest an indecision of frontier between friendship and love. Such enthusiasms, of which his last, for Hawthorne, is the most intimately documented expression, he celebrated with neither reticence, nor, in so far as we have any evidence, with outspoken integrity. Failure in quest of his Platonic half was perhaps inevitable. In his old age, in *After the Pleasure Party* again, he makes this remarkable comment upon his destiny:

> *"Could I remake me! or set free*
> *This sexless bound in sex, then plunge*
> *Deeper than Sappho, in a lunge*
> *Piercing Pan's paramount mystery!*
> *For, Nature, in no shallow surge*
> *Against thee either sex may urge.*
> *Why hast thou made us but in halves —*
> *Co-relatives? This makes us slaves.*
> *If these co-relatives never meet*
> *Selfhood itself seems incomplete.*
> *And such the dicing of blind fate*
> *Few matching halves here meet and* **mate.**
> *What Cosmic jest or Anarch blunder*
> *The human integral clove asunder*
> *And shied the fractions through life's gate?"*

His last word upon the strange mystery of himself and of human destiny is *Billy Budd:* "A story," so Melville said in a pencilled note at the end, "not unwarranted by what happens in this incongruous world of ours—innocence and infirmity, spiritual depravity and fair respite." It is a brief and appealing narrative, unmatched among Melville's works in lucidity and inward peace. "With calm of mind, all passion spent," Melville turned again to the narrative of one who, like Pierre, reaps death as the wages of virtue. The scene is aboard ship, and the conflict is between the innocence of the handsome young sailor Billy Budd, and the "natural depravity" of Claggart, a subtle, dark, demon-haunted petty officer. Claggart's is the "natural depravity" of Plato's definition: "depravity according to nature." Primarily he had been moved against Billy by his significant personal beauty, but not by that alone; it was, more deeply, the simplicity of a nature which had never willed malice which pricked the malice of the master-at-arms. "One person excepted, the master-at-arms was perhaps the only man in the ship intellectually capable of adequately appreciating the moral phenomenon presented in Billy Budd, and the insight but intensified his passion, which, assuming various secret forms within him, at times assumed that of cynic disdain—disdain of innocence. To be nothing more than innocent!" Melville himself had known this "cynic disdain." For when he wrote *Pierre,* one part of him hated the youthful guilelessness of his earlier self as represented in the hero of that novel, even as Claggart hated Billy Budd.

To pass from a normal nature to one haunted as was Claggart one must cross, Melville says, "the deadly space between, and this is best done by indirection." In attempting this oblique passage, Melville tells how "long ago an honest scholar, my senior, said to me in reference to one who like himself is no more, a man so unimpeachably respectable that against him nothing was ever openly said, though among the few something was whispered, 'Yes, X—— is a nut not to be cracked by the tap of a lady's fan.'" And Melville's comment is as guarded as the rest of the passage: "At the time my inexperience was such that I did not quite see the drift of all this. It may be that I see it now."

But there are other and less ambiguous glimpses given us into Claggart's dark soul. "When Claggart's unobserved glance happened to light on belted Billy rolling along the upper gun-deck in the leisure of the second dog-watch, exchanging passing broadsides of fun with other promenaders in the crowd, that glance would follow the cheerful sea-Hyperion with a settled, meditative, and melancholy expression, his eyes strangely suffused with incipient feverish tears. Then would Claggart look like the man of sorrows. Yes, and sometimes the melancholy expression would have in it a touch of soft yearning, as if Claggart could even have loved Billy but for fate and ban." Claggart would seem to be an American forerunner of the Charlus of Marcel Proust. And as a study in abnormal psychology, *Billy Budd* is remarkably detached, subtle, and profound. In the writing of it, however, Melville's exclusive interest was not to probe clinically into "the mystery of iniquity."

Just as some theologians have presented the fall of man as evidence of the great glory of God, in similar manner Melville studies the evil in Claggart in vindication of the innocence in Billy Budd. For, primarily, Melville wrote *Billy Budd* in witness to his ultimate faith that evil is defeat and natural goodness invincible in the affections of man. *Billy Budd*, as *Pierre*, ends in disaster and death; in each case inexperience and innocence and seraphic impulse are wrecked against the malign forces of darkness that seem to preside over external human destiny. In *Pierre*, Melville had hurled himself into a fury of vituperation against the world; with *Billy Budd* he would justify the ways of God to man. Among the many parallels of contrast between these two books, each is a tragedy (as was Melville's life), but in opposed sense of the term. For tragedy may be viewed not as being essentially the representation of human misery, but rather as the representation of human goodness or nobility. All of the supremest art is tragic: but the tragedy is, in Aristotle's phrase, "the representation of Eudaimonia," or the highest kind of happiness. There is, of course, in this type of tragedy, with its essential quality of encouragement and triumph, no flinching of any horror of tragic life, no shirking of the truth by a feeble idealism, none of the compromises of the so-called "happy ending." The powers of evil and horror must be granted their fullest scope; it is only thus we can triumph over them. Even though in the end the tragic hero finds no friends among the living or dead, no help in God, only a deluge of calamity everywhere, yet in the very intensity of his affliction he may reveal the splendour undiscoverable in any gentler fate. Here he has reached, not the bottom, but the crowning peak of fortune—something which neither suffering nor misfortune can touch. Only when worldly disaster has worked its utmost can we realize that there remains something in man's soul which is for ever beyond the grasp of the accidents of existence, with power in its own right to make life beautiful. Only through tragedy of this type could Melville affirm his everlasting yea. The final great revelation—or great illusion—of his life, he uttered in *Billy Budd*.

RAYMOND WEAVER.

BUTLER HALL,
NEW YORK CITY,
7 *July*, 1928.

BENITO CERENO

First published anonymously in *Putnam's Monthly Magazine*, October, November, December, 1855.
Republished in "The Piazza Tales", 1856.

BENITO CERENO

In the year 1799, Captain Amasa Delano, of Duxbury, in Massachusetts, commanding a large sealer and general trader, lay at anchor, with a valuable cargo, in the harbour of St. Maria—a small, desert, uninhabited island towards the southern extremity of the long coast of Chili. There he had touched for water.

On the second day, not long after dawn, while lying in his berth, his mate came below, informing him that a strange sail was coming into the bay. Ships were then not so plenty in those waters as now. He rose, dressed, and went on deck.

The morning was one peculiar to that coast. Everything was mute and calm; everything grey. The sea, though undulated into long roods of swells, seemed fixed, and was sleeked at the surface like waved lead that has cooled and set in the smelter's mould. The sky seemed a grey mantle. Flights of troubled grey fowl, kith and kin with flights of troubled grey vapours among which they were mixed, skimmed low and fitfully over the waters, as swallows over meadows before storms. Shadows present, foreshadowing deeper shadows to come.

To Captain Delano's surprise, the stranger, viewed through the glass, showed no colours; though to do so upon entering a haven, however uninhabited in its shores, where but a single other ship might be lying, was the custom among peaceful seamen of all nations. Considering the lawlessness and loneliness of the spot, and the sort of stories, at that day, associated with those seas, Captain Delano's surprise might have deepened into some uneasiness had he not been a person of a singularly undistrustful good nature,

3

not liable, except on extraordinary and repeated excitement, and hardly then, to indulge in personal alarms, any way involving the imputation of malign evil in man. Whether, in view of what humanity is capable, such a trait implies, along with a benevolent heart, more than ordinary quickness and accuracy of intellectual perception, may be left to the wise to determine.

But whatever misgivings might have obtruded on first seeing the stranger, would almost, in any seaman's mind, have been dissipated by observing that, the ship, in navigating into the harbour, was drawing too near the land, for her own safety's sake, owing to a sunken reef making out off her bow. This seemed to prove her a stranger, indeed, not only to the sealer, but the island; consequently, she could be no wonted freebooter on that ocean. With no small interest, Captain Delano continued to watch her—a proceeding not much facilitated by the vapours partly mantling the hull, through which the far matin light from her cabin streamed equivocally enough; much like the sun—by this time crescented on the rim of the horizon, and apparently, in company with the strange ship, entering the harbour —which, wimpled by the same low, creeping clouds, showed not unlike a Lima intriguante's one sinister eye peering across the Plaza from the Indian loop-hole of her dusk *saya-y-manta*.

It might have been but a deception of the vapours, but, the longer the stranger was watched, the more singular appeared her manœuvres. Ere long it seemed hard to decide whether she meant to come in or no—what she wanted, or what she was about. The wind, which had breezed up a little during the night, was now extremely light and baffling, which the more increased the apparent uncertainty of her movements.

Surmising, at last, that it might be a ship in distress, Captain Delano ordered his whale-boat to be dropped, and, much to the wary opposition of his mate, prepared to board her, and, at the least, pilot her in. On the night previous, a fishing-party of the seamen had gone a long distance to some detached rocks out of sight from the sealer, and, an hour or two before day-break, had returned, having met with no small success. Presuming that the stranger might have been long off soundings, the good captain put several baskets of the fish, for presents, into his boat, and so pulled away. From her continuing too near the sunken reef, deeming her in danger, calling to his men, he made all haste to apprise those on board of their situation. But, some time ere the boat came up, the wind, light though it was, having shifted, had headed the vessel off, as well as partly broken the vapours from about her.

Upon gaining a less remote view, the ship, when made signally visible on the verge of the leaden-hued swells, with the shreds of fog here and there raggedly furring her, appeared like a white-washed monastery after a thunder-storm, seen perched upon some dun cliff among the Pyrenees. But it was no purely fanciful resemblance which now, for a moment, almost led Captain Delano to think that nothing less than a ship-load of monks was before him. Peering over the bulwarks were what really seemed, in the hazy distance, throngs of dark cowls; while, fitfully revealed through the open port-holes, other dark moving figures were dimly descried, as of Black Friars pacing the cloisters.

Upon a still nigher approach, this appearance was modified, and the true character of the vessel was plain—a Spanish merchantman of the first class; carrying negro slaves, amongst other valuable freight, from one colonial port to another. A very large, and, in its time, a very fine vessel, such as in those days were at intervals encountered along that main; sometimes superseded Acapulco treasure-ships, or retired frigates of the Spanish king's navy, which, like superannuated Italian palaces, still, under a decline of masters, preserved signs of former state.

As the whale-boat drew more and more nigh, the cause of the peculiar pipe-clayed aspect of the stranger was seen in the slovenly neglect pervading her. The spars, ropes, and great part of the bulwarks, looked woolly, from long unacquaintance with the scraper, tar, and the brush. Her keel seemed laid, her ribs put together, and she launched, from Ezekiel's Valley of Dry Bones.

In the present business in which she was engaged, the ship's general model and rig appeared to have undergone no material change from their original warlike and Froissart pattern. However, no guns were seen.

The tops were large, and were railed about with what had once been octagonal net-work, all now in sad disrepair. These tops hung overhead like three ruinous aviaries, in one of which was seen perched, on a ratlin, a white noddy, a strange fowl, so called from its lethargic somnambulistic character, being frequently caught by hand at sea. Battered and mouldy, the castellated forecastle seemed some ancient turret, long ago taken by assault, and then left to decay. Towards the stern, two high-raised quarter galleries —the balustrades here and there covered with dry, tindery sea-moss—opening out from the unoccupied state-cabin, whose dead lights, for all the mild weather, were hermetically closed and caulked—these tenantless balconies hung over the sea as if it were the grand Venetian canal. But the principal relic of faded grandeur was the ample oval of the shield-like stern-piece, intricately carved with the arms of Castile and Leon, medallioned about by groups of mythological or symbolical devices; uppermost and central of which was a dark satyr in a mask, holding his foot on the prostrate neck of a writhing figure, likewise masked.

Whether the ship had a figure-head, or only a plain beak, was not quite certain, owing to canvas wrapped about that part, either to protect it while undergoing a refurbishing, or else decently to hide its decay. Rudely painted or chalked, as in a sailor freak, along the forward side of a sort of pedestal below the canvas, was the sentence, *"Seguid vuestro jefe,"* (follow your leader); while upon the tarnished head-boards, near by, appeared, in stately capitals, once gilt, the ship's name, "SAN DOMINICK," each letter streakingly corroded with tricklings of copper-spike rust; while, like mourning weeds, dark festoons of sea-grass slimily swept to and fro over the name, with every hearse-like roll of the hull.

As at last the boat was hooked from the bow along toward the gangway amidship, its keel, while yet some inches separated from the hull, harshly grated as on a sunken coral reef. It proved a huge bunch of conglobated barnacles adhering below the water to the side like a wen; a token of baffling airs and long calms passed somewhere in those seas.

Climbing the side, the visitor was at once surrounded by a clamorous throng of whites and blacks, but the latter outnumbering the former more than could have been expected, negro transportation-ship as the stranger in port was. But, in one language, and as with one voice, all poured out a common tale of suffering; in which the negresses, of whom there were not a few, exceeded the others in their dolorous vehemence. The scurvy, together with a fever, had swept off a great part of their number, more especially the Spaniards. Off Cape Horn, they had narrowly escaped shipwreck; then, for days together, they had lain tranced without wind; their provisions were low; their water next to none; their lips that moment were baked.

While Captain Delano was thus made the mark of all eager tongues, his one eager glance took in all the faces, with every other object about him.

Always upon first boarding a large and populous ship at sea, especially a foreign one, with a nondescript crew such as Lascars or Manilla men, the impression varies in a peculiar way from that produced by first entering a strange house with strange inmates in a strange land. Both house and ship, the one by its walls and blinds, the other by its high bulwarks like ramparts, hoard from view their interiors till the last moment; but in the case of the ship there is this addition: that the living spectacle it contains, upon its sudden and complete disclosure, has, in contrast with the blank ocean which zones it, something of the effect of enchantment. The ship seems unreal; these strange costumes, gestures, and faces, but a shadowy tableau just emerged from the deep, which directly must receive back what it gave.

Perhaps it was some such influence as above is attempted to be described which, in Captain Delano's mind, heightened whatever, upon a staid scrutiny, might have seemed unusual; especially the conspicuous figures of four elderly grizzled negroes, their heads like black, doddered willow tops, who, in venerable contrast to the tumult below them, were couched sphynx-like, one on the starboard cat-head, another on the larboard, and the remaining pair face to face on the opposite bulwarks above the main-chains. They each had bits of unstranded old junk in their hands, and, with a sort of stoical self-content, were picking the junk into oakum, a small heap of which lay by their sides. They accompanied the task with a continuous, low, monotonous chant; droning and drooling away like so many grey-headed bag-pipers playing a funeral march.

The quarter-deck rose into an ample elevated poop, upon the forward verge of which, lifted, like the oakum-pickers, some eight feet above the general throng, sat along in a row, separated by regular spaces, the cross-legged figures of six other blacks; each with a rusty hatchet in his hand, which, with a bit of brick and a rag, he was engaged like a scullion in scouring; while between each two was a small stack of hatchets, their rusted edges turned forward awaiting a like operation. Though occasionally the four oakum-pickers would briefly address some person or persons in the crowd below, yet the six hatchet-polishers neither spoke to others, nor breathed a whisper among themselves, but sat intent upon their task, except at intervals, when, with the peculiar love in negroes of uniting industry with pastime, two-and-two they sideways clashed their hatchets together, like cymbals, with a barbarous din. All six, unlike the generality, had the raw aspect of unsophisticated Africans.

But that first comprehensive glance which took in those ten figures, with scores less conspicuous, rested but an instant upon them, as, impatient of the hubbub of voices, the visitor turned in quest of whomsoever it might be that commanded the ship.

But as if not unwilling to let nature make known her own case among his suffering charge, or else in despair of restraining it for the time, the Spanish captain, a gentlemanly, reserved-looking, and rather young man to a stranger's eye, dressed with singular richness, but bearing plain traces of recent sleepless cares and disquietudes, stood passively by, leaning against the main-mast, at one moment casting a dreary, spiritless look upon his excited people, at the next an unhappy glance toward his visitor. By his side stood

strange people [margin annotation]

a black of small stature, in whose rude face, as occasionally, like a shepherd's dog, he mutely turned it up into the Spaniard's, sorrow and affection were equally blended.

Struggling through the throng, the American advanced to the Spaniard, assuring him of his sympathies, and offering to render whatever assistance might be in his power. To which the Spaniard returned, for the present, but grave and ceremonious acknowledgments, his national formality dusked by the saturnine mood of ill health.

But losing no time in mere compliments, Captain Delano returning to the gangway, had his baskets of fish brought up; and as the wind still continued light, so that some hours at least must elapse ere the ship could be brought to the anchorage, he bade his men return to the sealer, and fetch back as much water as the whale-boat could carry, with whatever soft bread the steward might have, all the remaining pumpkins on board, with a box of sugar, and a dozen of his private bottles of cider.

Not many minutes after the boat's pushing off, to the vexation of all, the wind entirely died away, and the tide turning, began drifting back the ship helplessly seaward. But trusting this would not long last, Captain Delano sought with good hopes to cheer up the strangers, feeling no small satisfaction that, with persons in their condition he could— thanks to his frequent voyages along the Spanish main— converse with some freedom in their native tongue.

While left alone with them, he was not long in observing some things tending to heighten his first impressions; but surprise was lost in pity, both for the Spaniards and blacks, alike evidently reduced from scarcity of water and provisions; while long-continued suffering seemed to have brought out the less good-natured qualities of the negroes, besides, at the same time, impairing the Spaniard's authority

over them. But, under the circumstances, precisely this condition of things was to have been anticipated. In armies,
navies, cities, or families—in nature herself—nothing more
relaxes good order than misery. Still, Captain Delano was
not without the idea, that had Benito Cereno been a man
of greater energy, misrule would hardly have come to the
present pass. But the debility, constitutional or induced by
the hardships, bodily and mental, of the Spanish captain,
was too obvious to be overlooked. A prey to settled dejec-
tion, as if long mocked with hope he would not now indulge
it, even when it had ceased to be a mock, the prospect of
that day or evening at furthest, lying at anchor, with plenty
of water for his people, and a brother captain to counsel and
befriend, seemed in no perceptible degree to encourage him.
His mind appeared unstrung, if not still more seriously affected. Shut up in these oaken walls, chained to one dull
round of command, whose unconditionality cloyed him, like
some hypochondriac abbot he moved slowly about, at times
suddenly pausing, starting, or staring, biting his lip, biting
his finger-nail, flushing, paling, twitching his beard, with
other symptoms of an absent or moody mind. This distempered spirit was lodged, as before hinted, in as distempered
a frame. He was rather tall, but seemed never to have been
robust, and now with nervous suffering was almost worn
to a skeleton. A tendency to some pulmonary complaint appeared to have been lately confirmed. His voice was like
that of one with lungs half gone, hoarsely suppressed, a
husky whisper. No wonder that, as in this state he tottered
about, his private servant apprehensively followed him.
Sometimes the negro gave his master his arm, or took his
handkerchief out of his pocket for him; performing these
and similar offices with that affectionate zeal which trans-
mutes into something filial or fraternal acts in themselves

but menial; and which has gained for the negro the repute of making the most pleasing body servant in the world; one, too, whom a master need be on no stiffly superior terms with, but may treat with familiar trust; less a servant than a devoted companion.

Marking the noisy indocility of the blacks in general, as well as what seemed the sullen inefficiency of the whites, it was not without humane satisfaction that Captain Delano witnessed the steady good conduct of Babo.

But the good conduct of Babo, hardly more than the ill-behaviour of others, seemed to withdraw the half-lunatic Don Benito from his cloudy languor. Not that such precisely was the impression made by the Spaniard on the mind of his visitor. The Spaniard's individual unrest was, for the present, but noted as a conspicuous feature in the ship's general affliction. Still, Captain Delano was not a little concerned at what he could not help taking for the time to be Don Benito's unfriendly indifference toward himself. The Spaniard's manner, too, conveyed a sort of sour and gloomy disdain, which he seemed at no pains to disguise. But this the American in charity ascribed to the harassing effects of sickness, since, in former instances, he had noted that there are peculiar natures on whom prolonged physical suffering seems to cancel every social instinct of kindness; as if forced to black bread themselves, they deemed it but equity that each person coming nigh them should, indirectly, by some slight or affront, be made to partake of their fare.

But ere long Captain Delano bethought him that, indulgent as he was at the first, in judging the Spaniard, he might not, after all, have exercised charity enough. At bottom it was Don Benito's reserve which displeased him; but the same reserve was shown toward all but his personal attendant. Even the formal reports which, according to sea-usage, were at stated times made to him by some petty underling (either a white, mulatto or black), he hardly had patience enough to listen to, without betraying contemptuous aversion. His manner upon such occasions was, in its degree, not unlike that which might be supposed to have been his imperial countryman's, Charles V., just previous to the anchoritish retirement of that monarch from the throne.

This splenetic disrelish of his place was evinced in almost every function pertaining to it. Proud as he was moody, he condescended to no personal mandate. Whatever special orders were necessary, their delivery was delegated to his body-servant, who in turn transferred them to their ultimate destination, through runners, alert Spanish boys or slave boys, like pages or pilot-fish within easy call continually hovering round Don Benito. So that to have beheld this undemonstrative invalid gliding about, apathetic and mute, no landsman could have dreamed that in him was lodged a dictatorship beyond which, while at sea, there was no earthly appeal.

Thus, the Spaniard, regarded in his reserve, seemed as the involuntary victim of mental disorder. But, in fact, his reserve might, in some degree, have proceeded from design. If so, then in Don Benito was evinced the unhealthy climax of that icy though conscientious policy, more or less adopted by all commanders of large ships, which, except in signal emergencies, obliterates alike the manifestation of sway with every trace of sociality; transforming the man into a block, or rather into a loaded cannon, which, until there is call for thunder, has nothing to say.

Viewing him in this light, it seemed but a natural token of the perverse habit induced by a long course of such hard self-restraint, that, notwithstanding the present condition of his ship, the Spaniard should still persist in a demeanour,

which, however harmless—or it may be, appropriate—in a
well-appointed vessel, such as the *San Dominick* might have
been at the outset of the voyage, was anything but judicious
now.   But the Spaniard perhaps thought that it was with
captains as with gods: reserve, under all events, must still
be their cue.   But more probably this appearance of slumbering dominion might have been but an attempted disguise
to conscious imbecility—not deep policy, but shallow device.
But be all this as it might, whether Don Benito's manner
was designed or not, the more Captain Delano noted its
pervading reserve, the less he felt uneasiness at any particular manifestation of that reserve toward himself.

Neither were his thoughts taken up by the captain alone.
Wonted to the quiet orderliness of the sealer's comfortable
family of a crew, the noisy confusion of the *San Dominick's*
suffering host repeatedly challenged his eye.   Some promi-
nent breaches not only of discipline but of decency were observed.   These Captain Delano could not but ascribe, in
the main, to the absence of those subordinate deck-officers
to whom, along with higher duties, is entrusted what may
be styled the police department of a populous ship.   True,
the old oakum-pickers appeared at times to act the part of
monitorial constables to their countrymen, the blacks; but
though occasionally succeeding in allaying trifling outbreaks
now and then between man and man, they could do little or
nothing toward establishing general quiet.   The *San Dominick* was in the condition of a transatlantic emigrant ship,
among whose multitude of living freight are some individuals, doubtless, as little troublesome as crates and bales; but
the friendly remonstrances of such with their ruder companions are of not so much avail as the unfriendly arm of
the mate.   What the *San Dominick* wanted was, what the

emigrant ship has, stern superior officers. But on these decks not so much as a fourth mate was to be seen.

The visitor's curiosity was roused to learn the particulars of those mishaps which had brought about such absenteeism, with its consequences; because, though deriving some inkling of the voyage from the wails which at the first moment had greeted him, yet of the details no clear understanding had been had. The best account would, doubtless, be given by the captain. Yet at first the visitor was loth to ask it, unwilling to provoke some distant rebuff. But plucking up courage, he at last accosted Don Benito, renewing the expression of his benevolent interest, adding, that did he (Captain Delano) but know the particulars of the ship's misfortunes, he would, perhaps, be better able in the end to relieve them. Would Don Benito favour him with the whole story?

Don Benito faltered; then, like some somnambulist suddenly interfered with, vacantly stared at his visitor, and ended by looking down on the deck. He maintained this posture so long, that Captain Delano, almost equally disconcerted, and involuntarily almost as rude, turned suddenly from him, walking forward to accost one of the Spanish seamen for the desired information. But he had hardly gone five paces, when with a sort of eagerness Don Benito invited him back, regretting his momentary absence of mind, and professing readiness to gratify him.

While most part of the story was being given, the two captains stood on the after part of the main-deck, a privileged spot, no one being near but the servant.

"It is now a hundred and ninety days," began the Spaniard, in his husky whisper, "that this ship, well officered and well manned, with several cabin passengers—some fifty Spaniards in all—sailed from Buenos Ayres bound to Lima, with a general cargo, Paraguay tea and the like—and," pointing forward, "that parcel of negroes, now not more than a hundred and fifty, as you see, but then numbering over three hundred souls. Off Cape Horn we had heavy gales. In one moment, by night, three of my best officers, with fifteen sailors, were lost, with the main-yard; the spar snapping under them in the slings, as they sought, with heavers, to beat down the icy sail. To lighten the hull, the heavier sacks of mata were thrown into the sea, with most of the water-pipes lashed on deck at the time. And this last necessity it was, combined with the prolonged detentions afterwards experienced, which eventually brought about our chief causes of suffering. When——"

Here there was a sudden fainting attack of his cough, brought on, no doubt, by his mental distress. His servant sustained him, and drawing a cordial from his pocket placed it to his lips. He a little revived. But unwilling to leave him unsupported while yet imperfectly restored, the black with one arm still encircled his master, at the same time keeping his eye fixed on his face, as if to watch for the first sign of complete restoration, or relapse, as the event might prove.

The Spaniard proceeded, but brokenly and obscurely, as one in a dream.

—"Oh, my God! rather than pass through what I have, with joy I would have hailed the most terrible gales; but——"

His cough returned and with increased violence; this subsiding, with reddened lips and closed eyes he fell heavily against his supporter.

"His mind wanders. He was thinking of the plague that followed the gales," plaintively sighed the servant; "my poor, poor master!" wringing one hand, and with the other

wiping the mouth. "But be patient, Señor," again turning
to Captain Delano, "these fits do not last long; master will
soon be himself."

Don Benito reviving, went on; but as this portion of the
story was very brokenly delivered, the substance only will
here be set down.

It appeared that after the ship had been many days tossed
in storms off the Cape, the scurvy broke out, carrying off
numbers of the whites and blacks. When at last they had
worked round into the Pacific, their spars and sails were so
damaged, and so inadequately handled by the surviving mariners, most of whom were become invalids, that, unable to
lay her northerly course by the wind, which was powerful,
the unmanageable ship for successive days and nights was
blown northwestward, where the breeze suddenly deserted
her, in unknown waters, to sultry calms. The absence of the
water-pipes now proved as fatal to life as before their presence had menaced it. Induced, or at least aggravated, by the
more than scanty allowance of water, a malignant fever followed the scurvy; with the excessive heat of the lengthened
calm, making such short work of it as to sweep away, as by
billows, whole families of the Africans, and a yet larger number, proportionably, of the Spaniards, including, by a luckless fatality, every officer on board. Consequently, in the
smart west winds eventually following the calm, the already
rent sails having to be simply dropped, not furled, at need,
had been gradually reduced to the beggar's rags they were
now. To procure substitutes for his lost sailors, as well as
supplies of water and sails, the captain at the earliest opportunity had made for Baldivia, the southermost civilized port
of Chili and South America; but upon nearing the coast the
thick weather had prevented him from so much as sighting
that harbour. Since which period, almost without a crew,

and almost without canvas and almost without water, and at intervals giving its added dead to the sea, the *San Dominick* had been battle-dored about by contrary winds, inveigled by currents, or grown weedy in calms. Like a man lost in woods, more than once she had doubled upon her own track.

"But throughout these calamities," huskily continued Don Benito, painfully turning in the half embrace of his servant, "I have to thank those negroes you see, who, though to your inexperienced eyes appearing unruly, have, indeed, conducted themselves with less of restlessness than even their owner could have thought possible under such circumstances."

Here he again fell faintly back. Again his mind wandered: but he rallied, and less obscurely proceeded.

"Yes, their owner was quite right in assuring me that no fetters would be needed with his blacks; so that while, as is wont in this transportation, those negroes have always remained upon deck—not thrust below, as in the Guineamen—they have, also, from the beginning, been freely permitted to range within given bounds at their pleasure."

Once more the faintness returned—his mind roved—but, recovering, he resumed:

"But it is Babo here to whom, under God, I owe not only my own preservation, but likewise to him, chiefly, the merit is due, of pacifying his more ignorant brethren, when at intervals tempted to murmurings."

"Ah, master," sighed the black, bowing his face, "don't speak of me; Babo is nothing; what Babo has done was but duty."

"Faithful fellow!" cried Captain Delano. "Don Benito, I envy you such a friend; slave I cannot call him."

As master and man stood before him, the black upholding the white, Captain Delano could not but bethink him of the beauty of that relationship which could present such a spectacle of fidelity on the one hand and confidence on the other. The scene was heightened by the contrast in dress, denoting their relative positions. The Spaniard wore a loose Chili jacket of dark velvet; white small clothes and stockings, with silver buckles at the knee and instep; a high-crowned sombrero, of fine grass; a slender sword, silver mounted, hung from a knot in his sash; the last being an almost invariable adjunct, more for utility than ornament, of a South American gentleman's dress to this hour. Excepting when his occasional nervous contortions brought about disarray, there was a certain precision in his attire, curiously at variance with the unsightly disorder around; especially in the belittered Ghetto, forward of the main-mast, wholly occupied by the blacks.

The servant wore nothing but wide trousers, apparently, from their coarseness and patches, made out of some old topsail; they were clean, and confined at the waist by a bit of unstranded rope, which, with his composed, deprecatory air at times, made him look something like a begging friar of St. Francis.

However unsuitable for the time and place, at least in the blunt-thinking American's eyes, and however strangely surviving in the midst of all his afflictions, the toilette of Don Benito might not, in fashion at least, have gone beyond the style of the day among South Americans of his class. Though on the present voyage sailing from Buenos Ayres, he had avowed himself a native and resident of Chili, whose inhabitants had not so generally adopted the plain coat and once plebeian pantaloons; but, with a becoming modification, adhered to their provincial costume, picturesque as any in the world. Still, relatively to the pale history of the voyage, and his own pale face, there seemed something so incongruous in the Spaniard's apparel, as almost to suggest the image of an invalid courtier tottering about London streets in the time of the plague.

The portion of the narrative which, perhaps, most excited interest, as well as some surprise, considering the latitudes in question, was the long calms spoken of, and more particularly the ship's so long drifting about. Without communicating the opinion, of course, the American could not but impute at least part of the detentions both to clumsy seamanship and faulty navigation. Eyeing Don Benito's small, yellow hands, he easily inferred that the young captain had not got into command at the hawse-hole but the cabin-window, and if so, why wonder at incompetence, in youth, sickness, and aristocracy united? Such was his democratic conclusion.

But drowning criticism in compassion, after a fresh repetition of his sympathies, Captain Delano having heard out his story, not only engaged, as in the first place, to see Don Benito and his people supplied in their immediate bodily needs, but, also, now further promised to assist him in procuring a large permanent supply of water, as well as some sails and rigging; and, though it would involve no small embarrassment to himself, yet he would spare three of his best seamen for temporary deck officers; so that without delay the ship might proceed to Concepcion, there fully to refit for Lima, her destined port.

Such generosity was not without its effect, even upon the invalid. His face lighted up; eager and hectic, he met the honest glance of his visitor. With gratitude he seemed overcome.

"This excitement is bad for master," whispered the servant, taking his arm, and with soothing words gently drawing him aside.

When Don Benito returned, the American was pained to

observe that his hopefulness, like the sudden kindling in his cheek, was but febrile and transient.

Ere long, with a joyless mien, looking up toward the poop, the host invited his guest to accompany him there, for the benefit of what little breath of wind might be stirring.

As during the telling of the story, Captain Delano had once or twice started at the occasional cymballing of the hatchet-polishers, wondering why such an interruption should be allowed, especially in that part of the ship, and in the ears of an invalid; and, moreover, as the hatchets had anything but an attractive look, and the handlers of them still less so, it was, therefore, to tell the truth, not without some lurking reluctance, or even shrinking, it may be, that Captain Delano, with apparent complaisance, acquiesced in his host's invitation. The more so, since with an untimely caprice of punctilio, rendered distressing by his cadaverous aspect, Don Benito, with Castilian bows, solemnly insisted upon his guest's preceding him up the ladder leading to the elevation; where, one on each side of the last step, sat four armorial supporters and sentries, two of the ominous file. Gingerly enough stepped good Captain Delano between them, and in the instant of leaving them behind, like one running the gauntlet, he felt an apprehensive twitch in the calves of his legs.

But when, facing about, he saw the whole file, like so many organ-grinders, still stupidly intent on their work, unmindful of everything beside, he could not but smile at his late fidgeting panic.

Presently, while standing with Don Benito, looking forward upon the decks below, he was struck by one of those instances of insubordination previously alluded to. Three black boys, with two Spanish boys, were sitting together on the hatchets, scraping a rude wooden platter, in which some scanty mess had recently been cooked. Suddenly, one of the black boys, enraged at a word dropped by one of his white companions, seized a knife, and though called to forbear by one of the oakum-pickers, struck the lad over the head, inflicting a gash from which blood flowed.

In amazement, Captain Delano inquired what this meant. To which the pale Benito dully muttered, that it was merely the sport of the lad.

"Pretty serious sport, truly," rejoined Captain Delano. "Had such a thing happened on board the *Bachelor's Delight,* instant punishment would have followed."

At these words the Spaniard turned upon the American one of his sudden, staring, half-lunatic looks; then, relapsing into his torpor, answered, "Doubtless, doubtless, Señor."

Is it, thought Captain Delano, that this helpless man is one of those paper captains I've known, who by policy wink at what by power they cannot put down? I know no sadder sight than a commander who has little of command but the name.

, "I should think, Don Benito," he now said, glancing toward the oakum-picker who had sought to interfere with the boys, "that you would find it advantageous to keep all your blacks employed, especially the younger ones, no matter at what useless task, and no matter what happens to the ship. Why, even with my little band, I find such a course indispensable. I once kept a crew on my quarter-deck thrumming mats for my cabin, when, for three days, I had given up my ship—mats, men, and all—for a speedy loss, owing to the violence of a gale in which we could do nothing but helplessly drive before it."

"Doubtless, doubtless," muttered Don Benito.

"But," continued Captain Delano, again glancing upon the oakum-pickers and then at the hatchet-polishers, near by, "I see you keep some at least of your host employed."

"Yes," was again the vacant response.

"Those old men there, shaking their pows from their pulpits," continued Captain Delano, pointing to the oakum-pickers, "seem to act the part of old dominies to the rest, little heeded as their admonitions are at times. Is this voluntary on their part, Don Benito, or have you appointed them shepherds to your flock of black sheep?"

"What posts they fill, I appointed them," rejoined the Spaniard in an acrid tone, as if resenting some supposed satiric reflection.

"And these others, these Ashantee conjurors here," continued Captain Delano, rather uneasily eyeing the brandished steel of the hatchet-polishers, where in spots it had been brought to a shine, "this seems a curious business they are at, Don Benito?"

"In the gales we met," answered the Spaniard, "what of our general cargo was not thrown overboard was much damaged by the brine. Since coming into calm weather, I have had several cases of knives and hatchets daily brought up for overhauling and cleaning."

"A prudent idea, Don Benito. You are part owner of ship and cargo, I presume; but not of the slaves, perhaps?"

"I am owner of all you see," impatiently returned Don Benito, "except the main company of blacks, who belonged to my late friend, Alexandro Aranda."

As he mentioned this name, his air was heart-broken, his knees shook; his servant supported him.

Thinking he divined the cause of such unusual emotion, to confirm his surmise, Captain Delano, after a pause, said, "And may I ask, Don Benito, whether—since awhile ago you spoke of some cabin passengers—the friend, whose loss so afflicts you, at the outset of the voyage accompanied his blacks?"

"Yes."

"But died of the fever?"

"Died of the fever.—Oh, could I but—"

Again quivering, the Spaniard paused.

"Pardon me," said Captain Delano slowly, "but I think that, by a sympathetic experience, I conjecture, Don Benito, what it is that gives the keener edge to your grief. It was once my hard fortune to lose at sea a dear friend, my own brother, then supercargo. Assured of the welfare of his spirit, its departure I could have borne like a man; but that honest eye, that honest hand—both of which had so often met mine—and that warm heart; all, all—like scraps to the dogs—to throw all to the sharks! It was then I vowed never to have for fellow-voyager a man I loved, unless, unbeknown to him, I had provided every requisite, in case of a fatality, for embalming his mortal part for interment on shore. Were your friend's remains now on board this ship, Don Benito, not thus strangely would the mention of his name affect you."

"On board this ship?" echoed the Spaniard. Then, with horrified gestures, as directed against some spectre, he unconsciously fell into the ready arms of his attendant, who, with a silent appeal toward Captain Delano, seemed beseeching him not again to broach a theme so unspeakably distressing to his master.

This poor fellow now, thought the pained American, is the victim of that sad superstition which associates goblins with the deserted body of man, as ghosts with an abandoned house. How unlike are we made! What to me, in like case, would have been a solemn satisfaction, the bare suggestion, even, terrifies the Spaniard into this trance. Poor Alexandro Aranda! what would you say could you here see your friend —who, on former voyages, when you for months were left behind, has, I dare say, often longed, and longed, for one peep at you—now transported with terror at the least thought of having you anyway nigh him.

At this moment, with a dreary graveyard toll, betokening a flaw, the ship's forecastle bell, smote by one of the grizzled oakum-pickers, proclaimed ten o'clock through the leaden calm; when Captain Delano's attention was caught by the moving figure of a gigantic black, emerging from the general crowd below, and slowly advancing toward the elevated poop. An iron collar was about his neck, from which depended a chain, thrice wound round his body; the terminating links padlocked together at a broad band of iron, his girdle.

"How like a mute Atufal moves," murmured the servant.

The black mounted the steps of the poop, and, like a brave prisoner, brought up to receive sentence, stood in unquailing muteness before Don Benito, now recovered from his attack.

At the first glimpse of his approach, Don Benito had started, a resentful shadow swept over his face; and, as with the sudden memory of bootless rage, his white lips glued together

This is some mulish mutineer, thought Captain Delano, surveying, not without a mixture of admiration, the colossal form of the negro.

"See, he waits your question, master," said the servant.

Thus reminded, Don Benito, nervously averting his glance, as if shunning, by anticipation, some rebellious response, in a disconcerted voice, thus spoke:

"Atufal, will you ask my pardon now?"

The black was silent.

"Again, master," murmured the servant, with bitter upbraiding eyeing his countryman; "Again, master; he will bend to master yet."

"Answer," said Don Benito, still averting his glance, "say but the one word *pardon*, and your chains shall be off."

Upon this, the black, slowly raising both arms, let them lifelessly fall, his links clanking, his head bowed; as much as to say, "No, I am content."

"Go," said Don Benito, with inkept and unknown emotion.

Deliberately as he had come, the black obeyed.

"Excuse me, Don Benito," said Captain Delano, "but this scene surprises me; what means it, pray?"

"It means that that negro alone, of all the band, has given me peculiar cause of offence. I have put him in chains; I—"

Here he paused; his hand to his head, as if there were a swimming there, or a sudden bewilderment of memory had come over him; but meeting his servant's kindly glance seemed reassured, and proceeded:

"I could not scourge such a form. But I told him he must ask my pardon. As yet he has not. At my command, every two hours he stands before me."

"And how long has this been?"

"Some sixty days."

"And obedient in all else? And respectful?"

"Yes."

"Upon my conscience, then," exclaimed Captain Delano, impulsively, "he has a royal spirit in him, this fellow."

"He may have some right to it," bitterly returned Don Benito; "he says he was king in his own land."

"Yes," said the servant, entering a word, "those slits in Atufal's ears once held wedges of gold; but poor Babo here, in his own land, was only a poor slave; a black man's slave was Babo, who now is the white's."

Somewhat annoyed by these conversational familiarities, Captain Delano turned curiously upon the attendant, then glanced inquiringly at his master; but, as if long wonted to these little informalities, neither master nor man seemed to understand him.

"What, pray, was Atufal's offence, Don Benito?" asked Captain Delano; "if it was not something very serious, take a fool's advice, and, in view of his general docility, as well as in some natural respect for his spirit, remit his penalty."

"No, no, master never will do that," here murmured the servant to himself, "proud Atufal must first ask master's pardon. The slave there carries the padlock, but master here carries the key."

His attention thus directed, Captain Delano now noticed for the first time that, suspended by a slender silken cord, from Don Benito's neck hung a key. At once, from the servant's muttered syllables divining the key's purpose, he smiled and said: "So, Don Benito—padlock and key—significant symbols, truly."

Biting his lip, Don Benito faltered.

Though the remark of Captain Delano, a man of such native simplicity as to be incapable of satire or irony, had been dropped in playful allusion to the Spaniard's singularly evidenced lordship over the black; yet the hypochondriac seemed in some way to have taken it as a malicious reflection upon his confessed inability thus far to break down, at least, on a verbal summons, the entrenched will of the slave. Deploring this supposed misconception, yet despairing of correcting it, Captain Delano shifted the subject; but finding his companion more than ever withdrawn, as if still slowly digesting the lees of the presumed affront above-men-

tioned, by-and-by Captain Delano likewise became less talkative, oppressed, against his own will, by what seemed the
secret vindictiveness of the morbidly sensitive Spaniard. But
the good sailor himself, of a quite contrary disposition, refrained, on his part, alike from the appearance as from the
feeling of resentment, and if silent, was only so from con-
tagion.

Presently the Spaniard, assisted by his servant, somewhat
discourteously crossed over from Captain Delano; a procedure which, sensibly enough, might have been allowed to
pass for idle caprice of ill-humour, had not master and man,
lingering round the corner of the elevated skylight, begun
whispering together in low voices. This was unpleasing.
And more: the moody air of the Spaniard, which at times
had not been without a sort of valetudinarian stateliness, now
seemed anything but dignified; while the menial familiarity
of the servant lost its original charm of simple-hearted attachment.

In his embarrassment, the visitor turned his face to the
other side of the ship. By so doing, his glance accidentally
fell on a young Spanish sailor, a coil of rope in his hand,
just stepped from the deck to the first round of the mizzen-
rigging. Perhaps the man would not have been particularly
noticed, were it not that, during his ascent to one of the yards,
he, with a sort of covert intentness, kept his eye fixed on
Captain Delano, from whom, presently, it passed, as if by a
natural sequence, to the two whisperers.

His own attention thus redirected to that quarter, Captain
Delano gave a slight start. From something in Don Benito's
manner just then, it seemed as if the visitor had, at least
partly, been the subject of the withdrawn consultation going
on—a conjecture as little agreeable to the guest as it was
little flattering to the host.

The singular alternations of courtesy and ill-breeding in the Spanish captain were unaccountable, except on one of two suppositions—innocent lunacy, or wicked imposture.

But the first idea, though it might naturally have occurred to an indifferent observer, and, in some respects, had not hitherto been wholly a stranger to Captain Delano's mind, yet, now that, in an incipient way, he began to regard the stranger's conduct something in the light of an intentional affront, of course the idea of lunacy was virtually vacated. But if not a lunatic, what then? Under the circumstances, would a gentleman, nay, any honest boor, act the part now acted by his host? The man was an impostor. Some low-born adventurer, masquerading as an oceanic grandee; yet so ignorant of the first requisites of mere gentlemanhood as to be betrayed into the present remarkable indecorum. That strange ceremoniousness, too, at other times evinced, seemed not uncharacteristic of one playing a part above his real level. Benito Cereno—Don Benito Cereno—a sounding name. One, too, at that period, not unknown, in the surname, to supercargoes and sea captains trading along the Spanish Main, as belonging to one of the most enterprising and extensive mercantile families in all those provinces; several members of it having titles; a sort of Castilian Rothschild, with a noble brother, or cousin, in every great trading town of South America. The alleged Don Benito was in early manhood, about twenty-nine or thirty. To assume a sort of roving cadetship in the maritime affairs of such a house, what more likely scheme for a young knave of talent and spirit? But the Spaniard was a pale invalid. Never mind. For even to the degree of simulating mortal disease, the craft of some tricksters had been known to attain. To think that, under the aspect of infantile weakness, the most savage energies might be couched—those velvets of the Spaniard but the velvet paw to his fangs.

From no train of thought did these fancies come; not from within, but from without; suddenly, too, and in one throng, like hoar frost; yet as soon to vanish as the mild sun of Captain Delano's good-nature regained its meridian.

Glancing over once again toward Don Benito—whose side-face, revealed above the skylight, was now turned toward him—Captain Delano was struck by the profile, whose clearness of cut was refined by the thinness incident to ill-health, as well as ennobled about the chin by the beard. Away with suspicion. He was a true off-shoot of a true hidalgo Cereno.

Relieved by these and other better thoughts, the visitor, lightly humming a tune, now began indifferently pacing the poop, so as not to betray to Don Benito that he had at all mistrusted incivility, much less duplicity; for such mistrust would yet be proved illusory, and by the event; though, for the present, the circumstance which had provoked that distrust remained unexplained. But when that little mystery should have been cleared up, Captain Delano thought he might extremely regret it, did he allow Don Benito to become aware that he had indulged in ungenerous surmises. In short, to the Spaniard's black-letter text, it was best, for a while, to leave open margin.

Presently, his pale face twitching and overcast, the Spaniard, still supported by his attendant, moved over toward his guest, when, with even more than his usual embarrassment, and a strange sort of intriguing intonation in his husky whisper, the following conversation began:

"Señor, may I ask how long you have lain at this isle?"

"Oh, but a day or two, Don Benito."

"And from what port are you last?"

"Canton."

"And there, Señor, you exchanged your seal-skins for teas and silks, I think you said?"

"Yes. Silks, mostly."

"And the balance you took in specie, perhaps?"

Captain Delano, fidgeting a little, answered—

"Yes; some silver; not a very great deal, though."

"Ah—well. May I ask how many men have you on board, Señor?"

Captain Delano slightly started, but answered:

"About five-and-twenty, all told."

"And at present, Señor, all on board, I suppose?"

"All on board, Don Benito," replied the captain now with satisfaction.

"And will be to-night, Señor?"

At this last question, following so many pertinacious ones, for the soul of him Captain Delano could not but look very earnestly at the questioner, who, instead of meeting the glance, with every token of craven discomposure dropped his eyes to the deck; presenting an unworthy contrast to his servant, who, just then, was kneeling at his feet adjusting a loose shoe-buckle; his disengaged face meantime, with humble curiosity, turned openly up into his master's downcast one.

The Spaniard, still with a guilty shuffle, repeated his question:

"And—and will be to-night, Señor?"

"Yes, for aught I know," returned Captain Delano,— "but nay," rallying himself into fearless truth, "some of them talked of going off on another fishing party about midnight."

"Your ships generally go—go more or less armed, I believe, Señor?"

"Oh, a six-pounder or two, in case of emergency," was the intrepidly indifferent reply, "with a small stock of muskets, sealing-spears, and cutlasses, you know."

As he thus responded, Captain Delano again glanced at Don Benito, but the latter's eyes were averted; while abruptly and awkwardly shifting the subject, he made some peevish allusion to the calm, and then, without apology, once more, with his attendant, withdrew to the opposite bulwarks, where the whispering was resumed.

At this moment, and ere Captain Delano could cast a cool thought upon what had just passed, the young Spanish sailor before mentioned was seen descending from the rigging. In act of stooping over to spring inboard to the deck, his voluminous, unconfined frock, or shirt, of coarse woollen, much spotted with tar, opened out far down the chest, revealing a soiled under-garment of what seemed the finest linen, edged, about the neck, with a narrow blue ribbon, sadly faded and worn. At this moment the young sailor's eye was again fixed on the whisperers, and Captain Delano thought he observed a lurking significance in it, as if silent signs of some freemason sort had that instant been interchanged.

This once more impelled his own glance in the direction of Don Benito, and, as before, he could not but infer that himself formed the subject of the conference. He paused. The sound of the hatchet-polishing fell on his ears. He cast another swift side-look at the two. They had the air of conspirators. In connection with the late questionings, and the incident of the young sailor, these things now begat such return of involuntary suspicion, that the singular guilelessness of the American could not endure it. Plucking up a gay and humorous expression, he crossed over to the two rapidly, saying: "Ha, Don Benito, your black here seems high in your trust; a sort of privy-counsellor, in fact."

Upon this, the servant looked up with a good-natured grin, but the master started as from a venomous bite. It was a moment or two before the Spaniard sufficiently recovered himself to reply; which he did, at last, with cold constraint: "Yes, Señor, I have trust in Babo."

Here Babo, changing his previous grin of mere animal humour into an intelligent smile, not ungratefully eyed his master.

Finding that the Spaniard now stood silent and reserved, as if involuntarily, or purposely giving hint that his guest's proximity was inconvenient just then, Captain Delano, unwilling to appear uncivil even to incivility itself, made some trivial remark and moved off; again and again turning over in his mind the mysterious demeanour of Don Benito Cereno.

He had descended from the poop, and, wrapped in thought, was passing near a dark hatchway, leading down into the steerage, when, perceiving motion there, he looked to see what moved. The same instant there was a sparkle in the shadowy hatchway, and he saw one of the Spanish sailors, prowling there, hurriedly placing his hand in the bosom of his frock, as if hiding something. Before the man could have been certain who it was that was passing, he slunk below out of sight. But enough was seen of him to make it sure that he was the same young sailor before noticed in the rigging.

What was that which so sparkled? thought Captain Delano. It was no lamp—no match—no live coal. Could it have been a jewel? But how come sailors with jewels? —or with silk-trimmed under-shirts either? Has he been robbing the trunks of the dead cabin passengers? But if so, he would hardly wear one of the stolen articles on board ship here. Ah, ah—if now that was, indeed, a secret sign

I saw passing between this suspicious fellow and his captain awhile since; if I could only be certain that in my uneasiness my senses did not deceive me, then—

Here, passing from one suspicious thing to another, his mind revolved the point of the strange questions put to him concerning his ship.

By a curious coincidence, as each point was recalled, the black wizards of Ashantee would strike up with their hatchets, as in ominous comment on the white stranger's thoughts. Pressed by such enigmas and portents, it would have been almost against nature, had not, even into the least distrustful heart, some ugly misgivings obtruded.

Observing the ship now helplessly fallen into a current, with enchanted sails, drifting with increased rapidity seaward; and noting that, from a lately intercepted projection of the land, the sealer was hidden, the stout mariner began to quake at thoughts which he barely durst confess to himself. Above all, he began to feel a ghostly dread of Don Benito. And yet when he roused himself, dilated his chest, felt himself strong on his legs, and coolly considered it— what did all these phantoms amount to?

Had the Spaniard any sinister scheme, it must have reference not so much to him (Captain Delano) as to his ship (the *Bachelor's Delight*). Hence the present drifting away of the one ship from the other, instead of favouring any such possible scheme, was, for the time at least, opposed to it. Clearly any suspicion, combining such contradictions, must need be delusive. Beside, was it not absurd to think of a vessel in distress—a vessel by sickness almost dismanned of her crew—a vessel whose inmates were parched for water —was it not a thousand times absurd that such a craft should, at present, be of a piratical character; or her commander, either for himself or those under him, cherish any desire

but for speedy relief and refreshment? But then, might not
general distress, and thirst in particular, be affected? And
might not that same undiminished Spanish crew, alleged to
have perished off to a remnant, be at that very moment
lurking in the hold? On heart-broken pretence of entreating a cup of cold water, fiends in human form had got into
lonely dwellings, nor retired until a dark deed had been
done. And among the Malay pirates, it was no unusual
thing to lure ships after them into their treacherous harbours,
or entice boarders from a declared enemy at sea, by the
spectacle of thinly manned or vacant decks, beneath which
prowled a hundred spears with yellow arms ready to up-
thrust them through the mats. Not that Captain Delano
had entirely credited such things. He had heard of them—
and now, as stories, they recurred. The present destination
of the ship was the anchorage. There she would be near
his own vessel. Upon gaining that vicinity, might not the
San Dominick, like a slumbering volcano, suddenly let loose
energies now hid?

He recalled the Spaniard's manner while telling his story.
There was a gloomy hesitancy and subterfuge about it. It
was just the manner of one making up his tale for evil purposes, as he goes. But if that story was not true, what was
the truth? That the ship had unlawfully come into the
Spaniard's possession? But in many of its details, especially
in reference to the more calamitous parts, such as the fatali-
ties among the seamen, the consequent prolonged beating
about, the past sufferings from obstinate calms, and still continued suffering from thirst; in all these points, as well as
others, Don Benito's story had corroborated not only the
wailing ejaculations of the indiscriminate multitude, white
and black, but likewise—what seemed impossible to be coun-
terfeit—by the very expression and play of every human

feature, which Captain Delano saw. If Don Benito's story was throughout an invention, then every soul on board, down to the youngest negress, was his carefully drilled recruit in the plot: an incredible inference. And yet, if there was ground for mistrusting the Spanish captain's veracity, that inference was a legitimate one.

In short, scarce an uneasiness entered the honest sailor's mind but, by a subsequent spontaneous act of good sense, it was ejected. At last he began to laugh at these forebodings; and laugh at the strange ship for, in its aspect someway siding with them, as it were; and laugh, too, at the odd-looking blacks, particularly those old scissors-grinders, the Ashantees; and those bed-ridden old knitting-women, the oakum-pickers; and, in a human way, he almost began to laugh at the dark Spaniard himself, the central hobgoblin of all.

For the rest, whatever in a serious way seemed enigmatical, was now good-naturedly explained away by the thought that, for the most part, the poor invalid scarcely knew what he was about; either sulking in black vapours, or putting random questions without sense or object. Evidently, for the present, the man was not fit to be entrusted with the ship. On some benevolent plea withdrawing the command from him, Captain Delano would yet have to send her to Concepcion in charge of his second mate, a worthy person and good navigator—a plan which would prove no wiser for the *San Dominick* than for Don Benito; for—relieved from all anxiety, keeping wholly to his cabin—the sick man, under the good nursing of his servant, would probably, by the end of the passage, be in a measure restored to health and with that he should also be restored to authority.

Such were the American's thoughts. They were tranquillizing. There was a difference between the idea of Don

Benito's darky pre-ordaining Captain Delano's fate, and Captain Delano's lightly arranging Don Benito's. Nevertheless, it was not without something of relief that the good seaman presently perceived his whale-boat in the distance. Its absence had been prolonged by unexpected detention at the sealer's side, as well as its returning trip lengthened by the continual recession of the goal.

The advancing speck was observed by the blacks. Their shouts attracted the attention of Don Benito, who, with a return of courtesy, approaching Captain Delano, expressed satisfaction at the coming of some supplies, slight and temporary as they must necessarily prove.

Captain Delano responded; but while doing so, his attention was drawn to something passing on the deck below: among the crowd climbing the landward bulwarks, anxiously watching the coming boat, two blacks, to all appearances accidentally incommoded by one of the sailors, flew out against him with horrible curses, which the sailor someway resenting, the two blacks dashed him to the deck and jumped upon him, despite the earnest cries of the oakum-pickers.

"Don Benito," said Captain Delano quickly, "do you see what is going on there? Look!"

But, seized by his cough, the Spaniard staggered, with both hands to his face, on the point of falling. Captain Delano would have supported him, but the servant was more alert, who, with one hand sustaining his master, with the other applied the cordial. Don Benito, restored, the black withdrew his support, slipping aside a little, but dutifully remaining within call of a whisper. Such discretion was here evinced as quite wiped away, in the visitor's eyes, any blemish of impropriety which might have attached to the attendant, from the indecorous conferences before mentioned; showing, too, that if the servant were to blame, it might be more the master's fault than his own, since when left to himself he could conduct thus well.

His glance thus called away from the spectacle of disorder to the more pleasing one before him, Captain Delano could not avoid again congratulating Don Benito upon possessing such a servant, who, though perhaps a little too forward now and then, must upon the whole be invaluable to one in the invalid's situation.

"Tell me, Don Benito," he added, with a smile—"I should like to have your man here myself—what will you take for him? Would fifty doubloons be any object?"

"Master wouldn't part with Babo for a thousand doubloons," murmured the black, overhearing the offer, and taking it in earnest, and, with the strange vanity of a faithful slave appreciated by his master, scorning to hear so paltry a valuation put upon him by a stranger. But Don Benito, apparently hardly yet completely restored, and again interrupted by his cough, made but some broken reply.

Soon his physical distress became so great, affecting his mind, too, apparently, that, as if to screen the sad spectacle, the servant gently conducted his master below.

Left to himself, the American, to while away the time till his boat should arrive, would have pleasantly accosted some one of the few Spanish seamen he saw; but recalling something that Don Benito had said touching their ill conduct, he refrained, as a ship-master indisposed to countenance cowardice or unfaithfulness in seamen.

While, with these thoughts, standing with eye directed forward toward that handful of sailors—suddenly he thought that some of them returned the glance and with a sort of meaning. He rubbed his eyes, and looked again; but again seemed to see the same thing. Under a new form, but more obscure than any previous one, the old suspicions recurred, but, in the absence of Don Benito, with less of panic than before. Despite the bad account given of the sailors, Captain Delano resolved forthwith to accost one of them. Descending the poop, he made his way through the blacks, his movement drawing a queer cry from the oakum-pickers, prompted by whom the negroes, twitching each other aside, divided before him; but, as if curious to see what was the object of this deliberate visit to their Ghetto, closing in behind, in tolerable order, followed the white stranger up. His progress thus proclaimed as by mounted kings-at-arms, and escorted as by a Caffre guard of honour, Captain Delano, assuming a good-humoured, off-hand air, continued to advance; now and then saying a blithe word to the negroes, and his eye curiously surveying the white faces, here and there sparsely mixed in with the blacks, like stray white pawns venturously involved in the ranks of the chessmen opposed.

While thinking which of them to select for his purpose, he chanced to observe a sailor seated on the deck engaged in tarring the strap of a large block, with a circle of blacks squatted round him inquisitively eyeing the process.

The mean employment of the man was in contrast with something superior in his figure. His hand, black with continually thrusting it into the tar-pot held for him by a negro, seemed not naturally allied to his face, a face which would have been a very fine one but for its haggardness. Whether this haggardness had aught to do with criminality, could not be determined; since, as intense heat and cold, though unlike, produce like sensations, so innocence and guilt, when, through casual association with mental pain, stamping any visible impress, use one seal—a hacked one.

Not again that this reflection occurred to Captain Delano at the time, charitable man as he was. Rather another idea.

Because observing so singular a haggardness to be combined with a dark eye, averted as in trouble and shame, and then, however illogically, uniting in his mind his own private suspicions of the crew with the confessed ill-opinion on the part of their captain, he was insensibly operated upon by certain general notions, which, while disconnecting pain and abashment from virtue, as invariably link them with vice.

If, indeed, there be any wickedness on board this ship, thought Captain Delano, be sure that man there has fouled his hand in it, even as now he fouls it in the pitch. I don't like to accost him. I will speak to this other, this old Jack here on the windlass.

He advanced to an old Barcelona tar, in ragged red breeches and dirty night-cap, cheeks trenched and bronzed, whiskers dense as thorn hedges. Seated between two sleepy-looking Africans, this mariner, like his younger shipmate, was employed upon some rigging—splicing a cable—the sleepy-looking blacks performing the inferior function of holding the outer parts of the ropes for him.

Upon Captain Delano's approach, the man at once hung his head below its previous level; the one necessary for business. It appeared as if he desired to be thought absorbed, with more than common fidelity, in his task. Being addressed, he glanced up, but with what seemed a furtive, diffident air, which sat strangely enough on his weather-beaten visage, much as if a grizzly bear, instead of growling and biting, should simper and cast sheep's eyes. He was asked several questions concerning the voyage—questions purposely referring to several particulars in Don Benito's narrative—not previously corroborated by those impulsive cries greeting the visitor on first coming on board. The questions were briefly answered, confirming all that remained to be confirmed of the story. The negroes about the windlass joined in with the old sailor, but, as they became talkative, he by degrees became mute, and at length quite glum, seemed morosely unwilling to answer more questions, and yet, all the while, this ursine air was somehow mixed with his sheepish one.

Despairing of getting into unembarrassed talk with such a centaur, Captain Delano, after glancing round for a more promising countenance, but seeing none, spoke pleasantly to the blacks to make way for him; and so, amid various grins and grimaces, returned to the poop, feeling a little strange at first, he could hardly tell why, but upon the whole with regained confidence in Benito Cereno.

How plainly, thought he, did that old whiskerando yonder betray a consciousness of ill-desert. No doubt, when he saw me coming, he dreaded lest I, apprised by his captain of the crew's general misbehaviour, came with sharp words for him, and so down with his head. And yet—and yet, now that I think of it, that very old fellow, if I err not, was one of those who seemed so earnestly eyeing me here awhile since. Ah, these currents spin one's head round almost as much as they do the ship. Ha, there now's a pleasant sort of sunny sight; quite sociable, too.

His attention had been drawn to a slumbering negress, partly disclosed through the lace-work of some rigging, lying, with youthful limbs carelessly disposed, under the lee of the bulwarks, like a doe in the shade of a woodland rock. Sprawling at her lapped breasts was her wide-awake fawn, stark naked, its black little body half lifted from the deck, crosswise with its dam's; its hands, like two paws, clambering upon her; its mouth and nose ineffectually rooting to get at the mark; and meantime giving a vexatious half-grunt, blending with the composed snore of the negress.

The uncommon vigour of the child at length roused the

mother. She started up, at distance facing Captain Delano. But, as if not at all concerned at the attitude in which she had been caught, delightedly she caught the child up, with maternal transports, covering it with kisses.

There's naked nature, now; pure tenderness and love, thought Captain Delano, well pleased.

This incident prompted him to remark the other negresses more particularly than before. He was gratified with their manners; like most uncivilized women, they seemed at once tender of heart and tough of constitution; equally ready to die for their infants or fight for them. Unsophisticated as leopardesses; loving as doves. Ah! thought Captain Delano, these perhaps are some of the very women whom Mungo Park saw in Africa, and gave such a noble account of.

These natural sights somehow insensibly deepened his confidence and ease. At last he looked to see how his boat was getting on; but it was still pretty remote. He turned to see if Don Benito had returned; but he had not.

To change the scene, as well as to please himself with a leisurely observation of the coming boat, stepping over into the mizzen-chains he clambered his way into the starboard quarter-gallery; one of those abandoned Venetian-looking water-balconies previously mentioned; retreats cut off from the deck. As his foot pressed the half-damp, half-dry sea-mosses matting the place, and a chance phantom cats-paw— an islet of breeze, unheralded, unfollowed—as this ghostly cats-paw came fanning his cheek, as his glance fell upon the row of small, round dead-lights, all closed like coppered eyes of the coffined, and the state-cabin door, once connecting with the gallery, even as the dead-lights had once looked out upon it, but now caulked fast like a sarcophagus lid, to a purple-black, tarred-over panel, threshold, and post; and he bethought him of the time, when that state-cabin and this state-balcony had heard the voices of the Spanish king's officers, and the forms of the Lima viceroy's daughters had perhaps leaned where he stood—as these and other images flitted through his mind, as the cats-paw through the calm, gradually he felt rising a dreamy inquietude, like that of one who alone on the prairie feels unrest from the repose of the noon.

He leaned against the carved balustrade, again looking off toward his boat; but found his eye falling upon the ribboned grass, trailing along the ship's water-line, straight as a border of green box; and parterres of sea-weed, broad ovals and crescents, floating nigh and far, with what seemed long formal alleys between, crossing the terraces of swells, and sweeping round as if leading to the grottoes below. And overhanging all was the balustrade by his arm, which, partly stained with pitch and partly embossed with moss, seemed the charred ruin of some summer-house in a grand garden long running to waste.

Trying to break one charm, he was but becharmed anew. Though upon the wide sea, he seemed in some far inland country; prisoner in some deserted château, left to stare at empty grounds, and peer out at vague roads, where never wagon or wayfarer passed.

But these enchantments were a little disenchanted as his eye fell on the corroded main-chains. Of an ancient style, massy and rusty in link, shackle and bolt, they seemed even more fit for the ship's present business than the one for which probably she had been built.

Presently he thought something moved nigh the chains. He rubbed his eyes, and looked hard. Groves of rigging were about the chains; and there, peering from behind a great stay, like an Indian from behind a hemlock, a Spanish sailor, a marlingspike in his hand, was seen, who made what seemed an imperfect gesture toward the balcony—but immediately, as if alarmed by some advancing step along the deck within, vanished into the recesses of the hempen forest, like a poacher.

What meant this? Something the man had sought to communicate, unbeknown to any one, even to his captain. Did the secret involve aught unfavourable to his captain? Were those previous misgivings of Captain Delano's about to be verified? Or, in his haunted mood at the moment, had some random, unintentional motion of the man, while busy with the stay, as if repairing it, been mistaken for a significant beckoning?

Not unbewildered, again he gazed off for his boat. But it was temporarily hidden by a rocky spur of the isle. As with some eagerness he bent forward, watching for the first shooting view of its beak, the balustrade gave way before him like charcoal. Had he not clutched an outreaching rope he would have fallen into the sea. The crash, though feeble, and the fall, though hollow, of the rotten fragments, must have been overheard. He glanced up. With sober curiosity peering down upon him was one of the old oakum-pickers, slipped from his perch to an outside boom; while below the old negro—and, invisible to him, reconnoitring from a port-hole like a fox from the mouth of its den—crouched the Spanish sailor again. From something suddenly suggested by the man's air, the mad idea now darted into Captain Delano's mind; that Don Benito's plea of indisposition, in withdrawing below, was but a pretence: that he was engaged there maturing some plot, of which the sailor, by some means gaining an inkling, had a mind to warn the stranger against; incited, it may be, by gratitude for a kind word on first boarding the ship. Was it from foreseeing some possible interference like this, that Don Benito had, beforehand, given such a bad character of his sailors, while praising the negroes; though, indeed, the former seemed as docile as the latter the contrary? The whites, too, by nature, were the shrewder race. A man with some evil design, would not he be likely to speak well of that stupidity which was blind to his depravity, and malign that intelligence from which it might not be hidden? Not unlikely, perhaps. But if the whites had dark secrets concerning Don Benito, could then Don Benito be any way in complicity with the blacks? But they were too stupid. Besides, who ever heard of a white so far a renegade as to apostatize from his very species almost, by leaguing in against it with negroes? These difficulties recalled former ones. Lost in their mazes, Captain Delano, who had now regained the deck, was uneasily advancing along it, when he observed a new face: an aged sailor seated cross-legged near the main hatchway. His skin was shrunk up with wrinkles like a pelican's empty pouch; his hair frosted; his countenance grave and composed. His hands were full of ropes, which he was working into a large knot. Some blacks were about him obligingly dipping the strands for him, here and there, as the exigencies of the operation demanded.

Captain Delano crossed over to him, and stood in silence surveying the knot; his mind, by a not uncongenial transition, passing from its own entanglements to those of the hemp. For intricacy such a knot he had never seen in an American ship, or indeed any other. The old man looked like an Egyptian priest, making gordian knots for the temple of Ammon. The knot seemed a combination of double-bowline-knot, treble-crown-knot, back-handed-well-knot, knot-in-and-out-knot, and jamming-knot.

At last, puzzled to comprehend the meaning of such a knot, Captain Delano, addressed the knotter:—

"What are you knotting there, my man?"

"The knot," was the brief reply, without looking up.

"So it seems; but what is it for?"

"For some one else to undo," muttered back the old man, plying his fingers harder than ever, the knot being now nearly completed.

While Captain Delano stood watching him, suddenly the old man threw the knot toward him, and said in broken English,—the first heard in the ship,—something to this effect—"Undo it, cut it, quick." It was said lowly, but with such condensation of rapidity, that the long, slow words in Spanish, which had preceded and followed, almost operated as covers to the brief English between.

For a moment, knot in hand, and knot in head, Captain Delano stood mute; while, without further heeding him, the old man was now intent upon other ropes. Presently there was a slight stir behind Captain Delano. Turning, he saw the chained negro, Atufal, standing quietly there. The next moment the old sailor rose, muttering, and, followed by his subordinate negroes, removed to the forward part of the ship, where in the crowd he disappeared.

An elderly negro, in a clout like an infant's, and with a pepper and salt head, and a kind of attorney air, now approached Captain Delano. In tolerable Spanish, and with a good-natured, knowing wink, he informed him that the old knotter was simple-witted, but harmless; often playing his old tricks. The negro concluded by begging the knot, for of course the stranger would not care to be troubled with it. Unconsciously, it was handed to him. With a sort of congé, the negro received it, and turning his back ferreted into it like a detective Custom House officer after smuggled laces. Soon, with some African word, equivalent to pshaw, he tossed the knot overboard.

All this is very queer now, thought Captain Delano, with a qualmish sort of emotion; but as one feeling incipient sea-sickness, he strove, by ignoring the symptoms, to get rid of the malady. Once more he looked off for his boat. To his delight, it was now again in view, leaving the rocky spur astern.

The sensation here experienced, after at first relieving his uneasiness, with unforeseen efficiency, soon began to remove it. The less distant sight of that well-known boat—showing it, not as before, half blended with the haze, but with outline defined, so that its individuality, like a man's, was manifest; that boat, *Rover* by name, which, though now in strange seas, had often pressed the beach of Captain Delano's home, and, brought to its threshold for repairs, had familiarly lain there, as a Newfoundland dog; the sight of that household boat evoked a thousand trustful associations, which, contrasted with previous suspicions, filled him not only with lightsome confidence, but somehow with half humorous self-reproaches at his former lack of it.

"What, I, Amasa Delano—Jack of the Beach, as they called me when a lad—I, Amasa; the same that, duck-satchel in hand, used to paddle along the waterside to the school-house made from the old hulk;—I, little Jack of the Beach, that used to go berrying with cousin Nat and the rest; I to be murdered here at the ends of the earth, on board a haunted pirate-ship by a horrible Spaniard?—Too nonsensical to think of! Who would murder Amasa Delano? His conscience is clean. There is some one above. Fie, fie, Jack of the Beach! you are a child indeed; a child of the second childhood, old boy; you are beginning to dote and drule, I'm afraid."

Light of heart and foot, he stepped aft, and there was met by Don Benito's servant, who, with a pleasing expression, responsive to his own present feelings, informed him that his master had recovered from the effects of his coughing fit, and had just ordered him to go present his compliments to his good guest, Don Amasa, and say that he (Don Benito) would soon have the happiness to rejoin him.

There now, do you mark that? again thought Captain Delano, walking the poop. What a donkey I was. This kind gentleman who here sends me his kind compliments, he, but ten minutes ago, dark-lantern in hand, was dodging round some old grind-stone in the hold, sharpening a hatchet for me, I thought. Well, well; these long calms have a morbid effect on the mind, I've often heard, though I never believed it before. Ha! glancing toward the boat; there's *Rover;* a good dog; a white bone in her mouth. A pretty big bone though, seems to me.—What? Yes, she has fallen afoul of the bubbling tide-rip there. It sets her the other way, too, for the time. Patience.

It was now about noon, though, from the greyness of everything, it seemed to be getting toward dusk.

The calm was confirmed. In the far distance, away from the influence of land, the leaden ocean seemed laid out and leaded up, its course finished, soul gone, defunct. But the current from landward, where the ship was, increased; silently sweeping her further and further toward the tranced waters beyond.

Still, from his knowledge of those latitudes, cherishing hopes of a breeze, and a fair and fresh one, at any moment, Captain Delano, despite present prospects, buoyantly counted upon bringing the *San Dominick* safely to anchor ere night. The distance swept over was nothing; since, with a good wind, ten minutes' sailing would retrace more than sixty minutes' drifting. Meantime, one moment turning to mark "Rover" fighting the tide-rip, and the next to see Don Benito approaching, he continued walking the poop.

Gradually he felt a vexation arising from the delay of his boat; this soon merged into uneasiness; and at last, his eye falling continually, as from a stage-box into the pit, upon the strange crowd before and below him, and by-and-by recognizing there the face—now composed to indifference—of the Spanish sailor who had seemed to beckon from the main chains, something of his old trepidations returned.

Ah, thought he—gravely enough—this is like the ague: because it went off, it follows not that it won't come back.

Though ashamed of the relapse, he could not altogether subdue it; and so, exerting his good nature to the utmost, insensibly he came to a compromise.

Yes, this is a strange craft; a strange history, too, and strange folks on board. But—nothing more.

By way of keeping his mind out of mischief till the boat should arrive, he tried to occupy it with turning over and over, in a purely speculative sort of way, some lesser peculiarities of the captain and crew. Among others, four curious points recurred.

First, the affair of the Spanish lad assailed with a knife by the slave boy; an act winked at by Don Benito. Second, the tyranny in Don Benito's treatment of Atufal, the black; as if a child should lead a bull of the Nile by the ring in his nose. Third, the trampling of the sailor by the two negroes; a piece of insolence passed over without so much as a reprimand. Fourth, the cringing submission to their master of all the ship's underlings, mostly blacks; as if by the least inadvertence they feared to draw down his despotic displeasure.

Coupling these points, they seemed somewhat contradictory. But what then, thought Captain Delano, glancing toward his now nearing boat,—what then? Why, this Don Benito is a very capricious commander. But he is not the first of the sort I have seen; though it's true he rather exceeds any other. But as a nation—continued he in his reveries—these Spaniards are all an odd set; the very word Spaniard has a curious, conspirator, Guy-Fawkish twang to it. And yet, I dare say, Spaniards in the main are as good folks as any in Duxbury, Massachusetts. Ah, good! At last "Rover" has come.

As, with its welcome freight, the boat touched the side, the oakum-pickers, with venerable gestures, sought to restrain the blacks, who, at the sight of three gurried water-casks in its bottom, and a pile of wilted pumpkins in its bow, hung over the bulwarks in disorderly raptures.

Don Benito with his servant now appeared; his coming, perhaps, hastened by hearing the noise. Of him Captain Delano sought permission to serve out the water, so that all might share alike, and none injure themselves by unfair excess. But sensible, and, on Don Benito's account, kind as this offer was, it was received with what seemed impatience; as if aware that he lacked energy as a commander, Don Benito, with the true jealousy of weakness, resented as an affront any interference. So, at least, Captain Delano inferred.

In another moment the casks were being hoisted in, when some of the eager negroes accidentally jostled Captain Delano, where he stood by the gangway; so that, unmindful of Don Benito, yielding to the impulse of the moment, with good-natured authority he bade the blacks stand back; to enforce his words making use of a half-mirthful, half-menacing gesture. Instantly the blacks paused, just where they were, each negro and negress suspended in his or her posture, exactly as the word had found them—for a few seconds continuing so—while, as between the responsive posts of a telegraph, an unknown syllable ran from man to man among the perched oakum-pickers. While Captain Delano's attention was fixed by this scene, suddenly the hatchet-polishers half rose, and a rapid cry came from Don Benito.

Thinking that at the signal of the Spaniard he was about to be massacred, Captain Delano would have sprung for his boat, but paused, as the oakum-pickers, dropping down into the crowd with earnest exclamations, forced every white and every negro back, at the same moment, with gestures friendly and familiar, almost jocose, bidding him, in substance, not be a fool. Simultaneously the hatchet-polishers resumed their seats, quietly as so many tailors, and at once, as if nothing had happened, the work of hoisting in the casks was resumed, whites and blacks singing at the tackle.

Captain Delano glanced toward Don Benito. As he saw his meagre form in the act of recovering itself from reclining in the servant's arms, into which the agitated invalid had fallen, he could not but marvel at the panic by which himself had been surprised on the darting supposition that such a commander, who upon a legitimate occasion, so trivial, too, as it now appeared, could lose all self-command, was, with energetic iniquity, going to bring about his murder.

The casks being on deck, Captain Delano was handed a number of jars and cups by one of the steward's aides, who, in the name of Don Benito, entreated him to do as he had proposed: dole out the water. He complied, with republican impartiality as to this republican element, which always seeks one level, serving the oldest white no better than the youngest black; excepting, indeed, poor Don Benito, whose condition, if not rank, demanded an extra allowance. To him, in the first place, Captain Delano presented a fair pitcher of the fluid; but, thirsting as he was for fresh water, Don Benito quaffed not a drop until after several grave bows and salutes: a reciprocation of courtesies which the sight-loving Africans hailed with clapping of hands.

Two of the less wilted pumpkins being reserved for the cabin table, the residue were minced up on the spot for the general regalement. But the soft bread, sugar, and bottled cider, Captain Delano would have given the Spaniards alone, and in chief Don Benito; but the latter objected; which disinterestedness, on his part, not a little pleased the American; and so mouthfuls all around were given alike to whites and blacks; excepting one bottle of cider, which Babo insisted upon setting aside for his master.

Here it may be observed that as, on the first visit of the boat, the American had not permitted his men to board the ship, neither did he now; being unwilling to add to the confusion of the decks.

Not uninfluenced by the peculiar good humour at present prevailing, and for the time oblivious of any but benevolent thoughts, Captain Delano, who from recent indications counted upon a breeze within an hour or two at furthest, despatched the boat back to the sealer with orders for all the hands that could be spared immediately to set about rafting casks to the watering-place and filling them. Likewise he bade word be carried to his chief officer, that if against present expectation the ship was not brought to anchor by sunset, he need be under no concern, for as there was to be a full moon that night, he (Captain Delano) would remain on board ready to play the pilot, should the wind come soon or late.

As the two captains stood together, observing the departing boat——the servant as it happened having just spied a spot on his master's velvet sleeve, and silently engaged rubbing it out——the American expressed his regrets that the *San Dominick* had no boats; none, at least, but the unseaworthy old hulk of the long-boat, which, warped as a camel's skeleton in the desert, and almost as bleached, lay pot-wise inverted amidships, one side a little tipped, furnishing a subterraneous sort of den for family groups of the blacks, mostly women and small children; who, squatting on old mats below, or perched above in the dark dome, on the elevated seats, were descried, some distance within, like a social circle of bats, sheltering in some friendly cave; at intervals, ebon flights of naked boys and girls, three or four years old, darting in and out of the den's mouth.

"Had you three or four boats now, Don Benito," said Captain Delano, "I think that, by tugging at the oars, your negroes here might help along matters some.—Did you sail from port without boats, Don Benito?"

"They were stove in the gales, Señor."

"That was bad. Many men, too, you lost then. Boats and men.—Those must have been hard gales. Don Benito."

"Past all speech," cringed the Spaniard.

"Tell me, Don Benito," continued his companion with increased interest, "tell me, were these gales immediately off the pitch of Cape Horn?"

"Cape Horn?—who spoke of Cape Horn?"

"Yourself did, when giving me an account of your voyage," answered Captain Delano with almost equal astonishment at this eating of his own words, even as he ever seemed eating his own heart, on the part of the Spaniard. "You yourself, Don Benito, spoke of Cape Horn," he emphatically repeated.

The Spaniard turned, in a sort of stooping posture, pausing an instant, as one about to make a plunging exchange of elements, as from air to water.

At this moment a messenger-boy, a white, hurried by, in the regular performance of his function carrying the last expired half-hour forward to the forecastle, from the cabin time-piece, to have it struck at the ship's large bell.

"Master," said the servant, discontinuing his work on the coat sleeve, and addressing the rapt Spaniard with a sort of timid apprehensiveness, as one charged with a duty, the discharge of which, it was foreseen, would prove irksome to the very person who had imposed it, and for whose benefit it was intended, "master told me never mind where he was, or how engaged, always to remind him, to a minute, when shaving-time comes. Miguel has gone to strike the half-hour afternoon. It is *now*, master. Will master go into the cuddy?"

"Ah—yes," answered the Spaniard, starting, somewhat as from dreams into realities; then turning upon Captain Delano, he said that ere long he would resume the conversation.

"Then if master means to talk more to Don Amasa," said the servant, "why not let Don Amasa sit by master in the cuddy, and master can talk, and Don Amasa can listen, while Babo here lathers and strops."

"Yes," said Captain Delano, not unpleased with this sociable plan, "yes, Don Benito, unless you had rather not, I will go with you."

"Be it so, Señor."

As the three passed aft, the American could not but think it another strange instance of his host's capriciousness, this being shaved with such uncommon punctuality in the middle of the day. But he deemed it more than likely that the servant's anxious fidelity had something to do with the matter; inasmuch as the timely interruption served to rally his master from the mood which had evidently been coming upon him.

The place called the cuddy was a light deck-cabin formed by the poop, a sort of attic to the large cabin below. Part of it had formerly been the quarters of the officers; but since their death all the partitionings had been thrown down, and the whole interior converted into one spacious and airy marine hall; for absence of fine furniture and picturesque disarray, of odd appurtenances, somewhat answering to the wide, cluttered hall of some eccentric bachelor-squire in the country, who hangs his shooting-jacket and tobacco-pouch on deer antlers, and keeps his fishing-rod, tongs, and walking-stick in the same corner.

The similitude was heightened, if not originally suggested, by glimpses of the surrounding sea; since, in one aspect, the country and the ocean seem cousins-german.

The floor of the cuddy was matted. Overhead, four or five old muskets were stuck into horizontal holes along the beams. On one side was a claw-footed old table lashed to the deck; a thumbed missal on it, and over it a small, meagre crucifix attached to the bulkhead. Under the table lay a dented cutlass or two, with a hacked harpoon, among some melancholy old rigging, like a heap of poor friar's girdles. There were also two long, sharp-ribbed settees of malacca cane, black with age, and uncomfortable to look at as inquisitors' racks, with a large, misshapen arm-chair, which, furnished with a rude barber's crutch at the back, working with a screw, seemed some grotesque Middle Age engine of torment. A flag locker was in one corner, exposing various coloured bunting, some rolled up, others half unrolled, still others tumbled. Opposite was a cumbrous washstand, of black mahogany, all of one block, with a pedestal, like a font, and over it a railed shelf, containing combs, brushes, and other implements of the toilet. A torn hammock of stained grass swung near; the sheets tossed, and the pillow wrinkled up like a brow, as if whoever slept here slept but illy, with alternate visitations of sad thoughts and bad dreams.

The further extremity of the cuddy, overhanging the ship's stern, was pierced with three openings, windows or port holes, according as men or cannon might peer, socially or unsocially, out of them. At present neither men nor cannon were seen, though huge ring-bolts and other rusty iron fixtures of the wood-work hinted of twenty-four-pounders.

Glancing toward the hammock as he entered. Captain Delano said, "You sleep here, Don Benito?"

"Yes, Señor, since we got into mild weather."

"This seems a sort of dormitory, sitting-room, sail-loft, chapel, armoury, and private closet together. Don Benito," added Captain Delano, looking round.

"Yes, Señor; events have not been favourable to much order in my arrangements."

Here the servant, napkin on arm, made a motion as if waiting his master's good pleasure. Don Benito signified his readiness, when, seating him in the malacca arm-chair, and for the guest's convenience drawing opposite it one of the settees, the servant commenced operations by throwing back his master's collar and loosening his cravat.

There is something in the negro which, in a peculiar way, fits him for avocations about one's person. Most negroes are natural valets and hair-dressers; taking to the comb and brush congenially as to the castanets, and flourishing them apparently with almost equal satisfaction. There is, too, a smooth tact about them in this employment, with a marvellous, noiseless, gliding briskness, not ungraceful in its way, singularly pleasing to behold, and still more so to be the manipulated subject of. And above all is the great gift of good humour. Not the mere grin or laugh is here meant. Those were unsuitable. But a certain easy cheerfulness, harmonious in every glance and gesture; as though God had set the whole negro to some pleasant tune.

When to all this is added the docility arising from the unaspiring contentment of a limited mind, and that susceptibility of blind attachment sometimes inhering in indisputable inferiors, one readily perceives why those hypochondriacs, Johnson and Byron—it may be something like the hypochondriac, Benito Cereno—took to their hearts, almost to the exclusion of the entire white race, their serving men, the negroes, Barber and Fletcher. But if there be that in the negro which exempts him from the inflicted sourness of the morbid or cynical mind, how, in his most prepossessing aspects, must he appear to a benevolent one? When at ease with respect to exterior things, Captain Delano's nature was not only benign, but familiarly and humorously so. At home, he had often taken rare satisfaction in sitting in his door, watching some free man of colour at his work or play. If on a voyage he chanced to have a black sailor, invariably he was on chatty, and half-gamesome terms with him. In fact, like most men of a good, blithe heart, Captain Delano took to negroes, not philanthropically, but genially, just as other men to Newfoundland dogs.

Hitherto the circumstances in which he found the *San Dominick* had repressed the tendency. But in the cuddy, relieved from his former uneasiness, and, for various reasons, more sociably inclined than at any previous period of the day, and seeing the coloured servant, napkin on arm, so debonair about his master, in a business so familiar as that of shaving, too, all his old weakness for negroes returned.

Among other things, he was amused with an odd instance of the African love of bright colours and fine shows, in the black's informally taking from the flag-locker a great piece of bunting of all hues, and lavishly tucking it under his master's chin for an apron.

The mode of shaving among the Spaniards is a little different from what it is with other nations. They have a basin, specially called a barber's basin, which on one side is scooped out, so as accurately to receive the chin, against which it is closely held in lathering; which is done, not with a brush, but with soap dipped in the water of the basin and rubbed on the face.

In the present instance salt-water was used for lack of better; and the parts lathered were only the upper lip, and low down under the throat, all the rest being cultivated beard.

These preliminaries being somewhat novel to Captain Delano he sat curiously eyeing them, so that no conversation took place, nor for the present did Don Benito appear disposed to renew any.

Setting down his basin, the negro searched among the razors, as for the sharpest, and having found it, gave it an additional edge by expertly stropping it on the firm, smooth, oily skin of his open palm; he then made a gesture as if to begin, but midway stood suspended for an instant, one hand elevating the razor, the other professionally dabbling among the bubbling suds on the Spaniard's lank neck. Not unaffected by the close sight of the gleaming steel, Don Benito nervously shuddered, his usual ghastliness was heightened by the lather, which lather, again, was intensified in its hue by the contrasting sootiness of the negro's body. Altogether the scene was somewhat peculiar, at least to Captain Delano, nor, as he saw the two thus postured, could he resist the vagary, that in the black he saw a headsman, and in the white, a man at the block. But this was one of those antic conceits, appearing and vanishing in a breath, from which, perhaps, the best regulated mind is not free.

Meantime the agitation of the Spaniard had a little loosened the bunting from around him, so that one broad fold swept curtain-like over the chair-arm to the floor, revealing, amid a profusion of armorial bars and ground-colours—black, blue and yellow—a closed castle in a blood-red field diagonal with a lion rampant in a white.

"The castle and the lion," exclaimed Captain Delano—"why, Don Benito, this is the flag of Spain you use here. It's well it's only I, and not the King, that sees this," he added with a smile, "but"—turning toward the black,—"it's all one, I suppose, so the colours be gay," which playful remark did not fail somewhat to tickle the negro.

"Now, master," he said, readjusting the flag, and pressing the head gently further back into the crotch of the chair; "now master," and the steel glanced nigh the throat.

Again Don Benito faintly shuddered.

"You must not shake so, master.—See, Don Amasa, master always shakes when I shave him. And yet master knows I never yet have drawn blood, though it's true, if master will shake so, I may some of these times. Now, master," he continued. "And now, Don Amasa, please go on with your talk about the gale, and all that, master can hear, and between times master can answer."

"Ah yes, these gales," said Captain Delano; "but the more I think of your voyage, Don Benito, the more I wonder, not at the gales, terrible as they must have been, but at the disastrous interval following them. For here, by your account, have you been these two months and more getting from Cape Horn to St. Maria, a distance which I myself, with a good wind, have sailed in a few days. True, you had calms, and long ones, but to be becalmed for two months, that is, at least, unusual. Why, Don Benito, had almost any other gentleman told me such a story, I should have been half disposed to a little incredulity."

Here an involuntary expression came over the Spaniard, similar to that just before on the deck, and whether it was the start he gave, or a sudden gawky roll of the hull in the calm, or a momentary unsteadiness of the servant's hand; however it was, just then the razor drew blood, spots of which stained the creamy lather under the throat; immediately the black barber drew back his steel, and remaining in his professional attitude, back to Captain Delano, and face to Don Benito, held up the trickling razor, saying, with a sort of half humorous sorrow, "See, master,—you shook so—here's Babo's first blood."

No sword drawn before James the First of England, no assassination in that timid King's presence, could have produced a more terrified aspect than was now presented by Don Benito.

Poor fellow, thought Captain Delano, so nervous he can't even bear the sight of barber's blood; and this unstrung, sick man, is it credible that I should have imagined he meant to spill all my blood, who can't endure the sight of one little drop of his own? Surely, Amasa Delano, you have been beside yourself this day. Tell it not when you get home, sappy Amasa. Well, well, he looks like a murderer, doesn't he? More like as if himself were to be done for. Well, well, this day's experience shall be a good lesson.

Meantime, while these things were running through the honest seaman's mind, the servant had taken the napkin from his arm, and to Don Benito had said: "But answer Don Amasa, please, master, while I wipe this ugly stuff off the razor, and strop it again."

As he said the words, his face was turned half round, so

as to be alike visible to the Spaniard and the American, and seemed by its expression to hint, that he was desirous, by getting his master to go on with the conversation, considerately to withdraw his attention from the recent annoying accident. As if glad to snatch the offered relief, Don Benito resumed, rehearsing to Captain Delano, that not only were the calms of unusual duration, but the ship had fallen in with obstinate currents and other things he added, some of which were but repetitions of former statements, to explain how it came to pass that the passage from Cape Horn to St. Maria had been so exceedingly long, now and then mingling with his words, incidental praises, less qualified than before, to the blacks, for their general good conduct.

These particulars were not given consecutively, the servant now and then using his razor, and so, between the intervals of shaving, the story and panegyric went on with more than usual huskiness.

To Captain Delano's imagination, now again not wholly at rest, there was something so hollow in the Spaniard's manner, with apparently some reciprocal hollowness in the servant's dusky comment of silence, that the idea flashed across him, that possibly master and man, for some unknown purpose, were acting out, both in word and deed, nay, to the very tremor of Don Benito's limbs, some juggling play before him. Neither did the suspicion of collusion lack apparent support, from the fact of those whispered conferences before mentioned. But then, what could be the object of enacting this play of the barber before him? At last, regarding the notion as a whimsy, insensibly suggested, perhaps, by the theatrical aspect of Don Benito in his harlequin ensign, Captain Delano speedily banished it.

The shaving over, the servant bestirred himself with a small bottle of scented waters, pouring a few drops on the head, and then diligently rubbing; the vehemence of the exercise causing the muscles of his face to twitch rather strangely.

His next operation was with comb, scissors and brush; going round and round, smoothing a curl here, clipping an unruly whisker-hair there, giving a graceful sweep to the temple-lock, with other impromptu touches evincing the hand of a master; while, like any resigned gentleman in barber's hands, Don Benito bore all, much less uneasily, at least, than he had done the razoring; indeed, he sat so pale and rigid now, that the negro seemed a Nubian sculptor finishing off a white statue-head.

All being over at last, the standard of Spain removed, tumbled up, and tossed back into the flag-locker, the negro's warm breath blowing away any stray hair which might have lodged down his master's neck; collar and cravat readjusted; a speck of lint whisked off the velvet lapel; all this being done; backing off a little space, and pausing with an expression of subdued self-complacency, the servant for a moment surveyed his master, as, in toilet at least, the creature of his own tasteful hands.

Captain Delano playfully complimented him upon his achievement; at the same time congratulating Don Benito.

But neither sweet waters, nor shampooing, nor fidelity, nor sociality, delighted the Spaniard. Seeing him relapsing into forbidding gloom, and still remaining seated, Captain Delano, thinking that his presence was undesired just then, withdrew, on pretence of seeing whether, as he had prophesied, any signs of a breeze were visible.

Walking forward to the mainmast, he stood awhile thinking over the scene, and not without some undefined misgivings, when he heard a noise near the cuddy, and turning, saw the negro, his hand to his cheek. Advancing, Captain

Delano perceived that the cheek was bleeding. He was about to ask the cause, when the negro's wailing soliloquy enlightened him.

"Ah, when will master get better from his sickness; only the sour heart that sour sickness breeds made him serve Babo so; cutting Babo with the razor, because, only by accident, Babo had given master one little scratch; and for the first time in so many a day, too. Ah, ah, ah," holding his hand to his face.

Is it possible, thought Captain Delano; was it to wreak in private his Spanish spite against this poor friend of his, that Don Benito, by his sullen manner, impelled me to withdraw? Ah, this slavery breeds ugly passions in man! Poor fellow!

He was about to speak in sympathy to the negro, but with a timid reluctance he now re-entered the cuddy.

Presently master and man came forth; Don Benito leaning on his servant as if nothing had happened.

But a sort of love-quarrel, after all, thought Captain Delano.

He accosted Don Benito, and they slowly walked together. They had gone but a few paces, when the steward—a tall, rajah-looking mulatto, orientally set off with a pagoda turban formed by three or four Madras handkerchiefs wound about his head, tier on tier—approaching with a salaam, announced lunch in the cabin.

On their way thither, the two captains were preceded by the mulatto, who, turning round as he advanced, with continual smiles and bows, ushered them in, a display of elegance which quite completed the insignificance of the small bare-headed Babo, who, as if not unconscious of inferiority, eyed askance the graceful steward. But in part, Captain Delano imputed his jealous watchfulness to that peculiar feeling which the full-blooded African entertains for the adulterated one. As for the steward, his manner, if not bespeaking much dignity of self-respect, yet evidenced his extreme desire to please; which is doubly meritorious, as at once Christian and Chesterfieldian.

Captain Delano observed with interest that while the complexion of the mulatto was hybrid, his physiognomy was European; classically so.

"Don Benito," whispered he, "I am glad to see this usher-of-the-golden-rod of yours; the sight refutes an ugly remark once made to me by a Barbados planter that when a mulatto has a regular European face, look out for him; he is a devil. But see, your steward here has features more regular than King George's of England; and yet there he nods, and bows, and smiles; a king, indeed—the king of kind hearts and polite fellows. What a pleasant voice he has, too?"

"He has, Señor."

"But, tell me, has he not, so far as you have known him, always proved a good, worthy fellow?" said Captain Delano, pausing, while with a final genuflexion the steward disappeared into the cabin; "come, for the reason just mentioned, I am curious to know."

"Francesco is a good man," rather sluggishly responded Don Benito, like a phlegmatic appreciator, who would neither find fault nor flatter.

"Ah, I thought so. For it were strange indeed, and not very creditable to us white-skins, if a little of our blood mixed with the African's, should, far from improving the latter's quality, have the sad effect of pouring vitriolic acid into black broth; improving the hue, perhaps, but not the wholesomeness."

"Doubtless, doubtless, Señor, but"—glancing at Babo—"not to speak of negroes, your planter's remark I have heard applied to the Spanish and Indian intermixtures in our provinces. But I know nothing about the matter," he listlessly added.

And here they entered the cabin.

The lunch was a frugal one. Some of Captain Delano's fresh fish and pumpkins, biscuit and salt beef, the reserved bottle of cider, and the *San Dominick's* last bottle of Canary.

As they entered, Francesco, with two or three coloured aids, was hovering over the table giving the last adjustments. Upon perceiving their master they withdrew, Francesco making a smiling congé, and the Spaniard, without condescending to notice it, fastidiously remarking to his companion that he relished not superfluous attendance.

Without companions, host and guest sat down, like a childless married couple, at opposite ends of the table, Don Benito waving Captain Delano to his place, and, weak as he was, insisting upon that gentleman being seated before himself.

The negro placed a rug under Don Benito's feet, and a cushion behind his back, and then stood behind, not his master's chair, but Captain Delano's. At first, this a little surprised the latter. But it was soon evident that, in taking his position, the black was still true to his master; since by facing him he could the more readily anticipate his slightest want.

"This is an uncommonly intelligent fellow of yours, Don Benito," whispered Captain Delano across the table.

"You say true, Señor."

During the repast, the guest again reverted to parts of Don Benito's story, begging further particulars here and there. He inquired how it was that the scurvy and fever should have committed such wholesale havoc upon the whites, while destroying less than half of the blacks. As if this question reproduced the whole scene of plague before

the Spaniard's eyes, miserably reminding him of his solitude
in a cabin where before he had had so many friends and
officers round him, his hand shook, his face became hueless,
broken words escaped; but directly the sane memory of the
past seemed replaced by insane terrors of the present. With
starting eyes he stared before him at vacancy. For nothing
was to be seen but the hand of his servant pushing the
Canary over towards him. At length a few sips served partially to restore him. He made random reference to the
different constitutions of races, enabling one to offer more
resistance to certain maladies than another. The thought
was new to his companion.

Presently Captain Delano, intending to say something to
his host concerning the pecuniary part of the business he
had undertaken for him, especially—since he was strictly
accountable to his owners—with reference to the new suit
of sails, and other things of that sort; and naturally pre-
ferring to conduct such affairs in private, was desirous that
the servant should withdraw; imagining that Don Benito
for a few minutes could dispense with his attendance. He,
however, waited awhile; thinking that, as the conversation
proceeded, Don Benito, without being prompted, would perceive the propriety of the step.

But it was otherwise. At last catching his host's eye,
Captain Delano, with a slight backward gesture of his thumb,
whispered, "Don Benito, pardon me, but there is an interference with the full expression of what I have to say to
you."

Upon this the Spaniard changed countenance; which was
imputed to his resenting the hint, as in some way a reflection
upon his servant. After a moment's pause, he assured his
guest that the black's remaining with them could be of no
disservice; because since losing his officers he had made Babo

(whose original office, it now appeared, had been captain of the slaves) not only his constant attendant and companion, but in all things his confidant.

After this, nothing more could be said; though, indeed, Captain Delano could hardly avoid some little tinge of irritation upon being left ungratified in so inconsiderable a wish, by one, too, for whom he intended such solid services. But it is only his querulousness, thought he; and so filling his glass he proceeded to business.

The price of the sails and other matters was fixed upon. But while this was being done, the American observed that, though his original offer of assistance had been hailed with hectic animation, yet now when it was reduced to a business transaction, indifference and apathy were betrayed. Don Benito, in fact, appeared to submit to hearing the details more out of regard to common propriety, than from any impression that weighty benefit to himself and his voyage was involved.

Soon, this manner became still more reserved. The effort was vain to seek to draw him into social talk. Gnawed by his splenetic mood, he sat twitching his beard, while to little purpose the hand of his servant, mute as that on the wall, slowly pushed over the Canary.

Lunch being over, they sat down on the cushioned transom; the servant placing a pillow behind his master. The long continuance of the calm had now affected the atmosphere. Don Benito sighed heavily, as if for breath.

"Why not adjourn to the cuddy," said Captain Delano; "there is more air there." But the host sat silent and motionless.

Meantime his servant knelt before him, with a large fan of feathers. And Francesco, coming in on tiptoes, handed the negro a little cup of aromatic waters, with which at intervals he chafed his master's brow, smoothing the hair along the temples as a nurse does a child's. He spoke no word. He only rested his eye on his master's, as if, amid all Don Benito's distress, a little to refresh his spirit by the silent sight of fidelity.

Presently the ship's bell sounded two o'clock; and through the cabin-windows a slight rippling of the sea was discerned; and from the desired direction.

"There," exclaimed Captain Delano, "I told you so, Don Benito, look!"

He had risen to his feet, speaking in a very animated tone, with a view the more to rouse his companion. But though the crimson curtain of the stern-window near him that moment fluttered against his pale cheek, Don Benito seemed to have even less welcome for the breeze than the calm.

Poor fellow, thought Captain Delano, bitter experience has taught him that one ripple does not make a wind, any more than one swallow a summer. But he is mistaken for once. I will get his ship in for him, and prove it.

Briefly alluding to his weak condition, he urged his host to remain quietly where he was, since he (Captain Delano) would with pleasure take upon himself the responsibility of making the best use of the wind.

Upon gaining the deck, Captain Delano started at the unexpected figure of Atufal, monumentally fixed at the threshold, like one of those sculptured porters of black marble guarding the porches of Egyptian tombs.

But this time the start was, perhaps, purely physical. Atufal's presence, singularly attesting docility even in sullenness, was contrasted with that of the hatchet-polishers, who in patience evinced their industry; while both spectacles showed, that lax as Don Benito's general authority might be, still, whenever he chose to exert it, no man so savage or colossal but must, more or less, bow.

Snatching a trumpet which hung from the bulwarks, with a free step Captain Delano advanced to the forward edge of the poop, issuing his orders in his best Spanish. The few sailors and many negroes, all equally pleased, obediently set about heading the ship toward the harbour.

While giving some directions about setting a lower stu'n'-sail, suddenly Captain Delano heard a voice faithfully repeating his orders. Turning, he saw Babo, now for the time acting, under the pilot, his original part of captain of the slaves. This assistance proved valuable. Tattered sails and warped yards were soon brought into some trim. And no brace or halyard was pulled but to the blithe songs of the inspirited negroes.

Good fellows, thought Captain Delano, a little training would make fine sailors of them. Why see, the very women pull and sing, too. These must be some of those Ashantee negresses that make such capital soldiers, I've heard. But who's at the helm? I must have a good hand there.

He went to see.

The *San Dominick* steered with a cumbrous tiller, with large horizontal pullies attached. At each pulley-end stood a subordinate black, and between them, at the tiller-head, the responsible post, a Spanish seaman, whose countenance evinced his due share in the general hopefulness and confidence at the coming of the breeze.

He proved the same man who had behaved with so shamefaced an air on the windlass.

"Ah,—it is you, my man," exclaimed Captain Delano—"well, no more sheep's-eyes now;—look straightforward and keep the ship so. Good hand, I trust? And want to get into the harbour, don't you?"

"Sí Señor," assented the man with an inward chuckle, grasping the tiller-head firmly. Upon this, unperceived by the American, the two blacks eyed the sailor askance.

Finding all right at the helm, the pilot went forward to the forecastle, to see how matters stood there.

The ship now had way enough to breast the current. With the approach of evening, the breeze would be sure to freshen.

Having done all that was needed for the present, Captain Delano, giving his last orders to the sailors, turned aft to report affairs to Don Benito in the cabin; perhaps additionally incited to rejoin him by the hope of snatching a moment's private chat while his servant was engaged upon deck.

From opposite sides, there were, beneath the poop, two approaches to the cabin; one further forward than the other, and consequently communicating with a longer passage. Marking the servant still above, Captain Delano, taking the nighest entrance—the one last named, and at whose porch Atufal still stood—hurried on his way, till, arrived at the cabin threshold, he paused an instant, a little to recover from his eagerness. Then, with the words of his intended business upon his lips, he entered. As he advanced toward the Spaniard, on the transom, he heard another footstep, keeping time with his. From the opposite door, a salver in hand, the servant was likewise advancing.

"Confound the faithful fellow," thought Captain Delano; "what a vexatious coincidence."

Possibly, the vexation might have been something different, were it not for the buoyant confidence inspired by the breeze. But even as it was, he felt a slight twinge, from a sudden involuntary association in his mind of Babo with Atufal.

"Don Benito," said he, "I give you joy; the breeze will hold, and will increase. By the way, your tall man and time-piece, Atufal, stands without. By your order, of course?"

Don Benito recoiled, as if at some bland satirical touch, delivered with such adroit garnish of apparent good-breeding as to present no handle for retort.

He is like one flayed alive, thought Captain Delano; where may one touch him without causing a shrink?

The servant moved before his master, adjusting a cushion; recalled to civility, the Spaniard stiffly replied: "You are right. The slave appears where you saw him, according to my command; which is, that if at the given hour I am below, he must take his stand and abide my coming."

"Ah now, pardon me, but that is treating the poor fellow like an ex-king denied. Ah, Don Benito," smiling, "for all the license you permit in some things, I fear lest, at bottom, you are a bitter hard master."

Again Don Benito shrank; and this time, as the good sailor thought, from a genuine twinge of his conscience.

Conversation now became constrained. In vain Captain Delano called attention to the now perceptible motion of the keel gently cleaving the sea; with lack-lustre eye, Don Benito returned words few and reserved.

By-and-by, the wind having steadily risen, and still blowing right into the harbour, bore the *San Dominick* swiftly on. Rounding a point of land, the sealer at distance came into open view

Meantime Captain Delano had again repaired to the deck, remaining there some time. Having at last altered the ship's course, so as to give the reef a wide berth, he returned for a few moments below.

I will cheer up my poor friend, this time, thought he.

"Better and better, Don Benito," he cried as he blithely re-entered; "there will soon be an end to your cares, at least for awhile. For when, after a long, sad voyage, you know, the anchor drops into the haven, all its vast weight seems lifted from the captain's heart. We are getting on famously, Don Benito. My ship is in sight. Look through this side-light here; there she is; all a-taunt-o! The *Bachelor's Delight*, my good friend. Ah, how this wind braces one up. Come, you must take a cup of coffee with me this evening. My old steward will give you as fine a cup as ever any sultan tasted. What say you, Don Benito, will you?"

At first, the Spaniard glanced feverishly up, casting a longing look toward the sealer, while with mute concern his servant gazed into his face. Suddenly the old ague of cold-ness returned, and dropping back to his cushions he was silent.

"You do not answer. Come, all day you have been my host; would you have hospitality all on one side?"

"I cannot go," was the response.

"What? it will not fatigue you. The ships will lie to-gether as near as they can, without swinging foul. It will be little more than stepping from deck to deck; which is but as from room to room. Come, come, you must not refuse me."

"I cannot go," decisively and repulsively repeated Don Benito.

Renouncing all but the last appearance of courtesy, with a sort of cadaverous sullenness, and biting his thin nails to the quick, he glanced, almost glared, at his guest; as if impatient that a stranger's presence should interfere with the full indulgence of his morbid hour. Meantime the sound of the parted waters came more and more gurglingly and merrily in at the windows; as reproaching him for his dark spleen; as telling him that, sulk as he might, and go mad with it, nature cared not a jot; since, whose fault was it, pray?

But the foul mood was now at its depth. as the fair wind at its height.

There was something in the man so far beyond any mere unsociality or sourness previously evinced, that even the forbearing good-nature of his guest could no longer endure it. Wholly at a loss to account for such demeanour, and deeming sickness with eccentricity, however extreme, no adequate excuse, well satisfied, too, that nothing in his own conduct could justify it, Captain Delano's pride began to be roused. Himself became reserved. But all seemed one to the Spaniard. Quitting him, therefore, Captain Delano once more went to the deck.

The ship was now within less than two miles of the sealer. The whale-boat was seen darting over the interval.

To be brief, the two vessels, thanks to the pilot's skill, ere long in neighbourly style lay anchored together.

Before returning to his own vessel, Captain Delano had intended communicating to Don Benito the practical details of the proposed services to be rendered. But, as it was, unwilling anew to subject himself to rebuffs, he resolved, now that he had seen the *San Dominick* safely moored, immediately to quit her, without further allusion to hospitality or business. Indefinitely postponing his ulterior plans, he would regulate his future actions according to future circumstances. His boat was ready to receive him; but his host still tarried below. Well, thought Captain Delano, if he has little breeding, the more need to show mine. He descended to the cabin to bid a ceremonious, and, it may be, tacitly rebukeful adieu. But to his great satisfaction, Don Benito, as if he began to feel the weight of that treatment with which his slighted guest had, not indecorously, retaliated upon him, now supported by his servant, rose to his feet, and grasping

Captain Delano's hand, stood tremulous; too much agitated to speak. But the good augury hence drawn was suddenly dashed, by his resuming all his previous reserve, with augmented gloom, as, with half-averted eyes, he silently reseated himself on his cushions. With a corresponding return of his own chilled feelings, Captain Delano bowed and withdrew.

He was hardly midway in the narrow corridor, dim as a tunnel, leading from the cabin to the stairs, when a sound, as of the tolling for execution in some jail-yard, fell on his ears. It was the echo of the ship's flawed bell, striking the hour, drearily reverberated in this subterranean vault. Instantly, by a fatality not to be withstood, his mind, responsive to the portent, swarmed with superstitious suspicions. He paused. In images far swifter than these sentences, the minutest details of all his former distrusts swept through him.

Hitherto, credulous good-nature had been too ready to furnish excuses for reasonable fears. Why was the Spaniard, so superfluously punctilious at times, now heedless of common propriety in not accompanying to the side his departing guest? Did indisposition forbid? Indisposition had not forbidden more irksome exertion that day. His last equivocal demeanour recurred. He had risen to his feet, grasped his guest's hand, motioned toward his hat; then, in an instant, all was eclipsed in sinister muteness and gloom. Did this imply one brief, repentant relenting at the final moment, from some iniquitous plot, followed by remorseless return to it? His last glance seemed to express a calamitous, yet acquiescent farewell to Captain Delano for ever. Why decline the invitation to visit the sealer that evening? Or was the Spaniard less hardened than the Jew, who refrained not from supping at the board of him whom the same night he meant to betray? What imported all those day-long enigmas and contradictions, except they were intended to mystify, preliminary to some stealthy blow? Atufal, the pretended rebel, but punctual shadow, that moment lurked by the threshold without. He seemed a sentry, and more. Who, by his own confession, had stationed him there? Was the negro now lying in wait?

The Spaniard behind—his creature before: to rush from darkness to light was the involuntary choice.

The next moment, with clenched jaw and hand, he passed Atufal, and stood unarmed in the light. As he saw his trim ship lying peacefully at her anchor, and almost within ordinary call; as he saw his household boat, with familiar faces in it, patiently rising and falling on the short waves by the *San Dominick's* side; and then, glancing about the decks where he stood, saw the oakum-pickers still gravely plying their fingers; and heard the low, buzzing whistle and industrious hum of the hatchet-polishers, still bestirring themselves over their endless occupation; and more than all, as he saw the benign aspect of Nature, taking her innocent repose in the evening; the screened sun in the quiet camp of the west shining out like the mild light from Abraham's tent; as his charmed eye and ear took in all these, with the chained figure of the black, the clenched jaw and hand relaxed. Once again he smiled at the phantoms which had mocked him, and felt something like a tinge of remorse, that, by indulging them even for a moment, he should, by implication, have betrayed an almost atheist doubt of the ever-watchful Providence above.

There was a few minutes' delay, while, in obedience to his orders, the boat was being hooked along to the gangway. During this interval, a sort of saddened satisfaction stole over Captain Delano, at thinking of the kindly offices he had that day discharged for a stranger. Ah, thought he, after good actions one's conscience is never ungrateful, however much so the benefited party may be.

Presently, his foot, in the first act of descent into the boat, pressed the first round of the side-ladder, his face presented inward upon the deck. In the same moment, he heard his name courteously sounded; and, to his pleased surprise, saw Don Benito advancing—an unwonted energy in his air, as if, at the last moment, intent upon making amends for his recent discourtesy. With instinctive good feeling, Captain Delano, revoking his foot, turned and reciprocally advanced. As he did so, the Spaniard's nervous eagerness increased, but his vital energy failed; so that, the better to support him, the servant, placing his master's hand on his naked shoulder, and gently holding it there, formed himself into a sort of crutch.

When the two captains met, the Spaniard again fervently took the hand of the American, at the same time casting an earnest glance into his eyes, but, as before, too much overcome to speak.

I have done him wrong, self-reproachfully thought Captain Delano; his apparent coldness has deceived me; in no instance has he meant to offend.

Meantime, as if fearful that the continuance of the scene might too much unstring his master, the servant seemed anxious to terminate it. And so, still presenting himself as a crutch, and walking between the two captains, he advanced with them toward the gangway; while still, as if full of kindly contrition, Don Benito would not let go the hand of Captain Delano, but retained it in his, across the black's body.

Soon they were standing by the side, looking over into the boat, whose crew turned up their curious eyes. Waiting a moment for the Spaniard to relinquish his hold, the now embarrassed Captain Delano lifted his foot, to overstep the threshold of the open gangway; but still Don Benito would not let go his hand. And yet, with an agitated tone, he said, "I can go no further; here I must bid you adieu. Adieu, my dear, dear Don Amasa. Go—go!" suddenly tearing his hand loose, "go, and God guard you better than me, my best friend."

Not unaffected, Captain Delano would now have lingered; but catching the meekly admonitory eye of the servant, with a hasty farewell he descended into his boat, followed by the continual adieus of Don Benito, standing rooted in the gangway.

Seating himself in the stern, Captain Delano, making a last salute, ordered the boat shoved off. The crew had their oars on end. The bowsman pushed the boat a sufficient distance for the oars to be lengthwise dropped. The instant that was done, Don Benito sprang over the bulwarks, falling at the feet of Captain Delano; at the same time, calling towards his ship, but in tones so frenzied, that none in the boat could understand him. But, as if not equally obtuse, three Spanish sailors, from three different and distant parts of the ship, splashed into the sea, swimming after their captain, as if intent upon his rescue.

The dismayed officer of the boat eagerly asked what this meant. To which, Captain Delano, turning a disdainful smile upon the unaccountable Benito Cereno, answered that, for his part, he neither knew nor cared; but it seemed as if the Spaniard had taken it into his head to produce the impression among his people that the boat wanted to kidnap him. "Or else—give way for your lives," he wildly added, starting at a clattering hubbub in the ship, above which rang the tocsin of the hatchet-polishers; and seizing Don Benito by the throat he added, "this plotting pirate means murder!" Here, in apparent verification of the words, the servant, a dagger in his hand, was seen on the rail overhead, poised, in the act of leaping, as if with desperate fidelity to befriend his master to the last; while, seemingly to aid the black, the three Spanish sailors were trying to clamber into the hampered bow. Meantime, the whole host of negroes, as if inflamed at the sight of their jeopardized captain, impended in one sooty avalanche over the bulwarks.

All this, with what preceded, and what followed, occurred with such involutions of rapidity, that past, present, and future seemed one.

Seeing the negro coming, Captain Delano had flung the Spaniard aside, almost in the very act of clutching him, and, by the unconscious recoil, shifting his place, with arms thrown up, so promptly grappled the servant in his descent, that with dagger presented at Captain Delano's heart, the black seemed of purpose to have leaped there as to his mark. But the weapon was wrenched away, and the assailant dashed down into the bottom of the boat, which now, with disentangled oars, began to speed through the sea.

At this juncture, the left hand of Captain Delano, on one side, again clutched the half-reclined Don Benito, heedless that he was in a speechless faint, while his right foot, on the other side, ground the prostrate negro; and his right arm pressed for added speed on the after oar, his eye bent forward, encouraging his men to their utmost.

But here, the officer of the boat, who had at last succeeded in beating off the towing Spanish sailors, and was now, with face turned aft, assisting the bowsman at his oar, suddenly called to Captain Delano, to see what the black was about; while a Portuguese oarsman shouted to him to give heed to what the Spaniard was saying.

Glancing down at his feet, Captain Delano saw the freed hand of the servant aiming with a second dagger—a small one, before concealed in his wool—with this he was snakishly writhing up from the boat's bottom, at the heart of his master, his countenance lividly vindictive, expressing the centred purpose of his soul; while the Spaniard, half-choked, was vainly shrinking away, with husky words, incoherent to all but the Portuguese.

That moment, across the long benighted mind of Captain Delano, a flash of revelation swept, illuminating in unanticipated clearness Benito Cereno's whole mysterious demeanour, with every enigmatic event of the day, as well as the entire past voyage of the *San Dominick*. He smote Babo's hand down, but his own heart smote him harder. With infinite pity he withdrew his hold from Don Benito. Not Captain Delano, but Don Benito, the black, in leaping into the boat, had intended to stab.

Both the black's hands were held, as, glancing up toward the *San Dominick*, Captain Delano, now with the scales dropped from his eyes, saw the negroes, not in misrule, not in tumult, not as if frantically concerned for Don Benito, but with mask torn away, flourishing hatchets and knives, in ferocious piratical revolt. Like delirious black dervishes, the six Ashantees danced on the poop. Prevented by their foes from springing into the water, the Spanish boys were hurrying up to the topmost spars, while such of the few Spanish sailors, not already in the sea, less alert, were descried, helplessly mixed in, on deck, with the blacks.

Meantime Captain Delano hailed his own vessel, ordering the ports up, and the guns run out. But by this time the cable of the *San Dominick* had been cut; and the fag-end, in lashing out, whipped away the canvas shroud about the beak, suddenly revealing, as the bleached hull swung round toward the open ocean, death for the figurehead, in a human skeleton; chalky comment on the chalked words below, *"Follow your leader."*

At the sight, Don Benito, covering his face, wailed out: " 'Tis he, Aranda! my murdered, unburied friend!"

Upon reaching the sealer, calling for ropes, Captain Delano bound the negro, who made no resistance, and had him hoisted to the deck. He would then have assisted the now almost helpless Don Benito up the side; but Don Benito, wan as he was, refused to move, or be moved, until the negro should have been first put below out of view. When, presently assured that it was done, he no more shrank from the ascent.

The boat was immediately despatched back to pick up the three swimming sailors. Meantime, the guns were in readiness, though, owing to the *San Dominick* having glided somewhat astern of the sealer, only the aftermost one could be brought to bear. With this, they fired six times; thinking to cripple the fugitive ship by bringing down her spars. But only a few inconsiderable ropes were shot away. Soon the ship was beyond the guns' range, steering broad out of the bay; the blacks thickly clustering round the bowsprit, one moment with taunting cries toward the whites, the next with upthrown gestures hailing the now dusky expanse of ocean —cawing crows escaped from the hand of the fowler.

The first impulse was to slip the cables and give chase. But, upon second thought, to pursue with whale-boat and yawl seemed more promising.

Upon inquiring of Don Benito what firearms they had on board the *San Dominick*, Captain Delano was answered that they had none that could be used; because, in the earlier stages of the mutiny, a cabin-passenger, since dead, had secretly put out of order the locks of what few muskets there were. But with all his remaining strength, Don Benito entreated the American not to give chase, either with ship or boat; for the negroes had already proved themselves such desperadoes, that, in case of a present assault, nothing but a total massacre of the whites could be looked for. But, regarding this warning as coming from one whose spirit had been crushed by misery, the American did not give up his design.

The boats were got ready and armed. Captain Delano ordered twenty-five men into them. He was going himself when Don Benito grasped his arm.

"What! have you saved my life, Señor, and are you now going to throw away your own?"

The officers also, for reasons connected with their interests and those of the voyage, and a duty owing to the owners, strongly objected against their commander's going. Weighing their remonstrances a moment, Captain Delano felt bound to remain; appointing his chief mate—an athletic and resolute man, who had been a privateer's man, and, as his enemies whispered, a pirate—to head the party. The more to encourage the sailors, they were told, that the Spanish captain considered his ship as good as lost; that she and her cargo, including some gold and silver, were worth upwards of ten thousand doubloons. Take her, and no small part should be theirs. The sailors replied with a shout.

The fugitives had now almost gained an offing. It was nearly night; but the moon was rising. After hard, prolonged pulling, the boats came up on the ship's quarters, at a suitable distance laying upon their oars to discharge their muskets. Having no bullets to return, the negroes sent their yells. But, upon the second volley, Indian-like, they hurtled their hatchets. One took off a sailor's fingers. Another struck the whale-boat's bow, cutting off the rope there, and remaining stuck in the gunwale, like a woodman's axe.

Snatching it, quivering from its lodgment, the mate hurled it back. The returned gauntlet now stuck in the ship's broken quarter-gallery, and so remained.

The negroes giving too hot a reception, the whites kept a more respectful distance. Hovering now just out of reach of the hurtling hatchets, they, with a view to the close encounter which must soon come, sought to decoy the blacks into entirely disarming themselves of their most murderous weapons in a hand-to-hand fight, by foolishly flinging them, as missiles, short of the mark, into the sea. But ere long perceiving the stratagem, the negroes desisted, though not before many of them had to replace their lost hatchets with handspikes; an exchange which, as counted upon, proved in the end favourable to the assailants.

Meantime, with a strong wind, the ship still clove the water; the boats alternately falling behind, and pulling up, to discharge fresh volleys

The fire was mostly directed toward the stern, since there, chiefly, the negroes, at present, were clustering. But to kill or maim the negroes was not the object. To take them, with the ship, was the object. To do it, the ship must be boarded; which could not be done by boats while she was sailing so fast.

A thought now struck the mate. Observing the Spanish boys still aloft, high as they could get, he called to them to descend to the yards, and cut adrift the sails. It was done. About this time, owing to causes hereafter to be shown, two Spaniards, in the dress of sailors and conspicuously showing themselves, were killed; not by volleys, but by deliberate marksman's shots; while, as it afterwards appeared, during one of the general discharges, Atufal, the black, and the Spaniard at the helm likewise were killed. What now, with the loss of the sails, and loss of leaders, the ship became unmanageable to the negroes.

With creaking masts she came heavily round to the wind; the prow slowly swinging into view of the boats, its skeleton gleaming in the horizontal moonlight, and casting a gigantic ribbed shadow upon the water. One extended arm of the ghost seemed beckoning the whites to avenge it.

"Follow your leader!" cried the mate; and, one on each bow, the boats boarded. Scaling-spears and cutlasses crossed hatchets and handspikes. Huddled upon the long-boat amidships, the negresses raised a wailing chant, whose chorus was the clash of the steel.

For a time, the attack wavered; the negroes wedging themselves to beat it back; the half-repelled sailors, as yet unable to gain a footing, fighting as troopers in the saddle, one leg sideways flung over the bulwarks, and one without, plying their cutlasses like carters' whips. But in vain. They were almost overborne, when, rallying themselves into a squad as one man, with a huzza, they sprang inboard; where, entangled, they involuntarily separated again. For a few breaths' space there was a vague, muffled, inner sound as of submerged sword-fish rushing hither and thither through shoals of black-fish. Soon, in a reunited band, and joined by the Spanish seamen, the whites came to the surface, irresistibly driving the negroes toward the stern. But a barricade of casks and sacks, from side to side, had been thrown up by the mainmast. Here the negroes faced about, and though scorning peace or truce, yet fain would have had a respite. But, without pause, overleaping the barrier, the unflagging sailors again closed. Exhausted, the blacks now fought in despair. Their red tongues lolled, wolf-like, from their black mouths. But the pale sailors' teeth were set; not a word was spoken; and, in five minutes more, the ship was won.

Nearly a score of the negroes were killed. Exclusive of those by the balls, many were mangled; their wounds—mostly inflicted by the long-edged scaling-spears—resembling those shaven ones of the English at Preston Pans, made by the poled scythes of the Highlanders. On the other side, none were killed, though several were wounded; some severely, including the mate. The surviving negroes were temporarily secured, and the ship, towed back into the harbour at midnight, once more lay anchored.

Omitting the incidents and arrangements ensuing, suffice it that, after two days spent in refitting, the two ships sailed in company for Concepcion in Chili, and thence for Lima in Peru; where, before the vice-regal courts, the whole affair, from the beginning, underwent investigation.

Though, midway on the passage, the ill-fated Spaniard, relaxed from constraint, showed some signs of regaining health with free-will; yet, agreeably to his own foreboding, shortly before arriving at Lima, he relapsed, finally becoming so reduced as to be carried ashore in arms. Hearing of his story and plight, one of the many religious institutions of the City of Kings opened an hospitable refuge to him, where both physician and priest were his nurses, and a member of the order volunteered to be his one special guardian and consoler, by night and by day.

The following extracts, translated from one of the official Spanish documents, will, it is hoped, shed light on the preceding narrative, as well as, in the first place, reveal the true port of departure and true history of the *San Dominick's* voyage, down to the time of her touching at the island of Santa Maria.

But, ere the extracts come, it may be well to preface them with a remark.

The document selected, from among many others, for partial translation, contains the deposition of Benito Cereno; the first taken in the case. Some disclosures therein were, at the time, held dubious for both learned and natural reasons. The tribunal inclined to the opinion that the deponent, not undisturbed in his mind by recent events, raved of some things which could never have happened. But subsequent depositions of the surviving sailors, bearing out the revelations of their captain in several of the strangest particulars, gave credence to the rest. So that the tribunal, in its final decision, rested its capital sentences upon statements which, had they lacked confirmation, it would have deemed it but duty to reject.

. . . . . .

I, Don José de Abos and Padilla, His Majesty's Notary for the Royal Revenue, and Register of this Province, and Notary Public of the Holy Crusade of this Bishopric, etc.

Do certify and declare, as much as is requisite in law, that, in the criminal cause commenced the twenty-fourth of the month of September, in the year seventeen hundred and ninety-nine, against the Senegal negroes of the ship *San Dominick*, the following declaration before me was made.

Declaration of the first witness, Don Benito Cereno.

The same day, and month, and year, His Honour, Doctor Juan Martinez de Dozas, Councillor of the Royal Audience of this Kingdom, and learned in the law of this Intendancy, ordered the captain of the ship *San Dominick,* Don Benito Cereno, to appear; which he did in his litter, attended by the monk Infelez; of whom he received, before Don José de Abos and Padilla, Notary Public of the Holy Crusade, the oath, which he took by God, our Lord, and a sign of the Cross; under which he promised to tell the truth of whatever he should know and should be asked;—and being interrogated agreeably to the tenor of the act commencing the process, he said, that on the twentieth of May last, he set sail with his ship from the port of Valparaiso, bound to that of Callao; loaded with the produce of the country and one hundred and sixty blacks, of both sexes, mostly belonging to Don Alexandro Aranda, gentleman, of the city of Mendoza; that the crew of the ship consisted of thirty-six men, beside the persons who went as passengers; that the negroes were in part as follows:

[*Here, in the original, follows a list of some fifty names, descriptions, and ages, compiled from certain recovered documents of Aranda's, and also from recollections of the deponent, from which portions only are extracted.*]

—One, from about eighteen to nineteen years, named José, and this was the man that waited upon his master, Don Alexandro, and who speaks well the Spanish, having served him four or five years; . . . a mulatto, named Francesco, the cabin steward, of a good person and voice, having sung in the Valparaiso churches, native of the province of Buenos Ayres, aged about thirty-five years. . . . A smart negro, named Dago, who had been for many years a grave-digger among the Spaniards, aged forty-six years. . . . Four old negroes, born in Africa, from sixty to seventy, but sound, caulkers by trade, whose names are as follows:—the first was named Muri, and he was killed (as was also his son named Diamelo); the second, Nacta; the third, Yola, likewise killed; the fourth, Ghofan; and six full-grown negroes, aged from thirty to forty-five, all raw, and born among the Ashantees—Martinqui, Yan, Lecbe, Mapenda, Yambaio, Akim; four of whom were killed; . . . a powerful negro named Atufal, who, being supposed to have been a chief in Africa, his owners set great store by him. . . . And a small negro of Senegal, but some years among the Spaniards, aged about thirty, which negro's name was Babo; . . . that he does not remember the names of the others, but that still expecting the residue of Don Alexandro's papers will be found, will then take due account of them all, and remit to the court; . . . and thirty-nine women and children of all ages.

[_After the catalogue, the deposition goes on as follows:_]

. . . That all the negroes slept upon deck, as is customary in this navigation, and none wore fetters, because the owner, his friend Aranda, told him that they were all tractable; . . . that on the seventh day after leaving port, at three o'clock in the morning, all the Spaniards being asleep except the two officers on the watch, who were the boatswain, Juan Robles, and the carpenter, Juan Bautista Gayete, and the helmsman and his boy, the negroes revolted suddenly, wounded dangerously the boatswain and the carpenter, and successively killed eighteen men of those who were sleeping upon deck, some with handspikes and hatchets, and others by throwing them alive overboard, after tying them; that of the Spaniards upon deck, they left about seven, as he thinks, alive and tied, to manœuvre the ship and three or four more who hid themselves, remained also alive. Although in the act of revolt the negroes made themselves masters of the hatchway, six or seven wounded went through it to the cockpit, without any hindrance on their part; that in the act of revolt, the mate and another person, whose name he does not recollect, attempted to come up through the hatchway, but having been wounded at the onset, they were obliged to return to the cabin; that the deponent resolved at break of day to come up the companionway, where the negro Babo was, being the ringleader, and Atufal, who assisted him, and having spoken to them, exhorted them to cease committing such atrocities, asking them, at the same time, what they wanted and intended to do, offering, himself, to obey their commands; that, notwithstanding this, they threw, in his presence, three men, alive and tied, overboard; that they told the deponent to come up, and that they would not kill him; which having done, the negro Babo asked him whether there were in those seas any negro countries where they might be carried, and he answered them. No; that the negro Babo afterwards told him to carry them to Senegal, or to the neighbouring islands of St. Nicholas; and he answered, that this was impossible, on account of the great distance, the necessity involved of rounding Cape Horn, the bad condition of the vessel, the want of provisions, sails, and water; but that the negro Babo replied to him he must carry them in any way; that they would do and conform themselves to everything the deponent should require as to eating and drinking; that after a long conference, being absolutely compelled to please them, for they threatened him to kill all the whites if they were not, at all events, carried to Senegal, he told them that what was most wanting for the voyage was water; that they would go near the coast to take it, and hence they would proceed on their course; that the negro Babo agreed to it; and the deponent steered toward the intermediate ports, hoping to meet some Spanish or foreign vessel that would save them; that within ten or eleven days they saw the land, and continued their course by it in the vicinity of Nasca; that the deponent observed that the negroes were now restless and mutinous, because he did not effect the taking in of water, the negro Babo having required, with threats, that it should be done, without fail, the following day; he told him he saw plainly that the coast was steep, and the rivers designated in the maps were not to be found, with other reasons suitable to the circumstances; that the best way would be to go to the island of Santa Maria, where they might water and victual easily, it being a desert island, as the foreigners did; that the deponent did not go to Pisco, that was near, nor make any other port of the coast, because the negro Babo had intimated to him several times, that he would kill all the whites the very moment he should perceive any city, town, or settlement of any kind on the shores to which they should be carried: that having determined to go to the island of Santa Maria, as the deponent had planned, for the purpose of trying whether, in the passage or in the island itself, they could find any vessel that should favour them, or whether he could escape from it in a boat to the neighbouring coast of Arruco; to adopt the necessary means he immediately changed his course, steering for the island; that the negroes Babo and Atufal held daily conferences, in which they discussed what was necessary for their design of returning to Senegal, whether they were to kill all the Spaniards, and particularly the deponent; that eight days after parting from the coast of Nasca, the deponent being on the watch a little after day-break, and soon after the negroes had their meeting, the negro Babo came to the place where the deponent was, and told him that he had determined to kill his master, Don Alexandro Aranda, both because he and his companions could not otherwise be sure of their liberty, and that, to keep the seamen in subjection, he wanted to prepare a warning of what road they should be made to take did they or any of them oppose him; and that, by means of the death of Don Alexandro, that warning would best be given; but, that what this last meant, the deponent did not at the time comprehend, nor could not, further than that the death of Don Alexandro was intended; and moreover, the negro Babo proposed to the deponent to call the mate Raneds, who was sleeping in the cabin, before the thing was done, for fear, as the deponent understood it, that the mate, who was a good navigator, should be killed with Don Alexandro and the rest; that the deponent, who was the friend, from youth of Don Alexandro, prayed and conjured, but all was useless; for the negro Babo answered him that the thing could not be prevented, and that all the Spaniards risked their death if they should attempt to frustrate his will in this matter, or any other; that, in this conflict, the deponent called the mate, Raneds, who was forced to go apart, and immediately the negro Babo commanded the Ashantee Martinqui and the Ashantee Lecbe to go and commit the murder; that those two went down with hatchets to the berth of Don Alexandro; that, yet half alive and mangled, they dragged him on deck; that they were going to throw him overboard in that state, but the negro Babo stopped them, bidding the murder be completed on the deck before him, which was done, when, by his orders, the body was carried below, forward; that nothing more was seen of it by the deponent for three days; . . . that Don Alonzo Sidonia, an old man, long resident at Valparaiso, and lately appointed to a civil office in Peru, whither he had taken passage, was at the time sleeping in the berth opposite Don Alexandro's; that, awakening at his cries, surprised by them, and at the sight of the negroes with their bloody hatchets in their hands, he threw himself into the sea through a window which was near him, and was drowned, without it being in the power of the deponent to assist or take him up; . . . that, a short time after killing Aranda, they brought upon deck his german-cousin, of middle-age, Don Francisco Masa, of Mendoza, and the young Don Joaquin, Marques de Aramboalaza, then lately from Spain, with his Spanish servant Ponce, and the three young clerks of Aranda, José Mozairi, Lorenzo Bargas, and Hermenegildo Gandix, all of Cadiz; that Don Joaquin and Hermenegildo Gandix, the negro Babo for purposes hereafter to appear, preserved alive; but Don Francisco Masa, José Mozairi, and Lorenzo Bargas, with Ponce, the servant, beside the boatswain, Juan Robles, the boatswain's mates, Manuel Viscaya and Roderigo Hurta, and four of the sailors, the negro Babo ordered to be thrown alive into the sea, although they made no resistance, nor begged for anything else but mercy; that the boatswain, Juan Robles, who knew how to swim, kept the longest above water, making acts of contrition, and, in the last words he uttered, charged this deponent to cause mass to be said for his soul to our Lady of Succour: . . . that, during the three days which followed, the deponent, uncertain what fate had befallen the remains of Don Alexandro, frequently asked the negro Babo where they were, and, if still on board, whether they were to be preserved for interment ashore, entreating him so to order it; that the negro Babo answered nothing till the fourth day, when at sunrise, the deponent coming on deck, the negro Babo showed him a skeleton, which had been substituted for the ship's proper figure-head, the image of Christopher Colon, the discoverer of the New World; that the negro Babo asked him whose skeleton that was, and whether, from its whiteness, he should not think it a white's; that, upon his covering his face, the negro Babo, coming close, said words to this effect: "Keep faith with the blacks from here to Senegal, or you shall in spirit, as now in body, follow your leader," pointing to the prow; . . . that the same morning the negro Babo took by succession each Spaniard forward, and asked him whose skeleton that was, and whether, from its whiteness, he should not think it a white's; that each Spaniard covered his face; that then to each the negro Babo repeated the words in the first place said to the deponent; . . . that they (the Spaniards), being then assembled aft, the negro Babo harangued them, saying that he had now done all; that the deponent (as navigator for the negroes) might pursue his course, warning him and all of them that they should, soul and body, go the way of Don Alexandro if he saw them (the Spaniards) speak or plot anything against them (the negroes)—a threat which was repeated every day; that, before the events last mentioned, they had tied the cook to throw him overboard, for it is not known what thing they heard him speak, but finally the negro Babo spared his life, at the request of the deponent; that a few days after, the deponent, endeavouring not to omit any means to preserve the lives of the remaining whites, spoke to the negroes peace and tranquillity, and agreed to draw up a paper, signed by the deponent and the sailors who could write, as also by the negro Babo, for himself and all the blacks, in which the deponent obliged himself to carry them to Senegal, and they not to kill any more, and he formally to make over to them the ship, with the cargo, with which they were for that time satisfied and quieted. . . . But the next day, the more surely to guard against the sailors' escape, the negro Babo commanded all the boats to be destroyed but the long-boat, which was unseaworthy, and another, a cutter in good condition, which, knowing it would yet be wanted for lowering the water casks, he had it lowered down into the hold.

[*Various particulars of the prolonged and perplexed navigation ensuing here follow, with incidents of a calamitous calm, from which portion one passage is extracted, to wit:*]

—That on the fifth day of the calm, all on board suffering much from the heat, and want of water, and five having died in fits, and mad, the negroes became irritable, and for a chance gesture, which they deemed suspicious—though it was harmless—made by the mate, Raneds, to the deponent, in the act of handing a quadrant, they killed him; but that for this they afterwards were sorry, the mate being the only remaining navigator on board, except the deponent.

—That omitting other events, which daily happened, and which can only serve uselessly to recall past misfortunes and conflicts, after seventy-three days' navigation, reckoned from the time they sailed from Nasca, during which they navigated under a scanty allowance of water, and were afflicted with the calms before mentioned, they at last arrived at the island of Santa Maria, on the seventeenth of the month of August, at about six o'clock in the afternoon, at which hour they cast anchor very near the American ship, *Bachelor's Delight,* which lay in the same bay, commanded by the generous Captain Amasa Delano; but at six o'clock in the morning, they had already descried the port, and the negroes became uneasy, as soon as at distance they saw the ship, not having expected to see one there; that the negro Babo pacified them, assuring them that no fear need be had; that straightway he ordered the figure on the bow to be covered with canvas, as for repairs, and had the decks a little set in order; that for a time the negro Babo and the negro Atufal conferred; that the negro Atufal was for sailing away, but the negro Babo would not, and, by himself, cast about what to do; that at last he came to the deponent, proposing to him to say and do all that the deponent declares to have said and done to the American captain; . . . that the negro Babo warned him that if he varied in the least, or uttered any word, or gave any look that should give the least intimation of the past events or present state, he would instantly kill him, with all his companions, showing a dagger, which he carried hid, saying something which, as he understood it, meant that that dagger would be alert as his eye; that the negro Babo then announced the plan to all his companions, which pleased them; that he then, the better to disguise the truth, devised many expedients, in some of them uniting deceit and defence; that of this sort was the device of the six Ashantees before named, who were his bravos; that them he stationed on the break of the poop, as if to clean certain hatchets (in cases, which were part of the cargo), but in reality to use them, and distribute them at need, and at a given word he told them that, among other devices, was the device of presenting Atufal, his right-hand man, as chained, though in a moment the chains could be dropped; that in every particular he informed the deponent what part he was expected to enact in every device, and what story he was to tell on every occasion, always threatening him with instant death if he varied in the least: that, conscious that many of the negroes would be turbulent, the negro Babo appointed the four aged negroes, who were caulkers, to keep what domestic order they could on the decks; that again and again he harangued the Spaniards and his companions, informing them of his intent, and of his devices, and of the invented story that this deponent was to tell, charging them lest any of them varied from that story; that these arrangements were made and matured during the interval of two or three hours, between their first sighting the ship and the arrival on board of Captain Amasa Delano;

that this happened at about half-past seven in the morning, Captain Amasa Delano coming in his boat, and all gladly receiving him; that the deponent, as well as he could force himself, acting then the part of principal owner, and a free captain of the ship, told Captain Amasa Delano, when called upon, that he came from Buenos Ayres, bound to Lima, with three hundred negroes; that off Cape Horn, and in a subsequent fever, many negroes had died; that also, by similar casualties, all the sea officers and the greatest part of the crew had died.

. . . . .

[*And so the deposition goes on, circumstantially recounting the fictitious story dictated to the deponent by Babo, and through the deponent imposed upon Captain Delano; and also recounting the friendly offers of Captain Delano, with other things, but all of which is here omitted. After the fictitious, strange story, etc., the deposition proceeds:*]

—That the generous Captain Amasa Delano remained on board all the day, till he left the ship anchored at six o'clock in the evening, deponent speaking to him always of his pretended misfortunes, under the fore-mentioned principles, without having had it in his power to tell a single word, or give him the least hint, that he might know the truth and state of things; because the negro Babo, performing the office of an officious servant with all the appearance of submission of the humble slave, did not leave the deponent one moment; that this was in order to observe the deponent's actions and words, for the negro Babo understands well the Spanish; and besides, there were thereabout some others who were constantly on the watch, and likewise understood the Spanish; . . . that upon one occasion, while deponent was standing on the deck conversing with Amasa Delano, by a secret sign the negro Babo drew him (the deponent) aside, the act appearing as if originating with the deponent; that then, he being drawn aside, the negro Babo proposed to him to gain from Amasa Delano full particulars about his ship, and crew, and arms; that the deponent asked "For what?" that the negro Babo answered he might conceive; that, grieved at the prospect of what might overtake the generous Captain Amasa Delano, the deponent at first refused to ask the desired questions, and used every argument to induce the negro Babo to give up this new design; that the negro Babo showed the point of his dagger; that, after the information had been obtained, the negro Babo again drew him aside, telling him that that very night he (the deponent) would be captain of two ships instead of one, for that, great part of the American's ship's crew being to be absent fishing, the six Ashantees, without any one else, would easily take it; that at this time he said other things to the same purpose; that no entreaties availed; that before Amasa Delano's coming on board, no hint had been given touching the capture of the American ship: that to prevent this project the deponent was powerless; . . . —that in some things his memory is confused, he cannot distinctly recall every event; . . . —that as soon as they had cast anchor at six of the clock in the evening, as has before been stated, the American captain took leave to return to his vessel; that upon a sudden impulse, which the deponent believes to have come from God and his angels, he, after the farewell had been said, followed the generous Captain Amasa Delano as far as the gunwale, where he stayed, under the pretence of taking leave, until Amasa Delano should have been seated in his boat; that on shoving off, the deponent sprang from the gunwale, into the boat, and fell into it, he knows not how, God guarding him; that—

. . . . .

[*Here, in the original, follows the account of what further happened at the escape, and how the "San Dominick" was retaken, and of the passage to the coast; including in the recital many expressions of "eternal gratitude" to the "generous Captain Amasa Delano." The deposition then proceeds with recapitulatory remarks, and a partial renumeration of the negroes, making record of their individual part in the past events, with a view to furnishing, according to command of the court, the data whereon to found the criminal sentences to be pronounced. From this portion is the following:*]

—That he believes that all the negroes, though not in the first place knowing to the design of revolt, when it was accomplished, approved it. . . . That the negro, José, eighteen years old, and in the personal service of Don Alexandro, was the one who communicated the information to the negro Babo, about the state of things in the cabin, before the revolt; that this is known, because, in the preceding midnight, he used to come from his berth, which was under his master's, in the cabin, to the deck where the ringleader and his associates were, and had secret conversations with the negro Babo, in which he was several times seen by the mate; that, one night, the mate drove him away twice; . . . that this same negro José, was the one who, without being commanded to do so by the negro Babo, as Lecbe and Martinqui were, stabbed his master, Don Alexandro, after he had been dragged half-lifeless to the deck; . . that the mulatto steward, Francesco, was of the first band of revolters, that he was, in all things, the creature and tool of the negro Babo; that, to make his court, he, just before a repast in the cabin, proposed, to the negro Babo, poisoning a dish for the generous Captain Amasa Delano; this is known and believed, because the negroes have said it; but that the negro Babo, having another design, forbade Francesco; . . . that the Ashantee Lecbe was one of the worst of them; for that, on the day the ship was retaken, he assisted in the defence of her, with a hatchet in each hand, with one of which he wounded, in the breast, the chief mate of Amasa Delano, in the first act of boarding; this all knew; that, in sight of the deponent, Lecbe struck, with a hatchet, Don Francisco Masa when, by the negro Babo's orders, he was carrying him to throw him overboard, alive; beside participating in the murder, before mentioned, of Don Alexandro Aranda, and others of the cabin-passengers; that, owing to the fury with which the Ashantees fought in the engagement with the boats, but this Lecbe and Yan survived; that Yan was bad as Lecbe; that Yan was the man who, by Babo's command, willingly prepared the skeleton of Don Alexandro, in a way the negroes afterwards told the deponent, but which he, so long as reason is left him, can never divulge; that Yan and Lecbe were the two who, in a calm by night, riveted the skeleton to the bow; this also the negroes told him; that the negro Babo was he who traced the inscription below it; that the negro Babo was the plotter from first to last; he ordered every murder, and was the helm and keel of the revolt; that Atufal was his lieutenant in all; but Atufal, with his own hand, committed no murder; nor did the negro Babo; . . that Atufal was shot, being killed in the fight with the boats, ere boarding; . . . that the negresses, of age, were knowing to the revolt, and testified themselves satisfied at the death of their master, Don Alexandro; that, had the negroes not restrained them, they would have tortured to death, instead of simply killing, the Spaniards slain by command of the negro Babo; that the negresses used their utmost influence to have the deponent made away with; that, in the various acts of murder, they sang songs and danced—

not gaily, but solemnly; and before the engagement with
the boats, as well as during the action, they sang melancholy
songs to the negroes, and that this melancholy tone was more
inflaming than a different one would have been, and was so
intended; that all this is believed, because the negroes have
said it.
—That of the thirty-six men of the crew—exclusive of the
passengers (all of whom are now dead), which the deponent had knowledge of—six only remained alive, with four
cabin-boys and ship-boys, not included with the crew; . . .
—that the negroes broke an arm of one of the cabin-boys
and gave him strokes with hatchets.

[*Then follow various random disclosures referring to
various periods of time. The following are extracted:*]

—That during the presence of Captain Amasa Delano
on board, some attempts were made by the sailors, and one
by Hermenegildo Gandix, to convey hints to him of the
true state of affairs; but that these attempts were ineffectual,
owing to fear of incurring death, and furthermore owing to
the devices which offered contradictions to the true state of
affairs; as well as owing to the generosity and piety of Amasa
Delano, incapable of sounding such wickedness; . . . that
Luys Galgo, a sailor about sixty years of age, and formerly
of the king's navy, was one of those who sought to convey
tokens to Captain Amasa Delano; but his intent, though undiscovered, being suspected, he was, on a pretence, made to
retire out of sight, and at last into the hold, and there was
made away with. This the negroes have since said; . . .
that one of the ship-boys feeling, from Captain Amasa Delano's presence, some hopes of release, and not having
enough prudence, dropped some chance-word respecting his

expectations, which being overheard and understood by a slave-boy with whom he was eating at the time, the latter struck him on the head with a knife, inflicting a bad wound, but of which the boy is now healing; that likewise, not long before the ship was brought to anchor, one of the seamen, steering at the time, endangered himself by letting the blacks remark a certain unconscious hopeful expression in his countenance, arising from some cause similar to the above; but this sailor, by his heedful after conduct, escaped; . . . that these statements are made to show the court that from the beginning to the end of the revolt, it was impossible for the deponent and his men to act otherwise than they did; . . . —that the third clerk, Hermenegildo Gandix, who before had been forced to live among the seamen, wearing a seaman's habit, and in all respects appearing to be one for the time; he, Gandix, was killed by a musket-ball fired through a mistake from the American boats before boarding; having in his fright ran up the mizzen-rigging, calling to the boats —"don't board," lest upon their boarding the negroes should kill him; that this inducing the Americans to believe he some way favoured the cause of the negroes, they fired two balls at him, so that he fell wounded from the rigging, and was drowned in the sea; . . . —that the young Don Joaquin, Marques de Arambaolaza, like Hermenegildo Gandix, the third clerk, was degraded to the office and appearance of a common seaman; that upon one occasion, when Don Joaquin shrank, the negro Babo commanded the Ashantee Lecbe to take tar and heat it, and pour it upon Don Joaquin's hands; . . . —that Don Joaquin was killed owing to another mistake of the Americans, but one impossible to be avoided, as upon the approach of the boats, Don Joaquin, with a hatchet tied edge out and upright to his hand, was made by the negroes to appear on the bulwarks; whereupon, seen with arms in his hands and in a questionable attitude, he was shot for a renegade seaman; . . . —that on the person of Don Joaquin was found secreted a jewel, which, by papers that were discovered, proved to have been meant for the shrine of our Lady of Mercy in Lima; a votive offering, beforehand prepared and guarded, to attest his gratitude, when he should have landed in Peru, his last destination, for the safe conclusion of his entire voyage from Spain; . . . —that the jewel, with the other effects of the late Don Joaquin, is in the custody of the brethren of the Hospital de Sacerdotes, awaiting the decision of the honourable court; . . . —that, owing to the condition of the deponent, as well as the haste in which the boats departed for the attack, the Americans were not forewarned that there were, among the apparent crew, a passenger and one of the clerks disguised by the negro Babo; . . . —that, beside the negroes killed in the action, some were killed after the capture and re-anchoring at night, when shackled to the ring-bolts on deck; that these deaths were committed by the sailors, ere they could be prevented. That so soon as informed of it, Captain Amasa Delano used all his authority, and, in particular with his own hand, struck down Martinez Gola, who, having found a razor in the pocket of an old jacket of his, which one of the shackled negroes had on, was aiming it at the negro's throat; that the noble Captain Amasa Delano also wrenched from the hand of Bartholomew Barlo, a dagger secreted at the time of the massacre of the whites, with which he was in the act of stabbing a shackled negro, who, the same day, with another negro, had thrown him down and jumped upon him; . . . —that, for all the events, befalling through so long a time, during which the ship was in the hands of the negro Babo, he cannot here give account; but that, what he has said is the most substantial of what occurs to him at present, and is the truth under the oath which he has taken; which declaration he affirmed and ratified, after hearing it read to him.

He said that he is twenty-nine years of age, and broken in body and mind; that when finally dismissed by the court, he shall not return home to Chili, but betake himself to the monastery on Mount Agonia without; and signed with his honour, and crossed himself, and, for the time, departed as he came, in his litter, with the monk Infelez, to the Hospital de Sacerdotes.

BENITO CERENO.

DOCTOR ROZAS.

If the deposition of Benito Cereno has served as the key to fit into the lock of the complications which preceded it, then, as a vault whose door has been flung back, the *San Dominick's* hull lies open to-day.

Hitherto the nature of this narrative, besides rendering the intricacies in the beginning unavoidable, has more or less required that many things, instead of being set down in the order of occurrence, should be restrospectively, or irregularly given; this last is the case with the following passages, which will conclude the account:

During the long, mild voyage to Lima, there was, as before hinted, a period during which Don Benito a little recovered his health, or, at least in some degree, his tranquillity. Ere the decided relapse which came, the two captains had many cordial conversations—their fraternal unreserve in singular contrast with former withdrawments.

Again and again, it was repeated, how hard it had been to enact the part forced on the Spaniard by Babo.

"Ah, my dear Don Amasa," Don Benito once said, "at those very times when you thought me so morose and ungrateful—nay when, as you now admit, you half thought me plotting your murder—at those very times my heart was frozen; I could not look at you, thinking of what, both on board this ship and your own, hung, from other hands, over my kind benefactor. And as God lives, Don Amasa, I know not whether desire for my own safety alone could have nerved me to that leap into your boat, had it not been for the thought that, did you, unenlightened, return to your ship, you, my best friend, with all who might be with you, stolen upon, that night, in your hammocks, would never in this world have wakened again. Do but think how you walked this deck, how you sat in this cabin, every inch of ground mined into honey-combs under you. Had I dropped the least hint, made the least advance toward an understanding between us, death, explosive death—yours as mine—would have ended the scene."

"True, true," cried Captain Delano, starting, "you saved my life, Don Benito, more than I yours; saved it, too, against my knowledge and will."

"Nay, my friend," rejoined the Spaniard, courteous even to the point of religion, "God charmed your life, but you saved mine. To think of some things you did—those smilings and chattings, rash pointings and gesturings. For less than these, they slew my mate, Raneds; but you had the Prince of Heaven's safe conduct through all ambuscades."

"Yes, all is owing to Providence, I know; but the temper of my mind that morning was more than commonly pleasant, while the sight of so much suffering—more apparent than real—added to my good nature, compassion, and charity, happily interweaving the three. Had it been otherwise, doubtless, as you hint, some of my interferences with the blacks might have ended unhappily enough. Besides that, those feelings I spoke of enabled me to get the better of momentary distrust, at times when acuteness might have cost me my life, without saving another's. Only at the end did my suspicions get the better of me, and you know how wide of the mark they then proved."

appearance + reality

"Wide, indeed," said Don Benito, sadly; "you were with me all day; stood with me, sat with me, talked with me, looked at me, ate with me, drank with me; and yet, your last act was to clutch for a villain, not only an innocent man, but the most pitiable of all men. To such degree may malign machinations and deceptions impose. So far may even the best men err, in judging the conduct of one with the recesses of whose condition he is not acquainted. But you were forced to it; and you were in time undeceived. Would that, in both respects, it was so ever, and with all men."

"I think I understand you; you generalize, Don Benito; and mournfully enough. But the past is passed; why moralize upon it? Forget it. See, yon bright sun has forgotten it all, and the blue sea, and the blue sky; these have turned over new leaves."

"Because they have no memory," he dejectedly replied; "because they are not human."

"But these mild trades that now fan your cheek, Don Benito, do they not come with a human-like healing to you? Warm friends, steadfast friends are the trades."

"With their steadfastness they but waft me to my tomb, Señor," was the foreboding response.

"You are saved, Don Benito," cried Captain Delano, more and more astonished and pained; "you are saved; what has cast such a shadow upon you?"

"The negro."

There was silence, while the moody man sat, slowly and

unconsciously gathering his mantle about him, as if it were a pall.

There was no more conversation that day.

But if the Spaniard's melancholy sometimes ended in muteness upon topics like the above, there were others upon which he never spoke at all; on which, indeed, all his old reserves were piled. Pass over the worst and, only to elucidate, let an item or two of these be cited. The dress so precise and costly, worn by him on the day whose events have been narrated, had not willingly been put on. And that silver-mounted sword, apparent symbol of despotic command, was not, indeed, a sword, but the ghost of one. The scabbard, artificially stiffened, was empty.

As for the black—whose brain, not body, had schemed and led the revolt, with the plot—his slight frame, inadequate to that which it held, had at once yielded to the superior muscular strength of his captor, in the boat. Seeing all was over, he uttered no sound, and could not be forced to. His aspect seemed to say: since I cannot do deeds, I will not speak words. Put in irons in the hold, with the rest, he was carried to Lima. During the passage Don Benito did not visit him. Nor then, nor at any time after, would he look at him. Before the tribunal he refused. When pressed by the judges he fainted. On the testimony of the sailors alone rested the legal identity of Babo. And yet the Spaniard would, upon occasion, verbally refer to the negro, as has been shown; but look on him he would not, or could not.

Some months after, dragged to the gibbet at the tail of a mule, the black met his voiceless end. The body was burned to ashes; but for many days, the head, that hive of subtlety, fixed on a pole in the Plaza, met, unabashed, the gaze of the whites; and across the Plaza looked toward St. Barthol-

omew's church, in whose vaults slept then, as now, the recovered bones of Aranda; and across the Rimac bridge
looked toward the monastery, on Mount Agonia without;
where, three months after being dismissed by the court,
Benito Cereno, borne on the bier, did, indeed, follow his
leader.

BARTLEBY THE SCRIVENER

A STORY OF WALL STREET

First published anonymously in *Putnam's Monthly Magazine*, November, 1853.

Reprinted in "The Piazza Tales," 1856.

BARTLEBY THE SCRIVENER

A Story of Wall Street

I AM a rather elderly man. The nature of my avocations for the last thirty years has brought me into more than ordinary contact with what would seem an interesting and somewhat singular set of men, of whom as yet nothing that I know of has ever been written:—I mean the law-copyists or scriveners. I have known very many of them, professionally and privately, and if I pleased, could relate divers histories, at which good-natured gentlemen might smile, and sentimental souls might weep. But I waive the biographies of all other scriveners for a few passages in the life of Bartleby, who was a scrivener the strangest I ever saw or heard of. While of other law-copyists I might write the complete life, of Bartleby nothing of that sort can be done. I believe that no materials exist for a full and satisfactory biography of this man. It is an irreparable loss to literature. Bartleby was one of those beings of whom nothing is ascertainable, except from the original sources, and in his case those are very small. What my own astonished eyes saw of Bartleby, *that* is all I know of him, except, indeed, one vague report which will appear in the sequel.

Ere introducing the scrivener, as he first appeared to me, it is fit I make some mention of myself, my *employés,* my business, my chambers, and general surroundings; because some such description is indispensable to an adequate understanding of the chief character about to be presented.

Imprimis: I am a man who, from his youth upward, has been filled with a profound conviction that the easiest way

109

of life is the best. Hence, though I belong to a profession proverbially energetic and nervous, even to turbulence, at times, yet nothing of that sort have I ever suffered to invade my peace. I am one of those unambitious lawyers who never addresses a jury, or in any way draws down public applause; but in the cool tranquillity of a snug retreat, do a snug business among rich men's bonds and mortgages and title-deeds. All who know me, consider me an eminently *safe* man. The late John Jacob Astor, a personage little given to poetic enthusiasm, had no hesitation in pronouncing my first grand point to be prudence; my next, method. I do not speak it in vanity, but simply record the fact, that I was not unemployed in my profession by the late John Jacob Astor; a name which, I admit, I love to repeat, for it hath a rounded and orbicular sound to it, and rings like unto bullion. I will freely add, that I was not insensible to the late John Jacob Astor's good opinion.

Some time prior to the period at which this little history begins, my avocations had been largely increased. The good old office, now extinct in the State of New York, of a Master in Chancery, had been conferred upon me. It was not a very arduous office, but very pleasantly remunerative. I seldom lose my temper; much more seldom indulge in dangerous indignation at wrongs and outrages; but I must be permitted to be rash here and declare, that I consider the sudden and violent abrogation of the office of Master in Chancery, by the new Constitution, as a —— premature act; inasmuch as I had counted upon a life-lease of the profits, whereas I only received those of a few short years. But this is by the way.

My chambers were upstairs at No. —— Wall Street. At one end they looked upon the white wall of the interior of a spacious sky-light shaft, penetrating the building from top to bottom. This view might have been considered rather tame than otherwise, deficient in what landscape painters call "life." But if so, the view from the other end of my chambers offered, at least, a contrast, if nothing more. In that direction my windows commanded an unobstructed view of a lofty brick wall, black by age and everlasting shade; which wall required no spy-glass to bring out its lurking beauties, but for the benefit of all near-sighted spectators, was pushed up to within ten feet of my window panes. Owing to the great height of the surrounding buildings, and my chambers being on the second floor, the interval between this wall and mine not a little resembled a huge square cistern.

At the period just preceding the advent of Bartleby, I had two persons as copyists in my employment, and a promising lad as an office-boy. First, Turkey; second, Nippers; third, Ginger Nut. These may seem names, the like of which are not usually found in the Directory. In truth they were nicknames, mutually conferred upon each other by my three clerks, and were deemed expressive of their respective persons or characters. Turkey was a short, pursy Englishman of about my own age, that is, somewhere not far from sixty. In the morning, one might say, his face was of a fine florid hue, but after twelve o'clock, meridian —his dinner hour—it blazed like a grate full of Christmas coals; and continued blazing—but, as it were, with a gradual wane—till 6 o'clock P.M. or thereabouts, after which I saw no more of the proprietor of the face, which, gaining its meridian with the sun, seemed to set with it, to rise, culminate, and decline the following day, with the like regularity and undiminished glory. There are many singular coincidences I have known in the course of my life, not the least among which was the fact, that exactly when Turkey

displayed his fullest beams from his red and radiant countenance, just then, too, at that critical moment, began the
daily period when I considered his business capacities as
seriously disturbed for the remainder of the twenty-four
hours. Not that he was absolutely idle, or averse to business then; far from it. The difficulty was, he was apt to
be altogether too energetic. There was a strange, inflamed,
flurried, flighty recklessness of activity about him. He would
be incautious in dipping his pen into his inkstand. All his
blots upon my documents, were dropped there after twelve
o'clock, meridian. Indeed, not only would he be reckless
and sadly given to making blots in the afternoon, but some
days he went further, and was rather noisy. At such times,
too, his face flamed with augmented blazonry, as if cannel
coal had been heaped on anthracite. He made an unpleasant
racket with his chair; spilled his sand-box; in mending his
pens, impatiently split them all to pieces, and threw them
on the floor in a sudden passion; stood up and leaned over
his table, boxing his papers about in a most indecorous manner, very sad to behold in an elderly man like him. Nevertheless, as he was in many ways a most valuable person to
me, and all the time before twelve o'clock, meridian, was
the quickest, steadiest creature, too, accomplishing a great
deal of work in a style not easy to be matched—for these
reasons, I was willing to overlook his eccentricities, though
indeed, occasionally, I remonstrated with him. I did this
very gently, however, because, though the civilest, nay, the
blandest and most reverential of men in the morning, yet
in the afternoon he was disposed, upon provocation, to be
slightly rash with his tongue, in fact, insolent. Now, valu-
ing his morning services as I did, and resolving not to lose
them—yet, at the same time, made uncomfortable by his
inflamed ways after twelve o'clock; and being a man of

peace, unwilling by my admonitions to call forth unseemly retorts from him—I took upon me, one Saturday noon (he was always worse on Saturdays), to hint to him, very kindly, that perhaps now that he was growing old, it might be well to abridge his labours; in short, he need not come to my chambers after twelve o'clock, but, dinner over, had best go home to his lodgings and rest himself till tea-time. But no; he insisted upon his afternoon devotions. His countenance became intolerably fervid, as he oratorically assured me—gesticulating, with a long ruler, at the other side of the room—that if his services in the morning were useful, how indispensable, then, in the afternoon?

"With submission, sir," said Turkey on this occasion, "I consider myself your right-hand man. In the morning I but marshal and deploy my columns; but in the afternoon I put myself at their head, and gallantly charge the foe, thus!"—and he made a violent thrust with the ruler.

"But the blots, Turkey," intimated I.

"True,—but, with submission, sir, behold these hairs! I am getting old. Surely, sir, a blot or two of a warm afternoon is not to be severely urged against grey hairs. Old age —even if it blot the page—is honourable. With submission, sir, we *both* are getting old."

This appeal to my fellow-feeling was hardly to be resisted. At all events, I saw that go he would not. So I made up my mind to let him stay, resolving, nevertheless, to see to it, that during the afternoon he had to do with my less important papers.

Nippers, the second on my list, was a whiskered, sallow, and, upon the whole, rather piratical-looking young man of about five and twenty. I always deemed him the victim of two evil powers—ambition and indigestion. The ambition was evinced by a certain impatience of the duties of a

mere copyist—an unwarrantable usurpation of strictly professional affairs, such as the original drawing up of legal
documents. The indigestion seemed betokened in an occasional nervous testiness and grinning irritability, causing the
teeth to audibly grind together over mistakes committed in
copying; unnecessary maledictions, hissed, rather than
spoken, in the heat of business; and especially by a continual
discontent with the height of the table where he worked.
Though of a very ingenious mechanical turn, Nippers could
never get this table to suit him. He put chips under it,
blocks of various sorts, bits of pasteboard, and at last went
so far as to attempt an exquisite adjustment by final pieces
of folded blotting-paper. But no invention would answer.
If, for the sake of easing his back, he brought the table lid
at a sharp angle well up toward his chin, and wrote there
like a man using the steep roof of a Dutch house for his
desk—then he declared that it stopped the circulation in his
arms. If now he lowered the table to his waistbands, and
stooped over it in writing, then there was a sore aching in
his back. In short, the truth of the matter was, Nippers
knew not what he wanted. Or, if he wanted anything, it
was to be rid of a scrivener's table altogether. Among the
manifestations of his diseased ambition was a fondness he
had for receiving visits from certain ambiguous-looking fellows in seedy coats, whom he called his clients. Indeed I
was aware that not only was he, at times, considerable of a
ward-politician, but he occasionally did a little business at
the Justices' courts, and was not unknown on the steps of
the Tombs. I have good reason to believe, however, that
one individual who called upon him at my chambers, and
who, with a grand air, he insisted was his client, was no
other than a dun, and the alleged title-deed, a bill. But
with all his failings, and the annoyances he caused me, Nip-

pers, like his compatriot Turkey, was a very useful man to me; wrote a neat, swift hand; and, when he chose, was not deficient in a gentlemanly sort of deportment. Added to this, he always dressed in a gentlemanly sort of way; and so, incidentally, reflected credit upon my chambers. Whereas with respect to Turkey, I had much ado to keep him from being a reproach to me. His clothes were apt to look oily and smell of eating-houses. He wore his pantaloons very loose and baggy in summer. His coats were execrable; his hat not to be handled. But while the hat was a thing of indifference to me, inasmuch as his natural civility and deference, as a dependent Englishman, always led him to doff it the moment he entered the room, yet his coat was another matter. Concerning his coats, I reasoned with him; but with no effect. The truth was, I suppose, that a man with so small an income, could not afford to sport such a lustrous face and a lustrous coat at one and the same time. As Nippers once observed, Turkey's money went chiefly for red ink. One winter day I presented Turkey with a highly-respectable looking coat of my own, a padded grey coat, of a most comfortable warmth, and which buttoned straight up from the knee to the neck. I thought Turkey would appreciate the favour, and abate his rashness and obstreperousness of afternoons. But no. I verily believe that buttoning himself up in so downy and blanket-like a coat had a pernicious effect upon him; upon the same principle that too much oats are bad for horses. In fact, precisely as a rash, restive horse is said to feel his oats, so Turkey felt his coat. It made him insolent. He was a man whom prosperity harmed.

Though concerning the self-indulgent habits of Turkey I had my own private surmises, yet touching Nippers I was well persuaded that whatever might be his faults in other respects, he was, at least, a temperate young man. But, indeed, nature herself seemed to have been his vintner, and at his birth charged him so thoroughly with an irritable, brandy-like disposition, that all subsequent potations were needless. When I consider how, amid the stillness of my chambers, Nippers would sometimes impatiently rise from his seat, and stooping over his table, spread his arms wide apart, seize the whole desk, and move it, and jerk it, with a grim, grinding motion on the floor, as if the table were a perverse voluntary agent, intent on thwarting and vexing him; I plainly perceive that for Nippers, brandy and water were altogether superfluous.

It was fortunate for me that, owing to its peculiar cause —indigestion—the irritability and consequent nervousness of Nippers, were mainly observable in the morning, while in the afternoon he was comparatively mild. So that Turkey's paroxysms only coming on about twelve o'clock, I never had to do with their eccentricities at one time. Their fits relieved each other like guards. When Nipper's was on, Turkey's was off; and *vice versa*. This was a good natural arrangement under the circumstances.

Ginger Nut, the third on my list, was a lad some twelve years old. His father was a carman, ambitious of seeing his son on the bench instead of a cart, before he died. So he sent him to my office as student at law, errand boy, and cleaner and sweeper, at the rate of one dollar a week. He had a little desk to himself, but he did not use it much. Upon inspection, the drawer exhibited a great array of the shells of various sorts of nuts. Indeed, to this quick-witted youth the whole noble science of the law was contained in a nut-shell. Not the least among the employments of Ginger Nut, as well as one which he discharged with the most alacrity, was his duty as cake and apple purveyor for Turkey and Nippers. Copying law papers being proverbially a dry,

husky sort of business, my two scriveners were fain to
moisten their mouths very often with Spitzenbergs to be had
at the numerous stalls nigh the Custom House and Post
Office. Also, they sent Ginger Nut very frequently for that
peculiar cake—small, flat, round, and very spicy—after
which he had been named by them. Of a cold morning,
when business was but dull, Turkey would gobble up scores
of these cakes, as if they were mere wafers—indeed they
sell them at the rate of six or eight for a penny—the scrape
of his pen blending with the crunching of the crisp particles
in his mouth. Of all the fiery afternoon blunders and
flurried rashness of Turkey, was his once moistening a gin-
ger-cake between his lips, and clapping it on to a mortgage
for a seal. I came within an ace of dismissing him then.
But he mollified me by making an oriental bow and saying
—"With submission, sir, it was generous of me to find you
in stationery on my own account."

Now my original business—that of a conveyancer and title
hunter, and drawer-up of recondite documents of all sorts
—was considerably increased by receiving the master's office.
There was now great work for scriveners. Not only must
I push the clerks already with me, but I must have additional
help. In answer to my advertisement, a motionless young
man one morning stood upon my office threshold, the door
being open, for it was summer. I can see that figure now—
pallidly neat, pitiably respectable, incurably forlorn! It
was Bartleby.

After a few words touching his qualifications, I engaged
him, glad to have among my corps of copyists a man of so
singularly sedate an aspect, which I thought might operate
beneficially upon the flighty temper of Turkey, and the
fiery one of Nippers.

I should have stated before that ground glass folding-doors divided my premises into two parts, one of which was occupied by my scriveners, the other by myself. According to my humour I threw open these doors, or closed them. I resolved to assign Bartleby a corner by the folding-doors, but on my side of them, so as to have this quiet man within easy call, in case any trifling thing was to be done. I placed his desk close up to a small side-window in that part of the room, a window which originally had afforded a lateral view of certain grimy back-yards and bricks, but which, owing to subsequent erections, commanded at present no view at all, though it gave some light. Within three feet of the panes was a wall, and the light came down from far above, between two lofty buildings, as from a very small opening in a dome. Still further to a satisfactory arrangement, I procured a high green folding screen, which might entirely isolate Bartleby from my sight, though not remove him from my voice. And thus, in a manner, privacy and society were conjoined.

At first Bartleby did an extraordinary quantity of writing. As if long famishing for something to copy, he seemed to gorge himself on my documents. There was no pause for digestion. He ran a day and night line, copying by sun-light and by candle-light. I should have been quite delighted with his application, had he been cheerfully industrious. But he wrote on silently, palely, mechanically.

It is, of course, an indispensable part of a scrivener's business to verify the accuracy of his copy, word by word. Where there are two or more scriveners in an office, they assist each other in this examination, one reading from the copy, the other holding the original. It is a very dull, wearisome, and lethargic affair. I can readily imagine that to some sanguine temperaments it would be altogether intolerable. For example, I cannot credit that the mettlesome poet Byron would have contentedly sat down with Bartleby to examine a law document of, say five hundred pages, closely written in a crimpy hand.

Now and then, in the haste of business, it had been my habit to assist in comparing some brief document myself, calling Turkey or Nippers for this purpose. One object I had in placing Bartleby so handy to me behind the screen, was to avail myself of his services on such trivial occasions. It was on the third day, I think, of his being with me, and before any necessity had arisen for having his own writing examined, that, being much hurried to complete a small affair I had in hand, I abruptly called to Bartleby. In my haste and natural expectancy of instant compliance, I sat with my head bent over the original on my desk, and my right hand sideways, and somewhat nervously extended with the copy, so that immediately upon emerging from his retreat, Bartleby might snatch it and proceed to business without the least delay.

In this very attitude did I sit when I called to him, rapidly stating what it was I wanted him to do—namely, to examine a small paper with me. Imagine my surprise, nay, my consternation, when without moving from his privacy, Bartleby in a singularly mild, firm voice, replied, "I would prefer not to."

I sat awhile in perfect silence, rallying my stunned faculties. Immediately it occurred to me that my ears had deceived me, or Bartleby had entirely misunderstood my meaning. I repeated my request in the clearest tone I could assume. But in quite as clear a one came the previous reply, "I would prefer not to."

"Prefer not to," echoed I, rising in high excitement, and crossing the room with a stride. "What do you mean? Are you moon-struck? I want you to help me compare this sheet here—take it," and I thrust it toward him.

"I would prefer not to," said he.

I looked at him steadfastly. His face was leanly composed; his grey eye dimly calm. Not a wrinkle of agitation rippled him. Had there been the least uneasiness, anger, impatience or impertinence in his manner; in other words, had there been anything ordinarily human about him; doubtless I should have violently dismissed him from the premises. But as it was, I should have as soon thought of turning my pale plaster-of-paris bust of Cicero out of doors. I stood gazing at him awhile, as he went on with his own writing, and then reseated myself at my desk. This is very strange, thought I. What had one best do? But my business hurried me. I concluded to forget the matter for the present, reserving it for my future leisure. So calling Nippers from the other room, the paper was speedily examined.

A few days after this, Bartleby concluded four lengthy documents, being quadruplicates of a week's testimony taken before me in my High Court of Chancery. It became necessary to examine them. It was an important suit, and great accuracy was imperative. Having all things arranged, I called Turkey, Nippers and Ginger Nut from the next room, meaning to place the four copies in the hands of my four clerks, while I should read from the original. Accordingly Turkey, Nippers and Ginger Nut had taken their seats in a row, each with his document in hand, when I called to Bartleby to join this interesting group.

"Bartleby! quick, I am waiting."

I heard a slow scrape of his chair legs on the uncarpeted floor, and soon he appeared standing at the entrance of his hermitage.

"What is wanted?" said he mildly.

"The copies, the copies," said I hurriedly. "We are going to examine them. There"—and I held toward him the fourth quadruplicate.

"I would prefer not to," he said, and gently disappeared behind the screen.

For a few moments I was turned into a pillar of salt, standing at the head of my seated column of clerks. Recovering myself, I advanced toward the screen, and demanded the reason for such extraordinary conduct.

"*Why* do you refuse?"

"I would prefer not to."

With any other man I should have flown outright into a dreadful passion, scorned all further words, and thrust him ignominiously from my presence. But there was something about Bartleby that not only strangely disarmed me, but in a wonderful manner touched and disconcerted me. I began to reason with him.

"These are your own copies we are about to examine. It is labour saving to you, because one examination will answer for your four papers. It is common usage. Every copyist is bound to help examine his copy. Is it not so? Will you not speak? Answer!"

"I prefer not to," he replied in a flute-like tone. It seemed to me that while I had been addressing him, he carefully revolved every statement that I made; fully comprehended the meaning; could not gainsay the irresistible conclusion; but, at the same time, some paramount consideration prevailed with him to reply as he did.

"You are decided, then, not to comply with my request—a request made according to common usage and common sense?"

He briefly gave me to understand that on that point my judgment was sound. Yes: his decision was irreversible.

It is not seldom the case that when a man is browbeaten in some unprecedented and violently unreasonable way, he begins to stagger in his own plainest faith. He begins, as it were, vaguely to surmise that, wonderful as it may be, all the justice and all the reason are on the other side. Accordingly, if any disinterested persons are present, he turns to them for some reinforcement for his own faltering mind.

"Turkey," said I, "what do you think of this? Am I not right?"

"With submission, sir," said Turkey, with his blandest tone, "I think that you are."

"Nippers," said I, "what do *you* think of it?"

'I think I should kick him out of the office."

(The reader of nice perceptions will here perceive that, it being morning, Turkey's answer is couched in polite and tranquil terms but Nippers's reply in ill-tempered ones. Or, to repeat a previous sentence, Nippers's ugly mood was on duty, and Turkey's off.)

"Ginger Nut," said I, willing to enlist the smallest suffrage in my behalf, "what do *you* think of it?"

"I think, sir, he's a little *luny*," replied Ginger Nut, with a grin.

"You hear what they say," said I, turning towards the screen, "come forth and do your duty."

But he vouchsafed no reply. I pondered a moment in sore perplexity. But once more business hurried me. I determined again to postpone the consideration of this dilemma to my future leisure. With a little trouble we made out to examine the papers without Bartleby, though at every page or two, Turkey deferentially dropped his opinion that this proceeding was quite out of the common; while Nippers, twitching in his chair with a dyspeptic nervousness, ground out between his set teeth occasional hissing maledictions against the stubborn oaf behind the screen. And for his (Nippers's) part, this was the first and the last time he would do another man's business without pay.

Meanwhile Bartleby sat in his hermitage, oblivious to everything but his own peculiar business there.

Some days passed, the scrivener being employed upon another lengthy work. His late remarkable conduct led me to regard his ways narrowly. I observed that he never went to dinner; indeed that he never went any where. As yet I had never of my personal knowledge known him to be outside of my office. He was a perpetual sentry in the corner. At about eleven o'clock though, in the morning, I noticed that Ginger Nut would advance towards the opening in Bartleby's screen, as if silently beckoned thither by a gesture invisible to me where I sat. The boy would then leave the office jingling a few pence, and reappear with a handful of ginger-nuts which he delivered in the hermitage, receiving two of the cakes for his trouble.

He lives, then, on ginger-nuts, thought I; never eats a dinner, properly speaking; he must be a vegetarian then; but no; he never eats even vegetables, he eats nothing but ginger-nuts. My mind then ran on in reveries concerning the probable effects upon the human constitution of living entirely on ginger-nuts. Ginger-nuts are so called because they contain ginger as one of their peculiar constituents, and the final flavouring one. Now what was ginger? A hot, spicy thing. Was Bartleby hot and spicy? Not at all. Ginger, then, had no effect upon Bartleby. Probably he preferred it should have none.

Nothing so aggravates an earnest person as a passive resistance. If the individual so resisted be of a not inhumane temper, and the resisting one perfectly harmless in his passivity; then, in the better moods of the former, he will endeavour charitably to construe to his imagination what proves impossible to be solved by his judgment. Even so, for the most part, I regarded Bartleby and his ways. Poor fellow! thought I, he means no mischief; it is plain he intends no insolence; his aspect sufficiently evinces that his eccentricities are involuntary. He is useful to me. I can get along with him. If I turn him away, the chances are he will fall in with some less indulgent employer, and then he will be rudely treated, and perhaps driven forth miserably to starve. Yes. Here I can cheaply purchase a delicious self-approval. To befriend Bartleby; to humour him in his strange wilfulness, will cost me little or nothing, while I lay up in my soul what will eventually prove a sweet morsel for my conscience. But this mood was not invariable with me. The passiveness of Bartleby sometimes irritated me. I felt strangely goaded on to encounter him in new opposition, to elicit some angry spark from him answerable to my own. But indeed I might as well have essayed to strike fire with my knuckles against a bit of Windsor soap. But one afternoon the evil impulse in me mastered me, and the following little scene ensued:

"Bartleby," said I, "when those papers are all copied, I will compare them with you."

"I would prefer not to."

"How? Surely you do not mean to persist in that mulish vagary?"

No answer.

I threw open the folding-doors near by, and turning upon Turkey and Nippers, exclaimed in an excited manner:

"He says, a second time, he won't examine his papers. What do you think of it, Turkey?"

It was afternoon, be it remembered. Turkey sat glowing

like a brass boiler, his bald head steaming, his hands reeling among his blotted papers.

"Think of it?" roared Turkey; "I think I'll just step behind his screen, and black his eyes for him!"

So saying, Turkey rose to his feet and threw his arms into a pugilistic position. He was hurrying away to make good his promise, when I detained him, alarmed at the effect of incautiously rousing Turkey's combativeness after dinner.

"Sit down, Turkey," said I, "and hear what Nippers has to say. What do you think of it, Nippers? Would I not be justified in immediately dismissing Bartleby?"

"Excuse me, that is for you to decide, sir. I think his conduct quite unusual, and indeed unjust, as regards Turkey and myself. But it may only be a passing whim."

"Ah," exclaimed I, "you have strangely changed your mind then—you speak very gently of him now."

"All beer," cried Turkey; "gentleness is effects of beer—Nippers and I dined together to-day. You see how gentle *I* am, sir. Shall I go and black his eyes?"

"You refer to Bartleby, I suppose. No, not to-day, Turkey," I replied; "pray, put up your fists."

I closed the doors, and again advanced towards Bartleby. I felt additional incentives tempting me to my fate. I burned to be rebelled against again. I remembered that Bartleby never left the office.

"Bartleby," said I, "Ginger Nut is away; just step round to the Post Office, won't you? (it was but a three minutes' walk), and see if there is anything for me."

"I would prefer not to."

"You *will* not?"

"I *prefer* not."

I staggered to my desk, and sat there in a deep study. My blind inveteracy returned. Was there any other thing in which I could procure myself to be ignominiously repulsed by this lean, penniless wight?—my hired clerk? What added thing is there, perfectly reasonable, that he will be sure to refuse to do?

"Bartleby!"

No answer.

"Bartleby," in a louder tone.

No answer.

"Bartleby," I roared.

Like a very ghost, agreeably to the laws of magical invocation, at the third summons, he appeared at the entrance of his hermitage.

"Go to the next room, and tell Nippers to come to me."

"I prefer not to," he respectfully and slowly said, and mildly disappeared.

"Very good, Bartleby," said I, in a quiet sort of serenely severe self-possessed tone, intimating the unalterable purpose of some terrible retribution very close at hand. At the moment I half intended something of the kind. But upon the whole, as it was drawing towards my dinner-hour, I thought it best to put on my hat and walk home for the day, suffering much from perplexity and distress of mind.

Shall I acknowledge it? The conclusion of this whole business was, that it soon became a fixed fact of my chambers, that a pale young scrivener, by the name of Bartleby, had a desk there; that he copied for me at the usual rate of four cents a folio (one hundred words); but he was permanently exempt from examining the work done by him, that duty being transferred to Turkey and Nippers, out of compliment doubtless to their superior acuteness; moreover, said Bartleby was never on any account to be despatched on the most trivial errand of any sort; and that even if entreated to take upon him such a matter, it was generally understood that he would prefer not to—in other words, that he would refuse point-blank.

As days passed on, I became considerably reconciled to Bartleby. His steadiness, his freedom from all dissipation, his incessant industry (except when he chose to throw himself into a standing revery behind his screen), his great stillness, his unalterableness of demeanour under all circumstances, made him a valuable acquisition. One prime thing was this,—*he was always there;*—first in the morning, continually through the day, and the last at night. I had a singular confidence in his honesty. I felt my most precious papers prefectly safe in his hands. Sometimes to be sure I could not, for the very soul of me, avoid falling into sudden spasmodic passions with him. For it was exceeding difficult to bear in mind all the time those strange peculiarities, privileges, and unheard of exemptions, forming the tacit stipulations on Bartleby's part under which he remained in my office. Now and then, in the eagerness of despatching pressing business, I would inadvertently summon Bartleby, in a short, rapid tone, to put his finger, say, on the incipient tie of a bit of red tape with which I was about compressing some papers. Of course, from behind the screen the usual answer, "I prefer not to," was sure to come; and then, how could a human creature with the common infirmities of our nature, refrain from bitterly exclaiming upon such perverseness—such unreasonableness. However, every added repulse of this sort which I received only tended to lessen the probability of my repeating the inadvertence.

Here it must be said, that according to the custom of most legal gentlemen occupying chambers in densely-populated law buildings, there were several keys to my door. One was kept by a woman residing in the attic, which person weekly scrubbed and daily swept and dusted my apartments. Another was kept by Turkey for convenience sake. The third I sometimes carried in my own pocket. The fourth I knew not who had.

Now, one Sunday morning I happened to go to Trinity Church, to hear a celebrated preacher, and finding myself rather early on the ground, I thought I would walk round to my chambers for awhile. Luckily I had my key with me; but upon applying it to the lock, I found it resisted by something inserted from the inside. Quite surprised, I called out; when to my consternation a key was turned from within; and thrusting his lean visage at me, and holding the door ajar, the apparition of Bartleby appeared, in his shirt sleeves, and otherwise in a strangely tattered dishabille, saying quietly that he was sorry, but he was deeply engaged just then, and—preferred not admitting me at present. In a brief word or two, he moreover added, that perhaps I had better walk round the block two or three times, and by that time he would probably have concluded his affairs.

Now, the utterly unsurmised appearance of Bartleby, tenanting my law-chambers of a Sunday morning, with his cadaverously gentlemanly *nonchalance*, yet withal firm and self-possessed, had such a strange effect upon me, that incontinently I slunk away from my own door, and did as desired. But not without sundry twinges of impotent rebellion against the mild effrontery of this unaccountable scrivener. Indeed, it was his wonderful mildness chiefly, which not only disarmed me, but unmanned me, as it were. For I consider that one, for the time, is in a way unmanned when he tranquilly permits his hired clerk to dictate to him, and order him away from his own premises. Furthermore, I was full of uneasiness as to what Bartleby could possibly be doing in my office in his shirt sleeves, and in an otherwise dismantled condition of a Sunday morning. Was anything amiss going on? Nay, that was out of the question. It was not to be thought of for a moment that Bartleby was an immoral person. But what could he be doing there—copying? Nay again, whatever might be his eccentricities, Bartleby was an eminently decorous person. He would be the last man to sit down to his desk in any state approaching to nudity. Besides, it was Sunday; and there was something about Bartleby that forbade the supposition that he would by any secular occupation violate the proprieties of the day.

Nevertheless, my mind was not pacified; and full of a restless curiosity, at last I returned to the door. Without hindrance I inserted my key, opened it, and entered. Bartleby was not to be seen. I looked round anxiously, peeped behind his screen; but it was very plain that he was gone. Upon more closely examining the place, I surmised that for an indefinite period Bartleby must have ate, dressed, and slept in my office, and that too without plate, mirror, or bed. The cushioned seat of a ricketty old sofa in one corner bore the faint impress of a lean, reclining form. Rolled away under his desk, I found a blanket; under the empty grate, a blacking box and brush; on a chair, a tin basin, with soap and a ragged towel; in a newspaper a few crumbs of ginger-nuts and a morsel of cheese. Yes, thought I, it is evident enough that Bartleby has been making his home here, keeping bachelor's hall all by himself. Immediately then the thought came sweeping across me, What miserable friendlessness and loneliness are here revealed! His poverty is great; but his solitude, how horrible! Think of it. Of a Sunday, Wall street is deserted as Petra; and every night of every day it is an emptiness. This building too, which of week-days hums with industry and life, at nightfall echoes with sheer vacancy, and all through Sunday is forlorn. And here Bartleby makes his home; sole spectator of a solitude which he has seen all populous—a sort of innocent and transformed Marius brooding among the ruins of Carthage!

For the first time in my life a feeling of overpowering stinging melancholy seized me. Before, I had never experienced aught but a not-unpleasing sadness. The bond of a common humanity now drew me irresistibly to gloom. A fraternal melancholy! For both I and Bartleby were sons of Adam. I remembered the bright silks and sparkling faces I had seen that day, in gala trim, swan-like sailing down the Mississippi of Broadway; and I contrasted them with the pallid copyist, and thought to myself, Ah, happiness courts the light, so we deem the world is gay; but misery hides aloof, so we deem that misery there is none. These sad fancyings—chimeras, doubtless, of a sick and silly brain—led on to other and more special thoughts, concerning the eccentricities of Bartleby. Presentiments of strange discoveries hovered round me. The scrivener's pale form appeared to me laid out, among uncaring strangers, in its shivering winding sheet.

Suddenly I was attracted by Bartleby's closed desk, the key in open sight left in the lock.

I mean no mischief, seek the gratification of no heartless curiosity, thought I; besides, the desk is mine, and its contents, too, so I will make bold to look within. Everything was methodically arranged, the papers smoothly placed. The pigeon holes were deep, and, removing the files of documents, I groped into their recesses. Presently I felt something there, and dragged it out. It was an old bandana handkerchief, heavy and knotted. I opened it, and saw it was a savings' bank.

I now recalled all the quiet mysteries which I had noted in the man. I remembered that he never spoke but to answer; that though at intervals he had considerable time to himself, yet I had never seen him reading—no, not even a newspaper; that for long periods he would stand looking out, at his pale window behind the screen, upon the dead brick wall; I was quite sure he never visited any refectory or eating-house; while his pale face clearly indicated that he never drank beer like Turkey, or tea and coffee even, like other men; that he never went anywhere in particular that I could learn; never went out for a walk, unless indeed that was the case at present; that he had declined telling who he was, or whence he came, or whether he had any relatives in the world; that though so thin and pale, he never complained of ill health. And more than all, I remembered a certain unconscious air of pallid—how shall I call it?—of pallid haughtiness, say, or rather an austere reserve about him, which had positively awed me into my tame compliance with his eccentricities, when I had feared to ask him to do the slightest incidental thing for me, even though I might know, from his long-continued motionlessness, that behind his screen he must be standing in one of those dead-wall reveries of his.

Revolving all these things, and coupling them with the recently discovered fact that he made my office his constant abiding place and home, and not forgetful of his morbid moodiness; revolving all these things, a prudential feeling began to steal over me. My first emotions had been those of pure melancholy and sincerest pity; but just in proportion as the forlornness of Bartleby grew and grew to my imagination, did that same melancholy merge into fear, that pity into repulsion. So true it is, and so terrible, too, that up to a certain point the thought or sight of misery enlists our best affections; but, in certain special cases, beyond that point it does not. They err who would assert that invariably this is owing to the inherent selfishness of the human heart.

It rather proceeds from a certain hopelessness of remedying excessive and organic ill. To a sensitive being, pity is not seldom pain. And when at last it is perceived that such pity cannot lead to effectual succour, common sense bids the soul be rid of it. What I saw that morning persuaded me that the scrivener was the victim of innate and incurable disorder. I might give alms to his body; but his body did not pain him; it was his soul that suffered, and his soul I could not reach.

I did not accomplish the purpose of going to Trinity Church that morning. Somehow, the things I had seen disqualified me for the time from church-going. I walked homeward, thinking what I would do with Bartleby. Finally, I resolved upon this:—I would put certain calm questions to him the next morning, touching his history, &c., and if he declined to answer them openly and unreservedly (and I supposed he would prefer not), then to give him a twenty dollar bill over and above whatever I might owe him, and tell him his services were no longer required; but that if in any other way I could assist him, I would be happy to do so, especially if he desired to return to his native place, wherever that might be, I would willingly help to defray the expenses. Moreover, if, after reaching home, he found himself at any time in want of aid, a letter from him would be sure of a reply.

The next morning came.

"Bartleby," said I, gently calling to him behind his screen.

No reply.

"Bartleby," said I, in a still gentler tone, "come here; I am not going to ask you to do anything you would prefer not to do—I simply wish to speak to you."

Upon this he noiselessly slid into view.

"Will you tell me, Bartleby, where you were born?"

"I would prefer not to."

"Will you tell me *anything* about yourself?"

"I would prefer not to."

"But what reasonable objection can you have to speak to me? I feel friendly towards you."

He did not look at me while I spoke, but kept his glance fixed upon my bust of Cicero, which, as I then sat, was directly behind me, some six inches above my head.

"What is your answer, Bartleby?" said I, after waiting a considerable time for a reply, during which his countenance remained immovable, only there was the faintest conceivable tremor of the white attenuated mouth.

"At present I prefer to give no answer," he said, and retired into his hermitage.

It was rather weak in me I confess, but his manner on this occasion nettled me. Not only did there seem to lurk in it a certain calm disdain, but his perverseness seemed ungrateful, considering the undeniable good usage and indulgence he had received from me.

Again I sat ruminating what I should do. Mortified as I was at his behaviour, and resolved as I had been to dismiss him when I entered my office, nevertheless I strangely felt something superstitious knocking at my heart, and forbidding me to carry out my purpose, and denouncing me for a villain if I dared to breathe one bitter word against this forlornest of mankind. At last, familiarly drawing my chair behind his screen, I sat down and said: "Bartleby, never mind then about revealing your history; but let me entreat you, as a friend, to comply as far as may be with the usages of this office. Say now you will help to examine papers to-morrow or next day: in short, say now that in a day or two you will begin to be a little reasonable:—say so, Bartleby."

"At present I would prefer not to be a little reasonable," was his mildly cadaverous reply.

Just then the folding-doors opened, and Nippers approached. He seemed suffering from an unusually bad night's rest, induced by severer indigestion than common. He overheard those final words of Bartleby.

"*Prefer not,* eh?" gritted Nippers—"I'd *prefer* him, if I were you, sir," addressing me—"I'd *prefer* him; I'd give him preferences, the stubborn mule! What is it, sir, pray, that he *prefers* not to do now?"

Bartleby moved not a limb.

"Mr. Nippers," said I, "I'd prefer that you would withdraw for the present."

Somehow, of late I had got into the way of involuntarily using this word "prefer" upon all sorts of not exactly suitable occasions. And I trembled to think that my contact with the scrivener had already and seriously affected me in a mental way. And what further and deeper aberration might it not yet produce? This apprehension had not been without efficacy in determining me to summary means.

As Nippers, looking very sour and sulky, was departing, Turkey blandly and deferentially approached.

"With submission, sir," said he, "yesterday I was thinking about Bartleby here, and I think that if he would but prefer to take a quart of good ale every day, it would do much towards mending him, and enabling him to assist in examining his papers."

"So you have got the word, too," said I, slightly excited.

"With submission, what word, sir," asked Turkey, respectfully crowding himself into the contracted space behind the screen, and by so doing, making me jostle the scrivener. "What word, sir?"

"I would prefer to be left alone here," said Bartleby, as if offended at being mobbed in his privacy.

"*That's* the word, Turkey," said I—"*that's* it."

"Oh, *prefer?* oh, yes—queer word. I never use it myself. But, sir, as I was saying, if he would but prefer—"

"Turkey," interrupted I, "you will please withdraw."

"Oh certainly, sir, if you prefer that I should."

As he opened the folding-door to retire, Nippers at his desk caught a glimpse of me, and asked whether I would prefer to have a certain paper copied on blue paper or white. He did not in the least roguishly accent the word prefer. It was plain that it involuntarily rolled from his tongue. I thought to myself, surely I must get rid of a demented man, who already has in some degree turned the tongues, if not the heads, of myself and clerks. But I thought it prudent not to break the dismission at once.

The next day I noticed that Bartleby did nothing but stand at his window in his dead-wall revery. Upon asking him why he did not write, he said that he had decided upon doing no more writing.

"Why, how now? what next?" exclaimed I, "do no more writing?"

"No more."

"And what is the reason?"

"Do you not see the reason for yourself?" he indifferently replied.

I looked steadfastly at him, and perceived that his eyes looked dull and glazed. Instantly it occurred to me, that his unexampled diligence in copying by his dim window for the first few weeks of his stay with me might have temporarily impaired his vision.

I was touched. I said something in condolence with him. I hinted that, of course, he did wisely in abstaining from writing for a while, and urged him to embrace that opportunity of taking wholesome exercise in the open air. This, however, he did not do. A few days after this, my other clerks being absent, and being in a great hurry to despatch certain letters by the mail, I thought that, having nothing else earthly to do, Bartleby would surely be less inflexible than usual, and carry these letters to the Post Office. But he blankly declined. So, much to my inconvenience, I went myself.

Still added days went by. Whether Bartleby's eyes improved or not, I could not say. To all appearance, I thought they did. But when I asked him if they did, he vouchsafed no answer. At all events, he would do no copying. At last, in reply to my urgings, he informed me that he had permanently given up copying.

"What!" exclaimed I; "suppose your eyes should get entirely well—better than ever before—would you not copy then?"

"I have given up copying," he answered and slid aside.

He remained, as ever, a fixture in my chamber. Nay—if that were possible—he became still more of a fixture than before. What was to be done? He would do nothing in the office: why should he stay there? In plain fact, he had now become a millstone to me, not only useless as a necklace, but afflictive to bear. Yet I was sorry for him. I speak less than truth when I say that, on his own account, he occasioned me uneasiness. If he would but have named a single relative or friend, I would instantly have written, and urged their taking the poor fellow away to some convenient retreat. But he seemed alone, absolutely alone in the universe. A bit of wreckage in the mid-Atlantic. At length, necessities connected with my business tyrannized over all other considerations. Decently as I could, I told Bartleby that in six days' time he must unconditionally leave the office. I warned him to take measures, in the interval, for procuring some other abode. I offered to assist him in this endeavour, if he himself would but take the first step towards a removal. "And when you finally quit me, Bartleby," added I. "I shall see that you go away not entirely unprovided. Six days from this hour, remember."

At the expiration of that period, I peeped behind the screen, and lo! Bartleby was there.

I buttoned up my coat, balanced myself; advanced slowly towards him, touched his shoulder, and said, "The time has come; you must quit this place; I am sorry for you; here is money; but you must go."

"I would prefer not," he replied, with his back still towards me.

"You *must*."

He remained silent.

Now I had an unbounded confidence in this man's common honesty. He had frequently restored to me sixpences and shillings carelessly dropped upon the floor, for I am apt to be very reckless in such shirt-button affairs. The proceeding then which followed will not be deemed extraordinary.

"Bartleby," said I, "I owe you twelve dollars on account; here are thirty-two; the odd twenty are yours.—Will you take it?" and I handed the bills towards him.

But he made no motion.

"I will leave them here then," putting them under a weight on the table. Then taking my hat and cane and going to the door, I tranquilly turned and added—"After you have removed your things from these offices, Bartleby, you will of course lock the door—since every one is now gone for the day but you—and if you please, slip your key underneath the mat, so that I may have it in the morning. I shall not see you again; so good-bye to you. If hereafter in your new place of abode I can be of any service to you, do not fail to advise me by letter. Good-bye, Bartleby, and fare you well."

But he answered not a word; like the last column of some ruined temple, he remained standing mute and solitary in the middle of the otherwise deserted room.

As I walked home in a pensive mood, my vanity got the better of my pity. I could not but highly plume myself on my masterly management in getting rid of Bartleby. Masterly I call it, and such it must appear to any dispassionate thinker. The beauty of my procedure seemed to consist in its perfect quietness. There was no vulgar bullying, no bravado of any sort, no choleric hectoring, no striding to and fro across the apartment, jerking out vehement commands for Bartleby to bundle himself off with his beggarly traps. Nothing of the kind. Without loudly bidding Bartleby depart—as an inferior genius might have done—I *assumed* the ground that depart he must; and upon that assumption built all I had to say. The more I thought over my procedure, the more I was charmed with it. Nevertheless, next morning, upon awakening, I had my doubts,—I had somehow slept off the fumes of vanity. One of the coolest and wisest hours a man has, is just after he awakes in the morning. My procedure seemed as sagacious as ever, —but only in theory. How it would prove in practice— there was the rub. It was truly a beautiful thought to have assumed Bartleby's departure; but, after all, that assumption was simply my own, and none of Bartleby's. The great point was, not whether I had assumed that he would quit me, but whether he would prefer so to do. He was more a man of preferences than assumptions.

After breakfast, I walked down town, arguing the probabilities *pro* and *con*. One moment I thought it would prove a miserable failure, and Bartleby would be found all alive at my office as usual; the next moment it seemed certain that I should see his chair empty. And so I kept veering about. At the corner of Broadway and Canal Street, I saw quite an excited group of people standing in earnest conversation.

"I'll take odds he doesn't," said a voice as I passed.

"Doesn't go?—done!" said I, "put up your money."

I was instinctively putting my hand in my pocket to produce my own, when I remembered that this was an election day. The words I had overheard bore no reference to Bartleby, but to the success or non-success of some candidate for the mayoralty. In my intent frame of mind, I had, as it were, imagined that all Broadway shared in my excitement, and were debating the same question with me. I passed on, very thankful that the uproar of the street screened my momentary absent-mindedness.

As I had intended, I was earlier than usual at my office door. I stood listening for a moment. All was still. He must be gone. I tried the knob. The door was locked. Yes, my procedure had worked to a charm; he indeed must be vanished. Yet a certain melancholy mixed with this: I was almost sorry for my brilliant success. I was fumbling under the door mat for the key, which Bartleby was to have left there for me, when accidentally my knee knocked against a panel, producing a summoning sound, and in response a voice came to me from within—"Not yet; I am occupied."

It was Bartleby.

I was thunderstruck. For an instant I stood like the man who, pipe in mouth, was killed one cloudless afternoon long ago in Virginia, by summer lightning; at his own warm open window he was killed, and remained leaning out there upon the dreamy afternoon, till some one touched him, and he fell.

"Not gone!" I murmured at last. But again obeying that wondrous ascendency which the inscrutable scrivener had over me—and from which ascendency, for all my chafing, I could not completely escape—I slowly went down stairs and out into the street, and while walking round the block, considered what I should next do in this unheard-of perplexity. Turn the man out by an actual thrusting I could not; to drive him away by calling him hard names would not do; calling in the police was an unpleasant idea; and yet, permit him to enjoy his cadaverous triumph over me,—this too I could not think of. What was to be done? or, if nothing could be done, was there anything further that I could *assume* in the matter? Yes, as before I had prospectively assumed that Bartleby would depart, so now I might retrospectively assume that departed he was. In the legitimate carrying out of this assumption, I might enter my office in a great hurry, and pretending not to see Bartleby at all, walk straight against him as if he were air. Such a proceeding would in a singular degree have the appearance of a home-thrust. It was hardly possible that Bartleby could withstand such an application of the doctrine of assumptions. But, upon second thought, the success of the plan seemed rather dubious. I resolved to argue the matter over with him again.

"Bartleby," said I, entering the office, with a quietly severe expression, "I am seriously displeased. I am pained, Bartleby. I had thought better of you. I had imagined you of such a gentlemanly organization, that in any delicate dilemma a slight hint would suffice—in short, an assumption; but it appears I am deceived. Why," I added, unaffectedly

starting, "you have not even touched that money yet," pointing to it, just where I had left it the evening previous.

He answered nothing.

"Will you, or will you not, quit me?" I now demanded
in a sudden passion, advancing close to him.

"I would prefer *not* to quit you," he replied, gently em-
phasizing the *not*.

"What earthly right have you to stay here? Do you pay
any rent? Do you pay my taxes? Or is this property
yours?"

He answered nothing.

"Are you ready to go on and write now? Are your eyes
recovered? Could you copy a small paper for me this morning? or help examine a few lines? or step round to the Post
Office? In a word, will you do any thing at all, to give a
colouring to your refusal to depart the premises?"

He silently retired into his hermitage.

I was now in such a state of nervous resentment that I
thought it but prudent to check myself, at present, from
further demonstrations. Bartleby and I were alone. I remembered the tragedy of the unfortunate Adams and the
still more unfortunate Colt in the solitary office of the latter;
and how poor Colt, being dreadfully incensed by Adams,
and imprudently permitting himself to get wildly excited,
was at unawares hurried into his fatal act—an act which certainly no man could possibly deplore more than the actor
himself. Often it had occurred to me in my ponderings upon
the subject, that had that altercation taken place in the public
street, or at a private residence, it would not have terminated
as it did. It was the circumstance of being alone in a solitary
office, upstairs, of a building entirely unhallowed by human-
izing domestic associations—an uncarpeted office, doubtless,
of a dusty, haggard sort of appearance;—this it must have

been, which greatly helped to enhance the irritable despera-
tion of the hapless Colt.

But when this old Adam of resentment rose in me and
tempted me concerning Bartleby, I grappled him and threw
him. How? Why, simply by recalling the divine injunction: "A new commandment give I unto you, that ye love
one another." Yes, this it was that saved me. Aside from
higher considerations, charity often operates as a vastly wise
and prudent principle—a great safeguard to its possessor.
Men have committed murder for jealousy's sake, and anger's
sake, and hatred's sake, and selfishness' sake, and spiritual
pride's sake; but no man that ever I heard of, ever committed a diabolical murder for sweet charity's sake. Mere
self-interest, then, if no better motive can be enlisted, should,
especially with high-tempered men, prompt all beings to
charity and philanthropy. At any rate, upon the occasion
in question, I strove to drown my exasperated feelings
toward the scrivener by benevolently construing his conduct.
Poor fellow, poor fellow! thought I, he doesn't mean any
thing; and besides, he has seen hard times, and ought to be
indulged.

I endeavoured also immediately to occupy myself, and at
the same time to comfort my despondency. I tried to fancy
that in the course of the morning, at such time as might prove
agreeable to him, Bartleby, of his own free accord, would
emerge from his hermitage, and take up some decided line
of march in the direction of the door. But no. Half-past
twelve o'clock came; Turkey began to glow in the face,
overturn his inkstand, and become generally obstreperous;
Nippers abated down into quietude and courtesy; Ginger
Nut munched his noon apple; and Bartleby remained standing at his window in one of his profoundest dead-wall
reveries. Will it be credited? Ought I to acknowledge it?

That afternoon I left the office without saying one further word to him.

Some days now passed, during which at leisure intervals I looked a little into "Edwards on the Will," and "Priestley on Necessity." Under the circumstances, those books induced a salutary feeling. Gradually I slid into the persuasion that these troubles of mine, touching the scrivener, had been all predestinated from eternity, and Bartleby was billeted upon me for some mysterious purpose of an all-wise Providence, which it was not for a mere mortal like me to fathom. Yes, Bartleby, stay there behind your screen, thought I; I shall persecute you no more; you are harmless and noiseless as any of these old chairs; in short, I never feel so private as when I know you are here. At least I see it, I feel it; I penetrate to the predestinated purpose of my life. I am content. Others may have loftier parts to enact; but my mission in this world, Bartleby, is to furnish you with office room for such period as you may see fit to remain.

I believe that this wise and blessed frame of mind would have continued with me had it not been for the unsolicited and uncharitable remarks obtruded upon me by my professional friends who visited the rooms. But thus it often is, that the constant friction of illiberal minds wears out at last the best resolves of the more generous. Though to be sure, when I reflected upon it, it was not strange that people entering my office should be struck by the peculiar aspect of the unaccountable Bartleby, and so be tempted to throw out some sinister observations concerning him. Sometimes an attorney having business with me, and calling at my office, and finding no one but the scrivener there, would undertake to obtain some sort of precise information from him touching my whereabouts; but without heeding his idle talk, Bartleby would remain standing immovable in the middle of the room.

So, after contemplating him in that position for a time, the attorney would depart, no wiser than he came.

Also, when a Reference was going on, and the room full of lawyers and witnesses and business was driving fast, some deeply occupied legal gentleman present, seeing Bartleby wholly unemployed, would request him to run round to his (the legal gentleman's) office and fetch some papers for him. Thereupon, Bartleby would tranquilly decline, and yet remain idle as before. Then the lawyer would give a great stare, and turn to me. And what could I say? At last I was made aware that all through the circle of my professional acquaintance, a whisper of wonder was running round, having reference to the strange creature I kept at my office. This worried me very much. And as the idea came upon me of his possibly turning out a long-lived man, and keep occupying my chambers, and denying my authority; and perplexing my visitors; and scandalizing my professional reputation; and casting a general gloom over the premises; keeping soul and body together to the last upon his savings (for doubtless he spent but half a dime a day), and in the end perhaps outlive me, and claim possession of my office by right of his perpetual occupancy: as all these dark anticipations crowded upon me more and more, and my friends continually intruded their relentless remarks upon the apparition in my room, a great change was wrought in me. I resolved to gather all my faculties together, and for ever rid me of this intolerable incubus.

Ere revolving any complicated project, however, adapted to this end, I first simply suggested to Bartleby the propriety of his permanent departure. In a calm and serious tone, I commended the idea to his careful and mature consideration. But having taken three days to meditate upon it, he apprised me that his original determination remained the same; in short, that he still preferred to abide with me.

What shall I do? I now said to myself, buttoning up my coat to the last button. What shall I do? what ought I to do? what does conscience say I *should* do with this man, or rather ghost? Rid myself of him, I must; go, he shall. But how? You will not thrust him, the poor, pale, passive mortal,—you will not thrust such a helpless creature out of your door? you will not dishonour yourself by such cruelty? No, I will not, I cannot do that. Rather would I let him live and die here, and then mason up his remains in the wall. What then will you do? For all your coaxing, he will not budge. Bribes he leaves under your own paper-weight on your table; in short, it is quite plain that he prefers to cling to you.

Then something severe, something unusual must be done. What! surely you will not have him collared by a constable, and commit his innocent pallor to the common jail? And upon what ground could you procure such a thing to be done? —a vagrant, is he? What! he a vagrant, a wanderer, who refuses to budge? It is because he will *not* be a vagrant, then, that you seek to count him *as* a vagrant. That is too absurd. No visible means of support: there I have him. Wrong again: for indubitably he *does* support himself, and that is the only unanswerable proof that any man can show of his possessing the means so to do. No more then. Since he will not quit me, I must quit him. I will change my offices; I will move elsewhere; and give him fair notice, that if I find him on my new premises I will then proceed against him as a common trespasser.

Acting accordingly, next day I thus addressed him: "I find these chambers too far from the City Hall; the air is un-wholesome. In a word, I propose to remove my offices next week, and shall no longer require your services. I tell you this now, in order that you may seek another place."

He made no reply, and nothing more was said.

On the appointed day I engaged carts and men, proceeded to my chambers, and having but little furniture, everything was removed in a few hours. Throughout all, the scrivener remained standing behind the screen, which I directed to be removed the last thing. It was withdrawn; and being folded up like a huge folio, left him the motionless occupant of a naked room. I stood in the entry watching him a moment, while something from within me upbraided me.

I re-entered, with my hand in my pocket—and—and my heart in my mouth.

"Good-bye, Bartleby; I am going—good-bye, and God some way bless you; and take that," slipping something in his hand. But it dropped upon the floor and then—strange to say—I tore myself from him whom I had so longed to be rid of.

Established in my new quarters, for a day or two I kept the door locked, and started at every footfall in the passages. When I returned to my rooms after any little absence, I would pause at the threshold for an instant, and attentively listen, ere applying my key. But these fears were needless. Bartleby never came nigh me.

I thought all was going well, when a perturbed looking stranger visited me, inquiring whether I was the person who had recently occupied rooms at No. —— Wall street.

Full of forebodings, I replied that I was.

"Then sir," said the stranger, who proved a lawyer, "you are responsible for the man you left there. He refuses to do any copying, he refuses to do anything; and he says he prefers not to; and he refuses to quit the premises."

"I am very sorry, sir," said I, with assumed tranquillity,

but an inward tremor, "but, really, the man you allude to is nothing to me—he is no relation or apprentice of mine, that you should hold me responsible for him."

"In mercy's name, who is he?"

"I certainly cannot inform you. I know nothing about him. Formerly I employed him as a copyist; but he has done nothing for me now for some time past."

"I shall settle him then,—good morning, sir."

Several days passed, and I heard nothing more; and though I often felt a charitable prompting to call at the place and see poor Bartleby, yet a certain squeamishness of I know not what withheld me.

All is over with him, by this time, thought I at last, when through another week no further intelligence reached me. But coming to my room the day after, I found several persons waiting at my door in a high state of nervous excitement.

"That's the man—here he comes," cried the foremost one, whom I recognized as the lawyer who had previously called upon me alone.

"You must take him away, sir, at once," cried a portly person among them, advancing upon me, and whom I knew to be the landlord of No. —— Wall street. "These gentlemen, my tenants, cannot stand it any longer; Mr. B——," pointing to the lawyer, "has turned him out of his room, and he now persists in haunting the building generally, sitting upon the banisters of the stairs by day, and sleeping in the entry by night. Everybody here is concerned; clients are leaving the offices; some fears are entertained of a mob; something you must do, and that without delay."

Aghast at this torrent, I fell back before it, and would fain have locked myself in my new quarters. In vain I persisted that Bartleby was nothing to me—no more than to any one else there. In vain:—I was the last person known to have anything to do with him, and they held me to the terrible account. Fearful then of being exposed in the papers (as one person present obscurely threatened) I considered the matter, and at length said, that if the lawyer would give me a confidential interview with the scrivener, in his (the lawyer's) own room, I would that afternoon strive my best to rid them of the nuisance they complained of.

Going up stairs to my old haunt, there was Bartleby silently sitting upon the banister at the landing.

"What are you doing here, Bartleby?" said I.

"Sitting upon the banister," he mildly replied.

I motioned him into the lawyer's room, who then left us.

"Bartleby," said I, "are you aware that you are the cause of great tribulation to me, by persisting in occupying the entry after being dismissed from the office?"

No answer.

"Now one of two things must take place. Either you must do something, or something must be done to you. Now what sort of business would you like to engage in? Would you like to re-engage in copying for some one?"

"No; I would prefer not to make any change."

"Would you like a clerkship in a dry-goods store?"

"There is too much confinement about that. No, I would not like a clerkship; but I am not particular."

"Too much confinement," I cried, "why you keep yourself confined all the time!"

"I would prefer not to take a clerkship," he rejoined, as if to settle that little item at once.

"How would a bartender's business suit you? There is no trying of the eyesight in that."

"I would not like it at all; though, as I said before, I am not particular."

His unwonted wordiness inspirited me. I returned to the charge.

"Well then, would you like to travel through the country collecting bills for the merchants? That would improve your health."

"No, I would prefer to be doing something else."

"How then would going as a companion to Europe to entertain some young gentleman with your conversation,— how would that suit you?"

"Not at all. It does not strike me that there is anything definite about that. I like to be stationary. But I am not particular."

"Stationary you shall be then," I cried, now losing all patience, and for the first time in all my exasperating connection with him fairly flying into a passion. "If you do not go away from these premises before night, I shall feel bound—indeed I *am* bound—to—to—to quit the premises myself!" I rather absurdly concluded, knowing not with what possible threat to try to frighten his immobility into compliance. Despairing of all further efforts, I was precipitately leaving him, when a final thought occurred to me— one which had not been wholly unindulged before.

"Bartleby," said I, in the kindest tone I could assume under such exciting circumstances, "will you go home with me now—not to my office, but my dwelling—and remain there till we can conclude upon some convenient arrangement for you at our leisure? Come, let us start now, right away."

"No: at present I would prefer not to make any change at all."

I answered nothing; but effectually dodging every one by the suddenness and rapidity of my flight, rushed from the building, ran up Wall street toward Broadway, and then jumping into the first omnibus was soon removed from pursuit. As soon as tranquillity returned I distinctly perceived that I had now done all that I possibly could, both in respect to the demands of the landlord and his tenants, and with regard to my own desire and sense of duty, to benefit Bartleby, and shield him from rude persecution. I now strove to be entirely care-free and quiescent; and my conscience justified me in the attempt; though indeed it was not so successful as I could have wished. So fearful was I of being again hunted out by the incensed landlord and his exasperated tenants, that, surrendering my business to Nippers, for a few days I drove about the upper part of the town and through the suburbs, in my rockaway; crossed over to Jersey City and Hoboken, and paid fugitive visits to Manhattanville and Astoria. In fact I almost lived in my rockaway for the time.

When again I entered my office, lo, a note from the landlord lay upon the desk. I opened it with trembling hands. It informed me that the writer had sent to the police, and had Bartleby removed to the Tombs as a vagrant. Moreover, since I knew more about him than any one else, he wished me to appear at that place, and make a suitable statement of the facts. These tidings had a conflicting effect upon me. At first I was indignant; but at last almost approved. The landlord's energetic, summary disposition had led him to adopt a procedure which I do not think I would have decided upon myself; and yet as a last resort, under such peculiar circumstances, it seemed the only plan.

As I afterwards learned, the poor scrivener, when told that he must be conducted to the Tombs, offered not the slightest obstacle, but in his own pale, unmoving way silently acquiesced.

Some of the compassionate and curious bystanders joined the party; and headed by one of the constables, arm-in-arm

with Bartleby the silent procession filed its way through all
the noise, and heat, and joy of the roaring thoroughfares
at noon.

The same day I received the note I went to the Tombs,
or, to speak more properly, the Halls of Justice. Seeking
the right officer, I stated the purpose of my call, and was
informed that the individual I described was indeed within.
I then assured the functionary that Bartleby was a perfectly
honest man, and greatly to be a compassionated (however
unaccountable) eccentric. I narrated all I knew, and closed
by suggesting the idea of letting him remain in as indulgent
confinement as possible till something less harsh might be
done—though indeed I hardly knew what. At all events,
if nothing else could be decided upon, the alms-house must
receive him. I then begged to have an interview.

Being under no disgraceful charge, and quite serene and
harmless in all his ways, they had permitted him freely to
wander about the prison, and especially in the inclosed grass-
platted yards thereof. And so I found him there, standing
all alone in the quietest of the yards, his face toward a high
wall—while all around, from the narrow slits of the jail
windows, I thought I saw peering out upon him the eyes of
murderers and thieves.

"Bartleby!"

"I know you," he said, without looking round,—"and I
want nothing to say to you."

"It was not I that brought you here, Bartleby," said I,
keenly pained at his implied suspicion. "And to you, this
should not be so vile a place. Nothing reproachful attaches
to you by being here. And see, it is not so sad a place as one
might think. Look, there is the sky and here is the grass."

"I know where I am," he replied, but would say nothing
more, and so I left him.

As I entered the corridor again a broad, meat-like man in an apron accosted me, and jerking his thumb over his shoulder said—"Is that your friend?"

"Yes."

"Does he want to starve? If he does, let him live on the prison fare, that's all."

"Who are you?" asked I, not knowing what to make of such an unofficially speaking person in such a place.

"I am the grub-man. Such gentlemen as have friends here, hire me to provide them with something good to eat."

"Is this so?" said I, turning to the turnkey.

He said it was.

"Well then," said I, slipping some silver into the grub-man's hands (for so they called him), "I want you to give particular attention to my friend there; let him have the best dinner you can get. And you must be as polite to him as possible."

"Introduce me, will you?" said the grub-man, looking at me with an expression which seemed to say he was all impatience for an opportunity to give a specimen of his breeding.

Thinking it would prove of benefit to the scrivener, I acquiesced; and asking the grub-man his name, went up with him to Bartleby.

"Bartleby, this is Mr. Cutlets; you will find him very useful to you."

"Your sarvant, sir, your sarvant," said the grub-man, making a low salutation behind his apron. "Hope you find it pleasant here, sir;—spacious grounds—cool apartments, sir—hope you'll stay with us some time—try to make it agreeable. May Mrs. Cutlets and I have the pleasure of your company to dinner, sir, in Mrs. Cutlets' private room?"

"I prefer not to dine to-day," said Bartleby, turning away. "It would disagree with me; I am unused to dinners." So saying, he slowly moved to the other side of the inclosure and took up a position fronting the dead-wall.

"How's this?" said the grub-man, addressing me with a stare of astonishment. "He's odd, ain't he?"

"I think he is a little deranged," said I, sadly.

"Deranged? deranged is it? Well now, upon my word, I thought that friend of yourn was a gentleman forger; they are always pale and genteel-like, them forgers. I can't help pity 'em—can't help it, sir. Did you know Monroe Edwards?" he added touchingly, and paused. Then, laying his hand pityingly on my shoulder, sighed, "he died of the consumption at Sing-Sing. So you weren't acquainted with Monroe?"

"No, I was never socially acquainted with any forgers. But I cannot stop longer. Look to my friend yonder. You will not lose by it. I will see you again."

Some few days after this, I again obtained admission to the Tombs, and went through the corridors in quest of Bartleby; but without finding him.

"I saw him coming from his cell not long ago," said a turnkey, "maybe he's gone to loiter in the yards."

So I went in that direction.

"Are you looking for the silent man?" said another turnkey passing me. "Yonder he lies—sleeping in the yard there. 'Tis not twenty minutes since I saw him lie down."

The yard was entirely quiet. It was not accessible to the common prisoners. The surrounding walls, of amazing thickness, kept off all sounds behind them. The Egyptian character of the masonry weighed upon me with its gloom. But a soft imprisoned turf grew under foot. The heart of the eternal pyramids, it seemed, wherein by some strange magic, through the clefts grass-seed, dropped by birds, had sprung.

Strangely huddled at the base of the wall—his knees drawn up, and lying on his side, his head touching the cold stones—I saw the wasted Bartleby. But nothing stirred. I paused; then went close up to him; stooped over, and saw that his dim eyes were open; otherwise he seemed profoundly sleeping. Something prompted me to touch him. I felt his hand, when a tingling shiver ran up my arm and down my spine to my feet.

The round face of the grub-man peered upon me now. "His dinner is ready. Won't he dine to-day, either? Or does he live without dining?"

"Lives without dining," said I, and closed the eyes.

"Eh!—He's asleep, ain't he?"

"With kings and counsellors," murmured I.

There would seem little need for proceeding further in this history. Imagination will readily supply the meagre recital of poor Bartleby's interment. But ere parting with the reader, let me say, that if this little narrative has sufficiently interested him, to awaken curiosity as to who Bartleby was, and what manner of life he led prior to the present narrator's making his acquaintance, I can only reply, that in such curiosity I fully share—but am wholly unable to gratify it. Yet here I hardly know whether I should divulge one little item of rumour, which came to my ear a few months after the scrivener's decease. Upon what basis it rested, I could never ascertain; and hence, how true it is I cannot now tell. But inasmuch as this vague report has not been without a certain strange suggestive interest to me, however sad, it may prove the same with some others; and so I will briefly mention it. The report was this: that Bartleby had been a subordinate clerk in the Dead Letter Office at Washington, from which he had been suddenly removed by a change in the administration. When I think over this rumour I cannot adequately express the emotions which seize me. Dead letters! does it not sound like dead men? Conceive a man by nature and misfortune prone to a pallid hopelessness: can any business seem more fitted to heighten it than that of continually handling these dead letters, and assorting them for the flames? For by the cartload they are annually burned. Sometimes from out the folded paper the pale clerk takes a ring:——the finger it was meant for, perhaps, moulders in the grave; a bank-note sent in swiftest charity:——he whom it would relieve, nor eats nor hungers any more; pardon for those who died despairing; hope for those who died unhoping; good tidings for those who died stifled by unrelieved calamities. On errands of life, these letters speed to death.

Ah Bartleby! Ah humanity!

does not explain anything - life is a sad mystery

maybe dead letters represent Melville's books which did not communicate with their readers - maybe Melville speculating what would happen if he just stopped writing and says "no" (in a world that says "yes")

THE ENCANTADAS

OR

ENCHANTED ISLES

BY

SALVATOR R. TARNMOOR

First published in *Putnam's Monthly Magazine*, March, April, May, 1854.

Republished in "The Piazza Tales," 1856.

THE ENCANTADAS,

OR ENCHANTED ISLES

Sketch First

THE ISLES AT LARGE

—*"That may not be, said then the ferryman,*
Least we unweeting hap to be fordonne;
For those same islands seeming now and than,
Are not firme land, nor any certein wonne,
But stragling plots which to and fro do ronne
In the wide waters; therefore are they hight
The Wandering Islands; therefore do them shonne;
For they have oft drawne many a wandring wight
Into most deadly daunger and distressed plight;
For whosoever once hath fastened
His foot thereon may never it secure
But wandreth evermore uncertain and unsure."

. . . .

"Darke, dolefull, dreary, like a greedy grave,
That still for carrion carcasses doth crave;
On top whereof ay dwelt the ghastly owl,
Shrieking his balefull note, which ever drave
Far from that haunt all other cheerful fowl,
And all about it wandring ghosts did wayle and howl."

TAKE five-and-twenty heaps of cinders dumped here and
there in an outside city lot; imagine some of them magni-
fied into mountains, and the vacant lot the sea; and you will
have a fit idea of the general aspect of the Encantadas, or
Enchanted Isles. A group rather of extinct volcanoes than
of isles; looking much as the world at large might, after a
penal conflagration.

It is to be doubted whether any spot of earth can, in desolateness, furnish a parallel to this group. Abandoned cemeteries of long ago, old cities by piecemeal tumbling to their ruin, these are melancholy enough; but, like all else which has but once been associated with humanity they still awaken in us some thoughts of sympathy, however sad. Hence, even the Dead Sea, along with whatever other emotions it may at times inspire, does not fail to touch in the pilgrim some of his less unpleasurable feelings.

And as for solitariness; the great forests of the north, the expanses of unnavigated waters, the Greenland ice-fields, are the profoundest of solitudes to a human observer; still the magic of their changeable tides and seasons mitigates their terror; because, though unvisited by men, those forests are visited by the May; the remotest seas reflect familiar stars even as Lake Erie does; and in the clear air of a fine Polar day, the irradiated, azure ice shows beautifully as malachite.

But the special curse, as one may call it, of the Encantadas, that which exalts them in desolation above Idumea and the Pole, is that to them change never comes; neither the change of seasons nor of sorrows. Cut by the Equator, they know not autumn and they know not spring; while already reduced to the lees of fire, ruin itself can work little more upon them. The showers refresh the deserts, but in these isles, rain never falls. Like split Syrian gourds, left withering in the sun, they are cracked by an everlasting drought beneath a torrid sky. "Have mercy upon me," the wailing spirit of the Encantadas seems to cry, "and send Lazarus that he may dip the tip of his finger in water and cool my tongue, for I am tormented in this flame."

Another feature in these isles is their emphatic uninhabitableness. It is deemed a fit type of all-forsaken overthrow, that the jackal should den in the wastes of weedy Babylon;

but the Encantadas refuse to harbour even the outcasts of
the beasts. Man and wolf alike disown them. Little but reptile life is here found:—tortoises, lizards, immense spiders,
snakes, and the strangest anomaly of outlandish Nature,
the *aguano*. No voice, no low, no howl is heard; the chief
sound of life here is a hiss.

On most of the isles where vegetation is found at all,
it is more ungrateful than the blankness of Aracama.
Tangled thickets of wiry bushes, without fruit and without
a name, springing up among deep fissures of calcined rock,
and treacherously masking them; or a parched growth of
distorted cactus trees.

In many places the coast is rock-bound, or more properly,
clinker-bound; tumbled masses of blackish or greenish stuff
like the dross of an iron-furnace, forming dark clefts and
caves here and there, into which a ceaseless sea pours a fury
of foam; overhanging them with a swirl of grey, haggard
mist, amidst which sail screaming flights of unearthly birds
heightening the dismal din. However calm the sea without,
there is no rest for these swells and those rocks, they lash and
are lashed, even when the outer ocean is most at peace with
itself. On the oppressive, clouded days such as are peculiar
to this part of the watery Equator, the dark vitrified masses,
many of which raise themselves among white whirlpools and
breakers in detached and perilous places off the shore, present
a most Plutonian sight. In no world but a fallen one could
such lands exist.

Those parts of the strand free from the marks of fire
stretch away in wide level beaches of multitudinous dead
shells, with here and there decayed bits of sugar-cane, bam-
boos, and cocoanuts, washed upon this other and darker
world from the charming palm isles to the westward and
southward; all the way from Paradise to Tartarus; while

mixed with the relics of distant beauty you will sometimes see fragments of charred wood and mouldering ribs of wrecks. Neither will any one be surprised at meeting these last, after observing the conflicting currents which eddy throughout nearly all the wide channels of the entire group. The capriciousness of the tides of air sympathizes with those of the sea. Nowhere is the wind so light, baffling, and every way unreliable, and so given to perplexing calms, as at the Encantadas. Nigh a month has been spent by a ship going from one isle to another, though but thirty miles between; for owing to the force of the current, the boats employed to tow barely suffice to keep the craft from sweeping upon the cliffs, but do nothing toward accelerating her voyage. Sometimes it is impossible for a vessel from afar to fetch up with the group itself, unless large allowances for prospective lee-way have been made ere its coming in sight. And yet, at other times, there is a mysterious indraft, which irresistibly draws a passing vessel among the isles, though not bound to them.

True, at one period, as to some extent at the present day, large fleets of whalemen cruised for Spermaceti upon what some seamen call the Enchanted Ground. But this, as in due place will be described, was off the great outer isle of Albemarle, away from the intricacies of the smaller isles, where there is plenty of sea-room; and hence, to that vicinity, the above remarks do not altogether apply; though even there the current runs at times with singular force, shifting, too, with as singular a caprice. Indeed, there are seasons when currents quite unaccountable prevail for a great distance round about the total group, and are so strong and irregular as to change a vessel's course against the helm, though sailing at the rate of four or five miles the hour. The difference in the reckonings of navigators produced by these causes, along

with the light and variable winds, long nourished a persuasion that there existed two distinct clusters of isles in the
parallel of the Encantadas, about a hundred leagues apart.
Such was the idea of their earlier visitors, the Buccaneers;
and as late as 1750, the charts of that part of the Pacific
accorded with the strange delusion. And this apparent fleet-
ingness and unreality of the locality of the isles was most
probably one reason for the Spaniards calling them the
Encantada, or Enchanted Group.

But not uninfluenced by their character, as they now con-
fessedly exist, the modern voyager will be inclined to fancy
that the bestowal of this name might have in part originated
in that air of spell-bound desertness which so significantly
invests the isles. Nothing can better suggest the aspect of
once living things malignly crumbled from ruddiness into
ashes. Apples of Sodom, after touching, seem these isles.

However wavering their place may seem by reason of the
currents, they themselves, at least to one upon the shore,
appear invariably the same: fixed, cast, glued into the very
body of cadaverous death.

Nor would the appellation, enchanted, seem misapplied in
still another sense. For concerning the peculiar reptile inhabitant of these wilds—whose presence gives the group its
second Spanish name, Gallipagos—concerning the tortoises
found here, most mariners have long cherished a superstition, not more frightful than grotesque. They earnestly
believe that all wrecked sea-officers, more especially com-
modores and captains, are at death (and in some cases, before
death) transformed into tortoises; thenceforth dwelling upon
these hot aridities, sole solitary Lords of Asphaltum.

Doubtless so quaintly dolorous a thought was originally
inspired by the woe-begone landscape itself, but more particularly, perhaps, by the tortoises. For apart from their

strictly physical features, there is something strangely self-condemned in the appearance of these creatures. Lasting sorrow and penal hopelessness are in no animal form so suppliantly expressed as in theirs; while the thought of their wonderful longevity does not fail to enhance the impression.

Nor even at the risk of meriting the charge of absurdly believing in enchantments, can I restrain the admission that sometimes, even now, when leaving the crowded city to wander out July and August among the Adirondack Mountains, far from the influences of towns and proportionally nigh to the mysterious ones of Nature; when at such times I sit me down in the mossy head of some deep-wooded gorge, surrounded by prostrate trunks of blasted pines, and recall, as in a dream, my other and far-distant rovings in the baked heart of the charmed isles; and remember the sudden glimpses of dusky shells, and long languid necks protruded from the leafless thickets; and again have beheld the vitreous inland rocks worn down and grooved into deep ruts by ages and ages of the slow draggings of tortoises in quest of pools of scanty water; I can hardly resist the feeling that in my time I have indeed slept upon evilly enchanted ground.

Nay, such is the vividness of my memory, or the magic of my fancy, that I know not whether I am not the occasional victim of optical delusion concerning the Gallipagos. For often in scenes of social merriment, and especially at revels held by candle light in old-fashioned mansions—when the shadows are thrown into the further recesses of an angular and spacious room, making them put on a look of haunted undergrowth of lonely woods—I have drawn the attention of my comrades by my fixed gaze and sudden change of air, as I have seemed to see, slowly emerging from those imagined solitudes, and heavily crawling along the floor, the ghost of a gigantic tortoise, with "Memento . . ." burning in live letters upon his back.

Sketch Second

TWO SIDES TO A TORTOISE

"Most ugly shapes and horrible aspects,
Such as Dame Nature selfe mote feare to see,
Or shame, that ever should so fowle defects
From her most cunning hand escaped bee;
All dreadfull pourtraicts of deformitee.

. . . . . .

Ne wonder if these do a man appall;
For all that here at home we dreadfull hold
Be but as bugs to fearen babes withall
Compared to the creatures in these isles' entrall

. . . . . .

Fear naught, then said the palmer, well avized,
For these same monsters are not there indeed,
But are into these fearfull shapes disguized.

. . . . . .

And lifting up his vertuous staffe on high,
Then all that dreadfull armie fast gan flye
Into great Zethy's bosom, where they hidden lye."

IN view of the description given, may one be gay upon the Encantadas? Yes: that is, find one the gaiety, and he will be gay. And indeed, sackcloth and ashes as they are, the isles are not perhaps unmitigated gloom. For while no spectator can deny their claims to a most solemn and superstitious consideration, no more than my firmest resolutions can decline to behold the spectre-tortoise when emerging from its shadowy recess; yet even the tortoise, dark and melancholy as it is upon the back, still possesses a bright side; its calapee or breast-plate being sometimes of a faint yellowish or golden tinge. Moreover, every one knows that tortoises as well as turtles are of such a make, that if you but put them on their backs you thereby expose their bright sides without the possibility of their recovering themselves, and turning into view the other. But after you have done this, and because you have done this, you should not swear that the tortoise has no dark side. Enjoy the bright, keep it turned up perpetually if you can, but be honest and don't deny the black. Neither should he who cannot turn the tortoise from its natural position so as to hide the darker and expose his livelier aspect, like a great October pumpkin in the sun, for that cause declare the creature to be one total inky blot. The tortoise is both black and bright. But let us to particulars.

Some months before my first stepping ashore upon the group, my ship was cruising in its close vicinity. One noon we found ourselves off the South Head of Albemarle, and not very far from the land. Partly by way of freak, and partly by way of spying out so strange a country, a boat's crew was sent ashore, with orders to see all they could, and besides, bring back whatever tortoises they could conveniently transport.

It was after sunset when the adventurers returned. I looked down over the ship's high side as if looking down over the curb of a well, and dimly saw the damp boat deep in the sea with some unwonted weight. Ropes were dropped over, and presently three huge antediluvian-looking tortoises, after much straining, were landed on deck. They seemed hardly of the seed of earth. We had been abroad upon the waters for five long months, a period amply sufficient to make all things of the land wear a fabulous hue to the dreamy mind. Had three Spanish custom-house officers boarded us then, it is not unlikely that I should have curiously stared at them, felt of them, and stroked them much as savages observe civilized guests. But instead of three custom-house officers, behold these really wondrous tortoises —none of your schoolboy mud-turtles—but black as widower's weeds, heavy as chests of plate, with vast shells medallioned and orbed like shields, and dented and blistered like shields that have breasted a battle—shaggy too, here and there, with dark green moss, and slimy with the spray of the sea. These mystic creatures, suddenly translated by night from unutterable solitudes to our peopled deck, affected me in a manner not easy to unfold. They seemed newly crawled forth from beneath the foundations of the world. Yea, they seemed the identical tortoises whereon the Hindoo plants this total sphere. With a lantern I inspected them more closely. Such worshipful venerableness of aspect! Such furry greenness mantling the rude peelings and healing the fissures of their shattered shells. I no more saw three tortoises. They expanded—became transfigured. I seemed to see three Roman Coliseums in magnificent decay.

Ye oldest inhabitants of this or any other isle, said I, pray give me the freedom of your three-walled towns.

The great feeling inspired by these creatures was that of age:—dateless, indefinite endurance. And, in fact, that any other creature can live and breathe as long as the tortoise of the Encantadas, I will not readily believe. Not to hint of their known capacity of sustaining life, while going without food for an entire year, consider that impregnable armour of their living mail. What other bodily being possesses such a citadel wherein to resist the assaults of Time?

As, lantern in hand, I scraped among the moss and beheld the ancient scars of bruises, received in many a sullen fall among the marly mountains of the isle—scars strangely widened, swollen, half obliterate, and yet distorted like those sometimes found in the bark of very hoary trees—I seemed an antiquary of a geologist, studying the bird tracks and ciphers upon the exhumed slates trod by incredible creatures whose very ghosts are now defunct.

As I lay in my hammock that night, overhead I heard the slow, weary draggings of the three ponderous strangers along the encumbered deck. Their stupidity or their resolution was so great that they never went aside for any impediment. One ceased his movements altogether just before the mid-watch. At sunrise I found him butted like a battering-ram against the immovable foot of the foremast, and still striv-ing, tooth and nail, to force the impossible passage. That these tortoises are the victims of a penal, or malignant, or perhaps a downright diabolical enchanter, seems in nothing more likely than in that strange infatuation of hopeless toil which so often possesses them. I have known them in their journeyings to ram themselves heroically against rocks and long abide there, nudging, wriggling, wedging, in order to displace them, and so hold on their inflexible path. Their crowning curse is their drudging impulse to straightforward-ness in a belittered world.

Meeting with no such hindrance as their companion did, the other tortoises merely fell foul of small stumbling-blocks; buckets, blocks, and coils of rigging; and at times in the act of crawling over them would slip with an astounding rattle to the deck. Listening to these draggings and concus-sions, I thought me of the haunt from which they came; an isle full of metallic ravines and gulches, sunk bottomlessly into the hearts of splintered mountains, and covered for many miles with inextricable thickets. I then pictured these three straightforward monsters, century after century, writh-ing through the shades, grim as blacksmiths; crawling so slowly and ponderously, that not only did toadstools and all fungous things grow beneath their feet, but a sooty moss sprouted upon their backs. With them I often lost myself in volcanic mazes; brushed away endless boughs of rotting thickets; till finally in a dream I found myself sitting cross-legged upon the foremost, a Brahmin similarly mounted upon either side, forming a tripod of foreheads which upheld the universal cope.

Such was the wild nightmare begot by my first impression of the Encantadas tortoise. But next evening, strange to say, I sat down with my shipmates and made a merry repast from tortoise steaks and tortoise stews; and supper over, out knife, and helped convert the three mighty concave shells into three fanciful soup-tureens, and polished the three flat yellowish calapees into three gorgeous salvers.

Sketch Third

ROCK RODONDO

"For they this hight the Rock of vile Reproach,
A dangerous and dreadfull place,
To which nor fish nor fowl did once approach,
But yelling meaws with sea-gulls hoars and bace
And cormoyrants with birds of ravenous race,
Which still sit waiting on that dreadful clift."

. . . . .

"With that the rolling sea resounding soft
In his big vase them fitly answered,
And on the Rock, the waves breaking aloft,
A solemn meane unto them measured."

. . . . .

"Then he the boteman bad row easily,
And let him heare some part of that rare melody."

. . . . .

"Suddeinly an innumerable flight
Of harmefull fowles about them fluttering cride,

> *And with their wicked wings them oft did smight*
> *And sore annoyed, groping in that griesly night."*
>
> *"Even all the nation of unfortunate*
> *And fatal birds about them flocked were."*

To go up into a high stone tower is not only a very fine thing in itself, but the very best mode of gaining a comprehensive view of the region round about. It is all the better if this tower stand solitary and alone, like that mysterious Newport one, or else be sole survivor of some perished castle.

Now, with reference to the Enchanted Isles, we are fortunately supplied with just such a noble point of observation in a remarkable rock, from its peculiar figure called of old by the Spaniards, Rock Rodondo, or Round Rock. Some two hundred and fifty feet high, rising straight from the sea ten miles from land, with the whole mountainous group to the south and east, Rock Rodondo occupies, on a large scale, very much the position which the famous Campanile or detached Bell Tower of Saint Mark does with respect to the tangled group of hoary edifices around it.

Ere ascending, however, to gaze abroad upon the Encantadas, this sea-tower itself claims attention. It is visible at the distance of thirty miles; and, fully participating in that enchantment which pervades the group, when first seen afar invariably is mistaken for a sail. Four leagues away, on a golden, hazy noon, it seems some Spanish Admiral's ship, stacked up with glittering canvas. Sail ho! Sail ho! Sail ho! from all three masts. But coming nigh, the enchanted frigate is transformed apace into a craggy keep.

My first visit to the spot was made in the grey of the morning. With a view of fishing, we had lowered three boats, and pulling some two miles from our vessel found ourselves, just before dawn of day, close under the moon-shadow of Rodondo. Its aspect was heightened, and yet softened, by the strange double twilight of the hour. The great full moon burned in the low west like a half-spent beacon casting a soft mellow tinge upon the sea, like that cast by a waning fire of embers upon a midnight hearth; while along the entire east the invisible sun sent pallid intimations of his coming. The wind was light; the waves languid; the stars twinkled with a faint effulgence; all nature seemed supine with the long night watch, and half-suspended in jaded expectation of the sun. This was the critical hour to catch Rodondo in his perfect mood. The twilight was just enough to reveal every striking point, without tearing away the dim investiture of wonder.

From a broken, stair-like base, washed, as the steps of a water-palace, by the waves, the tower rose in entablatures of strata to a shaven summit. These uniform layers which compose the mass form its most peculiar feature. For at their lines of junction they project flatly into encircling shelves, from top to bottom, rising one above another in graduated series. And as the eaves of any old barn or abbey are alive with swallows, so were all these rocky ledges with unnumbered sea-fowl. Eaves upon eaves, and nests upon nests. Here and there were long birdlime streaks of a ghostly white staining the tower from sea to air, readily accounting for its sail-like look afar. All would have been bewitchingly quiescent, were it not for the demoniac din created by the birds. Not only were the eaves rustling with them, but they flew densely overhead, spreading themselves into a winged and continually shifting canopy. The tower is the resort of aquatic birds for hundreds of leagues around. To the north, to the east, to the west, stretches nothing but eternal ocean; so that the man-of-war hawk coming from the coasts of North America, Polynesia, or Peru, makes his first land at

Rodondo. And yet though Rodondo be terra-firma, no land-bird ever lighted on it. Fancy a red-robin or a canary there! What a falling into the hands of the Philistines, when the poor warbler should be surrounded by such locust-flights of strong bandit birds, with long bills cruel as daggers.

I know not where one can better study the Natural History of strange sea-fowl than at Rodondo. It is the aviary of Ocean. Birds light here which never touched mast or tree; hermit-birds, which ever fly alone, cloud-birds, familiar with unpierced zones of air.

Let us first glance low down to the lowermost shelf of all, which is the widest too, and but a little space from high-water mark. What outlandish beings are these? Erect as men, but hardly as symmetrical, they stand all round the rock like sculptured caryatides, supporting the next range of eaves above. Their bodies are grotesquely misshapen; their bills short; their feet seemingly legless; while the members at their sides are neither fin, wing, nor arm. And truly neither fish, flesh nor fowl is the penguin; as an edible, per-taining neither to Carnival nor Lent; without exception the most ambiguous and least lovely creature yet discovered by man. Though dabbling in all three elements, and indeed possessing some rudimental claims to all, the penguin is at home in none. On land it stumps; afloat it sculls; in the air it flops. As if ashamed of her failure Nature keeps this ungainly child hidden away at the ends of the earth, in the Straits of Magellan and on the abased sea-story of Rodondo.

But look, what are yon woe-begone regiments drawn up on the next shelf above? What rank and file of large strange fowl? What sea Friars of Orders Grey? Pelicans. Their elongated bills, and heavy leathern pouches, suspended thereto, give them the most lugubrious expression. A pen-sive race, they stand for hours together without motion.

Their dull, ashy plumage imparts an aspect as if they had been powdered over with cinders. A penitential bird indeed —fitly haunting the shores of the clinkered Encantadas— whereon tormented Job himself might have well sat down and scraped himself with potsherds.

Higher up now we mark the gony, or grey albatross, anomalously so called, an unsightly unpoetic bird, unlike its storied kinsman, which is the snow-white ghost of the haunted Capes of Hope and Horn.

As we still ascend from shelf to shelf we find the tenants of the tower serially disposed in order of their magnitude:— gannets, black and speckled haglets, jays, sea-hens, sperm-whale-birds, gulls of all varieties:—thrones, princedoms, powers, dominating one above another in senatorial array; while sprinkled over all, like an ever-repeated fly in a great piece of broidery, the stormy petrel or Mother Cary's chicken sounds his continual challenge and alarm. That this mysterious humming-bird of ocean, which had it but brilliancy of hue might from its evanescent liveliness be almost called its butterfly, yet whose chirrup under the stern is ominous to mariners as to the peasant the death-tick sounding from behind the chimney-jam—should have its special haunt at the Encantadas, contributes in the seaman's mind not a little to their dreary spell.

As day advances the dissonant din augments. With ear-splitting cries the wild birds celebrate their matins. Each moment, flights push from the tower, and join the aerial choir hovering overhead, while their places below are supplied by darting myriads. But down through all this discord of commotion I hear clear silver bugle-like notes unbrokenly falling, like oblique lines of swift slanting rain in a cascading shower. I gaze far up, and behold a snow-white angelic thing, with one long lance-like feather thrust out behind.

It is the bright inspiriting chanticleer of ocean, the beauteous bird, from its bestirring whistle of musical invocation, fitly styled the "Boatswain's Mate."

The winged life clouding Rodondo on that well-remembered morning, I saw had its full counterpart in the finny hosts which people the waters at its base. Below the water-line, the rock seemed one honey-comb of grottoes, affording labyrinthine lurking places for swarms of fairy fish. All were strange; many exceedingly beautiful; and would have well graced the costliest glass globes in which goldfish are kept for a show. Nothing was more striking than the complete novelty of many individuals of this multitude. Here hues were seen as yet unpainted, and figures which are unengraved.

To show the multitude, avidity, and nameless fearlessness and tameness of these fish, let me say that often, marking through clear spaces of water—temporarily made so by the concentric dartings of the fish above the surface—certain larger and less unwary wights, which swam slow and deep, our anglers would cautiously essay to drop their lines down to these last. But in vain; there was no passing the uppermost zone. No sooner did the hook touch the sea than a hundred infatuates contended for the honour of capture. Poor fish of Rodondo! in your victimized confidence you are of the number of those who inconsiderately trust while they do not understand, human nature.

But the dawn is now fairly day. Band after band the sea-fowl sail away to forage the deep for their food. The tower is left solitary, save the fish caves at its base. Its birdlime gleams in the golden rays like the whitewash of a tall lighthouse, or the lofty sails of a cruiser. This moment, doubtless, while we know it to be a dead desert rock, other voyagers are taking oaths it is a glad populous ship.

But ropes now, and let us ascend. Yet soft, this is not so easy.

Sketch Fourth

A PISGAH VIEW FROM THE ROCK

—*"That done, he leads him to the highest mount,*
From whence, far off he unto him did show:"——

If you seek to ascend Rock Rodondo, take the following prescription. Go three voyages round the world as a main-royalman of the tallest frigate that floats; then serve a year or two apprenticeship to the guides who conduct strangers up the Peak of Teneriffe; and as many more, respectively, to a rope-dancer, an Indian Juggler, and a chamois. This done, come and be rewarded by the view from our tower. How we get there, we alone know. If we sought to tell others, what the wiser were they? Suffice it, that here at the summit you and I stand. Does any balloonist, does the outlooking man in the moon, take a broader view of space? Much thus, one fancies, looks the universe from Milton's celestial battlements. A boundless watery Kentucky. Here Daniel Boone would have dwelt content.

Never heed for the present yonder Burnt District of the Enchanted Isles. Look edgeways, as it were, past them, to the south. You see nothing; but permit me to point out the direction, if not the place, of certain interesting objects in the vast sea, which kissing this tower's base, we behold unscrolling itself towards the Antarctic Poles.

We stand now ten miles from the Equator. Yonder, to the East, some six hundred miles, lies the continent; this Rock being just about on the parallel of Quito.

Observe another thing here. We are at one of three uninhabited clusters, which, at pretty nearly uniform distances from the main, sentinel, at long intervals from each other, the entire coast of South America. In a peculiar manner, also, they terminate the South American character of country. Of the unnumbered Polynesian chains to the westward, not one partakes of the qualities of the Encantadas or Gallipagos, the isles St. Felix and St. Ambrose, the isles Juan Fernandes and Massafuero. Of the first it needs not here to speak. The second lie a little above the Southern Tropic; lofty, inhospitable, and uninhabitable rocks, one of which, presenting two round hummocks connected by a low reef, exactly resembles a huge double-headed shot. The last lie in the latitude of 33°; high, wild and cloven. Juan Fernandes is sufficiently famous without further description. Massafuero is a Spanish name, expressive of the fact, that the isle so called lies *more without*, that is, further off the main than its neighbour Juan. This isle Massafuero has a very imposing aspect at a distance of eight or ten miles. Approached in one direction, in cloudy weather, its great overhanging height and rugged contour, and more especially a peculiar slope of its broad summits, give it much the air of a vast iceberg drifting in tremendous poise. Its sides are split with dark cavernous recesses, as an old cathedral with its gloomy lateral chapels. Drawing nigh one of these gorges from sea after a long voyage, and beholding some tatterdemalion outlaw, staff in hand, descending its steep rocks towards you, conveys a very queer emotion to a lover of the picturesque.

On fishing parties from ships, at various times, I have chanced to visit each of these groups. The impression they give to the stranger pulling close up in his boat under their grim cliffs is, that surely he must be their first discoverer, such for the most part is the unimpaired . . . silence and solitude. And here, by the way, the mode in which these

isles were really first lighted upon by Europeans is not unworthy mention, especially as what is about to be said, likewise applies to the original discovery of our Encantadas.

Prior to the year 1563, the voyages made by Spanish ships
from Peru to Chili, were full of difficulty. Along this coast
the winds from the South most generally prevail; and it had
been an invariable custom to keep close in with the land, from
a superstitious conceit on the part of the Spaniards, that were
they to lose sight of it, the eternal trade wind would waft
them into unending waters, from whence would be no return. Here, involved among tortuous capes and headlands,
shoals and reefs, beating too against a continual head wind,
often light, and sometimes for days and weeks sunk into
utter calm, the provincial vessels, in many cases, suffered the
extremest hardships, in passages, which at the present day
seem to have been incredibly protracted. There is on record
in some collections of nautical disasters, an account of one of
these ships, which starting on a voyage whose duration was
estimated at ten days, spent four months at sea, and indeed
never again entered harbour, for in the end she was cast
away. Singular to tell, this craft never encountered a gale,
but was the vexed sport of malicious calms and currents.
Thrice, out of provisions, she put back to an intermediate
port, and started afresh, but only yet again to return. Frequent fogs enveloped her; so that no observation could be
had of her place, and once, when all hands were joyously an-
ticipating sight of their destination, lo! the vapours lifted and
disclosed the mountains from which they had taken their
first departure. In the like deceptive vapours she at last
struck upon a reef, whence ensued a long series of calamities
too sad to detail.

It was the famous pilot, Juan Fernandes, immortalized by
the island named after him, who put an end to these coast-

ing tribulations, by boldly venturing the experiment—as De Gama did before him with respect to Europe—of standing broad out from land. Here he found the winds favourable for getting to the south, and by running westward till beyond the influence of the trades, he regained the coast without difficulty; making the passage which, though in a high degree circuitous, proved far more expeditious than the nominally direct one. Now it was upon these new tracks, and about the year 1670 or thereabouts, that the Enchanted Isles and the rest of the sentinel groups, as they may be called, were discovered. Though I know of no account as to whether any of them were found inhabited or no, it may be reasonably concluded that they have been immemorial solitudes. But let us return to Rodondo.

Southwest from our tower lies all Polynesia, hundreds of leagues away; but straight west, on the precise line of his parallel, no land rises till your keel is beached upon the Kingsmills, a nice little sail of say five thousand miles.

Having thus by such distant references—with Rodondo the only possible ones—settled our relative place on the sea, let us consider objects not quite so remote. Behold the grim and charred Enchanted Isles. This nearest crater-shaped headland is part of Albemarle, the largest of the group, being some sixty miles or more long, and fifteen broad. Did you ever lay eye on the real genuine Equator? Have you ever, in the largest sense , toed the Line? Well, that identical crater-shaped headland there, all yellow lava, is cut by the Equator exactly as a knife cuts straight through the centre of a pumpkin pie. If you could only see so far, just to one side of that same headland, across yon low dykey ground, you would catch sight of the isle of Narborough, the loftiest land of the cluster; no soil whatever; one seamed clinker from top to bottom; abounding in black caves like smithies;

its metallic shore ringing under foot like plates of iron; its central volcanoes standing grouped like a gigantic chimney-stack.

Narborough and Albemarle are neighbours after a quite curious fashion. A familiar diagram will illustrate this strange neighbourhood.

Cut a channel at the above letter joint, and the middle transverse limb is Narborough, and all the rest is Albemarle. Volcanic Narborough lies in the black jaws of Albemarle like a wolf's red tongue in his open mouth.

If now you desire the population of Albemarle, I will give you, in round numbers, the statistics, according to the most reliable estimates made upon the spot:

Men	none
Ant-eaters	unknown
Man-haters	unknown
Lizards	500,000
Snakes	500,000
Spiders	10,000,000
Salamanders	unknown
Devils	do.
Making a clean total of	11,000,000

exclusive of an incomputable host of fiends, ant-eaters, man-haters, and salamanders.

Albemarle opens his mouth towards the setting sun. His distended jaws form a great bay, which Narborough, his tongue divides into halves, one whereof is called Weather Bay, the other Lee Bay; while the volcanic promontories terminating his coasts are styled South Head and North Head. I note this, because these Bays are famous in the annals of the Sperm Whale Fishery. The whales come here at certain seasons to calve. When ships first cruised hereabouts, I am told, they used to blockade the entrance of Lee Bay, —when, their boats going round by Weather Bay, passed through Narborough channel,—and so had the Leviathans very neatly in a pen.

The day after we took fish at the base of this Round Tower, we had a fine wind, and, shooting round the north headland, suddenly descried a fleet of full thirty sail, all beating to windward like a squadron in line. A brave sight as ever man saw. A most harmonious concord of rushing keels. Their thirty kelsons hummed like thirty harp-strings, and looked as straight whilst they left their parallel traces on the sea. But there proved too many hunters for the game. The fleet looked up and went their separate ways out of sight, leaving my own ship and two trim gentlemen of London. These last, finding no luck either, likewise vanished; and Lee Bay, with all its appurtenances, and without a rival, devolved to us.

The way of cruising here is this. You keep hovering about the entrance of the bay, in one beat and out the next. But at times—not always, as in other parts of the group—a racehorse of a current sweeps right across its mouth. So, with all sails set, you carefully ply your tacks. How often, standing at the foremast head at sunrise, with our patient prow pointed in between these isles, did I gaze upon that land, not of cakes but of clinkers, not of streams of sparkling water, but arrested torrents of tormented lava.

As the ship runs in from the open sea, Narborough presents its side in one dark craggy mass, soaring up some five or six thousand feet, at which point it hoods itself in heavy clouds, whose lowest level fold is as clearly defined against the rocks, as the snow-line against the Andes. There is dire mischief going on in that upper dark. There toil the demons of fire, who at intervals irradiate the nights with a strange spectral illumination for miles and miles around, but unaccompanied by any further demonstration; or else, suddenly announce themselves by terrific concussions, and the full drama of a volcanic eruption. The blacker that cloud by day, the more may you look for light by night. Often whalemen have found themselves cruising nigh that burning mountain when all aglow with a ball-room blaze. Or, rather, glassworks, you may call this same vitreous isle of Narborough, with its tall chimney-stacks.

Where we still stand, here on Rodondo, we cannot see all the other isles, but it is a good place from which to point out where they lie. Yonder, though, to the E.N.E., I mark a distant dusky ridge. It is Abington Isle, one of the most northerly of the group; so solitary, remote, and blank, it looks like No-Man's Land seen off our northern shore. I doubt whether two human beings ever touched upon that spot. So far as yon Abington Isle is concerned, Adam and his billions of posterity remain uncreated.

Ranging south of Abington, and quite out of sight behind the long spire of Albemarle, lies James's Isle, so called by the early Buccaneers after the luckless Stuart, Duke of York. Observe here, by the way, that, excepting the isles particularized in comparatively recent times, and which mostly received the names of famous Admirals, the Encantadas were first christened by the Spaniards; but these Spanish names were generally effaced on English charts by the subsequent christenings of the Buccaneers, who, in the middle of the seventeenth century, called them after English noblemen and kings. Of these loyal freebooters and the things which associate their name with the Encantadas, we shall hear anon. Nay, for one little item, immediately; for between James's Isle and Albemarle, lies a fantastic islet, strangely known as "Cowley's Enchanted Isle." But as all the group is deemed enchanted, the reason must be given for the spell within a spell involved by this particular designation. The name was bestowed by that excellent Buccaneer himself, on his first visit here. Speaking in his published voyages of this spot, he says—"My fancy led me to call it Cowley's Enchanted Isle, for we having had a sight of it upon several points of the compass, it appeared always in so many different forms; sometimes like a ruined fortification; upon another point like a great city," etc. No wonder though, that among the Encantadas all sorts of ocular deceptions and mirages should be met.

That Cowley linked his name with this self-transforming and bemocking isle, suggests the possibility that it conveyed to him some meditative image of himself. At least, as is not impossible, if he were any relative of the mildly thoughtful, and self-upbraiding poet Cowley, who lived about his time, the conceit might seem unwarranted; for that sort of thing evinced in the naming of this isle runs in the blood, and may be seen in pirates as in poets.

Still south of James's Isle lie Jervis Isle, Duncan Isle, Crossman's Isle, Brattle Isle, Wood's Isle, Chatham Isle, and various lesser isles, for the most part an archipelago of aridities, without inhabitant, history, or hope of either in all time to come. But not far from these are rather notable isles —Barrington, Charles's, Norfolk, and Hood's. Succeeding chapters will reveal some ground for their notability.

Sketch Fifth

THE FRIGATE, AND SHIP "FLYAWAY"

"Looking far forth into the ocean wide,
A goodly ship with banners bravely dight,
And flag in her top-gallant I espide,
Through the main sea making her merry flight."

ERE quitting Rodondo, it must not be omitted that here, in 1813, the U.S. frigate *Essex*, Captain David Porter, came near leaving her bones. Lying becalmed one morning with a strong current setting her rapidly towards the rock, a strange sail was descried, which—not out of keeping with alleged enchantments of the neighbourhood—seemed to be staggering under a violent wind, while the frigate lay lifeless as if spell-bound. But a light air springing up, all sail was made by the frigate in chase of the enemy, as supposed —he being deemed an English whale-ship—but the rapidity of the current was so great, that soon all sight was lost of him; and at meridian the *Essex*, spite of her drags, was driven so close under the foam-lashed cliffs of Rodondo that for a time all hands gave her up. A smart breeze, however, at last helped her off, though the escape was so critical as to seem almost miraculous.

Thus saved from destruction herself, she now made use of that salvation to destroy the other vessel, if possible. Renewing the chase in the direction in which the stranger had disappeared, sight was caught of him the following morning. Upon being descried he hoisted American colours and stood away from the *Essex*. A calm ensued; when, still confident that the stranger was an Englishman, Porter despatched a cutter, not to board the enemy, but drive back his boats engaged in towing him. The cutter succeeded.

Cutters were subsequently sent to capture him; the stranger now showing English colours in place of American. But when the frigate's boats were within a short distance of their hoped-for prize, another sudden breeze sprang up; the stranger under all sail bore off to the westward, and ere night was hull down ahead of the *Essex,* which all this time lay perfectly becalmed.

This enigmatic craft—American in the morning, and English in the evening—her sails full of wind in a calm—was never again beheld. An enchanted ship no doubt. So at least the sailors swore.

This cruise of the *Essex* in the Pacific during the war of 1812, is perhaps the strangest and most stirring to be found in the history of the American navy. She captured the furthest wandering vessels; visited the remotest seas and isles; long hovered in the charmed vicinity of the enchanted group; and finally valiantly gave up the ghost fighting two English frigates in the harbour of Valparaiso. Mention is made of her here for the same reason that the Buccaneers will likewise receive record; because, like them, by long cruising among the isles, tortoise-hunting upon their shores, and generally exploring them; for these and other reasons, the *Essex* is peculiarly associated with the Encantadas.

Here be it said that you have but three eye-witness authorities worth mentioning touching the Enchanted Isles:—Cowley, the Buccaneer (1684); Colnet, the whaling-ground explorer (1798); Porter, the post captain (1813). Other than these you have but barren, bootless allusions from some few passing voyagers or compilers.

Sketch Sixth

BARRINGTON ISLE AND THE BUCCANEERS

> "Let us all servile base subjection scorn,
>   And as we be sons of the earth so wide,
>   Let us our father's heritage divide,
>   And challenge to ourselves our portions dew
>   Of all the patrimony, which a few
>   Now hold on hugger-mugger in their hand."
>
> .   .   .   .   .
>
> "Lords of the world, and so will wander free,
>   Where—so us listeth, uncontroll'd of any."
>
> .   .   .   .   .

"How brave now we live, how jocund, how near the first inheritance, without fear, how free from little troubles!"

NEAR two centuries ago Barrington Isle was the resort of that famous wing of the West Indian Buccaneers, which, upon their repulse from the Cuban waters, crossing the Isthmus of Darien, ravaged the Pacific side of the Spanish colonies, and, with the regularity and timing of a modern mail, waylaid the royal treasure ships plying between Manilla and Acapulco. After the toils of piratic war, here they came to say their prayers, enjoy their free-and-easies, count their crackers from the cask, their doubloons from the keg, and measure their silks of Asia with long Toledos for their yard-sticks.

As a secure retreat, an undiscoverable hiding place, no spot in those days could have been better fitted. In the centre of a vast and silent sea, but very little traversed; surrounded by islands, whose inhospitable aspect might well drive away the chance navigator; and yet within a few days' sail of the opulent countries which they made their prey;

the unmolested Buccaneers found here that tranquillity which they fiercely denied to every civilized harbour in that part of the world.   Here, after stress of weather, or a temporary drubbing at the hands of their vindictive foes, or in swift flight with golden booty, those old marauders came, and lay snugly out of all harm's reach.   But not only was the place a harbour of safety, and a bower of ease, but for utility in other things it was most admirable.

Barrington Isle is in many respects singularly adapted to careening, refitting, refreshing, and other seamen's purposes. Not only has it good water, and good anchorage, well sheltered from all winds by the high land of Albemarle, but it is the least unproductive isle of the group.   Tortoises good for food, trees good for fuel, and long grass good for bedding, abound here, and there are pretty natural walks, and several landscapes to be seen.   Indeed, though in its locality belonging to the Enchanted group, Barrington Isle is so unlike most of its neighbours that it would hardly seem of kin to them.

"I once landed on its western side," says a sentimental voyager long ago, "where it faces the black buttress of Albemarle.   I walked beneath groves of trees; not very lofty, and not palm trees, or orange trees, or peach trees, to be sure; but for all that, after long sea-faring very beautiful to walk under, even though they supplied no fruit. And here, in calm spaces at the heads of glades, and on the shaded tops of slopes commanding the most quiet scenery— what do you think I saw?   Seats which might have served Brahmins and presidents of peace societies.   Fine old ruins of what had once been symmetric lounges of stone and turf; they bore every mark both of artificialness and age, and were undoubtedly made by the Buccaneers.   One had been a long sofa, with back and arms, just such a sofa as the poet Gray might have loved to throw himself upon, his Crebillon in hand.

"Though they sometimes tarried here for months at a time, and used the spot for a storing-place for spare spars, sails, and casks; yet it is highly improbable that the buccaneers ever erected dwelling-houses upon the isle. They never were here except their ships remained, and they would most likely have slept on board. I mention this, because I cannot avoid the thought that it is hard to impute the construction of these romantic seats to any other motive than one of pure peacefulness and kindly fellowship with nature. That the buccaneers perpetrated the greatest outrages is very true; that some of them were mere cut-throats is not to be denied; but we know that here and there among their host was a Dampier, a Wafer, and a Cowley, and likewise other men, whose worst reproach was their desperate fortunes; whom persecution, or adversity, or secret and unavengeable wrongs, had driven from Christian society to seek the melancholy solitude or the guilty adventures of the sea. At any rate, long as those ruins of seats on Barrington remain, the most singular monuments are furnished to the fact, that all of the buccaneers were not unmitigated monsters.

"But during my ramble on the isle I was not long in discovering other tokens, of things quite in accordance with those wild traits, popularly—and no doubt truly enough—imputed to the freebooters at large. Had I picked up old sails and rusty hoops I would only have thought of the ship's carpenter and cooper. But I found old cutlasses and daggers reduced to mere threads of rust, which doubtless had stuck between Spanish ribs ere now. These were signs of the murderer and robber; the reveller likewise had left his trace. Mixed with shells, fragments of broken jars were lying here and there, high up upon the beach. They were precisely like the jars now used upon the Spanish coast for the wine and Pisco spirits of that country.

"With a rusty dagger-fragment in one hand, and a bit of a wine-jar in another, I sat me down on the ruinous green sofa I have spoken of, and bethought me long and deeply of these same buccaneers. Could it be possible, that they robbed and murdered one day, revelled the next, and rested themselves by turning meditative philosophers, rural poets, and seat-builders on the third? Not very improbable, after all. For consider the vacillations of a man. Still, strange as it may seem, I must also abide by the more charitable thought; namely, that among these adventurers were some gentlemanly, companionable souls, capable of genuine tranquillity and virtue."

Sketch Seventh

CHARLES'S ISLE AND THE DOG-KING

————————*So with outragious cry,*
A thousand villeins round about him swarmed
Out of the rocks and caves adjoining nye;
Vile caitive wretches, ragged, rude, deformed;
All threatening death, all in straunge manner armed;
Some with unweldy clubs, some with long speares,
Some rusty knives, some staves in fier warmd.

*   *   *   *   *

We will not be of any occupation,
Let such vile vassals, born to base vocation,
Drudge in the world, and for their living droyle,
Which have no wit to live withouten toyle.

SOUTHWEST of Barrington lies Charles's Isle. And hereby hangs a history which I gathered long ago from a shipmate learned in all the lore of outlandish life.

During the successful revolt of the Spanish provinces from Old Spain, there fought on behalf of Peru a certain Creole adventurer from Cuba, who by his bravery and good fortune at length advanced himself to high rank in the patriot army. The war being ended, Peru found herself —like many valorous gentlemen—free and independent enough, but with few shot in the locker. In other words, she had not wherewithal to pay off her troops. But the Creole—I forget his name—volunteered to take his pay in lands. So they told him he might have his pick of the Enchanted Isles, which were then, as they still remain, the nominal appanage of Peru. The soldier straightway embarks thither, explores the group, returns to Callao, and says he will take a deed of Charles's Isle. Moreover, this deed must stipulate that thenceforth said Charles's Isle is not only the sole property of the Creole, but is forever free of Peru, even as Peru of Spain. To be short, this adventurer procures himself to be made in effect Supreme Lord of the Island, one of the princes of the powers of the earth.*

He now sends forth a proclamation inviting subjects to his as yet unpopulated kingdom. Some eighty souls, men and women, respond; and being provided by their leader with necessaries, and tools of various sorts, together with a few cattle and goats, take ship for the promised land; the last arrival on board, prior to sailing, being the Creole himself, accompanied, strange to say, by a disciplined cavalry company of large grim dogs. These, it was observed on the passage, refusing to consort with the emigrants, remained aristocratically grouped around their master on the elevated

* The American Spaniards have long been in the habit of making presents of islands to deserving individuals. The pilot Juan Fernandes procured a deed of the isle named after him, and for some years resided there before Selkirk came. It is supposed, however, that he eventually contracted the blues upon his princely property, for after a time he returned to the main, and as report goes, became a very garrulous barber in the city of Lima.

quarter-deck, casting disdainful glances forward upon the inferior rabble there; much as from the ramparts, the soldiers of a garrison thrown into a conquered town, eye the inglorious citizen-mob over which they are set to watch.

Now Charles's Isle not only resembles Barrington Isle in being much more inhabitable than other parts of the group, but it is double the size of Barrington; say forty or fifty miles in circuit.

Safely debarked at last, the company, under direction of their lord and patron, forthwith proceeded to build their capital city. They make considerable advance in the way of walls of clinkers, and lava floors, nicely sanded with cinders. On the least barren hills they pasture their cattle, while the goats, those adventurers by nature, explore the far inland solitudes for a scanty livelihood of lofty herbage. Meantime, abundance of fish and an inexhaustible tribe of tortoises, supply the adventurer's other wants.

The disorders incident to settling all primitive regions, in the present case were heightened by the peculiarly untoward character of many of the pilgrims. His Majesty was forced at last to proclaim martial law, and actually hunted and shot with his own hand several of his rebellious subjects, who, with most questionable intentions, had clandestinely encamped in the interior; whence they stole by night, to prowl barefooted on tiptoe round the precincts of the lava-palace. It is to be remarked, however, that prior to such stern proceedings, the more reliable men had been judiciously picked out for an infantry body-guard, subordinate to the cavalry body-guard of dogs. But the state of politics in this unhappy nation may be somewhat imagined from the circumstance that all who were not of the body-guard were downright plotters and malignant traitors. At length the death penalty was tacitly abolished, owing to the timely thought, that were strict sportsman's justice to be dispensed among such subjects, ere long the Nimrod King would have little or no remaining game to shoot. The human part of the life-guard was now disbanded, and set to work cultivating the soil, and raising potatoes; the regular army now solely consisting of the dog-regiment. These, as I have heard, were of a singularly ferocious character, though by severe training rendered docile to their master. Armed to the teeth, the Creole now goes in state, surrounded by his canine janizaries, whose terrific bayings prove quite as serviceable as bayonets in keeping down the surgings of revolt.

But the census of the isle, sadly lessened by the dispensation of justice, and not materially recruited by matrimony, began to fill his mind with sad mistrust. In some way the population must be increased. Now, from its possessing a little water, and its comparative pleasantness of aspect, Charles's Isle at this period was occasionally visited by foreign whalers. These His Majesty had always levied upon for port charges, thereby contributing to his revenue. But now he had additional designs. By insidious arts he, from time to time, cajoles sailors to desert their ships and enlist beneath his banner. Soon as missed, their captains crave permission to go and hunt them up. Whereupon His Majesty first hides them very carefully away, and then freely permits the search. In consequence, the delinquents are never found, and the ships retire without them.

Thus, by a two-edged policy of this crafty monarch, foreign nations were crippled in the number of their subjects, and his own greatly multiplied. He then particularly petted these renegado strangers. But alas for the deep-laid schemes of ambitious princes, and alas for the vanity of glory. As the foreign-born Pretorians of the Roman state, unwisely introduced into the commonwealth, and still more

unwisely made favourites of the Emperors, at last insulted
and overturned the throne, even so these lawless mariners,
with all the rest of the body-guard and all the populace,
broke out into a terrible mutiny, and defied their master. He
marched against them with all his dogs. A deadly battle
ensued upon the beach. It raged for three hours, the dogs
fighting with determined valour, and the sailors reckless
of everything but victory. Three men and thirteen dogs
were left dead upon the field, many on both sides were
wounded, and the king was forced to fly with the remainder
of his canine regiment. The enemy pursued, stoning the
dogs with their master into the wilderness of the interior.
Discontinuing the pursuit, the victors returned to the village
on the shore, stove the spirit-casks, and proclaimed a Republic. The dead men were interred with the honours of war,
and the dead dogs ignominiously thrown into the sea. At
last, forced by stress of suffering, the fugitive Creole came
down from the hills and offered to treat for peace. But
the rebels refused it on any other terms than his uncondi-
tional banishment. Accordingly, the next ship that arrived
carried away the ex-king to Peru.

The history of the king of Charles's Island furnishes another illustration of the difficulty of colonizing barren islands
with unprincipled pilgrims.

Doubtless for a long time the exiled monarch, pensively
ruralizing in Peru, which afforded him a safe asylum in his
calamity, watched every arrival from the Encantadas, to
hear news of the failure of the Republic, the consequent
penitence of the rebels, and his own recall to royalty. Doubtless he deemed the Republic but a miserable experiment
which would soon explode. But no, the insurgents had now
confederated themselves into a democracy neither Grecian,
Roman, nor American. Nay, it was no democracy at all,

but a permanent *Riotocracy,* which gloried in having no law
but lawlessness. Great inducements being offered to deserters,
their ranks were swelled by accessions of scamps from every
ship which touched their shores. Charles's Island was proclaimed the asylum of the oppressed of all navies. Each
runaway tar was hailed as a martyr in the cause of freedom,
and became immediately installed a ragged citizen of this
universal nation. In vain the captains of absconding seamen strove to regain them. Their new compatriots were
ready to give any number of ornamental eyes in their behalf.
They had few cannon, but their fists were not to be trifled
with. So, at last, it came to pass that no vessels acquainted
with the character of that country durst touch there, however sorely in want of refreshment. It became Anathema—
a sea Alsatia—the unassailed lurking-place of all sorts of
desperadoes, who in the name of liberty did just what they
pleased. They continually fluctuated in their numbers.
Sailors deserting ships at other islands—or in boats at sea
anywhere in that vicinity—steered for Charles's Isle as to
their sure home of refuge; while sated with the life of the
isle, numbers from time to time crossed the water to the
neighbouring ones, and there presenting themselves to
strange captains as shipwrecked seamen, often succeeded in
getting on board vessels bound to the Spanish coast; and
having a compassionate purse made up for them on landing
there.

One warm night during my first visit to the group, our
ship was floating along the languid stillness, when some one
on the forecastle shouted "Light ho!" We looked and saw
a beacon burning on some obscure land off the beam. Our
third mate was not intimate with this part of the world.
Going to the captain he said, "Sir, shall I put off in a boat?
These must be shipwrecked men."

The captain laughed rather grimly, as, shaking his fist towards the beacon, he rapped out an oath and said—"No, no, you precious rascals, you don't juggle one of my boats ashore this blessed night. You do well, you thieves—you do benevolently to hoist a light yonder as on a dangerous shoal. It tempts no wise man to pull off and see what's the matter, but bids him steer small and keep off shore— that is, Charles's Island; brace up, Mr. Mate, and keep the light astern."

Sketch Eighth

NORFOLK ISLE AND THE CHOLA WIDOW

> *"At last they in a island did espy*
> *A seemly woman sitting by the shore,*
> *That with great sorrow and sad agony*
> *Seemed some great misfortune to deplore,*
> *And loud to them for succor called evermore."*

> *"Black his eyes as the midnight sky,*
> *White his neck as the driven snow,*
> *Red his cheek as the morning light;—*
> *Cold he lies in the ground below.*
> *My love is dead,*
> *Gone to his death-bed,*
> *All under the cactus tree."*

FAR to the northeast of Charles's Isle, sequestered from the rest, lies Norfolk Isle; and, however insignificant to most voyagers, to me, through sympathy, that lone island has become a spot made sacred by the strongest trials of humanity.

It was my first visit to the Encantadas. Two days had been spent ashore in hunting tortoises. There was not time to capture many; so on the third afternoon we loosed our sails. We were just in the act of getting under way, the uprooted anchor yet suspended and invisibly swaying beneath the wave, as the good ship gradually turned her heel to leave the isle behind, when the seaman who heaved with me at the windlass paused suddenly, and directed my attention to something moving on the land, not along the beach, but somewhat back, fluttering from a height.

In view of the sequel of this little story, be it here narrated how it came to pass, that an object which partly from its being so small was quite lost to every other man on board, still caught the eye of my handspike companion. The rest of the crew, myself included, merely stood up to our spikes in heaving; whereas, unwontedly exhilarated at every turn of the ponderous windlass, my belted comrade leaped atop of it, with might and main giving a downward, thewey, perpendicular heave, his raised eye bent in cheery animation upon the slowly receding shore. Being high lifted above all others was the reason he perceived the object, otherwise unperceivable: and this elevation of his eye was owing to the elevation of his spirits; and this again—for truth must out—to a dram of Peruvian pisco, in guerdon for some kindness done, secretly administered to him that morning by our mulatto steward. Now, certainly, pisco does a deal of mischief in the world; yet seeing that, in the present case, it was the means, though indirect, of rescuing a human being from the most dreadful fate, must we not also needs admit that sometimes pisco does a deal of good?

Glancing across the water in the direction pointed out, I saw some white thing hanging from an inland rock, perhaps half a mile from the sea.

"It is a bird; a white-winged bird; perhaps a—no; it is—it is a handkerchief!"

"Aye, a handkerchief!" echoed my comrade, and with a louder shout apprised the captain.

Quickly now—like the running out and training of a great gun—the long cabin spy-glass was thrust through the mizzen rigging from the high platform of the poop; whereupon a human figure was plainly seen upon the inland rock, eagerly waving towards us what seemed to be the handkerchief.

Our captain was a prompt, good fellow. Dropping the glass, he lustily ran forward, ordering the anchor to be dropped again; hands to stand by a boat, and lower away.

In a half-hour's time the swift boat returned. It went with six and came with seven; and the seventh was a woman.

It is not artistic heartlessness, but I wish I could but draw in crayons; for this woman was a most touching sight; and crayons, tracing softly melancholy lines, would best depict the mournful image of the dark-damasked Chola widow.

Her story was soon told, and though given in her own strange language was as quickly understood, for our captain from long trading on the Chilian coast was well versed in the Spanish. A *cholo*, or half-breed Indian woman of Payta in Peru, three years gone by, with her young new-wedded husband Felipe, of pure Castilian blood, and her one only Indian brother, Truxill, Hunilla had taken passage on the main in a French whaler, commanded by a joyous man; which vessel, bound to the cruising grounds beyond the Enchanted Isles, proposed passing close by their vicinity. The object of the little party was to procure tortoise oil, a fluid which for its great purity and delicacy is held in high estimation wherever known; and it is well known all along this part of the Pacific coast. With a chest of clothes, tools, cooking utensils, a rude apparatus for trying out the oil, some casks of biscuit, and other things, not omitting two favourite dogs, of which faithful animal all the Cholos are very fond, Hunilla and her companions were safely landed at their chosen place; the Frenchman, according to the contract made ere sailing, engaged to take them off upon returning from a four months' cruise in the westward seas; which interval the three adventurers deemed quite sufficient for their purposes.

On the isle's lone beach they paid him in silver for their passage out, the stranger having declined to carry them at all except upon that condition; though willing to take every means to insure the due fulfilment of his promise. Felipe had striven hard to have this payment put off to the period of the ship's return. But in vain. Still, they thought they had, in another way, ample pledge of the good faith of the Frenchman. It was arranged that the expenses of the passage home should not be payable in silver, but in tortoises; one hundred tortoises ready captured to the returning captain's hand. These the Cholos meant to secure after their own work was done, against the probable time of the Frenchman's coming back; and no doubt in prospect already felt, that in those hundred tortoises—now somewhere ranging in the isle's interior—they possessed one hundred hostages. Enough: the vessel sailed; the gazing three on shore answered the loud glee of the singing crew; and ere evening, the French craft was hull down in the distant sea, its masts three faintest lines which quickly faded from Hunilla's eye.

The stranger had given a blithesome promise, and had anchored it with oaths; but oaths and anchors equally will drag; nought else abides on fickle earth but unkept promises of joy. Contrary winds from out unstabled skies, or contrary moods of his more varying mind, or shipwreck and sudden death in solitary waves; whatever was the cause, the blithe stranger never was seen again.

Yet, however dire a calamity was here in store, misgivings of it ere due time never disturbed the Cholos's busy mind, now all intent upon the toilsome matter which had brought them hither. Nay, by swift doom coming like the thief at night, ere seven weeks went by, two of the little party were removed from all anxieties of land or sea. No more they sought to gaze with feverish fear, or still more feverish hope, beyond the present's horizon line; but into the furthest future their own silent spirits sailed. By persevering labour beneath that burning sun, Felipe and Truxill had brought down to their hut many scores of tortoises, and tried out the oil, when, elated with their good success, and to reward themselves for such hard work, they, too hastily, made a catamaran, or Indian raft, much used on the Spanish main, and merrily started a fishing trip just without a long reef with many jagged gaps, running parallel with the shore, about half a mile from it. By some bad tide or hap—or natural negligence of joyfulness (for though they could not be heard, yet by their gestures they seemed singing at the time), forced in deep water against that iron bar—the ill-made catamaran was overset, and came all to pieces; when, dashed by broad-chested swells between their broken logs and the sharp teeth of the reef, both adventurers perished before Hunilla's eyes.

Before Hunilla's eyes they sank. The real woe of this event passed before her sight as some sham tragedy on the stage. She was seated on a rude bower among the withered thickets, crowning a lofty cliff, a little back from the beach. The thickets were so disposed, that in looking upon the sea at large she peered out from among the branches as from the lattice of a high balcony. But, upon the day we speak of here, the better to watch the adventure of those two hearts she loved, Hunilla had withdrawn the branches to one side and held them so. They formed an oval frame through which the bluey boundless sea rolled like a painted one. And

there, the invisible painter painted to her view the wave-
tossed and disjointed raft, its once level logs slantingly up-
heaved, as raking masts, and the four struggling arms undis-
tinguishable among them; and then all subsided into smooth-
flowing creamy waters, slowly drifting the splintered wreck;
while first and last, no sound of any sort was heard. Death
in a silent picture; a dream of the eye; such vanishing shapes
as the mirage shows.

So instant was the scene, so trance-like its mild pictorial
effect, so distant from her blasted tower and her common
sense of things, that Hunilla gazed and gazed, nor raised
a finger or a wail. But as good to sit thus dumb, in stupor
staring on that dumb show, for all that otherwise might be
done. With half a mile of sea between, could her two enchanted arms aid those four fated ones? The distance long,
the time one sand. After the lightning is beheld, what fool
shall ever stay the thunderbolt? Felipe's body was washed
ashore, but Truxill's never came; only his gay, braided hat
of golden straw—that same sunflower thing he waved to
her, pushing from the strand—and now, to the last gallant,
it still saluted her. But Felipe's body floated to the marge,
with one arm encirclingly outstretched. Lock-jawed in grim
death, the lover-husband softly clasped his bride—true to
her even in death's dream. Ah, Heaven, when man thus
keeps his faith, wilt thou be faithless who created the faithful one? But they cannot break faith who never plighted it.

It needs not to be said what nameless misery now wrapped
the lonely widow. In telling her own story she passed this
almost entirely over, simply recounting the event. Construe
the comment of her features as you might; from her mere
words little would you have weened that Hunilla was herself the heroine of her tale. But not thus did she defraud
us of our tears. All hearts bled that grief could be so brave.

She but showed us her soul's lid, and the strange ciphers thereon engraved; all within, with pride's timidity, was withheld. Yet was there one exception. Holding out her small olive hand before our captain, she said in mild and slowest Spanish, "Señor, I buried him;" then paused, struggled as against the writhed coilings of a snake, and cringing suddenly, leaped up, repeating in impassioned pain, "I buried him, my life, my soul!"

Doubtless it was by half-unconscious, automatic motions of her hands, that this heavy-hearted one performed the final offices for Felipe, and planted a rude cross of withered sticks—no green ones might be had—at the head of that lonely grave, where rested now in lasting uncomplaint and quiet haven he whom untranquil seas had overthrown.

But some dull sense of another body that should be interred, of another cross that should hallow another grave—unmade as yet; some dull anxiety and pain touching her undiscovered brother now haunted the oppressed Hunilla. Her hands fresh from the burial earth, she slowly went back to the beach, with unshaped purposes wandered there, her spellbound eye bent upon the incessant waves. But they bore nothing to her but a dirge, which maddened her to think that murderers should mourn. As time went by, and these things came less dreamingly to her mind, the strong persuasions of her Romish faith, which sets peculiar store by consecrated urns, prompted her to resume in waking earnest that pious search which had but been begun as in somnambulism. Day after day, week after week, she trod the cindery beach, till at length a double motive edged every eager glance. With equal longing she now looked for the living and the dead; the brother and the captain; alike vanished, never to return. Little accurate note of time had Hunilla taken under such emotions as were hers, and little,

outside herself, served for calendar or dial. As to poor
Crusoe in the self-same sea, no saint's bell pealed forth the
lapse of week or month; each day went by unchallenged; no
chanticleer announced those sultry dawns, no lowing herds
those poisonous nights. All wonted and steadily recurring
sounds, human or humanized by sweet fellowship with man,
but one stirred that torrid trance,—the cry of dogs; save
which nought but the rolling sea invaded it, an all pervading
monotone; and to the widow that was the least loved voice
she could have heard.

No wonder that as her thoughts now wandered to the
unreturning ship, and were beaten back again, the hope
against hope so struggled in her soul, that at length she
desperately said, "Not yet, not yet; my foolish heart runs
on too fast." She she forced patience for some further
weeks. But to those whom earth's sure indraft draws, patience or impatience is still the same.

Hunilla now sought to settle precisely in her mind, to
an hour, how long it was since the ship had sailed; and
then, with the same precision, how long a space remained
to pass. But this proved impossible. What present day or
month it was she could not say. Time was her labyrinth,
in which Hunilla was entirely lost.

And now follows—

Against my own purposes a pause descends upon me here.
One knows not whether nature doth not impose some secrecy
upon him who has been privy to certain things. At least,
it is to be doubted whether it be good to blazon such. If
some books are deemed most baneful and their sale forbid,
how then with deadlier facts, not dreams of doting men?
Those whom books will hurt will not be proof against events.
Events, not books, should be forbid. But in all things man
sows upon the wind, which bloweth just there whither it

listeth; for ill or good man cannot know. Often ill comes from the good, as good from ill.

When Hunilla—

Dire sight it is to see some silken beast long dally with a golden lizard ere she devour. More terrible, to see how feline Fate will sometimes dally with a human soul, and by a nameless magic make it repulse one sane despair with another which is but mad. Unwittingly I imp this cat-like thing, sporting with the heart of him who reads; for if he feel not, he does read in vain.

—"The ship sails this day, to-day," at last said Hunilla to herself; "this gives me certain time to stand on; without certainty I go mad. In loose ignorance I have hoped and hoped; now in firm knowledge I will but wait. Now I live and no longer perish in bewilderings. Holy Virgin, aid me! Thou wilt waft back the ship. Oh, past length of weary weeks—all to be dragged over—to buy the certainty of to-day, I freely give ye, though I tear ye from me!"

As mariners tossed in tempest on some desolate ledge patch them a boat out of the remnants of their vessel's wreck, and launch it in the self-same waves—see here Hunilla, this lone shipwrecked soul, out of treachery invoking trust. Humanity, thou strong thing. I worship thee, not in the laurelled victor, but in this vanquished one.

Truly, Hunilla leaned upon a reed, a real one; no metaphor; a real Eastern reed. A piece of hollow cane, drifted from unknown isles, and found upon the beach, its once jagged ends rubbed smoothly even as by sand-paper; its golden glazing gone. Long ground between the sea and land, upper and nether stone, the unvarnished substance was filed bare, and wore another polish now, one with itself, the polish of its agony. Circular lines at intervals cut all round this surface, divided it into six panels of unequal length. In the first were scored the days, each tenth one marked by a longer and deeper notch; the second was scored for the number of sea-fowl eggs for sustenance, picked out from the rocky nests; the third, how many fish had been caught from the shore; the fourth, how many small tortoises found inland; the fifth, how many days of sun; the sixth, of clouds; which last, of the two, was the greater one. Long night of busy numbering, misery's mathematics, to weary her too-wakeful soul to sleep; yet sleep for that was none.

The panel of the days was deeply worn, the long tenth notches half effaced, as alphabets of the blind. Ten thousand times the longing widow had traced her finger over the bamboo—dull flute, which played on, gave no sound—as if counting birds flown by in air, would hasten tortoises creeping through the woods.

After the one hundred and eightieth day no further mark was seen; that last one was the faintest, as the first the deepest.

"There were more days," said our Captain; "many, many more; why did you not go on and notch them too, Hunilla?"

"Señor, ask me not."

"And meantime, did no other vessel pass the isle?"

"Nay, Señor;—but—"

"You do not speak; but *what*, Hunilla?"

"Ask me not, Señor."

"You saw ships pass, far away; you waved to them; they passed on;—was that it, Hunilla?"

"Señor, be it as you say."

Braced against her woe, Hunilla would not—durst not—trust the weakness of her tongue. Then when our Captain asked whether any whale-boats had——

But no, I will not file this thing complete for scoffing souls to quote, and call it firm proof upon their side. The half shall here remain untold. Those two unnamed events which befell Hunilla on this isle, let them abide between her and her God. In nature, as in law, it may be libellous to speak some truths.

Still, how it was that, although our vessel had lain three days anchored nigh the isle, its one human tenant should not have discovered us till just upon the point of sailing, never to revisit so lone and far a spot; this needs explaining ere the sequel come.

The place where the French captain had landed the little party was on the farther and opposite end of the isle. There too it was that they had afterwards built their hut. Nor did the widow in her solitude desert the spot where her loved ones had dwelt with her, and where the dearest of the twain now slept his last long sleep, and all her plaints awaked him not, and he of husbands the most faithful during life.

Now, high broken land rises between the opposite extremities of the isle. A ship anchored at one side is invisible from the other. Neither is the isle so small but a considerable company might wander for days through the wilderness of one side, and never be seen, or their halloos heard, by any stranger holding aloof on the other. Hence Hunilla, who naturally associated the possible coming of ships with her own part of the isle, might to the end have remained quite ignorant of the presence of our vessel, were it not for a mysterious presentiment, borne to her, so our mariners averred, by this isle's enchanted air. Nor did the widow's answer undo the thought.

"How did you come to cross the isle this morning then, Hunilla?" said our Captain.

"Señor, something came flitting by me. It touched my cheek, my heart, Señor."

"What do you say, Hunilla?"

"I have said, Señor; something came through the air."

It was a narrow chance. For when in crossing the isle Hunilla gained the high land in the centre, she must then for the first have perceived our masts, and also marked that their sails were being loosed, perhaps even heard the echoing chorus of the windlass song. The strange ship was about to sail, and she behind. With all haste she now descends the height on the hither side, but soon loses sight of the ship among the sunken jungles at the mountain's base. She struggles on through the withered branches, which seek at every step to bar her path, till she comes to the isolated rock, still some way from the water. This she climbs, to re-assure herself. The ship is still in plainest sight. But now, worn out with over tension, Hunilla all but faints; she fears to step down from her giddy perch; she is feign to pause, there where she is, and as a last resort catches the turban from her head, unfurls and waves it over the jungles towards us.

During the telling of her story the mariners formed a voiceless circle round Hunilla and the Captain; and when at length the word was given to man the fastest boat, and pull round to the isle's thither side, to bring away Hunilla's chest and the tortoise-oil—such alacrity of both cheery and sad obedience seldom before was seen. Little ado was made. Already the anchor had been recommitted to the bottom and the ship swung calmly to it.

But Hunilla insisted upon accompanying the boat as indis-pensable pilot to her hidden hut. So, being refreshed with the best the steward could supply, she started with us. Nor did ever any wife of the most famous admiral in her hus-band's barge receive more silent reverence of respect, than poor Hunilla from this boat's crew.

Rounding many a vitreous cape and bluff, in two hours' time we shot inside the fatal reef; wound into a secret cove, looked up along a green many-gabled lava wall, and saw the island's solitary dwelling.

It hung upon an impending cliff, sheltered on two sides by tangled thickets, and half-screened from view in front by juttings of the rude stairway, which climbed the precipice from the sea. Built of canes, it was thatched with long, mildewed grass. It seemed an abandoned hayrick, whose haymakers were now no more. The roof inclined but one way; the eaves coming to within two feet of the ground. And here was a simple apparatus to collect the dews, or rather doubly-distilled and finest winnowed rains, which, in mercy or in mockery, the night skies sometimes drop upon these blighted Encantadas. All along beneath the eave, a spotted sheet, quite weather-stained, was spread, pinned to short, upright stakes, set in the shallow sand. A small clinker, thrown into the cloth, weighed its middle down, thereby straining all moisture into a calabash placed below. This vessel supplied each drop of water ever drunk upon the isle by the Cholos. Hunilla told us the calabash would sometimes, but not often, be half filled over-night. It held six quarts, perhaps. "But," said she, "we were used to thirst. At Sandy Payta, where I live, no shower from heaven ever fell; all the water there is brought on mules from the inland vales."

Tied among the thickets were some twenty moaning tortoises, supplying Hunilla's lonely larder; while hundreds of vast tableted black bucklers, like displaced, shattered tombstones of dark slate, were also scattered round. These were the skeleton backs of those great tortoises from which Felipe and Truxill had made their precious oil. Several large calabashes and two goodly kegs were filled with it. In a pot near by were the caked crusts of a quantity which had been permitted to evaporate. "They meant to have strained it off next day," said Hunilla, as she turned aside.

I forgot to mention the most singular sight of all, though the first that greeted us after landing; memory keeps not in all things to the order of occurrence.

Some ten small, soft-haired, ringleted dogs, of a beautiful breed, peculiar to Peru, set up a concert of glad welcomings when we gained the beach, which was responded to by Hunilla. Some of these dogs had, since her widowhood, been born upon the isle, the progeny of the two brought from Payta. Owing to the jagged steeps and pitfalls, tortuous thickets, sunken clefts and perilous intricacies of all sorts in the interior, Hunilla, admonished by the loss of one favourite among them, never allowed these delicate creatures to follow her in her occasional bird's-nests climbs and other wanderings; so that, through long habituation, they offered not to follow, when that morning she crossed the land; and her own soul was then too full of other things to heed their lingering behind. Yet, all along she had so clung to them, that, besides what moisture they lapped up at early daybreak from the small scoop-holes among the adjacent rocks, she had shared the dew of her calabash among them; never laying by any considerable store against those prolonged and utter droughts, which in some disastrous seasons warp these isles.

Having pointed out, at our desire, what few things she would like transported to the ship—her chest, the oil, not omitting the live tortoises which she intended for a grateful present to our Captain—we immediately set to work, carrying them to the boat down the long, sloping stair of deeply-shadowed rock. While my comrades were thus employed, I looked, and Hunilla had disappeared.

It was not curiosity alone, but, it seems to me, something

different mingled with it, which prompted me to drop my tortoises and once more gaze slowly around. I remembered the husband buried by Hunilla's hands. A narrow pathway led into a dense part of the thickets. Following it through many mazes, I came out upon a small, round, open space, deeply chambered there.

The mound rose in the middle; a bare heap of finest sand, like that unverdured heap found at the bottom of an hourglass run out. At its head stood the cross of withered sticks; the dry, peeled bark still fraying from it; its transverse limb tied up with rope, and forlornly adroop in the silent air.

Hunilla was partly prostrate upon the grave; her dark head bowed, and lost in her long, loosened Indian hair; her hands extended to the cross-foot, with a little brass crucifix clasped between; a crucifix worn featureless, like an ancient graven knocker long plied in vain. She did not see me, and I made no noise but slid aside and left the spot.

A few moments, ere all was ready for our going, she reappeared among us. I looked into her eyes, but saw no tear. There was something which seemed strangely haughty in her air, and yet it was the air of woe. A Spanish and an Indian grief, which would not visibly lament. Pride's height in vain abased to proneness on the rock; nature's pride subduing nature's torture.

Like pages the small and silken dogs surrounded her, as she slowly descended towards the beach. She caught the two most eager creatures in her arms:—"Mia Teeta! Mia Tomoteeta!" and fondling them, inquired how many could we take on board.

The mate commanded the boat's crew; not a hard-hearted man, but his way of life had been such that in most things, even in the smallest, simple utility was his leading motive.

"We cannot take them all, Hunilla; our supplies are

short; the winds are unreliable; we may be a good many days going to Tombez. So take those you have, Hunilla; but no more."

She was in the boat; the oarsmen too were seated; all save one, who stood ready to push off and then spring himself. With the sagacity of their race, the dogs now seemed aware that they were in the very instant of being deserted upon a barren strand. The gunwales of the boat were high; its prow—presented inland—was lifted; so, owing to the water, which they seemed instinctively to shun, the dogs could not well leap into the little craft. But their busy paws hard scraped the prow, as it had been some farmer's door shutting them out from shelter in a winter storm. A clamorous agony of alarm. They did not howl, or whine; they all but spoke.

"Push off! Give way!" cried the mate. The boat gave one heavy drag and lurch, and next moment shot swiftly from the beach, turned on her heel, and sped. The dogs ran howling along the water's marge; now pausing to gaze at the flying boat, then motioning as if to leap in chase, but mysteriously withheld themselves; and again ran howling along the beach. Had they been human beings hardly would they have more vividly inspired the sense of desolation. The oars were plied as confederate feathers of two wings. No one spoke. I looked back upon the beach, and then upon Hunilla, but her face was set in a stern dusky calm. The dogs crouching in her lap vainly licked her rigid hands. She never looked behind her; but sat motionless, till we turned a promontory of the coast and lost all sights and sounds astern. She seemed as one who, having experienced the sharpest of mortal pangs, was henceforth content to have all lesser heartstrings riven, one by one. To Hunilla, pain seemed so necessary, that pain in other beings—though by love and sympathy made her own—was unrepiningly to be borne. A heart of yearning in a frame of steel. A heart of earthly yearning, frozen by the frost which falleth from the sky.

The sequel is soon told. After a long passage, vexed by calms and baffling winds, we made the little port of Tombez in Peru, there to recruit the ship. Payta was not very distant. Our captain sold the tortoise oil to a Tombez merchant; and adding to the silver a contribution from all hands, gave it to our silent passenger, who knew not what the mariners had done.

The last seen of lone Hunilla she was passing into Payta town, riding upon a small gray ass; and before her on the ass's shoulders, she eyed the jointed workings of the beast's armorial cross.

Sketch Ninth

HOOD'S ISLE AND THE HERMIT OBERLUS

> *"That darkesome glen they enter, where they find*
> *That cursed man low sitting on the ground,*
> *Musing full sadly in his sullein mind;*
> *His griesly lockes long grouen and unbound,*
> *Disordered hong about his shoulders round,*
> *And hid his face, through which his hollow eyne*
> *Lookt deadly dull, and stared as astound;*
> *His raw-bone cheekes, through penurie and pine,*
> *Were shronke into the jawes, as he did never dine.*
> *His garments nought but many ragged clouts,*
> *With thornes together pind and patched reads,*
> *The which his naked sides he wrapt abouts."*

To southeast of Crossman's Isle lies Hood's Isle, or McCain's Beclouded Isle; and upon its south side is a vitreous cove with a wide strand of dark pounded black lava, called Black Beach, or Oberlus's Landing. It might fitly have been styled Charon's.

It received its name from a wild white creature who spent many years here; in the person of a European bringing into this savage region qualities more diabolical than are to be found among any of the surrounding cannibals.

About half a century ago, Oberlus deserted at the above-named island, then, as now, a solitude. He built himself a den of lava and clinkers, about a mile from the Landing, subsequently called after him, in a vale, or expanded gulch, containing here and there among the rocks about two acres of soil capable of rude cultivation; the only place on the isle not too blasted for that purpose. Here he succeeded in raising a sort of degenerate potatoes and pumpkins, which from time to time he exchanged with needy whalemen passing, for spirits or dollars.

His appearance, from all accounts, was that of the victim of some malignant sorceress; he seemed to have drunk of Circe's cup; beast-like; rags insufficient to hide his nakedness; his befreckled skin blistered by continual exposure to the sun; nose flat; countenance contorted, heavy, earthy; hair and beard unshorn, profuse, and of a fiery red. He struck strangers much as if he were a volcanic creature thrown up by the same convulsion which exploded into sight the isle. All bepatched and coiled asleep in his lonely lava den among the mountains, he looked, they say, as a heaped drift of withered leaves, torn from autumn trees, and so left in some hidden nook by the whirling halt for an instant of a fierce night-wind, which then ruthlessly sweeps on, some-were else to repeat the capricious act. It is also reported to have been the strangest sight, this same Oberlus, of a sultry, cloudy morning, hidden under his shocking old black tar-paulin hat, hoeing potatoes among the lava. So warped and crooked was his strange nature, that the very handle of his hoe seemed gradually to have shrunk and twisted in his grasp, being a wretched bent stick, elbowed more like a savage's war-sickle than a civilized hoe-handle. It was his mysterious custom upon a first encounter with a stranger ever to present his back; possibly, because that was his better side, since it revealed the least. If the encounter chanced in his garden, as it sometimes did—the new-landed strangers going from the sea-side straight through the gorge, to hunt up the queer green-grocer reported doing business here— Oberlus for a time hoed on, unmindful of all greeting, jovial or bland; as the curious stranger would turn to face him, the recluse, hoe in hand, as diligently would avert himself; bowed over, and sullenly revolving round his murphy hill. Thus far for hoeing. When planting, his whole aspect and all his gestures were so malevolently and uselessly sinister and secret, that he seemed rather in act of dropping poison into wells than potatoes into soil. But among his lesser and more harmless marvels was an idea he ever had, that his visitors came equally as well led by longings to behold the mighty hermit Oberlus in his royal state of solitude, as simply to obtain potatoes, or find whatever company might be upon a barren isle. It seems incredible that such a being should possess such vanity; a misanthrope be conceited; but he really had his notion; and upon the strength of it, often gave himself amusing airs to captains. But after all, this is somewhat of a piece with the well-known eccentricity of some convicts, proud of that very hatefulness which makes them notorious. At other times, another unaccountable whim would seize him, and he would long dodge advancing strangers round the clinkered corners of his hut; sometimes like a stealthy bear, he would slink through the withered thickets up the mountains, and refuse to see the human face.

Except his occasional visitors from the sea—for a long period—the only companions of Oberlus were the crawling tortoises; and he seemed more than degraded to their level, having no desires for a time beyond theirs, unless it were for the stupor brought on by drunkenness. But sufficiently debased as he appeared, there yet lurked in him, only awaiting occasion for discovery, a still further proneness. Indeed the sole superiority of Oberlus over the tortoises was his possession of a larger capacity of degradation; and along with that, something like an intelligent will to it. Moreover, what is about to be revealed, perhaps will show, that selfish ambition, or the love of rule for its own sake, far from being the peculiar infirmity of noble minds, is shared by beings which have no mind at all. No creatures are so selfishly tyrannical as some brutes; as any one who has observed the tenants of the pasture must occasionally have observed.

"This island's mine by·Sycorax my mother;" said Oberlus to himself, glaring round upon his haggard solitude. By some means, barter or theft—for in those days ships at intervals still kept touching at his Landing—he obtained an old musket, with a few charges of powder and ball. Possessed of arms, he was stimulated to enterprise, as a tiger that first feels the coming of its claws. The long habit of sole dominion over every object round him, his almost unbroken solitude, his never encountering humanity except on terms of misanthropic independence, or mercantile craftiness, and even such encounters being comparatively but rare; all this must have gradually nourished in him a vast idea of his own importance, together with a pure animal sort of scorn for all the rest of the universe.

The unfortunate Creole, who enjoyed his brief term of royalty at Charles's Isle, was perhaps in some degree influenced by not unworthy motives; such as prompt other adventurous spirits to lead colonists into distant regions and assume political pre-eminence over them. His summary execution of many of his Peruvians is quite pardonable, considering the desperate characters he had to deal with; while his offering canine battle to the banded rebels seems under the circumstances altogether just. But for this King Oberlus and what shortly follows, no shade of palliation can be given. He acted out of mere delight in tyranny and cruelty, by virtue of a quality in him inherited from Sycorax his mother. Armed now with that shocking blunderbuss, strong in the thought of being master of that horrid isle, he panted for a chance to prove his potency upon the first specimen of humanity which should fall unbefriended into his hands.

Nor was he long without it. One day he spied a boat upon the beach, with one man, a negro, standing by it. Some distance off was a ship, and Oberlus immediately knew how matters stood. The vessel had put in for wood, and the boat's crew had gone into the thickets for it. From a convenient spot he kept watch of the boat, till presently a straggling company appeared loaded with billets. Throwing these on the beach, they again went into the thickets, while the negro proceeded to load the boat.

Oberlus now makes all haste and accosts the negro, who, aghast at seeing any living being inhabiting such a solitude, and especially so horrific a one, immediately falls into a panic, not at all lessened by the ursine suavity of Oberlus, who begs the favour of assisting him in his labours. The negro stands with several billets on his shoulder, in act of shouldering others; and Oberlus, with a short cord concealed in his bosom, kindly proceeds to lift those other billets to their place. In so doing he persists in keeping behind the negro, who rightly suspicious of this, in vain dodges about to gain the front of Oberlus; but Oberlus dodges also; till at last, weary of this bootless attempt at treachery, or fearful of being surprised by the remainder of the party, Oberlus runs off a little space to a bush, and fetching his blunderbuss, savagely demands the negro to desist work and follow him. He refuses. Whereupon, presenting his piece, Oberlus snaps at him. Luckily the blunderbuss misses fire; but by this time, frightened out of his wits, the negro, upon a second intrepid summons, drops his billets, surrenders at discretion, and follows on. By a narrow defile familiar to him, Oberlus speedily removes out of sight of the water.

On their way up the mountains, he exultingly informs the negro, that henceforth he is to work for him, and be his slave, and that his treatment would entirely depend on his future conduct. But Oberlus, deceived by the first impulsive cowardice of the black, in an evil moment slackens his vigilance. Passing through a narrow way, and perceiving his leader quite off his guard, the negro, a powerful fellow, suddenly grasps him in his arms, throws him down, wrests his musketoon from him, ties his hands with the monster's own cord, shoulders him, and returns with him down to the boat. When the rest of the party arrive, Oberlus is carried on board the ship. This proved him an Englishman and a smuggler—a sort of craft not apt to be over-charitable. Oberlus is severely whipped, then handcuffed, taken ashore, and compelled to make known his habitation and produce his property. His potatoes, pumpkins, and tortoises, with a pile of dollars he had hoarded from his mercantile operations, were secured on the spot. But while the too vindictive smugglers were busy destroying his hut and garden, Oberlus makes his escape into the mountains, and conceals himself there in impenetrable recesses, only known to himself, till the ship sails, when he ventures back, and by means of an old file which he sticks into a tree, contrives to free himself from his handcuffs.

Brooding among the ruins of his hut, and the desolate clinkers and extinct volcanoes of this outcast isle, the insulted misanthrope now meditates a signal revenge upon humanity, but conceals his purposes. Vessels still touch the Landing at times; and by and by Oberlus is enabled to supply them with some vegetables.

Warned by his former failure in kidnapping strangers, he now pursues a quite different plan. When seamen come ashore, he makes up to them like a free-and-easy comrade, invites them to his hut, and with whatever affability his red-haired grimness may assume, entreats them to drink his liquor and be merry. But his guests need little pressing; and so, soon as rendered insensible, are tied hand and foot, and pitched among the clinkers, are there concealed till the ship departs, when—finding themselves entirely dependent upon Oberlus, alarmed at his changed demeanour, his savage threats, and above all that shocking blunderbuss—they willingly enlist under him, becoming his humble slaves, and Oberlus the most incredible of tyrants. So much so, that two or three perish beneath his initiating process. He sets the remainder—four of them—to breaking the caked soil; transporting upon their backs loads of loamy earth, scooped up in moist clefts among the mountains; keeps them on the roughest fare; presents his piece at the slightest hint of insurrection; and in all respects converts them into reptiles at his feet; plebeian garter-snakes to this Lord Anaconda.

At last, Oberlus contrives to stock his arsenal with four rusty cutlasses, and an added supply of powder and ball intended for his blunderbuss. Remitting in good part the labour of his slaves, he now approves himself a man—or rather devil—of great abilities in the way of cajoling or coercing others into acquiescence with his own ulterior designs, however at first abhorrent to them. But indeed, prepared for almost any eventual evil by their previous lawless life, as a sort of ranging Cow-Boys of the sea, which had dissolved within them the whole moral man, so that they were ready to concrete in the first offered mould of baseness now; rotted down from manhood by their hopeless misery on the isle; wonted to cringe in all things to their lord, himself the worst of slaves; these wretches were now become wholly corrupted to his hands. He used them as creatures of an inferior race; in short, he gaffles his four animals, and makes murderers of them; out of cowards fitly manufacturing bravos.

Now, sword or dagger, human arms are but artificial claws and fangs, tied on like false spurs to the fighting cock. So, we repeat, Oberlus, czar of the isle, gaffles his four subjects; that is, with intent of glory, puts four rusty cutlasses into their hands. Like any other autocrat, he had a noble army now.

It might be thought a servile war would hereupon ensue. Arms in the hands of trodden slaves? how indiscreet of Emperors, Oberlus! Nay, they had but cutlasses—sad old scythes enough—he a blunderbuss, which by its blind scatterings of all sorts of boulders, clinkers and other scoria would annihilate all four mutineers, like four pigeons at one shot. Besides, at first he did not sleep in his accustomed hut; every lurid sunset, for a time, he might have been seen wending his way among the riven mountains, there to secrete himself till dawn in some sulphurous pitfall, undiscoverable to his gang; but finding this at last too troublesome, he now each evening tied his slaves hand and foot, hid the cutlasses, and thrusting them into his barracks, shut to the door, and lying down before it, beneath a rude shed lately added, slept out the night, blunderbuss in hand.

It is supposed that not content with daily parading over a cindery solitude at the head of his fine army, Oberlus now meditated the most active mischief; his probable object being to surprise some passing ship touching at his dominions, massacre the crew, and run away with her to parts unknown. While these plans were simmering in his head, two ships touch in company at the isle, on the opposite side to his; when his designs undergo a sudden change.

The ships are in want of vegetables, which Oberlus promises in great abundance, provided they send their boats round to his landing, so that the crews may bring the vegetables from his garden; informing the two captains, at the same time, that his rascals—slaves and soldiers—had become so abominably lazy and good-for-nothing of late, that he could not make them work by ordinary inducements, and did not have the heart to be severe with them.

The arrangement was agreed to, and the boats were sent and hauled upon the beach. The crews went to the lava hut; but to their surprise nobody was there. After waiting till their patience was exhausted, they returned to the shore, when lo, some stranger—not the Good Samaritan either—seems to have very recently passed that way. Three of the boats were broken in a thousand pieces, and the fourth was missing. By hard toil over the mountains and through the clinkers, some of the strangers succeeded in returning to that side of the isle where the ships lay, when fresh boats are sent to the relief of the rest of the hapless party.

However, amazed at the treachery of Oberlus, the two captains, afraid of new and still more mysterious atrocities,—and indeed, half imputing such strange events to the enchantments associated with these isles,—perceive no security but in instant flight; leaving Oberlus and his army in quiet possession of the stolen boat.

On the eve of sailing they put a letter in a keg, giving the Pacific Ocean intelligence of the affair, and moored the keg in the bay. Some time subsequent, the keg was opened by another captain chancing to anchor there, but not until after he had dispatched a boat round to Oberlus's Landing. As may be readily surmised, he felt no little inquietude till the boat's return; when another letter was handed him, giving Oberlus's version of the affair. This precious document had been found pinned half-mildewed to the clinker wall of the sulphurous and deserted hut. It ran as follows; showing that Oberlus was at least an accomplished writer, and no mere boor; and what is more, was capable of the most tristful eloquence.

"Sir: I am the most unfortunate ill-treated gentleman that lives. I am a patriot, exiled from country by the cruel hand of tyranny.

"Banished to these Enchanted Isles, I have again and again besought captains of ships to sell me a boat, but always have been refused, though I offered the handsomest prices in Mexican dollars. At length an opportunity presented of possessing myself of one, and I did not let it slip.

"I have been long endeavouring by hard labour and much solitary suffering to accumulate something to make myself comfortable in a virtuous though unhappy old age; but at various times have been robbed and beaten by men professing to be Christians.

"To-day I sail from the Enchanted group in the good boat Charity bound to the Feejee Isles.

"FATHERLESS OBERLUS.

"P.S.—Behind the clinkers, nigh the oven, you will find the old fowl. Do not kill it; be patient; I leave it setting;

if it shall have any chicks, I hereby bequeathe them to you, whoever you may be. But don't count your chicks before they are hatched."

The fowl proved a starveling rooster, reduced to a sitting posture by sheer debility.

Oberlus declares that he was bound to the Feejee Isles; but this was only to throw pursuers on a false scent. For after a long time he arrived, alone in his open boat, at Guayaquil. As his miscreants were never again beheld on Hood's Isle, it is supposed, either that they perished for want of water on the passage to Guayaquil, or, what is quite as probable, were thrown overboard by Oberlus, when he found the water growing scarce.

From Guayaquil Oberlus proceeded to Payta; and there, with that nameless witchery peculiar to some of the ugliest animals, wound himself into the affections of a tawny damsel; prevailing upon her to accompany him back to his Enchanted Isle; which doubtless he painted as a Paradise of flowers, not a Tartarus of clinkers.

But unfortunately for the colonization of Hood's Isle with a choice variety of animated nature, the extraordinary and delivish aspect of Oberlus made him to be regarded in Payta as a highly suspicious character. So that being found concealed one night, with matches in his pocket, under the hull of a small vessel just ready to be launched, he was seized and thrown into jail.

The jails in most South American towns are generally of the least wholesome sort. Built of huge cakes of sunburnt brick, and containing but one room, without windows or yard, and but one door heavily grated with wooden bars, they present both within and without the grimmest aspect. As public edifices they conspicuously stand upon the hot and dusty Plaza, offering to view, through the gratings, their villainous and hopeless inmates, burrowing in all sorts of tragic squalor. And here, for a long time, Oberlus was seen; the central figure of a mongrel and assassin band; a creature whom it is religion to detest, since it is philanthropy to hate a misanthrope.

Note.—They who may be disposed to question the possibility of the character above depicted, are referred to the 2d vol. of Porter's Voyage into the Pacific, where they will recognize many sentences, for expedition's sake derived verbatim from thence, and incorporated here; the main difference—save a few passing reflections—between the two accounts being, that the present writer had added to Porter's facts accessory ones picked up in the Pacific from reliable sources; and where facts conflict, has naturaly preferred his own authorities to Porter's. As, for instance, *his* authorities place Oberlus on Hood's Isle: Porter's, on Charles's Isle. The letter found in the hut is also somewhat different, for while at the Encantadas he was informed that not only did it evince a certain clerkliness, but was full of the strangest satiric effrontery which does not adequately appear in Porter's version. I accordingly altered it to suit the general character of its author.

Sketch Tenth

RUNAWAYS, CASTAWAYS, SOLITAIRES, GRAVESTONES, ETC.

> *"And all about old stocks and stubs of trees,*
> *Whereon nor fruit nor leaf was ever seen,*
> *Did hang upon the ragged knotty knees,*
> *On which had many wretches hanged been."*

SOME relics of the hut of Oberlus partially remain to this day at the head of the clinkered valley. Nor does the stranger wandering among other of the Enchanted Isles fail to stumble upon still other solitary abodes, long abandoned to the tortoise and the lizard. Probably few parts of earth have in modern times sheltered so many solitaries. The reason is, that these isles are situated in a distant sea, and the vessels which occasionally visit them are mostly all whalers, or ships bound on dreary and protracted voyages, exempting them in a good degree from both the oversight and the memory of human law. Such is the character of some commanders and some seamen, that under these untoward circumstances, it is quite impossible but that scenes of unpleasantness and discord should occur between them. A sullen hatred of the tyrannic ship will seize the sailor, and he gladly exchanges it for the isles, which though blighted as by a continual sirocco and burning breeze, still offer him in their labyrinthine interior, a retreat beyond the possibility of capture. To flee the ship in any Peruvian or Chilian port, even the smallest and most rustical, is not unattended with great risk of apprehension, not to speak of jaguars. A reward of five pesos sends fifty dastardly Spaniards into the woods, who with long knives scour them day and night in eager hopes of securing their prey. Neither is it, in general, much easier to escape pursuit at the isles of Polynesia. Those of them which have felt a civilizing influence present the same difficulty to the runaway with the Peruvian ports. The advanced natives being quite as mercenary and keen of knife and scent as the retrograde Spaniards; while, owing to the bad odour in which all Europeans lie in the minds of aboriginal savages who have chanced to hear aught of them, to desert the ship among primitive Polynesians, is, in most cases, a hope not unforlorn. Hence the Enchanted Isles become the voluntary tarrying places of all sorts of refugees; some of whom too sadly experience the fact that flight from tyranny does not of itself insure a safe asylum, far less a happy home.

Moreover, it has not seldom happened that hermits have been made upon the isles by the accidents incident to tortoise-hunting. The interior of most of them is tangled and difficult of passage beyond description; the air is sultry and stifling; an intolerable thirst is provoked, for which no running stream offers its kind relief. In a few hours, under an equatorial sun, reduced by these causes to entire exhaustion, woe betide the straggler at the Enchanted Isles! Their extent is such as to forbid an adequate search unless weeks are devoted to it. The impatient ship waits a day or two; when, the missing man remaining undiscovered, up goes a stake on the beach, with a letter of regret, and a keg of crackers and another of water tied to it, and away sails the craft.

Nor have there been wanting instances where the inhumanity of some captains has led them to wreak a secure revenge upon seamen who have given their caprice or pride some singular offence. Thrust ashore upon the scorching marl, such mariners are abandoned to perish outright, unless by solitary labours they succeed in discovering some precious dribblets of moisture oozing from a rock or stagnant in a mountain pool.

I was well acquainted with a man, who, lost upon the Isle of Narborough, was brought to such extremes by thirst, that at last he only saved his life by taking that of another being. A large hair-seal came upon the beach. He rushed upon it, stabbed it in the neck, and then throwing himself upon the panting body quaffed at the living wound; the palpitations of the creature's dying heart injecting life into the drinker.

Another seaman thrust ashore in a boat upon an isle at which no ship ever touched, owing to its peculiar sterility and the shoals about it, and from which all other parts of the group were hidden; this man feeling that it was sure death to remain there, and that nothing worse than death menaced him in quitting it, killed two seals, and inflating their skins, made a float, upon which he transported himself to Charles's Island, and joined the republic there.

But men not endowed with courage equal to such desperate attempts, find their only resource in forthwith seeking for some watery place, however precarious or scanty; building a hut; catching tortoises and birds; and in all respects preparing for hermit life, till tide or time, or a passing ship, arrives to float them off.

At the foot of precipices on many of the isles, small rude basins in the rocks are found, partly filled with rotted rubbish or vegetable decay, or overgrown with thickets, and sometimes a little moist; which, upon examination, reveal plain tokens of artificial instruments employed in hollowing them out, by some poor castaway or still more miserable runaway. These basins are made in places where it was supposed some scanty drops of dew might exude into them from the upper crevices.

The relics of hermitages and stone basins are not the only signs of vanishing humanity to be found upon the isles. And curious to say, that spot which of all others in settled communities is most animated, at the Enchanted Isles presents the most dreary of aspects. And though it may seem very strange to talk of post-offices in this barren region, yet post-offices are occasionally to be found there. They consist of a stake and bottle. The letters being not only sealed, but corked. They are generally deposited by captains of Nantucketers for the benefit of passing fisherman; and contain statements as to what luck they had in whaling or tortoise-hunting. Frequently, however, long months and months, whole years glide by and no applicant appears. The stake rots and falls, presenting no very exhilarating object.

If now it be added that grave-stones, or rather grave-boards, are also discovered upon some of the isles, the picture will be complete.

Upon the beach of James's Isle for many years was to be seen a rude finger-post pointing inland. And perhaps taking it for some signal of possible hospitality in this otherwise desolate spot—some good hermit living there with his maple dish—the stranger would follow on in the path thus indicated, till at last he would come out in a noiseless nook, and find his only welcome, a dead man; his sole greeting the inscription over a grave: "Here, in 1813, fell in a daybreak duel, a Lieutenant of the U.S. frigate Essex, aged twenty-one: attaining his majority in death."

It is but fit that—like those old monastic institutions of Europe, whose inmates go not out of their own walls to be inurned, but are entombed there where they die—the Encantadas too should bury their own dead, even as the great general monastery of earth does hers.

It is known that burial in the ocean is a pure necessity of sea-faring life, and that it is only done when land is far astern, and not clearly visible from the bow. Hence, to vessels cruising in the vicinity of the Enchanted Isles, they afford a convenient Potter's Field. The interment over, some good-natured forecastle poet and artist seizes his paint-brush, and inscribes a doggerel epitaph. When after a long lapse of time, other good-natured seamen chance to come upon the spot, they usually make a table of the mound, and quaff a friendly can to the poor soul's repose.

As a specimen of these epitaphs take the following, found in a bleak gorge of Chatham Isle:—

> "*Oh Brother Jack, as you pass by,*
> *As you are now, so once was I.*
> *Just so game and just so gay,*
> *But now, alack, they've stopped my pay.*
> *No more I peep out of my blinkers,*
> *Here I bee—tucked in with clinkers!*"

BILLY BUDD, FORETOPMAN

WHAT BEFELL HIM IN THE YEAR OF THE GREAT MUTINY

Begun—Friday, November 16, 1888.
Revision begun—March 2, 1889.
Finished—April 19, 1891.

DEDICATED
TO
JACK CHASE
ENGLISHMAN

WHEREVER THAT GREAT HEART MAY NOW BE
HERE ON EARTH OR HARBOURED IN PARA-
DISE. CAPTAIN OF THE MAINTOP IN THE YEAR
1843 IN THE U.S. FRIGATE "UNITED STATES"

Preface

THE year 1797, the year of this narrative, belongs to a period which, as every thinker now feels, involved a crisis for Christendom not exceeded in its undetermined momentousness at the time by any other era whereof there is record. The opening proposition made by the Spirit of that Age * involved rectification of the Old World's hereditary wrongs. In France, to some extent, this was bloodily effected. But what then? Straightway the Revolution itself became a wrongdoer, one more oppressive than the kings. Under Napoleon it enthroned upstart kings, and initiated that prolonged agony of continual war whose final throe was Waterloo. During those years not the wisest could have foreseen that the outcome of all would be what to some thinkers apparently it has since turned out to be—a political advance along nearly the whole line for Europeans.

Now, as elsewhere hinted, it was something caught from the Revolutionary Spirit that at Spithead emboldened the man-of-war's men to rise against real abuses, long-standing ones, and afterwards at the Nore to make inordinate and aggressive demands—successful resistance to which was confirmed only when the ringleaders were hung for an admonitory spectacle to the anchored fleet. Yet in a way analogous to the operation of the Revolution at large—the Great Mutiny, though by Englishmen naturally deemed monstrous at the time, doubtless gave the first latent prompting to most important reforms in the British navy.

* Crossed out; was one hailed by the noblest men of it. Even the dry tinder of a Wordsworth took fire.

BILLY BUDD, FORETOPMAN

WHAT BEFELL HIM IN THE YEAR OF **THE**
GREAT MUTINY, ETC.

CHAPTER I

(An inside Narrative)

In the time before steamships, or then more frequently
than now, a stroller along the docks of any considerable
seaport would occasionally have his attention arrested by a
group of bronzed marines, man-of-war's men or merchant-
sailors in holiday attire ashore on liberty.   In certain instances they would flank, or, like a bodyguard, quite sur-
round some superior figure of their own class, moving along
with them like Aldebaran among the lesser lights of his
constellation.   That signal object was the "Handsome Sailor"
of the less prosaic time, alike of the military and merchant
navies.   With no perceptible trace of the vainglorious about
him, rather with the off-hand unaffectedness of natural re-
gality, he seemed to accept the spontaneous homage of his
shipmates.   A somewhat remarkable instance recurs to me.
In Liverpool, now half a century ago I saw under the shadow
of the great dingy street-wall of Prince's Dock (an obstruc-
tion long since removed) a common sailor, so intensely
black that he must needs have been a native African of the
unadulterated blood of Ham.   A symmetric figure, much
above the average in height.   The two ends of a gay silk
handkerchief thrown loose about the neck danced upon the
displayed ebony of his chest; in his ears were big hoops of

gold, and a Scotch Highland bonnet with a tartan band set off his shapely head.

It was a hot noon in July, and his face, lustrous with perspiration, beamed with barbaric good-humour. In jovial sallies right and left, his white teeth flashing into view, he rollicked along, the centre of a company of his shipmates. These were made up of such an assortment of tribes and complexions as would have well fitted them to be marched up by Anacharsis Cloots before the bar of the first French Assembly as Representatives of the Human Race. At each spontaneous tribute rendered by the wayfarers to this black pagod of a fellow—the tribute of a pause and stare, and less frequent an exclamation—the motley retinue showed that they took that sort of pride in the evoker of it which the Assyrian priests doubtless showed for their grand sculptured Bull when the faithful prostrated themselves. To return—

If in some cases a bit of a nautical Murat in setting forth his person ashore, the Handsome Sailor of the period in question evinced nothing of the dandified Billy-be-Damn—an amusing character all but extinct now, but occasionally to be encountered, and in a form yet more amusing than the original, at the tiller of the boats on the tempestuous Erie Canal or, more likely, vapouring in the groggeries along the tow-path. Invariably a proficient in his perilous calling, he was also more or less of a mighty boxer or wrestler. It was strength and beauty. Tales of his prowess were recited. Ashore he was the champion; afloat the spokesman; on every suitable occasion always foremost. Close-reefing topsails in a gale, there he was—astride the weather yard-arm-end, foot in "stirrup," both hands tugging at the "ear-ring" as at a bridle, in very much the attitude of the young Alexander curbing the fiery Bucephalus. A superb figure, tossed up as by the horns of Taurus against the thunderous sky, cheerily ballooning to the strenuous file along the spar.

The moral nature was seldom out of keeping with the physical make. Indeed, except as toned by the former, the comeliness and power, always attractive in masculine perfection, hardly could have drawn the sort of homage the Handsome Sailor, in some examples, received from his less gifted associates.

Such a cynosure, at least in aspect, and something such too in nature, though with important variations made apparent as the story proceeds, was welkin-eyed Billy Budd, or Baby Budd—as more familiarly, under circumstances hereafter to be given, he at last came to be called—aged twenty-one, a foretopman of the fleet towards the close of the last decade of the eighteenth century. It was not very long prior to the time of the narration that follows, that he had entered the King's Service, having been impressed on the Narrow Seas from a homeward-bound English merchantman into a seventy-four outward-bound, H.M.S. *Indomitable*; which ship, as was not unusual in those hurried days, had been obliged to put to sea short of her proper complement of men. Plump upon Billy at first sight in the gangway the boarding officer, Lieutenant Ratcliffe, pounced, even before the merchantman's crew formally was mustered on the quarter-deck for his deliberate inspection. And him only he elected. For whether it was because the other men when ranged before him showed to ill advantage after Billy, or whether he had some scruples in view of the merchantman being rather short-handed; however it might be, the officer contented himself with his first spontaneous choice. To the surprise of the ship's company, though much to the Lieutenant's satisfaction, Billy made no demur. But indeed any demur would have been as idle as the protest of a goldfinch popped into a cage.

Noting this uncomplaining asquiescence, all but cheerful one might say, the shipmates turned a surprised glance of silent reproach at the sailor. The shipmaster was one of those worthy mortals found in every vocation,—even the humbler ones,—the sort of person whom everybody agrees in calling "a respectable man." And—nor so strange to report as it may appear to be—though a ploughman of the troubled waters, life-long contending with the intractable elements, there was nothing this honest soul at heart loved better than simple peace and quiet. For the rest, he was fifty or thereabouts, a little inclined to corpulence, a pre-possessing face, unwhiskered, and of an agreeable colour—a rather full face, humanely intelligent in expression. On a fair day with a fair wind and all going well, a certain musical chime in his voice seemed to be the veritable unobstructed outcome of the innermost man. He had much prudence, much conscientiousness, and there were occasions when these virtues were the cause of overmuch disquietude in him. On a passage, so long as his craft was in any proximity to land, there was no sleep for Captain Graveling. He took to heart those serious responsibilities not so heavily borne by some shipmasters.

Now, while Billy Budd was down in the forecastle, getting his kit together, the *Indomitable's* Lieutenant—burly and bluff, nowise disconcerted by Captain Graveling's omitting to profer the customary hospitalities on an occasion so unwelcome to him; an omission simply caused by preoccupation of thought—unceremoniously invited himself into the cabin, and also to a flask from the spirit locker, a receptacle which his experienced eye instantly discovered. In fact, he was one of those sea-dogs in whom all the hardship and peril of naval life in the great prolonged wars of his time never impaired the natural instinct for sensuous enjoyment. His duty he always faithfully did; but duty is sometimes a dry obligation, and he was for irrigating its aridity whensoever possible with a fertilizing decoction of strong waters. For the cabin's proprietor there was nothing left but to play the part of the enforced host with whatever grace and alacrity were practicable. As necessary adjuncts to the flask he silently placed tumbler and water-jug before the irrepressible guest. But excusing himself from partaking just then, he dismally watched the unembarrassed officer deliberately diluting his grog a little, then tossing it off in three swallows, pushing the empty tumbler away, yet not so far as to be beyond easy reach, at the same time settling himself in his seat and smacking his lips with high satisfaction, looking straight at the host.

These proceedings over the Master broke the silence; and there lurked a rueful reproach in the tone of his voice: "Lieutenant, you are going to take my best man from me, the jewel of 'em."

"Yes, I know," rejoined the other, immediately drawing back the tumbler preliminary to a replenishing; "Yes, I know. Sorry."

"Beg pardon, but you don't understand, Lieutenant. See here now. Before I shipped that young fellow, my forecastle was a rat-pit of quarrels. It was black times, I tell you, aboard the *"Rights"* here. I was worried to that degree my pipe had no comfort for me. But Billy came; and it was like a Catholic priest striking peace in an Irish shindy. Not that he preached to them or said or did anything in particular; but a virtue went out of him, sugaring the sour ones. They took to him like hornets to treacle; all but the bluffer of the gang, the big shaggy chap with the fire-red whiskers. He, indeed, out of envy perhaps of the newcomer, and thinking such a "sweet and pleasant fellow," as he mockingly designated him to the others, could hardly have the spirit of a game-cock, must needs bestir himself in trying to get up an ugly row with him. Billy forebore with him and reasoned with him in a pleasant way—he is something like myself, Lieutenant, to whom aught like a quarrel is hateful—but nothing served. So, in the second dog-watch one day the Red-Whiskers, in the presence of the others, under pretence of showing Billy just whence a sirloin steak was cut—for the fellow had once been a butcher—insultingly gave him a dig under the ribs. Quick as lightning Billy let fly his arm. I dare say he never meant to do quite as much as he did, but anyhow he gave the burly fool a terrible drubbing. It took about half a minute, I should think. And, Lord bless you, the lubber was astonished at the celerity. And will you believe it, Lieutenant, the Red-Whiskers now really loves Billy—loves him, or is the biggest hypocrite that ever I heard of. But they all love him. Some of 'em do his washing, darn old trousers for him; the carpenter is at odd times making a pretty little chest of drawers for him. Anybody will do anything for Billy Budd; and it's the happy family here. Now, Lieutenant, if that young fellow goes—I know how it will be aboard the *"Rights."* Not again very soon shall I, coming up from dinner, lean over the capstan smoking a quiet pipe—no, not very soon again, I think. Ay, Lieutenant, you are going to take away the jewel of 'em; you are going to take away my peacemaker." And with that the good soul had really some ado in checking a rising sob.

"Well," answered the Lieutenant, who had listened with amused interest to all this, and now waxing merry with his tipple, "Well, blessed are the peacemakers, especially the

fighting peacemakers! And such are the seventy-four beauties, some of which you see poking their noses out of the
portholes of yonder warship lying-to there for me," pointing
through the cabin window at the *Indomitable*. "But courage! don't look so down-hearted, man. Why, I pledge you
in advance the royal approbation. Rest assured that His
Majesty will be delighted to know that in a time when his
hard-tack is not sought for by sailors with such avidity as
should be; a time also when some shipmasters privily resent
the borrowing from them of a tar or two for the service;
His Majesty, I say, will be delighted to learn that *one* ship-
master, at least, cheerfully surrenders to the King the flower
of his flock: a sailor who with equal loyalty makes no dissent.
—But where's my beauty? Ah," looking through the cabin's
open door. "Here he comes; and, by Jove—lugging along
his chest—Apollo with his portmanteau! "My man,"
stepping out to him, "you can't take that big box on board
a warship. The boxes there are mostly shot-boxes. Put up
your duds in a bag, lad. Boot and saddle for the cavalry-
man, bag and hammock for the man-of-war's man."

The transfer from chest to bag was made. And, after
seeing his man into the cutter, and then following him down,
the Lieutenant pushed off from the *Rights-of-Man*. That
was the merchant ship's name; though by her master and
crew abbreviated in sailor fashion into the "*Rights*." The
hard-headed Dundee owner was a staunch admirer of
Thomas Paine, whose book in rejoinder to Burke's arraign-
ment of the French Revolution had then been published for
some time and had gone everywhere. In christening his vessel after the title of Paine's volume, the man of Dundee
was something like his contemporary shipowner, Stephen
Girard of Philadelphia, whose sympathies alike with his na-

tive land and its liberal philosophies he evinced by naming his ships after Voltaire, Diderot, and so forth.

But now, when the boat swept under the merchantman's stern, and officer and oarsmen were noting,—some bitterly and others with a grin,—the name emblazoned there; just then it was that the new recruit jumped up from the bow where the coxswain had directed him to sit, waving his hat to his silent shipmates sorrowfully looking over at him from the taffrail, and bade the lads a genial good-bye. Then making a salutation as to the ship herself, "And good-bye to you too, old *Rights-of-Man!*"

"Down, Sir," roared the Lieutenant, instantly assuming all the rigour of his rank, though with difficulty repressing a smile.

To be sure, Billy's action was a terrible breach of naval decorum. But in that decorum he had never been instructed; in consideration of which the Lieutenant would hardly have been so energetic in reproof but for the concluding farewell to the ship. This he rather took as meant to convey a covert sally on the new recruit's part—a sly slur at impressment in general, and that of himself in especial. And yet, more likely, if satire it was in effect, it was hardly so by intention, for Billy (though happily endowed with the gaiety of high health, youth and a free heart) was yet by no means of a satirical turn. The will to it and the sinister dexterity were alike wanting. To deal in double meaning and insinuations of any sort was quite foreign to his nature.

As to his enforced enlistment—that he seemed to take pretty much as he was wont to take any vicissitude of weather. Like the animals, though no philosopher, he was, without knowing it, practically a fatalist. And, it may be, that he rather liked this adventurous turn in his affairs which promised an opening into novel scenes and martial excitements.

Aboard the *Indomitable* our merchant-sailor was forthwith rated as an able seaman, and assigned to the starboard watch of the foretop. He was soon at home in the service, not at all disliked for his unpretentious good looks and his rather genial happy-go-lucky air. No merrier man in his mess; in marked contrast to certain other individuals included like himself among the impressed portions of the ship's company; for these when not actively employed were sometimes—and more particularly in the last dog-watch, when the drawing near of twilight induced revery—apt to fall into a saddish mood which in some partook of sullenness. But they were not so young as our foretopman, and no few of them must have known a hearth of some sort, others may have had wives and children left, too probably, in uncertain circumstances, and hardly any but must have acknowledged kith and kin; while for Billy, as will shortly be seen, his entire family was practically invested in himself.

CHAPTER II

THOUGH our new-made foretopman was well received in the top and on the gun-decks, hardly here was he that cynosure he had previously been among those minor ship's companies of the merchant marine, with which companies only had he hitherto consorted.

He was young; and despite his all but fully developed frame, in aspect looked even younger than he really was. This was owing to a lingering adolescent expression in the as yet smooth face, all but feminine in purity of natural complexion, but where, thanks to his seagoing, the lily was quite suppressed and the rose had some ado visibly to flush through the tan.

To one essentially such a novice in the complexities of

factitious life, the abrupt transition from his former and simpler sphere to the ampler and more knowing world of a great war-ship—this might well have abashed him had there been any conceit or vanity in his composition. Among her miscellaneous multitude, the *Indomitable* mustered several individuals who, however inferior in grade, were of no common natural stamp: sailors more signally susceptive of that air which continuous martial discipline and repeated presence in battle can in some degree impart even to the average man. As the "Handsome Sailor" Billy Budd's position aboard the seventy-four was something analogous to that of a rustic beauty transplanted from the provinces and brought into competition with the high-born dames of the court. But this change of circumstances he scarce noted. As little did he observe that something about him provoked an ambiguous smile in one or two harder faces among the bluejackets. Nor less unaware was he of the peculiar favourable effect his person and demeanour had upon the more intelligent gentlemen of the quarter-deck. Nor could this well have been otherwise. Cast in a mould peculiar to the finest physical examples of those Englishmen in whom the Saxon strain would seem not at all to partake of any Norman or other admixture, he showed in face that humane look of reposeful good nature which the Greek sculptor in some instances gave to his heroic strong man, Hercules. But this again was subtly modified by another and pervasive quality. The ear, small and shapely, the arch of the foot, the curve in mouth and nostril, even the indurated hand dyed to the orange-tawny of the toucan's bill, a hand telling of the halyards and tar-buckets. But, above all, something in the mobile expression, and every chance attitude and movement, something suggestive of a mother eminently favoured by Love and the Graces; all this strangely indicated a lineage

in direct contradiction to his lot. The mysteriousness here
became less mysterious through a matter of fact elicited when
Billy at the capstan was being formally mustered into the
service. Asked by the officer, a small, brisk little gentleman
as it chanced, among other questions, his place of birth, he
replied, "Please, Sir, I don't know."

"Don't know where you were born? Who was your
father?"

"God knows, Sir."

Struck by the straightforward simplicity of these replies,
the officer next asked, "Do you know anything about your
beginning?"

"No, Sir. But I have heard that I was found in a pretty
silk-lined basket hanging one morning from the knocker of
a good man's door in Bristol."

" 'Found,' say you? Well," throwing back his head and
looking up and down the new recruit; "well it turns out to
have been a pretty good find. Hope they'll find some more
like you, my man; the fleet sadly needs them."

Yes, Billy Budd was a foundling, a presumable by-blow,
and, evidently, no ignoble one. Noble descent was as evident in him as in a blood horse.

For the rest, with little or no sharpness of faculty or any
trace of the wisdom of the serpent, nor yet quite a dove,
he possessed that kind and degree of intelligence which goes
along with the unconventional rectitude of a sound human
creature—one to whom not as yet had been proffered the
questionable apple of knowledge. He was illiterate. He
could not read, but he could sing, and like the illiterate night-
ingale was sometimes the composer of his own song.

Of self-consciousness he seemed to have little or none, or
about as much as we may reasonably impute to a dog of St.
Bernard's breed.

Habitually being with the elements, and knowing little more of the land than as a beach, or, rather, that portion of the terraqueous globe, providentially set apart for dance-houses, doxies and tapsters, in short what sailors call a "fiddlers' green," his simple nature remained unsophisticated by those moral obliquities which are not in every case incomparable with that manufacturable thing known as respectability. But are sailors, frequenters of fiddlers' greens without vices? No; but less often than with landsmen do their vices, so called, partake of crookedness of heart, seeming less to proceed from viciousness than from exuberance of vitality after long restraint, frank manifestations in accordance with natural law. By his original constitution aided by the coöperating influences of his lot, Billy in many respects was little more than a sort of upright barbarian, much such perhaps as Adam presumably might have been ere the urbane Serpent wriggled himself into his company.

And here be it submitted that, apparently going to corroborate the doctrine of man's fall—a doctrine now popularly ignored—it is observable that where certain virtues pristine and unadulterate peculiarly characterize anybody in the external uniform of civilization, they will upon scrutiny seem not to be derived from custom or convention but rather to be out of keeping with these, as if indeed exceptionally transmitted from a period prior to Cain's City and citified man. The character marked by such qualities has to an unvitiated taste an untampered-with flavour like that of berries, while the man thoroughly civilized, even in a fair specimen of the breed, has to the same moral palate a questionable smack as of a compounded wine. To any stray inheritor of these primitive qualities found, like Caspar Hauser, wandering dazed in any Christian capital of our time, the poet's famous invocation, near two thousand years ago, of the good rustic

out of his latitude in the Rome of the Cæsars, still appropri-
ately holds:—

> *"Faithful in word and thought,*
> *What has Thee, Fabian, to the city brought."*

Though our Handsome Sailor had as much of masculine
beauty as one can expect anywhere to see; nevertheless, like
the beautiful woman in one of Hawthorne's minor tales,
there was just one thing amiss in him. No visible blemish,
indeed, as with the lady; no, but an occasional liability to a
vocal defect. Though in the hour of elemental uproar or
peril, he was everything that a sailor should be, yet under
sudden provocation of strong heart-feeling his voice, otherwise singularly musical, as if expressive of the harmony
within, was apt to develop an organic hesitancy,—in fact
more or less of a stutter or even worse. In this particular
Billy was a striking instance that the arch interpreter, the
envious marplot of Eden, still has more or less to do with
every human consignment to this planet of earth. In every
case, one way or another, he is sure to slip in his little card,
as much as to remind us—I too have a hand here.

The avowal of such an imperfection in the Handsome
Sailor should be evidence not alone that he is not presented
as a conventional hero, but also that the story in which he
is the main figure is no romance.

CHAPTER III

At the time of Billy Budd's arbitrary enlistment into the
Indomitable that ship was on her way to join the Mediterranean fleet. No long time elapsed before the junction was
effected. As one of that fleet the seventy-four participated
in its movements: though at times on account of her superior

sailing qualities, in the absence of frigates, despatched on separate duty as a scout—and at times on less temporary service. But with all this the story has little concernment, restricted as it is to the inner life of one particular ship and the career of an individual sailor.

It was the summer of 1797. In April of that year had occurred the commotion at Spithead followed in May by a second and yet more serious outbreak in the fleet at the Nore. The latter is known, and without exaggeration in the epithet, as the Great Mutiny. It was indeed a demonstration more menacing to England than the contemporary manifestoes and conquering and proselyting armies of the French Directory.

To the Empire, the Nore Mutiny was what a strike in the fire-brigade would be to London threatened by general arson. In a crisis when the Kingdom might well have anticipated the famous signal that some years later published along the naval line of battle what it was that upon occasion England expected of Englishmen; *that* was the time when at the mast-heads of the three-deckers and seventy-fours moored in our own roadstead—a fleet, the right arm of a Power then all but the sole free conservative one of the Old World, the blue-jackets, to be numbered by thousands, ran up with hurras the British colours with the union and cross wiped out; by that cancellation transmuting the flag of founded law and freedom defined, into the enemy's red meteor of unbridled and unbounded revolt. Reasonable discontent growing out of practical grievances in the fleet had been ignited into irrational combustion as by live cinders blown across the Channel from France in flames.

The event converted into irony for a time those spirited strains of Dibdin—as a song-writer no mean auxiliary to the English Government—at the European conjuncture, strains celebrating, among other things, the patriotic devotion of the British tar:

"*And as for my life, 'tis the King's!*"

Such an episode in the Island's grand naval story her naval historians naturally abridge; one of them (G. P. R. James) candidly acknowledging that fain would he pass it over did not "impartiality forbid fastidiousness." And yet his mention is less a narration than a reference, having to do hardly at all with details. Nor are these readily to be found in the libraries. Like some other events in every age befalling states everywhere, including America, the Great Mutiny was of such character that national pride along with views of policy would fain shade it off into the historical background. Such events cannot be ignored, but there is a considerate way of historically treating them. If a well-constituted individual refrains from blazoning aught amiss or calamitous in his family, a nation in the like circumstance may without reproach be equally discreet.

Though after parleyings between Government and the ring-leaders, and concessions by the former as to some glaring abuses, the first uprising—that at Spithead—with difficulty was put down, or matters for a time pacified; yet at the Nore the unforseen renewal of insurrection on a yet larger scale, and emphasized in the conferences that ensued by demands deemed by the authorities not only inadmissible but aggressively insolent, indicated, if the red flag did not sufficiently do so, what was the spirit animating the men. Final suppression, however, there was, but only made possible perhaps by the unswerving loyalty of the marine corps, and a voluntary resumption of loyalty among influential sections of the crews. To some extent the Nore Mutiny may be regarded as analogous to the distempering *irruption* of contagious fever in a frame constitutionally sound, and which anon throws it off.

At all events, of these thousands of mutineers were some of the tars who not so very long afterwards—whether wholly prompted thereto by patriotism, or pugnacious instinct, or by both,—helped to win a coronet for Nelson at the Nile, and the naval crown of crowns for him at Trafalgar. To the mutineers those battles, and especially Trafalgar, were a plenary absolution; and a grand one; for all that goes to make up scenic naval display is heroic magnificence in arms. Those battles, especially Trafalgar, stand unmatched in human annals.

CHAPTER IV

Concerning *"The greatest sailor since the world began"*—TENNYSON.

IN this matter of writing, resolve as one may to keep to the main road, some bypaths have an enticement not readily to be withstood. Beckoned by the genius of Nelson, I am going to err into such a bypath. If the reader will keep me company I shall be glad. At the least we can promise ourselves that pleasure which is wickedly said to be in sinning, for a literary sin the divergence will be.

Very likely it is no new remark that the inventions of our time have at last brought about a change in sea warfare in degree corresponding to the revolution in all warfare effected by the original introduction from China into Europe of gunpowder. The first European firearm, a clumsy contrivance, was, as is well known, scouted by no few of the knights as a base implement, good enough peradventure for weavers too craven to stand up crossing steel with steel in frank fight. But as ashore knightly valour, though shorn of its blazonry, did not cease with the knights, neither on the seas, though nowadays in encounters there a certain kind of displayed gallantry be fallen out of date as hardly applicable under changed circumstances, did the nobler qualities of such naval magnates as Don John of Austria, Doria, Van Tromp, Jean Bart, the long line of British admirals and the American Decaturs of 1812 become obsolete with their wooden walls.

Nevertheless, to anybody who can hold the Present at its worth without being inappreciative of the Past, it may be forgiven, if to such an one the solitary old hulk at Portsmouth, Nelson's *Victory*, seems to float there, not alone as the decaying monument of a fame incorruptible, but also as a poetic reproach, softened by its picturesqueness, to the *Monitors* and yet mightier hulls of the European ironsides. And this not altogether because such craft are unsightly, unavoidably lacking the symmetry and grand lines of the old battleships, but equally for other reasons.

There are some, perhaps, who while not altogether inaccessible to that poetic reproach just alluded to, may yet on behalf of the new order be disposed to parry it; and this to the extent of iconoclasm, if need be. For example, prompted by the sight of the star inserted in the *Victory's* deck designing the spot where the Great Sailor fell, these martial utilitarians may suggest considerations implying that Nelson's ornate publication of his person in battle was not only unnecessary, but not military, nay, savoured of foolhardiness and vanity. They may add, too, that at Trafalgar it was in effect nothing less than a challenge to death: and death came; and that but for his bravado the victorious admiral might possibly have survived the battle, and so, instead of having his sagacious dying injunction overruled by his immediate successor in command, he himself when the contest was decided might have brought his shattered fleet to anchor, a proceeding which might have averted the deplorable loss of life by shipwreck in the elemental tempest that followed the martial one.

Well, should we set aside the more disputable point whether for various reasons it was possible to anchor the fleet, then plausibly enough the Benthamites of war may urge the above.

But it *might have been* is but boggy ground to build on. And certainly in foresight as to the larger issue of an encounter, and anxious preparation for it—buoying the deadly way and mapping it out, as at Copenhagen—few commanders have been so painstakingly circumspect as this reckless declarer of his person in fight.

Personal prudence, even when dictated by quite other than selfish considerations, is surely no special virtue in a military man; while an excessive love of glory, exercising to the uttermost heartfelt sense of duty, is the first. If the name of *Wellington* is not so much a trumpet to the blood as the simpler name of *Nelson*, the reason for this may be inferred from the above. Alfred in his funeral ode on the victor of Waterloo ventures not to call him the greatest soldier of all time, though in the same ode he invokes Nelson as "the greatest sailor since the world began."

At Trafalgar, Nelson, on the brink of opening the fight, sat down and wrote his last brief will and testament. If under the presentiment of the most magnificent of all victories, to be crowned by his own glorious death, a sort of priestly motive led him to dress his person in the jewelled vouchers of his own shining deeds; if thus to have adorned himself for the altar and the sacrifice were indeed vainglory, then affectation and fustian is each truly heroic line in the great epics and dramas, since in such lines the poet but embodies in verse those exaltations of sentiment that a nature like Nelson, the opportunity being given, vitalizes into acts.

CHAPTER V

THE outbreak at the Nore was put down. But not every grievance was redressed. If the contractors, for example, were no longer permitted to ply some practices peculiar to their tribe everywhere, such as providing shoddy cloth, rations not sound, or false in the measure; not the less impressment, for one thing, went on. By custom sanctioned for centuries, and judicially maintained by a Lord Chancellor as late as Mansfield, that mode of manning the fleet, a mode now fallen into a sort of abeyance but never formally renounced, it was not practicable to give up in those years. Its abrogation would have crippled the indispensable fleet, one wholly under canvas, no steam-power, its innumerable sails and thousands of cannon, everything, in short, worked by muscle alone; a fleet the more insatiate in demand for men, because then multiplying its ships of all grades against contingencies present and to come of the convulsed Continent.

Discontent foreran the Two Mutinies, and more or less it lurkingly survived them. Hence it was not unreasonable to apprehend some return of trouble, sporadic or general. One instance of such apprehensions: In the same year with this story, Nelson, then Vice-Admiral Sir Horatio, being with the fleet off the Spanish coast, was directed by the Admiral in command to shift his pennant from the *Captain* to the *Theseus*; and for this reason: that the latter ship having newly arrived in the station from home where it had taken part in the Great Mutiny, danger was apprehended from the temper of the men; and it was thought that an officer like

Nelson was the one, not indeed to terrorize the crew into base subjection, but to win them by force of his mere presence back to an allegiance, if not as enthusiastic as his own, yet as true. So it was that for a time on more than one quarter-deck anxiety did exist. At sea precautionary vigilance was strained against relapse. At short notice an engagement might come on. When it did, the lieutenants assigned to batteries felt it incumbent on them in some instances to stand with drawn swords behind the men working the guns.

But on board the seventy-four in which Billy now swung his hammock, very little in the manner of the men and nothing obvious in the demeanour of the officers would have suggested to an ordinary observer that the Great Mutiny was a recent event. In their general bearing and conduct the commissioned officers of a war-ship naturally take their tone from the commander, that is if he has that ascendency of character that ought to be his.

Captain the Honourable Edward Fairfax Vere, to give his full title, was a bachelor of forty or thereabouts, a sailor of distinction, even in a time prolific of renowned seamen. Though allied to the higher nobility, his advancement had not been altogether owing to influences connected with that circumstance. He had seen much service, been in various engagements, always acquitting himself as an officer mindful of the welfare of his men, but never tolerating an infraction of discipline; thoroughly versed in the science of his profession, and intrepid to the verge of temerity, though never injudiciously so. For his gallantry in the West Indian waters as flag-lieutenant under Rodney in that Admiral's crowning victory, over De Grasse, he was made a post-captain.

Ashore in the garb of a civilian, scarce any one would have taken him for a sailor, more especially that he never garnished unprofessional talk with nautical terms, and grave in his bearing, evinced little appreciation of mere humour. It was not out of keeping with these traits that on a passage when nothing demanded his paramount action, he was the most undemonstrative of men. Any landsman observing this gentleman not conspicuous by his stature and wearing no pronounced insignia, emerging from his retreat to the open deck, and noting the silent deference of the officers retiring to leeward, might have taken him for the King's guest, a civilian aboard the King's ship, some highly honourable discreet envoy on his way to an important post. But, in fact, this unobtrusivness of demeanour may have proceeded from a certain unaffected modesty of manhood sometimes accompanying a resolute nature, a modesty evinced at all times not calling for pronounced action, and which shown in any rank of life suggests a virtue aristocratic in kind.

As with some others engaged in various departments of the world's more heroic activities, Captain Vere, though practical enough upon occasion, would at times betray a certain dreaminess of mood. Standing alone on the weather-side of the greater deck, one hand holding by the rigging, he would absently gaze off at the black sea. At the presentation to him then of some minor matter interrupting the current of his thoughts, he would show more or less irascibility; but instantly he would control it.

In the navy he was popularly known by the appellation— Starry Vere. How such a designation happened to fall upon one who, whatever his sturdy qualities, was without any brilliant ones, was in this wise: a favourite kinsman, Lord Denton, a free-handed fellow, had been the first to meet and congratulate him upon his return to England from the West Indian cruise; and but the day previous turning over a copy of Andrew Marvell's poems had lighted, not for the first time, however, upon the lines entitled "Appleton House," the name of one of the seats of their common ancestor, a hero in the German wars of the seventeenth century, in which poem occur the lines,

> *"This 'tis to have been from the first*
> *In a domestic heaven nursed,*
> *Under the discipline severe*
> *Of Fairfax and the starry Vere."*

And so, upon embracing his cousin fresh from Rodney's victory, wherein he had played so gallant a part, brimming over with just family pride in the sailor of their house, he exuberantly exclaimed, "Give ye joy, Ed; give ye joy, my starry Vere!" This got currency, and the novel prefix serving in familiar parlance readily to distinguish the *Indomitable's* Captain from another Vere, his senior, a distant relative, an officer of like rank in the navy, it remained permanently attached to the surname.

CHAPTER VI

In view of the part that the commander of the *Indomitable* plays in scenes shortly to follow, it may be well to fill out that sketch of him outlined in the previous chapter. Aside from his qualities as a sea-officer Captain Vere was an exceptional character. Unlike no few of England's renowned sailors, long and arduous service with signal devotion to it, had not resulted in absorbing and *salting* the entire man. He had a marked leaning towards everything intellectual. He loved books, never going to sea without a newly replenished library, compact but of the best. The isolated leisure, in some cases so wearisome, falling at intervals to commanders even during a war-cruise, never was tedious to Captain Vere. With nothing of that literary taste which less heeds the thing conveyed than the vehicle, his bias was towards those books to which every serious mind of superior order occupying any active post of authority in the world, naturally inclines; books treating of actual men and events, no matter of what era—history, biography and unconventional writers, who, free from cant and convention, like Montaigne, honestly, and in the spirit of common sense, philosophize upon realities.

In this love of reading he found confirmation of his own more reserved thoughts—confirmation which he had vainly sought in social converse, so that as touching most fundamental topics, there had got to be established in him some positive convictions which he forefelt would abide in him essentially unmodified so long as his intelligent part remained unimpaired. In view of the humbled position in which his lot was cast, this was well for him. His settled convictions were as a dyke against those invading waters of novel opinion social, political, and otherwise, which carried away as in a torrent no few minds in those days, minds by nature not inferior to his own. While other members of that aristocracy to which by birth he belonged were incensed at the innovators mainly because their theories were inimical to the privileged classes, Captain Vere disinterestedly opposed them because they seemed to him incapable of embodiment in lasting institutions, but at war with the peace of the world and the good of mankind.

With minds less stored than his and less earnest, some officers of his rank, with whom at times he would necessarily consort, found him lacking in the companionable quality, a dry and bookish gentleman as they deemed. Upon any chance withdrawal from their company one would be apt to say to another something like this: "Vere is a noble fellow,

Starry Vere. 'Spite the gazettes, Sir Horatio is at bottom scarce a better seaman or fighter. But between you and me now, don't you think there is a queer streak of the pedantic running through him? Yes, like the King's yarn in a coil of navy-rope?"

Some apparent ground there was for this sort of confidential criticism; since not only did the Captain's discourse never fall into the jocosely familiar, but in illustrating any point touching the stirring personages and events of the time, he would cite some historic character or incident of antiquity with the same easy air that he would cite from the moderns. He seemed unmindful of the circumstance that to his bluff company such remote allusions, however pertinent they might really be, were altogether alien to men whose reading was mainly confined to the journals. But considerateness in such matters is not easy to natures constituted like Captain Vere's. Their honesty prescribes to them directness, sometimes far-reaching, like that of a migratory fowl that in its flight never heeds when it crosses a frontier.

CHAPTER VII

THE lieutenants and other commissioned gentlemen forming Captain Vere's staff it is not necessary here to particularize nor needs it to make mention of any of the warrant-officers. But among the petty officers was one who, having much to do with the story, may as well be forthwith introduced. This portrait I essay, but shall never hit it.

This was John Claggart, the master-at-arms. But that sea-title may to landsmen seem somewhat equivocal. Originally, doubtless, that petty-officer's function was the instruction of the men in the use of arms, sword, or cutlass. But very long ago, owing to the advance in gunnery making hand-to-hand encounters less frequent—and giving to nitre and sulphur the pre-eminence over steel—that function ceased; the master-at-arms of a great war-ship becoming a sort of Chief of Police charged, among other matters, with the duty of preserving order on the populous lower gun-decks.

Claggart was a man of about five-and-thirty, somewhat spare and tall yet of no ill figure upon the whole. His hand was too small and shapely to have been accustomed to hard toil. The face was a notable one; the features, all except the chin, cleanly cut as those on a Greek medallion; yet the chin, beardless as Tecumseh's, had something of the strange protuberant heaviness in its make that recalled the prints of the Rev. Dr. Titus Oates, the historical deponent with the clerical drawl in the time of Charles II, and the fraud of the alleged Popish Plot. It served Claggart in his office that his eye could cast a tutoring glance. His brow was of the sort phrenologically associated with more than average intellect; silken jet curls partly clustering over it, making a foil to the pallor below, a pallor tinged with a faint shade of amber akin to the hue of time-tinted marbles of old.

This complexion singularly contrasting with the red or deeply bronzed visages of the sailors, and in part the result of his official seclusion from the sunlight, though it was not exactly displeasing, nevertheless seemed to hint of something defective or abnormal in the constitution and blood. But his general aspect and manner were so suggestive of an education and career incongruous with his naval function, that when not actively engaged in it he looked like a man of high quality, social and moral, who for reasons of his own was keeping incog. Nothing was known of his former life. It might be that he was an Englishman; and yet there lurked a bit of accent in his speech suggesting that possibly he was not such by birth, but through naturalization in early child-hood. Among certain grizzled sea-gossips of the gun-decks and forecastle went a rumour perdue that the master-at-arms was a chevalier who had volunteered into the King's navy by way of compounding for some mysterious swindle whereof he had been arraigned at the King's bench. The fact that nobody could substantiate this report was, of course, nothing against its secret currency. Such a rumour once started on the gun-decks in reference to almost any one below the rank of a commissioned officer would, during the period assigned to this narrative, have seemed not altogether wanting in credibility to the tarry old wiseacres of a man-of-war crew. And indeed a man of Claggart's accomplishments, without prior nautical experience entering the navy at mature life, as he did, and necessarily allotted at the start to the lowest grade in it; a man, too, who never made allusion to his previous life ashore; these were circumstances which in the dearth of exact knowledge as to his true antecedents opened to the invidious a vague field for unfavourable surmise.

But the sailors' dog-watch gossip concerning him derived a vague plausibility from the fact that now, for some period, the British Navy could so little afford to be squeamish in the matter of keeping up the muster-rolls, that not only were press-gangs notoriously abroad both afloat and ashore, but there was little or no secret about another matter, namely, that the London police were at liberty to capture any able-bodied suspect, and any questionable fellow at large, and summarily ship him to the dock-yard or fleet. Furthermore, even among voluntary enlistments, there were instances where the motive thereto partook neither of patriotic impulse nor yet of a random desire to experience a bit of sea-life and martial adventure. Insolvent debtors of minor grade, to-gether with the promiscuous lame ducks of morality, found in the navy a convenient and secure refuge. Secure, because once enlisted aboard a King's-Ship, they were as much in sanctuary, as the transgressor of the middle ages harbouring himself under the shadow of the altar. Such sanctioned irregularities, which for obvious reasons the Government would hardly think to parade at the time—and which consequently, and as affecting the least influential class of mankind, have all but dropped into oblivion—lends colour to something for the truth whereof I do not vouch, and hence have some scruple in stating; something I remember having seen in print, though the book I cannot recall; but the same thing was personally communicated to me now more than forty years ago by an old pensioner in a cocked hat, with whom I had a most interesting talk on the terrace at Greenwich, a Baltimore negro, a Trafalgar man. It was to this effect: In the case of a war-ship short of hands, whose speedy sailing was imperative, the deficient quota, in lack of any other way of making it good, would be eked out by drafts called direct from the jails. For reasons previously suggested it would not perhaps be very easy at the present day directly to prove or disprove the allegation. But allowed as a verity, how significant would it be of England's straits at the time, confronted by those wars which, like a flight of harpies, rose shrieking from the din and dust of the fallen Bastille. That era appears measurably clear to us who look back at it, and but read of it. But to the grandfathers of us greybeards, the thoughtful of them, the genius of it presented an aspect like that of Camoen's "Spirit of the Cape," an eclipsing menace, mysterious and prodigious. Not America even was exempt from apprehension. At the height of Napoleon's unexampled conquests, there were Americans who had fought at Bunker Hill, who looked forward to the possibility that the Atlantic might prove no barrier against the ultimate schemes of this portentous upstart from the revolutionary chaos, who seemed in act of fulfilling the judgment prefigured in the Apocalypse.

But the less credence was to be given to the gun-deck talk touching Claggart, seeing that no man holding his office in a man-of-war can ever hope to be popular with the crew. Besides, in derogatory comments upon any one against whom they have a grudge, or for any reason or no reason mislike, sailors are much like landsmen: they are apt to exaggerate or romance it.

About as much was really known to the *Indomitable's* tars of the Master-at-arms' career before entering the service as an astronomer knows about a comet's travels prior to its first observable appearance in the sky. The verdict of the sea *guid nunc's* has been cited only by way of showing what sort of moral impression the man made upon rude uncultivated natures whose conceptions of human wickedness were necessarily of the narrowest, limited to ideas of vulgar rascality, —a thief among the swinging hammocks during a nightwatch, or the man-brokers and land-sharks of the seaports.

It was no gossip, however, but fact, that though, as before hinted, Claggart upon his entrance into the navy was, as a novice, assigned to the least honourable section of a man-of-war's crew, embracing the drudges, he did not long remain there.

The superior capacity he immediately evinced, his constitutional sobriety, his ingratiating deference to superiors, together with a peculiar ferreting genius manifested on a singular occasion, all this capped by a certain austere patriotism, abruptly advanced him to the position of Master-at-arms.

Of this maritime Chief of Police the ship's-corporals, so called, were the immediate subordinates, and compliant ones;

and this—as is to be noted in some business departments
ashore—almost to a degree inconsistent with entire moral
volition. His place put various converging wires of under-
ground influence under the Chief's control, capable when
astutely worked through his understrappers of operating to
the mysterious discomfort, if nothing worse, of any of the
sea-commonalty.

CHAPTER VIII

LIFE in the foretop well agreed with Billy Budd. There,
when not actually engaged on the yards yet higher aloft,
the topmen, who as such had been picked out for youth and
activity, constituted an aerial club, lounging at ease against
the smaller stun'sails rolled up into cushions, spinning yarns
like the lazy gods, and frequently amused with what was
going on in the busy world of the decks below. No wonder
then that a young fellow of Billy's disposition was well content in such society. Giving no cause of offence to anybody,
he was always alert at a call. So in the merchant service it
had been with him. But now such punctiliousness in duty
was shown that his topmates would sometimes good-
naturedly laugh at him for it. This heightened alacrity had
its cause, namely, the impression made upon him by the first
formal gangway-punishment he had ever witnessed, which
befell the day following his impressment. It had been in-
curred by a little fellow, young, a novice, an after-guardsman
absent from his assigned post when the ship was being put
about, a dereliction resulting in a rather serious hitch to that
manœuvre, one demanding instantaneous promptitude in
letting go and making fast. When Billy saw the culprit's
naked back under the scourge gridironed with red welts,
and worse; when he marked the dire expression in the

liberated man's face, as with his woolen shirt flung over him by the executioner, he rushed forward from the spot to bury himself in the crowd, Billy was horrified. He resolved that never through remissness would he make himself liable to such a visitation, or do or omit aught that might merit even verbal reproof. What then was his surprise and concern when ultimately he found himself getting into petty trouble occasionally about such matters as the stowage of his bag, or something amiss in his hammock, matters under the police oversight of the ship's-corporals of the lower decks, and which brought down on him a vague threat from one of them.

So heedful in all things as he was, how could this be? He could not understand it, and it more than vexed him. When he spoke to his young topmates about it, they were either lightly incredulous, or found something comical in his unconcealed anxiety. "Is it your bag, Billy?" said one; "well, sew yourself up in it, Billy boy, and then you'll be sure to know if anybody meddles with it."

Now there was a veteran aboard who, because his years began to disqualify him for more active work, had been recently assigned duty as mainmast-man in his watch, looking to the gear belayed at the rail round about that great spar near the deck. At off-times the foretopman had picked up some acquaintance with him, and now in his trouble it occurred to him that he might be the sort of person to go to for wise council. He was an old Dansker long anglicized in the service, of few words, many wrinkles and some honourable scars. His wizened face, time-tinted and weather-stormed to the complexion of an antique parchment, was here and there peppered blue by the chance explosion of a gun-cartridge in action. He was an *Agamemnon*-man; some two years prior to the time of this story having served under Nelson, when but Sir Horatio, in that ship immortal in naval memory, and which, dismantled and in part broken up to her bare ribs, is seen a grand skeleton in Hayden's etching. As one of a boarding-party from the *Agamemnon* he had received a cut slantwise along one temple and cheek, leaving a long pale scar like a streak of dawn's light falling athwart the dark visage. It was on account of that scar and the affair in which it was known that he had received it, as well as from his blue-peppered complexion, that the Dansker went among the *Indomitable's* crew by the name of "Board-her-in-the-smoke."

Now the first time that his small weazel-eyes happened to light on Billy Budd, a certain grim internal merriment set all his ancient wrinkles into antic play. Was it that his eccentric unsentimental old sapience, primitive in its kind, saw, or thought it saw, something which in contrast with the war-ship's environment looked oddly incongruous in the Handsome Sailor? But after slyly studying him at intervals, the old Merlin's equivocal merriment was modified. For now when the twain would meet, it would start in his face a quizzing sort of look, but it would be but momentary, and sometimes replaced by an expression of speculative query as to what might eventually befall a nature like that, dropped into a world not without some man-traps and against whose subtleties simple courage lacking experience and address and without any touch of defensive ugliness, is of little avail; and where such innocence as man is capable of does yet, in a moral emergency, not always sharpen the faculties or enlighten the will.

However it was, the Dansker in his ascetic way rather took to Billy. Nor was this only because of a certain philosophic interest in such a character. There was another cause. While the old man's eccentricities, sometimes bordering on the ursine, repelled the juniors, Billy, undeterred thereby, would make advances, never passing the old *Aga-memnon*-man without a salutation marked by that respect which is seldom lost on the aged, however crabbed at times, or whatever their station in life. There was a vein of dry humour, or what not, in the mast-man; and whether in freak of patriarchal irony touching Billy's youth and athletic frame, or for some other and more recondite reason, from the first in addressing him he always substituted Baby for Billy. The Dansker, in fact, being the originator of the name by which the foretopman eventually became known aboard ship.

Well then, in his mysterious little difficulty going in quest of the wrinkled one, Billy found him off duty in a dog-watch ruminating by himself, seated on a shot-box of the upper gun-deck, now and then surveying with a somewhat cynical regard certain of the more swaggering promenaders there. Billy recounted his trouble, again wondering how it all happened. The salt seer attentively listened, accompanying the foretopman's recitals with queer twitchings of his wrinkles and problematical little sparkles of his small ferret eyes. Making an end of his story, the foretopman asked, "And now, Dansker, do tell me what you think of it."

The old man, shoving up the front of his tarpaulin and deliberately rubbing the long slant scar at the point where it entered the thin hair, laconically said, "Baby Budd, *Jimmy Legs*" (meaning the master-at-arms) "is down on you."

"*Jimmy Legs!*" ejaculated Billy his welkin eyes expanding; "what for? Why he calls me *the sweet and pleasant young fellow*, they tell me."

"Does he so?" grinned the grizzled one; then said, "Ay, Baby Lad, a sweet voice has *Jimmy Legs*."

"No, not always. But to me he has. I seldom pass him but there comes a pleasant word."

"And that's because he's down upon you, Baby Budd."

Such reiteration, along with the manner of it (incomprehensible to a novice), disturbed Billy almost as much as the mystery for which he had sought explanation. Something less unpleasingly oracular he tried to extract. But the old sea-chiron, thinking perhaps that for the nonce he had sufficiently instructed his young Achilles, pursed his lips, gathered all his wrinkles together, and would commit himself to nothing further.

Years, and those experiences which befall certain shrewder men subordinated life-long to the will of superiors, all this had developed in the Dansker the pithy guarded cynicism that was his leading characteristic.

CHAPTER IX

THE next day an incident served to confirm Billy Budd in his incredulity as to the Dansker's strange summing up of the case submitted.

The ship at noon going large before the wind was rolling on her course, and he, below at dinner and engaged in some sportful talk with the members of his mess, chanced in a sudden lurch to spill the entire contents of his soup-pan upon the new scrubbed deck. Claggart, the master-at-arms, official rattan in hand, happened to be passing along the battery, in a bay of which the mess was lodged, and the greasy liquid streamed just across his path. Stepping over it, he was proceeding on his way without comment, since the matter was nothing to take notice of under the circumstances, when he happened to observe who it was that had done the spilling. His countenance changed. Pausing, he was about to ejaculate something hasty at the sailor, but checked himself, and pointing down to the streaming soup, playfully tapped him from behind with his rattan, saying, in a low musical voice, peculiar to him at times, "Handsomely done, my lad! And handsome is as handsome did it, too!" and with that passed on. Not noted by Billy as not coming within his view was the involuntary smile, or rather grimace, that accompanied Claggart's equivocal words. Aridly it drew down the thin corners of his shapely mouth. But everybody taking his remark as meant for humorous, and at which therefore as coming from a superior they were bound to laugh, "with counterfeited glee" acted accordingly; and Billy tickled, it may be, by the allusion to his being the handsome sailor, merrily joined in; then addressing his messmates exclaimed, "There now, who says that Jimmy Legs is down on me!"

"And who said he was, Beauty?" demanded one Donald with some surprise. Whereat the foretopman looked a little foolish, recalling that it was only one person, Board-her-in-the-smoke, who had suggested what to him was the smoky idea that this master-at-arms was in any peculiar way hostile to him. Meantime that functionary resuming his path must have momentarily worn some expression less guarded than that of the bitter smile and, usurping the face from the heart, some distorting expression perhaps—for a drummer-boy, heedlessly frolicking along from the opposite direction, and chancing to come into light collision with his person was strangely disconcerted by his aspect. Nor was the impression lessened when the official, impulsively giving him a sharp cut with the rattan, vehemently exclaimed, "Look where you go!"

CHAPTER X

WHAT was the matter with the Master-at-arms? And, be the matter what it might, how could it have direct relation to Billy Budd, with whom prior to the affair of the spilled soup he had never come into any special contact, official or otherwise? What indeed could the trouble have to do with one so little inclined to give offence as the merchant-ship's *peacemaker*, even him who in Claggart's own phrase was "The sweet and pleasant young fellow"? Yes, why should *Jimmy Legs*, to borrow the Dansker's expression, be *down* on the Handsome Sailor?

But at heart and not for nothing, as the late chance encounter may indicate to the discerning, down on him, secretly down on him, he assuredly was.

Now to invent something touching the more private career of Claggart—something involving Billy Budd, of which something the latter should be wholly ignorant, some romantic incident implying that Claggart's knowledge of the young blue-jacket began at some period anterior to catching sight of him on board the seventy-four—all this, not so difficult to do, might avail in a more or less interesting way to account for whatever enigma may appear to lurk in the case. But, in fact, there was nothing of the sort. And yet the cause, necessarily to be assumed as the sole one assignable, is in its very realism as much charged with that prime element of Radcliffian romance, *the mysterious*, as any that the ingenuity of the author of the "Mysteries of Udolpho" could devise. For what can more partake of the mysterious than an antipathy spontaneous and profound such as is evoked in certain exceptional mortals by the mere aspect of some other mortal, however harmless he may be?—if not called forth by that very harmlessness itself.

Now there can exist no irritating juxtaposition of dissimilar personalities comparable to that which is possible aboard a great war-ship fully manned and at sea. There, every day, among all ranks. almost every man comes into more or less of contact with almost every other man. Wholly there to avoid even the sight of an aggravating object one must needs give it Jonah's toss, or jump overboard himself. Imagine how all this might eventually operate on some peculiar human creature the direct reverse of a saint?

But for the adequate comprehending of Claggart by a normal nature, these hints are insufficient. To pass from a normal nature to him one must cross "The deadly space between," and this is best done by indirection.

Long ago an honest scholar, my senior, said to me in reference to one who like himself is now no more, a man so unimpeachably respectable that against him nothing was ever openly said, though among the few something was whispered, "Yes, X—— is a nut not to be cracked by the tap of a lady's fan. You are aware that I am the adherent of no organized religion, much less of any philosophy built into a system. Well, for all that, I think that to try and get into X——, enter his labyrinth and get out again, without a clue derived from some source other than what is known as *knowledge of the world*—that were hardly possible, at least for me."

"Why," said I, "X——, however singular a study to some, is yet human, and knowledge of the world assuredly implies the knowledge of human nature, and in most of its varieties."

"Yes, but a superficial knowledge of it, serving ordinary purposes. But for anything deeper, I am not certain whether to know the world and to know human nature be not two distinct branches of knowledge, which while they may coexist in the same heart, yet either may exist with little or nothing of the other. Nay, in an average man of the world, his constant rubbing with it blunts that fine spiritual insight indispensable to the understanding of the essential in certain exceptional characters, whether evil ones or good. In a matter of some importance I have seen a girl wind an old lawyer about her little finger. Nor was it the dotage of senile love. Nothing of the sort. But he knew law better than he knew the girl's heart. Coke and Blackstone hardly shed so much light into obscure spiritual places as the Hebrew prophets. And who were they? Mostly recluses."

At the time my inexperience was such that I did not quite see the drift of all this. It may be that I see it now. And, indeed, if that lexicon which is based on Holy Writ were any longer popular, one might with less difficulty define and denominate certain phenomenal men. . . As it is, one must turn to some authority not liable to the charge of being tinctured with the Biblical element.

In a list of definitions included in the authentic translation of Plato, a list attributed to him, occurs this: "Natural Depravity: a depravity according to nature." A definition which though savouring of Calvinism by no means involves Calvin's dogma as to total mankind. Evidently its intent makes it applicable but to individuals. Not many are the examples of this depravity which the gallows and jail supply. At any rate, for notable instances,—since these have no vulgar alloy of the brute in them, but invariably are dominated by intellectuality,—one must go elsewhere. Civilization, especially if of the austerer sort, is auspicious to it. It folds itself in the mantle of respectability. It has its certain negative virtues serving as silent auxiliaries. It never allows wine to get within its guard. It is not going too far to say that it is without vices or small sins. There is a phenomenal pride in it that excludes them from anything. Never mercenary or avaricious. In short, the depravity here meant partakes nothing of the sordid or sensual. It is serious, but free from acerbity. Though no flatterer of mankind it never speaks ill of it.

But the thing which in eminent instances signalizes so exceptional a nature is this: though the man's even temper and discreet bearing would seem to intimate a mind peculiarly subject to the law of reason, not the less in his soul's recesses he would seem to riot in complete exemption from that law, having apparently little to do with reason further than to employ it as an ambidexter implement for effecting the irrational. That is to say: towards the accomplishment of an aim which in wantonness of malignity would seem to partake of the insane, he will direct a cool judgment sagacious and sound.

These men are true madmen, and of the most dangerous sort, for their lunacy is not continuous, but occasional; evoked by some special object; it is secretive and self-contained: so that when most active it is, to the average mind, not distinguished from sanity, and for the reason above suggested that whatever its aims may be (and the aim is never disclosed) the method and the outward proceeding is always perfectly rational.

Now something such was Claggart, in whom was the mania of an evil nature, not engendered by vicious training or corrupting books or licentious living, but born with him and innate, in short, "a depravity according to nature."

Can it be this phenomenon, disowned or not acknowledged, that in some criminal cases puzzles the courts? For this cause have our juries at times not only to endure the prolonged contentions of lawyers with their fees, but also the yet more perplexing strife of the medical experts with theirs? And why leave it to them? Why not subpoena as well the clerical proficients? Their vocation bringing them into peculiar contact with so many human beings, and sometimes in their least guarded hour, in interviews very much more confidential than those of physician and patient; this would seem to qualify them to know something about those intricacies involved in the question of moral responsibility; whether in a given case, say, the crime proceeded from manis in the brain or rabies of the heart. As to any differences among themselves which clerical proficients might develop on the stand, these could hardly be greater than the direct contradictions exchanged between the remunerated medical experts.

Dark sayings are these, some will say. But why? It is because they somewhat savour of Holy Writ in its phrase "mysteries of iniquity."

The point of the story turning on the hidden nature of the Master-at-arms has necessitated this chapter. With an added hint or two in connection with the incident at the mess, the resumed narrative must be left to vindicate as it may, its own credibility.

CHAPTER XI

(Pale ire, envy and despair)

THAT Claggart's figure was not amiss, and his face, save the chin, well moulded, has already been said. Of these favourable points he seemed not insensible, for he was not only neat but careful in his dress. But the form of Billy Budd was heroic; and if his face was without the intellectual look of the pallid Claggart's, not the less was it lit, like his, from within, though from a different source. The bonfire in his heart made luminous the rose-tan in his cheek.

In view of the marked contrast between the persons of the twain, it is more than probable that when the Master-at-arms in the scene last given applied to the sailor the proverb *Handsome is as handsome does* he there let escape an ironic inkling, not caught by the young sailors who heard it, as to what it was that had first moved him against Billy, namely, his significant personal beauty.

Now envy and antipathy, passions irreconcilable in reason, nevertheless in fact may spring conjoined like Chang and Eng in one birth. Is Envy then such a monster? Well, though many an arraigned mortal has in hopes of mitigated penalty pleaded guilty to horrible actions, did ever anybody seriously confess to envy? Something there is in it universally felt to be more shameful than even felonious crime. And not only does everybody disown it, but the better sort are inclined to incredulity when it is in earnest imputed to an intelligent man. But since its lodgment is in the heart, not the brain, no degree of intellect supplies a guarantee against it. But Claggart's was no vulgar form of the passion. Nor, as directed toward Billy Budd, did it partake of that streak of apprehensive jealousy which marred Saul's visage perturbedly brooding on the comely young David. Claggart's envy struck deeper. If askance he eyed the good looks, cheery health and frank enjoyment of young life in Billy Budd, it was because these happened to go along with a nature that, as Claggart magnetically felt, had in its simplicity never willed malice or experienced the reactionary bite of that serpent. To him, the spirit lodged within Billy, and looking out from his welkin eyes as from windows—that ineffability it was which made the dimple in his dyed cheeks, suppled his joints, and dancing in his yellow curls made him pre-eminently the Handsome Sailor. One person excepted, the Master-at-arms was perhaps the only man in the ship intellectually capable of adequately appreciating the moral phenomenon presented in Billy Budd, and the insight but intensified his passion, which, assuming various secret forms within him, at times assumed that of cynic disdain—disdain of innocence. To be nothing more than innocent! Yet in all æsthetic way he saw the charm of it, the courageous free-and-easy temper of it, and fain would have shared it, but he despaired of it.

With no power to annul the elemental evil in himself, though readily enough he could hide it; apprehending the good, but powerless to be it; a nature like Claggart's, surcharged with energy as such natures almost invariably are, what recourse is left to it but to recoil upon itself and like the scorpion for which the Creator alone is responsible, act out to the end the part allotted it.

Passion, and passion in its profoundest, is not a thing demanding a palatial stage whereon to play its part. Down among the groundlings, among the beggars and rakers of the garbage, profound passion is enacted. And the circumstances that provoke it, however trivial or mean, are no measure of its power. In the present instance the stage is a scrubbed gundeck, and one of the external provocations a man-of-war's man's spilled soup.

Now when the Master-at-arms noticed whence came that greasy fluid streaming before his feet, he must have taken it—to some extent wilfully perhaps—not for the mere accident it assuredly was, but for the sly escape of a spontaneous feeling on Billy's part more or less answering to the antipathy on his own. In effect a foolish demonstration he must have thought, and very harmless, like the futile kick of a heifer, which yet were the heifer a shod stallion would not be so harmless. Even so was it that into the gall of envy Claggart infused the vitriol of his contempt. But the incident confirmed to him certain tell-tale reports purveyed to his ear by *Squeak*, one of his more cunning corporals, a grizzled little man, so nicknamed by the sailors on account of his squeakv voice and sharp visage ferreting about the dark corners of the lower decks after interlopers, satirically suggesting to them the idea of a rat in a cellar.

Now his chief's employing him as an implicit tool in laying little traps for the worriment of the foretopman—for it was from the Master-at-arms that the petty persecutions heretofore adverted to had proceeded—the corporal, having naturally enough concluded that his master could have no love for the sailor, made it his business, faithful understrapper that he was, to ferment the ill blood by perverting to his chief certain innocent frolics of the good-natured foretopman, besides inventing for his master sundry contumelious epithets he claimed to have overheard him let fall. The Master-at-arms never suspected the veracity of these reports, more especially as to the epithets, for he well knew how secretly unpopular may become a Master-at-arms—at least a Master-at-arms of those days, zealous in his function—how the blue-jackets shot at him in private their raillery and wit; the nickname by which he goes among them (*Jimmy Legs*) implying under the form of merriment their cherished direspect and dislike.

But in view of the greediness of hate for provocation, it hardly needed a purveyor to feed Claggart's passion. An uncommon prudence is habitual with the subtler depravity, for it has everything to hide. And in case of any merely suspected injury its secretiveness voluntarily cuts it off from enlightenment or disillusion; and not unreluctantly, action is taken upon surmise as upon certainty. And the retaliation is apt to be in monstrous disproportion to the supposed offence; for when in anybody was revenge in its exactions aught else but an inordinate usurer? But how with Claggart's conscience? For though consciences are unlike as foreheads, every intelligence, not including the Scriptural devils who "believe and tremble," has one. But Claggart's conscience

being but the lawyer to his will, made ogres of trifles, probably arguing that the motive imputed to Billy in spilling the
soup just when he did, together with the epithets alleged—
these, if nothing more, made a strong case against him; nay,
justified animosity into a sort of retributive righteousness.
The Pharisee is the Guy Fawkes prowling in the hid chambers underlying some natures like Claggart's. And they
can really form no conception of an unreciprocated malice.
Probably, the Master-at-arms' clandestine persecutions of
Billy were started to try the temper of the man; but they had
not developed any quality in him that enmity could make
official use of, or ever pervert into even plausible self-justi-
fication; so that the occurrence at the mess, petty if it were,
was a welcome one to that peculiar conscience assigned to be
the private mentor of Claggart; and for the rest, not im-
probably it put him upon new experiments.

CHAPTER XII

Not many days after the last incident narrated, something
befell Billy Budd that more gravelled him than aught that
had previously occurred.

It was a warm night for the latitude; and the foretopman,
whose watch at the time was properly below, was dozing on
the uppermost deck whither he had ascended from his hot
hammock—one of hundreds suspended so closely wedged
together over a lower gun-deck that there was little or no
swing to them. He lay as in the shadow of a hill-side
stretched under the lee of the *booms*, a piled ridge of spare
spars, and among which the ship's largest boat, the launch,
was stowed. Alongside of three other slumberers from
below, he lay near one end of the booms which approached
from the foremast; his station aloft on duty as a foretopman

being just over the deck station of the forecastlemen entitling him according to usage to make himself more or less at home in that neighbourhood.

Presently he was stirred into semi-consciousness by some-body, who must have previously sounded the sleep of the others, touching his shoulder, and then as the foretopman raised his head, breathing into his ear in a quick whisper, "Slip into the lee fore-chains, Billy; there is something in the wind—don't speak. Quick. I will meet you there;" and disappeared.

Now Billy—like sundry other essentially good-natured ones—had some of the weakness inseparable from essential good nature; and among these was a reluctance, almost an incapacity of plumply saying *no* to an abrupt proposition not obviously absurd, on the face of it, nor obviously unfriendly, nor iniquitous. And being of warm blood he had not the phlegm to negative any proposition by unresponsive inaction. Like his sense of fear, his apprehension as to aught outside of the honest and natural was seldom very quick. Besides, upon the present occasion, the drowse from his sleep still hung upon him.

However it was, he mechanically rose and, sleepily won-dering what could be *in the wind*, betook himself to the desig-nated place, a narrow platform, one of six, outside of the high bulwarks and screened by the great dead-eyes and mul-tiple columned lanyards of the shrouds and back-stays; and, in a great war-ship of that time, of dimensions commensurate to the ample hull's magnitude; a tarry balcony, in short, overhanging the sea, and so secluded that one mariner of the *Indomitable*, a non-conformist old tar of serious turn, made it even in daytime his private oratory.

In this retired nook the stranger soon joined Billy Budd. There was no moon as yet; a haze obscured the star-light.

He could not distinctly see the stranger's face. Yet from something in the outline and carriage, Billy took him to be, and correctly, for one of the afterguard.

"Hist Billy!" said the man; in the same quick cautionary whisper as before; "You were impressed, weren't you? Well, so was I;" and he paused as to mark the effect. But Billy, not knowing exactly what to make of this, said nothing. Then the other: "We are not the only impressed ones, Billy. There's a gang of us. Couldn't you—help—at a pinch?"

"What do you mean?" demanded Billy here shaking off his drowse.

"Hist, hist!" the hurried whisper now growing husky, "see here;" and the man held up two small objects faintly twinkling in the night light; "See, they are yours, Bill, if you'll only—"

But Billy here broke in, and in his resentful eagerness to deliver himself his vocal infirmity somewhat intruded; "D-D-Damme, I don't know what you are d-driving at, or what you mean, but you had better g-g-go where you belong!" For the moment the fellow, as confounded, did not stir; and Billy, springing to his feet, said, "If you d-don't start, I'll t-t-toss you back over the r-rail!" There was no mistaking this, and the mysterious emissary decamped, disappearing in the direction of the mainmast in the shadow of the booms.

"Hallo, what's the matter?" here came growling from a forecastleman awakened from his deck-doze by Billy's raised voice. And as the foretopman reappeared and was recognized by him; "Ah, *Beauty*, is it you? Well, something must have been the matter for you st-st-stuttered."

"Oh," rejoined Billy, now mastering the impediment; "I found an afterguardsman in our part of the ship here and I bid him be off where he belongs."

"And is that all you did about it, foretopman?" gruffly demanded another, an irascible old fellow of brick-coloured visage and hair, and who was known to his associate forecastlemen as *Red Pepper*.

"Such sneaks I should like to marry to the gunner's daughter!" by that expression meaning that he would like to subject them to disciplinary castigation over a gun.

However, Billy's rendering of the matter satisfactorily accounted to these inquirers for the brief commotion, since of all the sections of a ship's company the forecastlemen, veterans for the most part, and bigoted in their sea-prejudices, are the most jealous in resenting territorial encroachments, especially on the part of any of the after guard, of whom they have but a sorry opinion, chiefly landsmen, never going aloft except to reef or furl the mainsail, and in no wise competent to handle a marlingspike or turn in a *dead-eye*, say.

CHAPTER XIII

THIS incident sorely puzzled Billy Budd. It was an entirely new experience—the first time in his life that he had ever been personally approached in underhanded intriguing fashion. Prior to this encounter he had known nothing of the afterguardsman, the two men being stationed wide apart, one forward and aloft during his watch, the other on deck and aft.

What could it mean? And could they really be guineas, those two glittering objects the interloper had held up to his (Billy's) eyes? Where could the fellow get guineas? Why, even buttons, spare buttons, are not so plentiful at sea. The more he turned the matter over, the more the was nonplussed, and made uneasy and discomfited. In his disgustful recoil from an overture which, though he but ill comprehended, he instinctively knew must involve evil of some sort—Billy Budd was like a young horse fresh from the pasture suddenly inhaling a vile whiff from some chemical factory and by repeated snortings trying to get it out of his nostrils and lungs. This frame of mind barred all desire of holding further parley with the fellow, even were it but for the purpose of gaining some enlightenment as to his design in approaching him. And yet he was not without natural curiosity to see how such a visitor in the dark would look in broad day.

He espied him the following afternoon in his first dog-watch below, one of the smokers on that forward part of the upper gun-deck allotted to the pipe. He recognized him by his general cut and build, more than by his round freckled face and glassy eyes of pale blue, veiled with lashes all but white. And yet Billy was a bit uncertain whether indeed it were he—yonder chap about his own age, chatting and laughing in a free-hearted way, leaning against a gun,—a genial young fellow enough to look at, and something of a rattle-brain, to all appearance. Rather chubby, too, for a sailor, even an afterguardsman. In short the last man in the world —one would think—to be overburthened with thoughts, especially those perilous thoughts that must needs belong to a conspirator in any serious project, or even to the underling of such a conspirator.

Although Billy was not aware of it, the fellow, with one sidelong watchful glance had perceived Billy first, and then noting that Billy was looking at him, thereupon nodded a familiar sort of friendly recognition as to an old acquaintance, without interrupting the talk he was engaged in with the group of smokers. A day or two afterwards, chancing in the evening promenade on a gun-deck, to pass Billy, he offered a flying word of good-fellowship, as it were, which by its unexpectedness, and equivocalness under the circumstances, so embarrassed Billy that he knew not how to respond to it, and let it go unnoticed.

Billy was now left more at a loss than before. The ineffectual speculations into which he was led were so disturbingly alien to him that he did his best to smother them. It never entered his mind that here was a matter, which, from its extreme questionableness, it was his duty as a loyal blue-jacket to report in the proper quarter. And, probably, had such a step been suggested to him, he would have been deterred from taking it by the thought—one of novice-magnanimity—that it would savour overmuch of the dirty work of a tell-tale. He kept the thing to himself. Yet upon one occasion he could not forbear a little disburthening himself to the old Dansker, tempted thereto perhaps by the influence of a balmy night when the ship lay becalmed; the twain, silent for the most part, sitting together on deck, their heads propped against the bulwarks. But it was only a partial and anonymous account that Billy gave— the unfounded scruples above referred to preventing full disclosure to anybody. Upon hearing Billy's version, the sage Dansker seemed to divine more than he was told; and after a little meditation, during which his wrinkles were pursed as into a point—quite effacing for the time that quizzing expression his face sometimes wore—answered: "Didn't I say so, Baby Budd?"

"Say what?" demanded Billy.

"Why, *Jimmy Legs* is *down* on you."

"And what," rejoined Billy in amazement, "has *Jimmy Legs* to do with that cracked afterguardsman?"

"Ho, it was an afterguardsman, then: a cat's-paw, only a cat's-paw!" And with that exclamation, which, whether it had reference to a light puff of air just then coming over the calm sea, or subtler relation to the afterguardsman, there is no telling. The old Merlin gave a twisting wrench with his black teeth at his plug of tobacco—vouchsafing no reply to Billy's impetuous question, though now repeated, for it was his wont to relapse into grim silence when interrogated in sceptical sort as to any of his sententious oracles, not always very clear ones, but rather partaking of that obscurity which invests most Delphic deliverances from any quarter.

CHAPTER XIV

LONG experience had very likely brought this old man to that bitter prudence which never interferes in aught, and never gives advice.

Yes, despite the Dansker's pithy insistence as to the Master-at-arms being at the bottom of these strange experiences of Billy on board the *Indomitable*, the young sailor was ready to ascribe them to almost anybody but the man who, to use Billy's own expression, "always had a pleasant word for him." This is to be wondered at. Yet not so much to be wondered at. In certain matters, some sailors even in mature life, remain unsophisticated enough. But a young seafarer of the disposition of our athletic foretopman is yet very much of a child-man. And yet a child's utter innocence is but its blank ignorance, and the innocence more or less wanes as intelligence waxes. But in Billy Budd intelligence, such as it was, had advanced, while yet his simple-mindedness remained for the most part unaffected. Experience is a teacher indeed; yet did Billy's years make his experience small. Besides, he had none of that intuitive knowledge of the bad which in natures not good or incompletely so, fore-runs experience, and therefore may pertain, as in some instances it too clearly does pertain, even to youth

And what could Billy know of man except of man as a mere sailor?   And the old-fashioned sailor, the veritable man-before-the-mast—the sailor from boyhood up—he, though indeed of the same species as a landsman, is in some respects singularly distinct from him.   The sailor is frankness, the landsman is finesse.   Life is not a game with the sailor, demanding the long head; no intricate game of chess where few moves are made in straightforwardness, and ends are attained by indirection; an oblique, tedious, barren game hardly worth that poor candle burnt out in playing it.

Yes, as a class, sailors are in character a juvenile race. Even their deviations are marked by juvenility.   And this more especially holding true with the sailors of Billy's time. Then, too, certain things which apply to all sailors, do more pointedly operate here and there upon the junior one.   Every sailor, too, is accustomed to obey orders without debating them; his life afloat is externally ruled for him; he is not brought into that promiscuous commerce with mankind where unobstructed free agency on equal terms—equal superficially, at least—soon teaches one that unless upon occasion he exercises a distrust keen in proportion to the fairness of the appearance, some foul turn may be served him. A ruled, undemonstrative distrustfulness is so habitual, not with business-men so much, as with men who know their kind in less shallow relations than business, namely certain men-of-the-world, that they come at last to employ it all but unconsciously; and some of them would very likely feel real surprise at being charged with it as one of their general characteristics.

CHAPTER XV

BUT after the little matter at the mess Billy Budd no more found himself in strange trouble at times about his hammock or his clothes-bag, or what not. While, as to that smile that occasionally sunned him, and the pleasant passing word: these were, if not more frequent, yet if anything more pronounced than before.

But for all that, there were certain other demonstrations now. When Claggart's unobserved glance happened to light on belted Billy rolling along the upper gun-deck in the leisure of the second dog-watch, exchanging passing broadsides of fun with other young promenaders in the crowd; that glance would follow the cheerful Sea Hyperion with a settled meditative and melancholy expression—his eyes strangely suffused with incipient feverish tears. Then would Claggart look like the man of sorrows. Yes, and sometimes the melancholy expression would have in it a touch of soft yearning, as if Claggart could even have loved Billy but for fate and ban. But this was an evanescence, and quickly repented of, as it were, by an immitigable look, pinching and shrivelling the visage into the momentary semblance of a wrinkled walnut. But sometimes, catching sight in advance of the foretopman coming in his direction, he would, upon their nearing, step aside a little to let him pass, dwelling upon Billy for the moment with the glittering dental satire of a Guise. Yet, upon an abrupt unforeseen encounter, a red light would flash forth from his eye, like a spark from an anvil in a dusky smithy. That quick fierce light was a strange one, darted from orbs which in repose were of a colour nearest approaching a deeper violet, the softest of shades.

Though some of these caprices of the pit could not but

be observed by their object, yet were they beyond the construing of such a nature. And the thews of Billy were hardly comparable with that sort of sensitive spiritual organization which in some cases instinctively conveys to ignorant innocence an admonition of the proximity of the malign. He thought the Master-at-arms acted in a manner rather queer at times. That was all. But the occasional frank air and pleasant word went for what they purported to be—the young sailor never having heard as yet of the "too fair-spoken man."

Had the foretopman been conscious of having done or said anything to provoke the ill will of the official, it would have been different with him, and his sight might have been purged if not sharpened.

So was it with him in yet another matter. Two minor officers, the Armourer, and Captain of the Hold, with whom he had never exchanged a word, his position on the ship not bringing him into contact with them; these men now for the first began to cast upon Billy—when they chanced to encounter him—that peculiar glance which evidences that the man from whom it comes has been some way tampered with, and to the prejudice of him upon whom the glance lights. Never did it occur to Billy as a thing to be noted, or a thing suspicious—though he well knew the fact that the Armourer and Captain of the Hold, with the ship's yeoman, apothecary, and others of that grade, were by naval usage, messmates of the Master-at-arms; men with ears convenient to his confidential tongue.

But the general popularity that our Handsome Sailor's manly forwardness upon occasion, and irresistible good nature, indicating no mental superiority tending to excite an invidious feeling; this good will on the part of most of his ship-mates made him the less to concern himself about such mute aspects toward him as those whereto allusion has just been made.

As to the afterguardsman, though Billy for reasons already given, necessarily saw little of him, yet when the two did happen to meet, invariably came the fellow's off-hand cheerful recognition, sometimes accompanied by a passing pleasant word or two. Whatever that equivocal young person's original design may really have been, or the design of which he might have been the deputy, certain it was from his manner upon these occasions, that he had wholly dropped it.

It was as if his precocity of crookedness (and every vulgar villain is precocious) had for once deceived him, and the man he had sought to entrap as a simpleton had, through his very simplicity, baffled him.

But shrewd ones may opine that it was hardly possible for Billy to refrain from going up to the afterguardsman and bluntly demanding to know his purpose in the initial interview, so abruptly closed in the fore-chains. Shrewd ones may also think it but natural in Billy to set about sounding some of the other impressed men of the ship in order to discover what basis, if any, there was for the emissary's obscure suggestions as to plotting disaffection aboard. The shrewd may so think. But something more, or rather, something else than mere shrewdness is perhaps needful for the due understanding of such a character as Billy Budd's.

As to Claggart, the monomania in the man—if that indeed it were—as involuntarily disclosed by stars in the manifestations detailed, yet in general covered over by his self-contained and rational demeanour; this, like a subterranean fire was eating its way deeper and deeper in him. Something decisive must come of it.

CHAPTER XVI

AFTER the mysterious interview in the fore-chains—the one so abruptly ended there by Billy—nothing especially germane to the story occurred until the events now about to be narrated.

Elsewhere it has been said that owing to the lack of frigates (of course better sailors than line-of-battle ships) in the English squadron up the Straits at that period, the *Indomitable* was occasionally employed not only as an available substitute for a scout, but at times on detached service of more important kind. This was not alone because of her sailing qualities, not common in a ship of her rate, but quite as much, probably, that the character of her commander—it was thought—specially adapted him for any duty where, under unforeseen difficulties, a prompt initiative might have to be taken in some matter demanding knowledge and ability in addition to those qualities employed in good seamanship. It was on an expedition of the latter sort, a somewhat distant one, and when the *Indomitable* was almost at her furthest remove from the fleet, that in the latter part of an afternoon-watch she unexpectedly came in sight of a ship of the enemy. It proved to be a frigate. The latter—perceiving through the glass that the weight of men and metal would be heavily against her—invoking her light heels, crowded on sail to get away. After a chase urged almost against hope—and lasting until about the middle of the first dog-watch she signally succeeded in effecting her escape.

Not long after the pursuit had been given up, and ere the excitement incident thereto had altogether waned away, the Master-at-arms, ascending from his cavernous sphere, made his appearance (cap in hand) by the mainmast: respectfully

awaiting the notice of Captain Vere—then solitary walking
the weather-side of the quarter-deck—doubtless somewhat
chafed at the failure of the pursuit. The spot where Claggart stood was the place allotted to the men of lesser grades
when seeking some more particular interview either with the
officer-of-the-deck or the Captain himself. But from the
latter it was not often that a sailor or petty-officer of those
days would seek a hearing; only some exceptional cause,
would, according to established custom, have warranted that.

Presently, just as the Commander, absorbed in his reflections, was on the point of turning aft in his promenade,
he became sensible of Claggart's presence, and saw the doffed
cap held in deferential expectancy. Here be it said that
Captain Vere's personal knowledge of this petty-officer had
only begun at the time of the ship's last sailing from home,
Claggart then for the first, in transfer from a ship detained
for repairs, supplying on board the *Indomitable* the place of
a previous Master-at-arms disabled and ashore.

No sooner did the Commander observe who it was that
now so deferentially stood awaiting his notice, than a
peculiar expression came over him. It was not unlike that
which uncontrollably will flit across the countenance of one
at unawares encountering a person, who, though known to
him, indeed, has hardly been long enough known for thor-
ough knowledge, but something in whose aspect nevertheless
now, for the first time, provokes a vaguely repellent distaste.
Coming to a stand and resuming much of his wonted official
manner, save that a sort of impatience lurked in the intonation of the opening word, he said, "Well? what is it, Master-
at-arms?"

With the air of a subordinate grieved at the necessity of
being a messenger of ill tidings, and while conscientiously
determined to be frank, yet equally resolved upon shunning

overstatement, Claggart at this invitation, or rather summons to disburthen, spoke up. What he said, conveyed in the language of no uneducated man, was to the effect following if not altogether in these words, namely, that during the chase and preparations for the possible encounter he had seen enough to convince him that at least one sailor aboard was a dangerous character in a ship mustering some who not only had taken a guilty part in the late serious trouble, but others also who, like the man in question, had entered His Majesty's service under another form than enlistment.

At this point Captain Vere, with some impatience, interrupted him:

"Be direct, man; say impressed men."

Claggart made a gesture of subservience and proceeded. Quite lately he (Claggart) had begun to suspect that some sort of movement prompted by the sailor in question was covertly going on, but he had not thought himself warranted in reporting the suspicion so long as it remained indistinct. But from what he had that afternoon observed in the man referred to, the suspicion of something clandestine going on had advanced to a point less removed from certainty. He deeply felt—he added—the serious responsibility assumed in making a report involving such possible consequences to the individual mainly concerned, besides tending to augment those natural anxieties which every naval commander must feel in view of the extraordinary outbreak so recent as those which, he sorrowfully said it, it needed not to name.

Now at the first broaching of the matter Captain Vere, taken by surprise, could not wholly dissemble his disquietude, but as Claggart went on, the former's aspect changed into restiveness under something in the testifier's manner in giving his testimony. However, he refrained from interrupting him. And Claggart, continuing, concluded with this:

"God forbid, your honour, that the *Indomitable's* should be the experience of the—"

"Never mind that!" here peremptorily broke in the superior, his face altering with anger instantly, divining the ship that the other was about to name, one in which the Nore Mutiny assumed a singularly tragical character that for a time jeopardized the life of its Commander. Under the circumstances he was indignant at the purposed allusion. When the commissioned officers themselves were on all occasions very heedful how they referred to the recent events, —for a petty-officer unnecessarily to allude to them in the presence of his Captain, this struck him as a most immodest presumption. Besides, to his quick sense of self-respect, it even looked under the circumstances something like an attempt to alarm him. Nor at that was he without some surprise that one who, so far as he had hitherto come under his notice, had shown considerable tact in his function, should in this particular evince such lack of it.

But these thoughts and kindred dubious ones flitting across his mind were suddenly replaced by an intuitional surmise, which though as yet obscure in form, served practically to affect his reception of the ill tidings. Certain it is that, long versed in everything pertaining to the complicated gun-deck life (which like every other form of life has its secret mines and dubious side; the side popularly disclaimed), Captain Vere did not permit himself to be unduly disturbed by the general tenor of his subordinate's report. Furthermore, if in view of recent events prompt action should be taken at the first palpable sign of recurring insubordination—for all that, not judicious would it be, he thought, to keep the idea of lingering disaffection alive by undue forwardness in crediting an informer, even if his own subordinate, and charged with police surveillance of the crew. This feeling would not perhaps have so prevailed with him were it not that upon a prior occasion the patriotic zeal officially evinced by Claggart had somewhat irritated him as appearing rather supersensible and strained. Furthermore, something even in the official's self-possessed and somewhat ostentatious manner in making his specifications strangely reminded him of a bandsman, a perjured witness in a capital case before a court-martial ashore of which when a lieutenant he, Captain Vere, had been a member.

Now the peremptory check given to Claggart in the matter of the arrested allusion was quickly followed up by this: "You say that there is at least one dangerous man aboard. Name him."

"William Budd, a foretopman, your honour——"

"William Budd," repeated Captain Vere with unfeigned astonishment, "and mean you the man our Lieutenant Ratcliffe took from the merchantman not very long ago—the young fellow who seems to be so popular with the men—Billy, the Handsome Sailor, as they call him?"

"The same, your honour; but for all his youth and good looks, a deep one. Not for nothing does he insinuate himself into the good will of his shipmates, since at the least they will at a pinch say a good word for him at all hazards. Did Lieutenant Ratcliffe happen to tell your honour of that adroit fling of Budd's jumping up in the Cutter's bow under the merchantman's stern when he was being taken off? It is even masqued by that sort of good-humoured air that at heart he resents his impressment. You have but noted his fair cheek. A man-trap may be under his fine ruddy-tipped daisies."

Now the *Handsome Sailor*, as a signal figure among the crew, had naturally enough attracted the Captain's attention from the first. Though in general not very demonstrative to his officers, he had congratulated Lieutenant Ratcliffe upon his good fortune in lighting on such a fine specimen of the *genus homo* who, in the nude, might have posed for a statue of young Adam before the fall.

As to Billy's adieu to the ship *Rights-of-Man*, which the boarding lieutenant had indeed reported to him, Captain Vere,—but in a deferential way—more as a good story than aught else,—though mistakenly understanding it as a satiric sally, had but thought so much the better of the impressed man for it; as a military sailor, admiring the spirit that could take an arbitrary enlistment so merrily and sensibly. The foretopman's conduct, too, so far as it had fallen under the Captain's notice had confirmed the first happy augury, while the new recruit's qualities as a *sailor-man* seemed to be such that he had thought of recommending him to the executive officer for promotion to a place that would more frequently bring him under his own observation, namely, the captaincy of the mizzen-top, replacing there in the star-board watch a man not so young whom partly for that reason he deemed less fitted for the post. Be it parenthesized here that since the mizzen-top-men have not to handle such breadths of heavy canvas as the lower sailors on the main-mast and fore-mast, a young man if of the right stuff not only seems best adapted to duty there, but, in fact, is generally selected for the captaincy of that top, and the company under him are light hands, and often but striplings. In sum, Captain Vere had from the beginning deemed Billy Budd to be what in the naval parlance of the times was called a *"King's bargain,"* that is to say, for His Britannic Majesty's navy a capital investment at small outlay or none at all.

After a brief pause—during which the reminiscences above mentioned passed vividly through his mind—he weighed the import of Claggart's last suggestion, conveyed in the phrase, "pitfall under the clover," and the more he weighed it the less reliance he felt in the informer's good faith. Suddenly he turned upon him: "Do you come to me, Master-at-arms, with so foggy a tale? As to Budd, cite me an act or spoken word of his confirmatory of what you here in general charge against him. Stay," drawing nearer to him, "heed what you speak. Just now and in a case like this, there is a yard-arm-end for the false-witness."

"Ah, your honour!" sighed Claggart mildly shaking his shapely head as in sad deprecation of such unmerited severity of tone. Then bridling—erecting himself as in virtuous self-assertion, he circumstantially alleged certain words and acts, which collectively if credited, led to presumptions mortally inculpating Budd, and for some of these averments, he added, substantiating proof was not far.

With grey eyes now impatient and distrustful, essaying to fathom to the bottom Claggart's calm violet ones, Captain Vere again heard him out; then for the moment stood ruminating. The mood he evinced, Claggart—himself for the time liberated from the other's scrutiny—steadily regarded with a look difficult to render:—a look curious of the operation of his tactics, a look such as might have been that of the spokesman of the envious children of Jacob deceptively imposing upon the troubled patriarch the blood-dyed coat of young Joseph.

Though something exceptional in the moral quality of Captain Vere made him, in earnest encounter with a fellow-man, a veritable touchstone of that man's essential nature, yet now as to Claggart and what was really going on in him his feeling partook less of intuitional conviction than of strong suspicion clogged by strange dubieties. The perplexity he evinced proceeded less from aught touching the man informed against—as Claggart doubtless opined—than from considerations how best to act in regard to the informer. At first, indeed, he was naturally for summoning that substantiation of his allegations which Claggart said was at hand. But such a proceeding would result in the matter at once getting abroad—which—in the present stage of it, he thought, might undesirably affect the ship's company. If Claggart was a false witness,—that closed the affair. And therefore, before trying the accusation, he would first practically test the accuser; and he thought this could be done in a quiet undemonstrative way.

The measure he determined upon involved a shifting of the scene—a transfer to a place less exposed to observation than the broad quarter-deck. For although the few gun-room officers there at the time had, in due observance of naval etiquette, withdrawn to leeward the moment Captain Vere had begun his promenade on the deck's weather side; and though during the colloquy with Claggart they of course ventured not to diminish the distance; and though throughout the interview Captain Vere's voice was far from high, and Claggart's silvery and low; and the wind in the cordage and the wash of the sea helped the more to put them beyond ear-shot; nevertheless, the interview's continuance already had attracted observation from some topmen aloft, and other sailors in the waist or further forward.

Having now determined upon his measures, Captain Vere forthwith took action. Abruptly turning to Claggart he asked, "Master-at-arms, is it now Budd's watch aloft?"

"No, your honour." Whereupon—"Mr. Wilkes," summoning the nearest midshipman, "tell Albert to come to me." Albert was the Captain's hammock-boy, a sort of sea-valet in whose discretion and fidelity his master had much confidence. The lad appeared. "You know Budd the foretopman?"

"I do, Sir."

"Go find him. It is his watch off. Manage to tell him out of ear-shot that he is wanted aft. Contrive it that he speaks to nobody. Keep him in talk yourself. And not till you get well aft here, not till then, let him know that the place where he is wanted is my cabin. You understand. Go.—Master-at-arms, show yourself on the decks below, and when you think it time for Albert to be coming with his man, stand by quietly to follow the sailor in."

CHAPTER XVII

Now when the foretopman found himself closeted, as it were, in the cabin with the Captain and Claggart, he was surprised enough. But it was a surprise unaccompanied by apprehension or distrust. To an immature nature, essentially honest and humane, forewarning intimations of subtler danger from one's kind come tardily, if at all. The only thing that took shape in the young sailor's mind was this: "Yes, the Captain, I have always thought, looks kindly upon me. I wonder if he's going to make me his coxswain. I should like that. And maybe now he is going to ask the Master-at-arms about me."

"Shut the door there, sentry," said the commander. "Stand without and let nobody come in.—Now, Master-at-arms, tell this man to his face what you told of him to me;" and stood prepared to scrutinize the mutually confronting visages.

With the measured step and calm collected air of an asylum physician approaching in the public hall some patient beginning to show indications of a coming paroxysm, Claggart deliberatley advanced within short range of Billy, and mesmerically looking him in the eye, briefly recapitulated the accusation.

Not at first did Billy take it in. When he did the rose-tan of his cheek looked struck as by white leprosy. He stood like one impaled and gagged. Meanwhile the accuser's eyes, removing not as yet from the blue, dilated ones, underwent a phenomenal change, their wonted rich violet colour blurring into a muddy purple. Those lights of human intelligence losing human expression, gelidly protruding like the alien eyes of certain uncatalogued creatures of the deep.

The first mesmeric glance was one of surprised fascination; the last was the the hungry lurch of the torpedo-fish.

"Speak, man!" said Captain Vere to the transfixed one, struck by his aspect even more than by Claggart's, "Speak! defend yourself." Which appeal caused but a strange, dumb gesturing and gurgling in Billy; amazement at such an accusation so suddenly sprung on inexperienced nonage; this, and it may be horror at the accuser, serving to bring out his lurking defect, and in this instance for the time intensifying it into a convulsed tongue-tie; while the intent head and entire form straining forward in an agony of ineffectual eagerness to obey the injunction to speak and defend himself, gave an expression to the face like that of a condemned vestal priestess in the moment of her being buried alive, and in the first struggle against suffocation.

Though at the time Captain Vere was quite ignorant of Billy's liability to vocal impediment, he now immediately divined it, since vividly Billy's aspect recalled to him that of a bright young schoolmate of his whom he had seen struck by much the same startling impotence in the act of eagerly rising in the class to be foremost in response to a testing question put to it by the master. Going close up to the young sailor, and laying a soothing hand on his shoulder, he said. "There is no hurry, my boy. Take your time, take your time." Contrary to the effect intended, these words, so fatherly in tone, doubtless touching Billy's heart to the quick, prompted yet more violent efforts at utterance—efforts soon ending for the time in confirming the paralysis, and bringing to the face an expression which was as a crucifixion to behold. The next instant, quick as the flame from a discharged cannon at night—his right arm shot out and Claggart dropped to the deck. Whether intentionally, or but owing to the young athlete's superior height, the blow had taken effect full upon the forehead, so shapely and intellectual-looking a feature in the Master-at-arms; so that the body fell over lengthwise, like a heavy plank tilted from erectness. A gasp or two and he lay motionless.

"Fated boy," breathed Captain Vere in a tone so low as to be almost a whisper, "what have you done!   But here, help me."

The twain raised the felled one from the loins up into a sitting position. The spare form flexibly acquiesced, but inertly. It was like handling a dead snake. They lowered it back. Regaining erectness, Captain Vere with one hand covering his face stood to all appearance as impassive as to the object at his feet. Was he absorbed in taking in all the bearings of the event, and what was best not only now at once to be done, but also in the sequel? Slowly he uncovered his face; forthwith the effect was as if the moon, emerging from eclipse, should reappear with quite another aspect than that which had gone into hiding. The father in him, manifested towards Billy thus far in the scene, was replaced by the military disciplinarian. In his official tone he bade the foretopman retire to a state-room aft, (pointing it out), and there remain till thence summoned. This order Billy in silence mechanically obeyed. Then, going to the cabin door where it opened on the quarter-deck, Captain Vere said to the sentry without, "Tell somebody to send Albert here."

When the lad appeared his master so contrived it that he should not catch sight of the prone one. "Albert," he said to him, "tell the surgeon I wish to see him. You need not come back till called."

When the surgeon entered—a self-poised character of that grave sense and experience that hardly anything could take him aback—Captain Vere advanced to meet him, thus unconsciously interrupting his view of Claggart and interrupting the other's wonted ceremonious salutation, said, "Nay, tell me how it is with yonder man," directing his attention to the prostrate one.

The surgeon looked, and for all his self-command, somewhat started at the abrupt revelation. On Claggart's always pallid complexion, thick black blood was now oozing from mouth and ear. To the gazer's professional eyes it was unmistakably no living man that he saw.

"Is it so, then?" said Captain Vere intently watching him. "I thought it. But verify it." Whereupon the customary tests confirmed the surgeon's first glance, who now looking up in unfeigned concern, cast a look of intense inquisitiveness upon his superior. But Captain Vere, with one hand to his brow, was standing motionless. Suddenly, catching the surgeon's arm convulsively, he exclaimed pointing down to the body,—"It is the divine judgment of Ananias! Look!"

Disturbed by the excited manner he had never before observed in the *Indomitable's* Captain, and as yet wholly ignorant of the affair, the prudent surgeon nevertheless held his peace, only again looking an earnest interrogation as to what it was that had resulted in such a tragedy.

But Captain Vere was now again motionless, standing absorbed in thought. Once again starting, he vehemently exclaimed—"Struck dead by an angel of God. Yet the angel must hang!"

At these interjections, incoherences to the listener as yet unapprised of the antecedent events, the surgeon was profoundly discomfited. But now, as recollecting himself, Captain Vere in less harsh tone briefly related the circumstances leading up to the event.

"But come; we must despatch," he added, "help me to remove him (meaning the body) to yonder compartment"—designating one opposite where the foretopman remained immured. Anew disturbed by a request that, as implying a desire for secrecy, seemed unaccountably strange to him, there was nothing for the subordinate to do but comply.

"Go now," said Captain Vere, with something of his wonted manner, "Go now. I shall presently call a drumhead court. Tell the lieutenants what has happened, and tell Mr. Morton"—meaning the captain of marines. "And charge them to keep the matter to themselves."

Full of disquietude and misgivings, the surgeon left the cabin. Was Captain Vere suddenly affected in his mind, or was it but a transient excitement brought about by so strange and extraordinary a happening? As to the drum-head court, it struck the surgeon as impolitic, if nothing more. The thing to do, he thought, was to place Billy Budd in confinement, and in a way dictated by usage, and postpone further action in so extraordinary a case to such time as they should again join the squadron, and then transfer it to the Admiral. He recalled the unwonted agitation of Captain Vere and his exciting exclamations so at variance with his normal manner. Was he unhinged? But assuming that he was, it were not so susceptible of proof. What then could he do? No worse trying situation is conceivable than that of an officer subordinated under a Captain whom he suspects to be, not mad indeed, but yet not quite unaffected in his intellect. To argue his order to him would be insolence. To resist him would be

mutiny. In obedience to Captain Vere he communicated to
the lieutenants and captain of marines what had happened;
saying nothing as to the Captain's state. They stared at
him in surprise and concern. Like him they seemed to think
that such a matter should be reported to the Admiral.

Who in the rainbow can draw the line where the violet tint
ends and the orange tint begins? Distinctly we see the difference of the colour, but where exactly does the first one
visibly enter into the other? So with sanity and insanity. In
pronounced cases there is no question about them. But in
some cases, in various degrees supposedly less pronounced, to
draw the line of demarkation few will undertake, though for
a fee some professional experts will. There is nothing nam-
able but that some men will undertake to do for pay. In
other words, there are instances where it is next to impossible
to determine whether a man is sane or beginning to be otherwise.

Whether Captain Vere, as the surgeon professionally surmised, was really the sudden victim of any degree of aberration, one must determine for himself by such light as this
narrative may afford.

CHAPTER XVIII

THE unhappy event which has been narrated could not
have happened at a worse juncture. For it was close on the
heel of the suppressed insurrections, an after-time very critical to naval authority, demanding from every English sea-
commander two qualities not readily interfusable—prudence
and rigour. Moreover, there was something crucial in the
case.

In the jugglery of circumstances preceding and attending
the event on board the *Indomitable* and in the light of that

martial code whereby it was formally to be judged, innocence and guilt, personified in Claggart and Budd, in effect changed places.

In the legal view the apparent victim of the tragedy was he who had sought to victimize a man blameless; and the indisputable deed of the latter, navally regarded, constituted the most heinous of military crimes. Yet more. The essential right and wrong involved in the matter, the clearer that might be, so much the worse for the responsibility of a loyal sea-commander; inasmuch as he was authorized to determine the matter on that primitive legal basis.

Small wonder then that the *Indomitable's* Captain, though in general a man of rigid decision, felt that circumspectness not less than promptitude was necessary. Until he could decide upon his course, and in each detail; and not only so, but until the concluding measure was upon the point of being enacted he deemed it advisable, in view of all the circumstances, to guard as much as possible against publicity. Here he may or may not have erred. Certain it is, however, that subsequently in the confidential talk of more than one or two gunrooms and cabins he was not a little criticized by some officers, a fact imputed by his friends, and vehemently by his cousin Jack Denton, to professional jealousy of Starry Vere. Some imaginative ground for invidious comment there was. The maintenance of secrecy in the matter, the confining all knowledge of it for a time to the place where the homicide occurred—the quarter-deck cabin; in these particulars lurked some resemblance to the policy adopted in those tragedies of the palace which have occurred more than once in the capital founded by Peter the Barbarian, great chiefly by his crimes.

The case was such that fain would the *Indomitable's* Captain have deferred taking any action whatever respecting it further than to keep the foretopman a close prisoner till the ship rejoined the squadron, and then submitting the matter to the judgment of his Admiral.

But a true military officer is, in one particular, like a true monk. Not with more of self-abnegation will the latter keep his vows of monastic obedience than the former his vows of allegiance to martial duty.

Feeling that unless quick action were taken on it, the deed of the foretopman, as soon as it should be known on the gun-decks, would tend to awaken any slumbering embers of the Nore among the crews—a sense of the urgency of the case overruled in Captain Vere all other considerations. But though a conscientious disciplinarian, he was no lover of authority for mere authority's sake. Very far was he from embracing opportunities for monopolizing to himself the perils of moral responsibility, none at least that could properly be referred to an official superior, or shared with him by his official equals or even subordinates. So thinking, he was glad it would not be at variance with usage to turn the matter over to a summary court of his own officers, reserving to himself, as the one on whom the ultimate accountability would rest, the right of maintaining a supervision of it, or formally or informally interposing at need. Accordingly a drum-head court was summarily convened, he electing the individuals composing it, the First Lieutenant, the Captain of Marines, and the Sailing Master.

In associating an officer of marines with the sea-lieutenants in a case having to do with a sailor, the Commander perhaps deviated from general custom. He was prompted thereto by the circumstances that he took that soldier to be a judicious person, thoughtful and not altogether incapable of gripping with a difficult case unprecedented in his prior experience. Yet even as to him he was not without some latent misgiving, for withal he was an extremely good-natured man, an enjoyer of his dinner, a sound sleeper, and inclined to obesity. The sort of man who, though he would always maintain his manhood in battle, might not prove altogether reliable in a moral dilemma involving aught of the tragic. As to the First Lieutenant and the Sailing Master, Captain Vere could not but be aware that though honest natures, of approved gallantry upon occasion, their intelligence was mostly confined to the matter of active seamanship, and the fighting demands of their profession. The court was held in the same cabin where the unfortunate affair had taken place. This cabin, the Commander's, embraced the entire area under the poop-deck. Aft, and on either side, was a small state-room—the one room temporarily a jail, and the other a dead-house—and a yet smaller compartment leaving a space between, expanding forward into a goodly oblong of length coinciding with the ship's beam. A sky-light of moderate dimension was overhead, and at each end of the oblong space were two sashed port-hole windows, easily converitable back into embrasures for short cannonades.

All being quickly in readiness, Billy Budd was arraigned, Captain Vere necessarily appearing as the sole witness in the case, and as such temporarily sinking his rank, though singularly maintaining it in a matter apparently trivial, namely, that he testified from the ship's weather-side, with that object having caused the court to sit on the lee-side. Concisely he narrated all that had led up to the catastrophe, omitting nothing in Claggart's accusation and deposing as to the manner in which the prisoner had received it. At this testimony the three officers glanced with no little surprise at Billy Budd, the last man they would have suspected, either of mutinous design alleged by Claggart, or of the undeniable deed he himself had done. The First Lieutenant, taking judicial primacy and turning towards the prisoner, said, "Captain Vere has spoken. Is it or is it not as Captain Vere says?" In response came syllables not so much impeded in the utterance as might have been anticipated. They were these:

"Captain Vere tells the truth. It is just as Captain Vere says, but it is not as the Master-at-arms said. I have eaten the King's bread and I am true to the King."

"I believe you, my man," said the witness, his voice indicating a suppressed emotion not otherwise betrayed.

"God will bless you for that, your honour!" not without stammering said Billy, and all but broke down. But immediately was recalled to self-control by another question, with which the same emotional difficulty of utterance came: "No, there was no malice between us. I never bore malice against the Master-at-arms. I am sorry that he is dead. I did not mean to kill him. Could I have used my tongue I would not have struck him. But he foully lied to my face, and in the presence of my Captain, and I had to say something, and I could only say it with a blow. God help me!"

In the impulsive above-board manner of the frank one the court saw confirmed all that was implied in words which just previously had perplexed them, coming as they did from the testifier to the tragedy, and promptly following Billy's impassioned disclaimer of mutinous intent—Captain Vere's words, "I believe you, my man."

Next it was asked of him whether he knew of or suspected aught savouring of incipient trouble (meaning a mutiny, though the explicit term was avoided) going on in any section of the ship's company.

The reply lingered. This was naturally imputed by the court to the same vocal embarrassment which had retarded or obstructed previous answers. But in main it was otherwise here; the question immediately recalling to Billy's mind the interview with the afterguardsman in the fore-chains.

But an innate repugnance to playing a part at all approaching that of an informer against one's own shipmates—the same erring sense of uninstructed honour which had stood in the way of his reporting the matter at the time; though as a loyal man-of-war man it was incumbent on him and failure so to do charged against him and, proven, would have subjected him to the heaviest of penalties. This, with the blind feeling now his, that nothing really was being hatched, prevailing with him. When the answer came it was a negative.

"One question more," said the officer of marines now first speaking and with a troubled earnestness. "You tell us that what the Master-at-arms said against you was a lie. Now why should he have so lied, so maliciously lied, since you declare there was no malice between you?"

At that question unintentionally touching on a spiritual sphere wholly obscure to Billy's thoughts, he was nonplussed, evincing a confusion indeed that some observers, such as can be imagined, would have construed into involuntary evidence of hidden guilt. Nevertheless he strove some way to answer, but all at once relinquished the vain endeavour, at the same time turning an appealing glance towards Captain Vere as deeming him his best helper and friend. Captain Vere, who had been seated for a time, rose to his feet, addressing the interrogator. "The question you put to him comes naturally enough. But can he rightly answer it?—or anybody else? unless indeed it be he who lies within there," designating the compartment where lay the corpse. "But the prone one there will not rise to our summons. In effect though, as it seems to me, the point you make is hardly material. Quite aside from any conceivable motive actuating the Master-at-arms, and irrespective of the provocation of the blow, a martial court must needs in the present case confine its attention to the blow's consequence, which consequence is to be deemed not otherwise than as the striker's deed!"

This utterance, the full significance of which it was not at all likely that Billy took in, nevertheless caused him to turn a wistful, interrogative look towards the speaker, a look in its dumb expressiveness not unlike that which a dog of generous breed might turn upon his master, seeking in his face some elucidation of a previous gesture ambiguous to the canine intelligence. Nor was the same utterance without marked effect upon the three officers, more especially the soldier. Couched in it seemed to them a meaning unanticipated, involving a prejudgment on the speaker's part. It served to augment a mental disturbance previously evident enough.

The soldier once more spoke, in a tone of suggestive dubiety addressing at once his associates and Captain Vere: "Nobody is present—none of the ship's company, I mean, who might shed lateral light, if any is to be had, upon what remains mysterious in this matter."

"That is thoughtfully put," said Captain Vere; "I see your drift. Ay, there is a mystery; but to use a Scriptural phrase, it is 'a mystery of iniquity,' a matter for only psychologic theologians to discuss. But what has a military court to do with it? Not to add that for us any possible investigation of it is cut off by the lasting tongue-tie of him in yonder," again designating the mortuary state-room. "The prisoner's deed. With that alone we have to do."

To this, and particularly the closing reiteration, the marine soldier, knowing not how aptly to reply, sadly abstained from saying aught. The First Lieutenant, who at the outset had not unnaturally assumed primacy in the court, now overrulingly instructed by a glance from Captain Vere (a glance more effective than words), resumed that primacy. Turning to the prisoner: "Budd," he said, and scarce in equable tones,

"Budd, if you have aught further to say for yourself, say it now."

Upon this the young sailor turned another quick glance towards Captain Vere; then, as taking a hint from that aspect, a hint confirming his own instinct that silence was now best, replied to the Lieutenant, "I have said all, Sir."

The marine—the same who had been the sentinel without the cabin-door at the time that the foretopman, followed by the Master-at-arms, entered it—he, standing by the sailor throughout their judicial proceedings, was now directed to take him back to the after compartment originally assigned to the prisoner and his custodian. As the twain disappeared from view, the three officers, as partially liberated from some inward constraint associated with Billy's mere presence—simultaneously stirred in their seats. They exchanged looks of troubled indecision, yet feeling that decide they must, and without long delay; for Captain Vere was for the time sitting unconsciously with his back towards them, apparently in one of his absent fits, gazing out from a sashed port-hole to windward upon the monotonous blank of the twilight sea. But the court's silence continuing, broken only at moments by brief consultations in low earnest tones, this seemed to assure him and encourage him. Turning, he to-and-fro paced the cabin athwart; in the returning ascent to windward, climbing the slant deck in the ship's lee roll; without knowing it symbolizing thus in his action a mind resolute to surmount difficulties even if against primitive instincts strong as the wind and the sea. Presently he came to a stand before the three. After scanning their faces he stood less as mustering his thoughts for expression, than as one in deliberating how best to put them to well-meaning men not intellectually mature—men with whom it was necessary to demonstrate certain principles that were axioms to himself. Similar impatience as to talking is perhaps one reason that deters some minds from addressing any popular assemblies; under which head is to be classed most legislatures in a Democracy.

When speak he did, something both in the substance of what he said and his manner of saying it, showed the influence of unshared studies, modifying and tempering the practical training of an active career. This, along with his phraseology now and then, was suggestive of the grounds whereon rested that imputation of a certain pedantry socially alleged against him by certain naval men of wholly practical cast, captains who nevertheless would frankly concede that His Majesty's Navy mustered no more efficient officers of their grade than "Starry Vere."

What he said was to this effect: "Hitherto I have been but the witness, little more; and I should hardly think now to take another tone, that of your coadjutor, for the time, did I not perceive in you—at the crisis too—a troubled hesitancy, proceeding, I doubt not, from the clashing of military duty with moral scruple—scruple vitalized by compassion. For the compassion, how can I otherwise but share it. But, mindful of paramount obligation, I strive against scruples that may tend to enervate decision. Not, gentlemen, that I hide from myself that the case is an exceptional one. Speculatively regarded, it well might be referred to a jury of casuists. But for us here, acting not as casuists or moralists, it is a case practical and under martial law practically to be dealt with.

"But your scruples! Do they move as in a dusk? Challenge them. Make them advance and declare themselves. Come now—do they import something like this: If, mindless of palliating circumstances, we are bound to regard the death of the Master-at-arms as the prisoner's deed, then does that deed constitute a capital crime whereof the penalty is a mortal one? But in natural justice is nothing but the prisoner's overt act to be considered? Now can we adjudge to summary and shameful death a fellow-creature innocent before God, and whom we feel to be so?—Does that state it aright? You sign sad assent. Well, I, too, feel that, the full force of that. It is Nature. But do these buttons that we wear attest that our allegiance is to Nature? No, to the King. Though the ocean, which is inviolate Nature primeval, though this be the element where we move and have our being as sailors, yet as the King's officers lies our duty in a sphere correspondingly natural? So little is that true, that in receiving our commissions we in the most important regards ceased to be natural free-agents. When war is declared, are we the commissioned fighters previously consulted? We fight at command. If our judgments approve the war, that is but coincidence. So in other particulars. So now, would it be so much we ourselves that would condemn as it would be martial law operating through us? For that law and the rigour of it, we are not responsible. Our vowed responsibility is in this: That however pitilessly that law may operate, we nevertheless adhere to it and administer it.

"But the exceptional in the matter moves the heart within you. Even so, too, is mine moved. But let not warm hearts betray heads that should be cool. Ashore in a criminal case will an upright judge allow himself when off the bench to be waylaid by some tender kinswoman of the accused seeking to touch him with her tearful plea? Well, the heart here is as that piteous woman. The heart is the feminine in man, and hard though it be, she must here be ruled out."

He paused, earnestly studying them for a moment; then resumed.

"But something in your aspect seems to urge that it is not solely that heart that moves in you, but also the conscience, the private conscience. Then, tell me whether or not, occupying the position we do, private conscience should not yield to that imperial one formulated in the code under which alone we officially proceed?"

Here the three men moved in their seats, less convinced than agitated by the course of an argument troubling but the more the spontaneous conflict within. Perceiving which, the speaker paused for a moment; then abruptly changing his tone, went on:

"To steady us a bit, let us recur to the facts.—In war-time at sea a man-of-war's man strikes his superior in grade, and the blow kills. Apart from its effect, the blow itself is, according to the Articles of War, a capital crime. Furthermore—"

"Ay, Sir," emotionally broke in the officer of marines, "in one sense it was. But surely Budd purposed neither mutiny nor homicide."

"Surely not, my good man. And before a court less arbitrary and more merciful than a martial one that plea would largely extenuate. At the Last Assizes it shall acquit. But how here? We proceed under the law of the Mutiny Act. In feature no child can resemble his father more than that Act resembles in spirit the thing from which it derives— War. In His Majesty's service—in this ship indeed—there are Englishmen forced to fight for the King against their will. Against their conscience, for aught we know. Though as their fellow-creatures some of us may appreciate their position, yet as Navy officers, what reck we of it? Still less recks the enemy. Our impressed men he would fain cut down in the same swath with our volunteers. As regards the enemy's naval conscripts, some of whom may even share our own abhorrence of the regicidal French Directory, it is the same on our side. War looks but to the frontage, the appearance. And the Mutiny Act, War's child, takes after the father. Budd's intent or non-intent is nothing to the purpose.

"But while, put to it by those anxieties in you which I cannot but respect, I only repeat myself—while thus strangely we prolong proceedings that should be summary, the enemy may be sighted and an engagement result. We must do; and one of two things must we do—condemn or let go."

"Can we not convict and yet mitigate the penalty?" asked the junior Lieutenant here speaking, and falteringly, for the first time.

"Lieutenant, were that clearly lawful for us under the circumstances, consider the consequences of such clemency. The people" (meaning the ship's company) "have native sense; most of them are familiar with our naval usage and tradition; and how would they take it? Even could you explain to them—which our official position forbids—they, long moulded by arbitrary discipline, have not that kind of intelligent responsiveness that might qualify them to comprehend and discriminate. No, to the people the foretopman's deed, however it be worded in the announcement, will be plain homicide committed in a flagrant act of mutiny. What penalty for that should follow, they know. But it does not follow. *Why?* they will ruminate. You know what sailors are. Will they not revert to the recent outbreak at the Nore? Ay, they know the well-founded alarm—the panic it struck throughout England. Your clement sentence they would account pusillanimous. They would think that we flinch, that we are afraid of them—afraid of practising a lawful rigour singularly demanded at this juncture lest it should provoke new troubles. What shame to us such a conjecture on their part, and how deadly to discipline. You see then whither, prompted by duty and the law, I steadfastly drive.

But I beseech you, my friends, do not take me amiss. I feel as you do for this unfortunate boy. But did he know our hearts, I take him to be of that generous nature that he would feel even for us on whom in this military necessity so heavy a compulsion is laid."

With that, crossing the deck, he resumed his place by the sashed port-hole, tacitly leaving the three to come to a decision. On the cabin's opposite side the troubled court sat silent. Loyal lieges, plain and practical, though at bottom they dissented from some points Captain Vere had put to them, they were without the faculty, hardly had the inclination to gainsay one whom they felt to be an earnest man— one, too, not less their superior in mind than in naval rank. But it is not improbable that even such of his words as were not without influence over them, less came home to them than his closing appeal to their instinct as sea-officers, in the forethought he threw out as to the practical consequences to discipline (considering the unconfirmed tone of the fleet at the time)—should a man-of-war's man's violent killing at sea of a superior in grade be allowed to pass for aught else than a capital crime, demanding prompt infliction of the penalty?

Not unlikely they were brought to something more or less akin to that harassed frame of mind which in the year 1842 actuated the commander of the U.S. brig-of-war *Somers* to resolve (under the so-called Articles of War—Articles modelled upon the English Mutiny Act) to resolve upon the execution at sea of a midshipman and two petty-officers as mutineers designing the seizure of the brig. Which resolution was carried out, though in a time of peace and within not many days' sail of home. An act vindicated by a naval court of inquiry subsequently convened ashore—history, and here cited without comment. True, the circumstances on board the *Somers* were different from those on board the

Indomitable. But the urgency felt, well-warranted or otherwise, was much the same.

Says a writer whom few know, "Forty years after a battle it is easy for a non-combatant to reason about how it ought to have been fought. It is another thing personally and under fire to direct the fighting while involved in the obscuring smoke of it. Much so with respect to other emergencies involving considerations both practical and moral, and when it is imperative promptly to act. The greater the fog, the more it imperils the steamer, and speed is put on though at the hazard of running somebody down. Little ween the snug card-players in the cabin of the responsibilities of the sleepless man on the bridge."

In brief, Billy Budd was formally convicted and sentenced to be hung at the yard-arm in the early morning-watch, it being now night. Otherwise, as is customary in such cases, the sentence would forthwith have been carried out. In war-time on the field or in the fleet, a mortal punishment decreed by a drum-head court—on the field sometimes decreed by but a nod from the General—follows without a delay on the heel of conviction without appeal.

CHAPTER XIX

IT was Captain Vere himself who, of his own motion, communicated the finding of the court to the prisoner; for that purpose going to the compartment where he was in custody, and bidding the marine there to withdraw for the time.

Beyond the communication of the sentence, what took place at this interview was never known. But, in view of the character of the twain briefly closeted in that state-room, each radically sharing in the rarer qualities of one nature—so rare, indeed, as to be all but incredible to average minds however much cultivated—some conjectures may be ventured.

It would have been in consonance with the spirit of our Captain Vere should he on this occasion have concealed nothing from the condemned one—should he indeed have frankly disclosed to him the part he himself had played in bringing about the decision, at the same time revealing his actuating motives. On Billy's side it is not improbable that such a confession would have been received in much the same spirit that prompted it. Not without a sort of joy indeed he might have appreciated the brave opinion of him implied in his Captain making such a confidant of him. Nor as to the sentence itself could he have been insensible that it was imparted to him as to one not afraid to die. Even more may have been. Captain Vere in the end may have developed the passion sometimes latent under an exterior stoical or indifferent. He was old enough to have been Billy's father. The austere devotee of military duty, letting himself melt back into what remains primeval in our formalized humanity, may in the end have caught Billy to heart, even as Abraham may have caught young Isaac on the brink of resolutely offering him up in obedience to the exacting behest. But there is no telling the sacrament—seldom if in any case revealed to the gadding world wherever under circumstances at all akin to those here attempted to be set forth—two of great Nature's nobler order embrace. There is privacy at the time, inviolable to the survivor, and holy oblivion (the sequel to each diviner magnanimity) providentially covers all at last.

The first to encounter Captain Vere in the act of leaving the compartment was the senior Lieutenant. The face he beheld, for the moment one expressive of the agony of the strong, was to that officer, though a man of fifty, a startling revelation. That the condemned one suffered less than he who mainly had effected the condemnation, was apparently indicated by the former's exclamation in the scene soon perforce to be touched upon.

Of a series of incidents within a brief term rapidly following each other, the adequate narration may take up a term less brief, especially if explanation or comment here and there seem requisite to the better understanding of such incidents. Between the entrance into the cabin of him who never left it alive, and him who when he did leave it left it as one condemned to die; between this and the closeted interview just given, less than an hour and a half had elapsed. It was an interval long enough, however, to awaken speculations among no few of the ship's company as to what it was that could be detaining in the cabin the Master-at-arms and the sailor, for it was rumoured that both of them had been seen to enter it and neither of them had been seen to emerge. This rumour had got abroad upon the gun-decks and in the tops; the people of a great war-ship being in one respect like villagers, taking microscopic note of every untoward movement or non-movement going on. When therefore in weather not at all tempestuous all hands were called in the second dog-watch, a summons under such circumstances not usual in those hours, the crew were not wholly unprepared for some announcement extraordinary, one having connection, too, with the continued absence of the two men from their wonted haunts.

There was a moderate sea at the time; and the moon, newly risen and near to being at its full, silvered the white spar-deck wherever not blotted by the clear-cut shadows horizontally thrown of fixtures and moving men. On either side of the quarter-deck the marine guard under arms was drawn up; and Captain Vere, standing up in his place surrounded by all the ward-room officers, addressed his men. In so doing his manner showed neither more nor less than that properly pertaining to his supreme position aboard his own ship. In clear terms and concise he told them what had taken place in the cabin; that the Master-at-arms was dead; that he who had killed him had been already tried by a summary court and condemned to death; and that the execution would take place in the early morning watch. The word *mutiny* was not named in what he said. He refrained, too, from making the occasion an opportunity for any preachment as to the maintenance of discipline, thinking, perhaps, that under existing circumstances in the navy the consequence of violating discipline should be made to speak for itself.

Their Captain's announcement was listened to by the throng of standing sailors in a dumbness like that of a seated congregation of believers in Hell listening to the clergyman's announcement of his Calvinistic text.

At the close, however, a confused murmur went up. It began to wax all but instantly, then, at a sign, was pierced and suppressed by shrill whistles of the Boatswain and his mates piping "Down one watch."

To be prepared for burial Claggart's body was delivered to certain petty-officers of his mess. And here, not to clog the sequel with lateral matters, it may be added that at a suitable hour, the Master-at-arms was committed to the sea with every funeral honour properly belonging to his naval grade.

In this proceeding, as in every public one growing out of the tragedy, strict adherence to usage was observed. Nor in any point could it have been at all deviated from, either with respect to Claggart or Billy Budd, without begetting undesirable speculations in the ship's company, the sailors, and more particularly the men-of-war's men, being of all men the greatest sticklers for usage.

For similar cause all communication between Captain Vere and the condemned one ended with the closeted interview already given, the latter being now surrendered to the ordinary routine preliminary to the end. This transfer under guard from the Captain's quarters was effected without unusual precautions—at least no visible ones.

If possible, not to let the men so much as surmise that their officers anticipate aught amiss from them, is the tacit rule in a military ship. And the more that some sort of trouble should really be apprehended, the more do the officers keep that apprehension to themselves; though not the less unostentatious vigilance may be augmented.

In the present instance the sentry placed over the prisoner had strict orders to let no one have communication with him but the Chaplain. And certain unobtrusive measures were taken absolutely to insure this point.

CHAPTER XX

In a seventy-four of the old order the deck known as the upper gun-deck was the one covered over by the spar-deck, which last, though not without its armament, was for the most part exposed to the weather. In general it was at all hours free from hammocks; those of the crew swinging on the lower gun-deck, and berth-deck, the latter being not only a dormitory but also the place for the stowing of the sailors' bags, and on both sides lined with the large chests or movable pantries of the many messes of the men.

On the starboard side of the *Indomitable's* upper gun-deck, behold Billy Budd under sentry lying prone in irons in one of the bays formed by the regular spacing of the guns comprising the batteries on either side. All these pieces were of the heavier calibre of that period. Mounted on lumbering wooden carriages, they were hampered with cumbersome harness of breeching and strong side-tackles for running them out. Guns and carriages, together with the long rammers and shorter lintstocks lodged in loops overhead —all these, as customary, were painted black; and the heavy hempen breechings, tarred to the same tint, wore the like livery of the undertakers. In contrast with the funereal tone of these surrounding the prone sailor's exterior apparel, white *jumper* and white duck trousers, each more or less soiled, dimly glimmered in the obscure light of the bay like a patch of discoloured snow in early April lingering at some upland cave's black mouth. In effect he is already in his shroud or the garments that shall serve him in lieu of one. Over him, but scarce illuminating him, two battle-lanterns swing from two massive beams of the deck above. Fed with the oil supplied by the war-contractors (whose gains, honest or otherwise, are in every land an anticipated portion of the harvest of death), with flickering splashes of dirty yellow light they pollute the pale moonshine all but ineffectually struggling in obstructed flecks through the open ports from which the tompined cannon protrude. Other lanterns at intervals serve but to bring out somewhat the obscurer bays which, like small confessionals or side-chapels in a cathedral, branch from the long, dim-vasted, broad aisle between the two batteries of that covered tire.

Such was the deck where now lay the Handsome Sailor. Through the rose-tan of his complexion, no pallor could have shown. It would have taken days of sequestration from the winds and the sun to have brought about the efface-ment of that young sea-bloom. But the skeleton in the cheek-bone at the point of its angle was just beginning delicately to be defined under the warm-tinted skin. In fervid hearts self-contained some brief experiences devour our human tissue as secret fire in a ship's hold consumes cotton in the bale.

But now, lying between the two guns, as nipped in the vice of fate, Billy's agony, mainly proceeding from a generous young heart's virgin experience of the diabolical incarnate and effective in some men—the tension of that agony was over now. It survived not the something healing in the closeted interview with Captain Vere. Without movement, he lay as in a trance, that adolescent expression previously noted as his, taking on something akin to the look of a slumbering child in the cradle when the warm hearth-glow of the still chamber of night plays on the dimples that at whiles mysteriously form in the cheek, silently coming and going there. For now and then in the gyved one's trance, a serene happy light born of some wandering reminiscence or dream would diffuse itself over his face, and then wane away only anew to return.

The Chaplain coming to see him and finding him thus, and perceiving no sign that he was conscious of his presence, attentively regarded him for a space, then slipping aside, withdrew for the time, peradventure feeling that even he, the minister of Christ, though receiving his stipend from wars, had no consolation to proffer which could result in a peace transcending that which he beheld. But in the small hours he came again. And the prisoner, now awake to his surroundings, noticed his approach, and civilly, all but cheerfully, welcomed him. But it was to little purpose that in the interview following the good man sought to bring Billy Budd to some Godly understanding that he must die, and at dawn. True, Billy himself freely referred to his death as a thing close at hand; but it was something in the way that children will refer to death in general, who yet among their other sports will play a funeral with hearse and mourners. Not that like children Billy was incapable of conceiving what death really is. No, but he was wholly without irrational fear of it, a fear more prevalent in highly civilized communities than those so-called barbarous ones which in all respects stand nearer to unadulterate Nature. And, as elsewhere said, a barbarian Billy radically was; as much so, for all the costume, as his countrymen the British captives, living trophies made to march in the Roman triumph of Germanicus. Quite as much so as those later barbarians, young men probably, and picked specimens among the earlier British converts to Christianity, at least nominally such, and taken to Rome (as to-day converts from lesser isles of the sea may be taken to London), of whom the Pope of that time, admiring the strangeness of their personal beauty—so unlike the Italian stamp, their clear, ruddy complexions and curled flaxen locks, explained, "Angles" (meaning in English the modern derivative)—"Angels do you call them? And is it because they look so like *angels?*" Had it been later in time one would think that the Pope had in mind Fra Angelico's seraphs, some of whom, plucking apples in gardens of Hesperides, have the faint rose-bud complexion of the more beautiful English girls.

CHAPTER XXI

IF in vain the kind Chaplain sought to impress the young barbarian with ideas of death akin to those conveyed in the skull, dial and cross-bones on old tombstones; equally futile to all appearances were his efforts to bring home to him the thought of salvation and a Saviour. Billy listened, but less out of awe or reverence, perhaps, than from a certain natural politeness; doubtless at bottom regarding all that in much the same way which most mariners of his class take any discourse abstract or out of the common tone of the workaday world. And this sailor way of taking clerical discourse is not wholly unlike the way in which the pioneer of Christianity—full of transcendant miracles—was received long ago on tropic isles by any superior *savage* so called: a Tahaitian say of Captain Cook's time or shortly after that time. Out of natural courtesy he received but did not appreciate. It was like a gift placed in the palm of an out-stretched hand upon which the fingers do not close.

But the *Indomitable's* Chaplain was a discreet man possessing the good sense of a good heart. So he insisted not in his vocation here. At the instance of Captain Vere, a lieutenant had apprised him of pretty much of everything as to Billy; and since he felt that innocence was even a better thing than religion wherewith to go to judgment, he reluctantly withdrew; but in his emotion not without performing an act strange enough in an Englishman, and under the circumstances yet more so in any regular priest. Stooping over, he kissed on the fair cheek his fellow man, a felon in martial law, one who, though in the confines of death, he felt he could never convert to a dogma; nor for all that he did fear for his future.

Marvel not that, having been made acquainted with the young sailor's essential innocence, the worthy man lifted not a finger to avert the doom of such a martyr to martial discipline. So to do would not only have been as idle as invoking the desert, but would also have been an audacious transgression of the bounds of his function—one as exactly prescribed to him by military law as that of any other naval officer. Bluntly put, a chaplain is the minister of the Prince of Peace serving in the host of the God of War—Mars.

As such, he is as incongruous as a musket would be on the altar at Christmas. Why then is he there? Because he indirectly subserves the purpose attested by the cannon; because, too, he lends the sanction of the religion of the meek to that which practically is the abrogation of everything but force.*

CHAPTER XXII

THE night so luminous on the spar-deck, but otherwise on the cavernous ones below—levels so very like the tiered galleries in a coal-mine—the luminous night passed away. Like the prophet in the chariot disappearing in heaven and dropping his mantle to Elisha, the withdrawing night transferred its pale robe to the peeping day. A meek shy light appeared in the East, where stretched a diaphanous fleece of white furrowed vapour. That light slowly waxed. Suddenly *one bell* was struck aft, responded to by one louder metallic stroke from forward. It was four o'clock in the morning. Instantly the silver whistles were heard summoning all hands to witness punishment. Up through the great hatchway rimmed with racks of heavy shot, the watch below came pouring, overspreading with the watch already on deck the space between the mainmast and foremast, including that occupied by the capacious *launch* and the black booms tiered on either side of it—boat and booms making a summit of observation for the powder boys and younger tars. A different group comprising one watch of topmen leaned over the side of the rail of that sea-balcony, no small one in a seventy-four, looking down on the crowd below. Man or boy, none spake but in whisper, and few spake at all. Captain Vere—as before, the central figure among the assembled com-

* Melville notes on this passage: "An irruption of heretic thought hard to suppress."

missioned officers—stood nigh the break of the poop-deck, facing forward. Just below him on the quarter-deck the marines in full equipment were drawn up much as at the scene of the promulgated sentence.

At sea in the old time, the execution by halter of a military sailor was generally from the fore-yard. In the present instance—for special reasons—the main-yard was assigned. Under an arm of that yard the prisoner was presently brought up, the Chaplain attending him. It was noted at the time, and remarked upon afterwards, that in this final scene the good man evinced little or nothing of the perfunctory. Brief speech indeed he had with the condemned one, but the genuine gospel was less on his tongue than in his aspect and manner towards him. The final preparations personal to the latter being speedily brought to an end by two boatswain's-mates, the consummation impended. Billy stood facing aft. At the penultimate moment, his words, his only ones, words wholly unobstructed in the utterance, were these —"God bless Captain Vere!" Syllables so unanticipated coming from one with the ignominious hemp about his neck —a conventional felon's benediction directed aft towards the quarters of honour; syllables, too, delivered in the clear melody of a singing-bird on the point of launching from the twig, had a phenomenal effect, not unenhanced by the rare personal beauty of the young sailor, spiritualized now through late experiences so poignantly profound.

Without volition, as it were, as if indeed the ship's populace were the vehicles of some vocal electric current, with one voice, from alow and aloft, came a resonant echo—"God bless Captain Vere!" And yet, at that instant, Billy alone must have been in their hearts, even as he was in their eyes.

At the pronounced words and the spontaneous echo that voluminously rebounded them, Captain Vere, either through stoic self-control or a sort of momentary paralysis induced by emotional shock, stood erectly rigid as a musket in the ship-armour's rack.

The hull, deliberately recovering from the periodic roll to leeward, was just regaining an even keel—when the last signal, the preconcerted dumb one, was given. At the same moment it chanced that the vapoury fleece hanging low in the East, was shot through with a soft glory as of the fleece of the Lamb of God seen in mystical vision; and simultaneously therewith, watched by the wedged mass of upturned faces, Billy ascended; and ascending, took the full rose of the dawn.

In the pinioned figure, arrived at the yard-end, to the wonder of all no motion was apparent save that created by the slow roll of the hull, in moderate weather so majestic in a great ship heavy-cannoned.

A DIGRESSION

WHEN, some days afterwards, in reference to the singularity just mentioned, the Purser (a rather ruddy, rotund person, more accurate as an accountant than profound as a philosopher) said at mess to the Surgeon, "What testimony to the force lodged in will-power," the latter, spare and tall, one in whom a discreet causticity went along with a manner less genial than polite, replied, "Your pardon, Mr. Purser. In a hanging so scientifically conducted—and, under special orders, I myself directed how Budd's was to be effected—any movement following the completed suspension and originating in the body suspended, such movement indicates mechanical spasm in the muscular system. Hence the absence of that is no more attributable to will-power, as you call it, than to horse-power—begging your pardon."

"But this muscular spasm you speak of—is not that, in a degree, more or less invariable in these cases?"

"Assuredly so, Mr. Purser."

"How then, my good sir, do you account for its absence in this instance?"

"Mr. Purser, it is clear that your sense of the singularity in this matter equals not mine. You account for it by what you call will-power, a term not yet included in the lexicon of science. As for me, I do not with my present knowledge pretend to account for it at all. Even should one assume the hypothesis that, at the first touch of the halyards, the action of Budd's heart, intensified by extraordinary emotion at its climax, abruptly stopped—much like a watch when in carelessly winding it up you strain at the finish, thus snapping the spring—even under that hypothesis, how account for the phenomenon that followed?"

"You admit, then, that the absence of spasmodic movement was phenomenal?"

"It was phenomenal, Mr. Purser, in the sense that it was an appearance, the cause of which is not immediately to be assigned."

"But tell me, my dear Sir," pertinaciously continued the other, "was the man's death effected by the halter, or was it a species of euthanasia?"

"*Euthanasia*, Mr. Purser, is something like your will-power; I doubt its authenticity as a scientific term—begging your pardon again. It is at once imaginative and metaphysical; in short, Greek. But," abruptly changing his tone, "there is a case in the sick-bay which I do not care to leave to my assistants. Begging your pardon, but excuse me." And rising from the mess he formally withdrew.

CHAPTER XXIII

THE silence at the moment of execution, and for a moment or two continuing thereafter (but emphasized by the regular wash of the sea against the hull, or the flutter of a sail caused by the helmsman's eyes being tempted astray), this emphasized silence was gradually disturbed by a sound not easily to be here verbally rendered. Whoever has heard the freshet-wave of a torrent suddenly swelled by pouring showers in tropical mountains, showers not shared by the plain; whoever has heard the first muffled murmur of its sloping advance through precipitous woods, may form some conception of the sound now heard. The seeming remoteness of its source was because of its murmurous indistinctness, since it came from close by, even from the men massed on the ship's open deck. Being inarticulate, it was dubious in significance further in that it seemed to indicate some capricious revulsion of thought or feeling such as mobs ashore are liable to—in the present instance possibly implying a sullen revocation on the men's part of their involuntary echoing of Billy's benediction. But ere the murmur had time to wax into clamour it was met by a strategic command, the more telling that it came with abrupt unexpectedness.

"Pipe down the starboard watch, Boatswain, and see that they go."

Shrill as the shriek of the sea-hawk the whistles of the Boatswain and his Mates pierced that ominous low sound, dissipating it; and yielding to the mechanism of discipline the throng was thinned by one half. For the remainder most of them were set to temporary employments connected with trimming the yards and so forth, business readily to be found upon occasion by any officer-of-the-deck.

Now each proceeding that follows a mortal sentence pronounced at sea by a drum-head court is characterized by a promptitude not perceptibly merging into hurry, though bordering that. The hammock—the one which had been Billy's bed when alive, having already been ballasted with shot and otherwise prepared to serve for his canvas coffin— the last offices of the sea-undertakers, the Sail-maker's Mates, were now speedily completed. When everything was in readiness, a second call for all hands, made necessary by the strategic movement before mentioned, was sounded: and now to witness burial.

The details of this closing formality it needs not to give. But when the tilted plank let slide its freight into the sea, a second strange human murmur was heard—blended now with another so inarticulate sound proceeding from certain larger sea-fowl, whose attention having been attracted by the peculiar commotion in the water resulting from the heavy sloped dive of the shotted hammock into the sea, flew screaming to the spot. So near the hull did they come, that the stridor or bony creak of their gaunt double-jointed pinions was audible. As the ship under light airs passed on, leaving the burial spot astern, they still kept circling it low down with the moving shadow of their outstretched wings and the cracked requiem of their cries.

Upon sailors as superstitious as those of the age preceding ours—all men-of-war's men, too, who had just beheld the prodigy of repose in the form suspended in air and now foundering in the deeps; to such mariners the action of the sea-fowl, though dictated by a mere animal greed for prey, was big with no prosaic significance. An uncertain movement began among them, in which some encroachment was made. It was tolerated but for a moment. For suddenly the drum beat to quarters—which familiar sound, happening at least twice every day, had upon the present occasion some signal peremptoriness in it. True martial discipline long continued superinduces in an average man a sort of impulse of docility, whose operation at the official tone of command much resembles in its promptitude the effect of an instinct.

The drum-beat dissolved the multitude, distributing most of them along the batteries of the two covered gun-decks. There, as wont, the gun crews stood by their respective cannon erect and silent. In due course the First officer, sword under arm and standing in his place on the quarter-deck, formally received the successive reports of the sworded Lieutenants commanding the sections of batteries below; the last of which reports being made, the summed report he delivered with the customary salute to the Commander. All of this occupied time, which, in the present case, was the object of beating to quarters at an hour prior to the customary one. That such variance from usage was authorized by an officer like Captain Vere (a martinet as some deemed him), was evidence of the necessity for unusual action implied in what he deemed to be temporarily the mood of his men. "With mankind," he would say, "forms, measured forms, are everything; and that is the import couched in the story of Orpheus, with his lyre, spell-binding the wild denizens of the woods." And this he once applied to the disruption of forms going on across the Channel and the consequence thereof.

At this unwonted muster at quarters, all proceeded as at the regular hour. The band on the quarter-deck played a sacred air. After which the Chaplain went through with the customary morning service. That done, the drum beat the retreat, and toned by music and religious rites subserving the discipline and purpose of war, the men in their wonted, orderly manner dispersed to the places alloted them when not at the guns.

And now it was full day. The fleece of low-hanging vapour had vanished, licked up by the sun that late had so glorified it. And the circumambient air in the clearness of its serenity was like smooth white marble in the polished block not yet removed from the marble-dealer's yard

CHAPTER XXIV

THE symmetry of form attainable in pure fiction cannot so readily be achieved in a narration essentially having less to do with fable than with fact. Truth uncompromisingly told will always have its ragged edges; hence the conclusion of such a narration is apt to be less finished than an architectural finial.

How it fared with the Handsome Sailor during the year of the great mutiny has been faithfully given. But though properly the story ends with his life, something in way of a sequel will not be amiss. Three brief chapters will suffice.

In the general re-christening under the Directory of the craft originally forming the navy of the French Monarchy, the *St. Louis* line-of-battle ship was named the *Athéiste*. Such a name, like some other substituted ones in the Revolutionary fleet, while proclaiming the infidel audacity of the ruling power, was yet (though not so intended to be) the aptest name, if one consider it, ever given to a war-ship; far more so, indeed, than the *Devastation* or the *Eritus* (the Hell) and similar names bestowed upon fighting ships.

On the return passage to the full English fleet from the detached cruise during which occurred the events already recorded, the *Indomitable* fell in with the *Athéiste*. An engagement ensued; during which Captain Vere, in the act of putting his ship alongside the enemy with a view of throwing his boarders across the bulwarks, was hit by a musket-ball from a port-hole of the enemy's main cabin. More than disabled, he dropped to the deck and was carried below to the same cock-pit where some of his men already lay. The senior Lieutenant took command. Under him the enemy was finally captured, and though much crippled, was by rare good fortune successfully taken into Gibraltar, an English fort not very distant from the scene of the fight. There Captain Vere with the rest of the wounded was put ashore. He lingered for some days, but the end came. Unhappily he was cut off too early for the Nile and Trafalgar. The spirit that, in spite of its philosophic austerity, may yet have indulged in the most secret of all passions—ambition—never attained to the fulness of fame.

Not long before death, while lying under the influence of that magical drug which, in soothing the physical frame, mysteriously operates on the subtler element in man, he was heard to murmur words inexplicable to his attendant—"Billy Budd, Billy Budd." That these were not the accents of remorse, would seem clear from what the attendant said to the *Indomitable's* potent senior officer of marines, who, as the most reluctant to condemn of the members of the drumhead court, too well knew (though here he kept the knowledge to himself) who Billy Budd was.

CHAPTER XXV

SOME few weeks after the execution, among other matters under the main head of *News from the Mediterranean*, there appeared in one naval chronicle of the time, an authorized weekly publication, an account of the affair. It was doubtless for the most part written in good faith, though the medium, partly rumour, through which the facts must have reached the writer, served to deflect and in part to falsify them. The account was as follows:—

"On the tenth of the last month a deplorable occurrence took place on board *H.M.S. Indomitable*. John Claggart, the ship's Master-at-arms, discovering that some sort of plot was incipient among an inferior section of the ship's company, and that the ringleader was one William Budd, he, Claggart, in the act of arraigning the man before the Captain was vindictively stabbed to the heart by the suddenly drawn sheath-knife of Budd.

"The deed and the implement employed sufficiently suggest that, though mustered into the service under an English name, the assassin was no Englishman but one of those aliens adopting English cognomen whom the present extraordinary necessities of the Service have caused to be admitted into it in considerable numbers.

"The enormity of the crime and the extreme depravity of the criminal, appear the greater in view of the character of the victim—a middle-aged man, respectable and discreet, belonging to that minor official grade, the petty-officers, upon whom, as none know better than the commissioned gentlemen, the efficiency of His Majesty's navy so largely depends. His function was a responsible one—at once onerous and thankless—and his fidelity in it the greater because of his strong patriotic impulse. In this instance, as in so many other instances in these days, the character of the unfortunate man signally refutes, if refutation were needed, that peevish saying attributed to the late Dr. Johnson, that patriotism is the last refuge of a scoundrel.

"The criminal paid the penalty of his crime. The promptitude of the punishment has proved salutary. Nothing amiss is now apprehended aboard the *H.M.S. Indomitable*."

The above item appearing in a publication, now long ago superannuated and forgotten in all that hitherto has stood in human record, to attest what manner of men respectively were John Claggart and Billy Budd.*

CHAPTER XXVI

EVERYTHING is for a season remarkable in navies. Any tangible object associated with some striking incident of the service is converted into a monument. The spar from which the foretopman was suspended was for some few years kept trace of by the bluejackets. Then knowledge followed it from ship to deck-yard, and again from deck-yard to ship, still pursuing it even when at last reduced to a mere deck-yard boom. To them a chip of it was as a piece of the Cross. Ignorant though they were of the real facts of the happening, and not thinking but that the penalty was unavoidably inflicted from the naval point of view, for all that they instinctively felt that Billy was a sort of man as incapable of mutiny as of wilful murder. They recalled the fresh young image of the Handsome Sailor, that face never deformed by a sneer or subtler vile freak of the heart within! This impression of him was doubtless deepened by the fact that he was gone, and in a measure mysteriously gone. On the gun-decks of the *Indomitable* the general estimate of his nature and its unconscious simplicity eventually found rude utterance from another foretopman, one of his own watch, gifted as some sailors are with an artless poetic temperament. Those tarry hands made some lines which, after circulating among the ship-board crew for a while, finally were rudely printed at

---

* An author's note, crossed out, here appears in the original MS. It reads: Here ends a story not unwarranted in this incongruous world of ours—innocence and infirmity, spiritual depravity and fair respite.

Portsmouth as a ballad.   The title given to it was the sailor's own:

BILLY IN THE DARBIES

Good of the Chaplain to enter Lone Bay .
And down on his marrow-bones here and pray
For the likes just o' me, Billy Budd,—But look:
Through the port comes the moon-shine astray!
It tips the guard's cutlass and silvers this nock;
But 'twill die in the dawning of Billy's last day.
A jewel-block they'll make of me to-morrow,
Pendant pearl from the yard-arm-end
Like the ear-drop I gave to Bristol Molly—
O, 'tis me, not the sentence, they'll suspend.
Ay, Ay, all is up; and I must up too
Early in the morning, aloft from alow.
On an empty stomach, now, never it would do.
They'll give me a nibble—bit o' biscuit ere I go.
Sure, a messmate will reach me the last parting cup;
But, turning heads away from the hoist and the belay,
Heaven knows who will have the running of me up!
No pipe to those halyards—but aren't it all sham?
A blur's in my eyes, it is dreaming that I am.
A hatchet to my panzer? all adrift to go?
The drum roll to grog, and Billy never know?
But Donald he has promised to stand by the plank;
So I'll shake a friendly hand ere I sink.
But—no! It is dead then I'll be, come to think.—
I remember Taff the Welshman when he sank.
And his cheek it was like the budding pink.
But me, they'll lash me in hammock, drop me deep
Fathoms down, fathoms down, how I'll dream fast asleep.
I feel it stealing now.   Sentry, are you there?
Just ease these darbies at the wrist.
And roll me over fair.
I am sleepy, and the oozy weeds about me twist.

END OF BOOK

April 19, 1891.

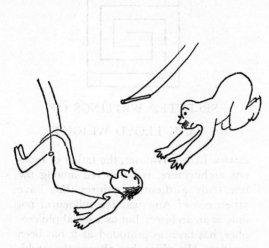

THE MIDDLE-AGED MAN ON
THE FYLING TRAPEZE

By James Thurber

Thurber is Thurber and there is none other.

To both the eye-minded and the ear-minded (to say nothing of the high- and low-minded) Thurber is one of the marvels of our age.

No one can read "If Grant Had Been Drinking at Appomattox," or "A Preface to Dogs," without realizing that things are not what they seem — or, for that matter, what they actually are. And the single chapter entitled "One Is a Wanderer" will make this book an unforgettable experience for any man — middle-aged or otherwise — or any woman.

UL-69

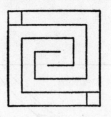

SELECTED WRITINGS OF
FRANK LLOYD WRIGHT

FRANK LLOYD WRIGHT, the father of modern architecture, is numbered among the few truly authentic geniuses that have arisen out of America. His influence, not only as an architect, but as a social philosopher, has been as profound as it has been limitless. His vision has altered the architectural landscape so completely, that one can easily consider him as one of the great revolutionaries of our time. In this volume of selected writings, which covers the greatest and most productive years of his life, is a compendium of the ideas that formed the basis of his philosophy of architecture. Here are expressed all of the famous concepts which have come to mean Modern Architecture for us: functional design, cantilever construction, the exploration of scale and proportion, the organic concept of space, the fresh expression of building materials, the exalted idea of lyric construction, the development of new and significant forms, and the humanization of buildings. All of these ideas, whether delivered in lectures, or written in articles or longer works, are expressed in Mr. Wright's unique style, which combines a passion for integrity with the poetic rhythms of a prophet and the practical vision of a master builder.

UL-70